THE AWAKENING

AN AUTHORITATIVE TEXT
CONTEXTS
CRITICISM

A NORTON CRITICAL EDITION

KATE CHOPIN

THE AWAKENING

AN AUTHORITATIVE TEXT
CONTEXTS
CRITICISM

Edited by

MARGARET CULLEY

UNIVERSITY OF MASSACHUSETTS AT AMHERST

W · W · NORTON & COMPANY · INC · New York

ACKNOWLEDGMENTS

George Arms: "Kate Chopin's *The Awakening* in the Perspective of Her Literary Career," from *Essays on American Literature in Honor of Jay B. Hubbell*, ed. Clarence Gohdes, pp. 215–17, 217–22. Copyright © 1967 by Duke University Press. Reprinted by permission of the publisher.

Jules Chametzky: "Our Decentralized Literature," from *Jahrbuch für America Studien*, 1972, pp. 70–71. Reprinted by permission of the author.

Kate Chopin: Facsimile of page from her notebooks printed by permission of the Missouri Historical Society.

Kenneth Eble: "A Forgotten Novel: Kate Chopin's *The Awakening*," from *The Western Humanities Review*, vol. IX, no. 3 (Summer 1956). Reprinted by permission of the publisher.

Marie Fletcher: "The Southern Woman in the Fiction of Kate Chopin," from *Louisiana History*, vol. VII (Spring 1966), pp. 123–25, 126, 131–32. Reprinted by permission of the publisher.

Lewis Leary: From *Southern Excursions: Essays on Mark Twain and Others* (Baton Rouge: Louisiana State University Press, 1971), pp. 169–74. Reprinted by permission.

John R. May: "Local Color in *The Awakening*," from *The Southern Review*, VI (Fall 1970), pp. 1031–40. Reprinted by permission of the author.

Daniel Rankin: From *Kate Chopin and Her Creole Stories* (Philadelphia: University of Pennsylvania Press, 1932), pp. 173–75, 178–82. Reprinted by permission of the University of Pennsylvania Press.

Donald A. Ringe: "Romantic Imagery in Kate Chopin's *The Awakening*," from *American Literature*, XLIII (1972), pp. 582–88. Reprinted by permission of Duke University Press.

Per Seyersted: From *Kate Chopin: A Critical Biography* (Baton Rouge: Louisiana State University Press, 1969), pp. 190–96. Reprinted by permission of the author.

George M. Spangler: "Kate Chopin's *The Awakening*: A Partial Dissent," from *Novel*, III (Spring 1970), pp. 249–55. Reprinted by permission of the author and the publisher.

Cynthia Griffin Wolff: "Thanatos and Eros: Kate Chopin's *The Awakening*," from *American Quarterly*, XXV (October 1973), pp. 460–71. Copyright © 1973 by the Trustees of the University of Pennsylvania. Reprinted by permission.

Published simultaneously in Canada by George J. McLeod Limited, Toronto. Printed in the United States of America.

Library of Congress Cataloging in Publication Data

Chopin, Kate O'Flaherty, 1851–1904.
    The awakening.

    (A Norton critical edition)
    Bibliography: p.
    I. Culley, Margaret. II. Title.
PZ3.C456Aw20   [PS1294.C63]   813'.4   76-55321
ISBN 0-393-04434-3
ISBN 0-393-09172-4 pbk.

2 3 4 5 6 7 8 9 0

Contents

Preface

Kate O'Flaherty was born in St. Louis in 1851. Her father was a successful St. Louis merchant who had married into an aristocratic family of French origin. Kate attended the best school available to young women in the city; then spent two years busy with the social activities appropriate to a person of her class; in 1870 she married Oscar Chopin, of a prominent Louisiana Creole family, and moved with him to New Orleans.

In the twelve years of their marrige she bore him six children; and upon his sudden death in the early 1880s, she assumed the management of the family plantation in Natchitoches, Louisiana. In 1884 she returned to her mother's home in St. Louis, and only after her mother's death the next year did she begin serious writing. Her first novel, *At Fault*, appeared in 1890 and was followed by two collections of short stories, *Bayou Folk* in 1894 and *A Night in Acadia* in 1897. By the time *The Awakening* appeared in 1899, she was the well-known author of over a hundred stories, sketches, and essays which had appeared in the popular and literary magazines of the period. She died in 1904.

Published in 1899 by Herbert S. Stone (Chicago), *The Awakening* met with widespread hostile criticism and the book was removed from the library shelves in St. Louis. Chopin herself was refused membership in the St. Louis Fine Arts Club because of the novel. In 1906 it was reprinted by Duffield (New York); but then it went out of print and remained so for more than half a century in this country.

Chopin worked quickly and without much revision, often in the family room surrounded by her children. These working habits, and the lack of a careful editor, left a number of inconsistencies in punctuation, and even errors in spelling, in the first edition. As no manuscript of the novel exists, the text here appears as it did in the first edition with the single addition of the word "of" on page 109. The text is accompanied in this edition by a selection of material contemporary to *The Awakening*, in order to establish the context in which the novel appeared and to help explain why the novel met such hostile criticism. As the selections demonstrate, everyone from economists to advice columnists was discussing "the woman question" in the 1890s in America. A novel in which a woman explored freedom from traditional modes raised questions on which everyone had strong opinions.

Also in this edition is a generous sample of the difficult-to-obtain, early reviews of *The Awakening*, including the recently discovered sympathetic reading of the novel by Willa Cather in 1899. Selections from the major critical essays on the novel which have appeared in the last twenty years trace the work's return to critical favor and acclaim. Chosen to represent a variety of approaches to the novel, the essays discuss influences upon the novel; its structure, theme, and imagery; and the major "problems" of the novel, particularly the problem of the ending.

In the preparation of this volume I am indebted to the consistently cheerful and expert assistance of the reference and interlibrary loan teams at the University of Massachusetts, Amherst. For assistance with the French phrases and allusions in the text I am grateful to Professors Carol Nolan Rigolot and Micheline Dufau, although they should not be thought responsible for any infelicities which may have persisted. From the women's studies faculty in the English Department at the University of Massachusetts, I have drawn energy and moral support as well as an intellectual context. In particular, the example of Kathleen Swaim has urged me to the highest standards of scholarship.

Margaret Culley

The Text of

The Awakening

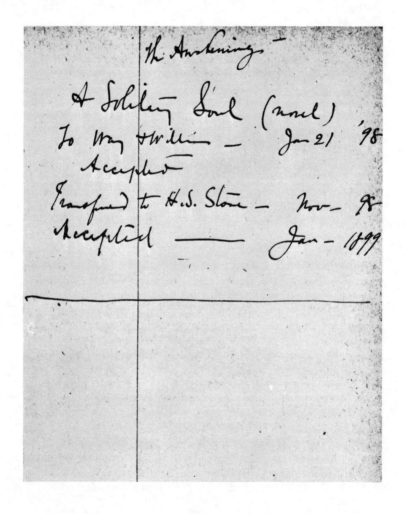

The page from a Chopin notebook where she recorded the original title of the novel, "A Solitary Soul." Used with permission of the Missouri Historical Society.

I

A green and yellow parrot, which hung in a cage outside the door, kept repeating over and over:

"*Allez vous-en! Allez vous-en! Sapristi!*[1] That's all right!"

He could speak a little Spanish, and also a language which nobody understood, unless it was the mocking-bird that hung on the other side of the door, whistling his fluty notes out upon the breeze with maddening persistence.

Mr. Pontellier, unable to read his newspaper with any degree of comfort, arose with an expression and an exclamation of disgust. He walked down the gallery and across the narrow "bridges" which connected the Lebrun cottages one with the other. He had been seated before the door of the main house. The parrot and the mocking-bird were the property of Madame Lebrun, and they had the right to make all the noise they wished. Mr. Pontellier had the privilege of quitting their society when they ceased to be entertaining.

He stopped before the door of his own cottage, which was the fourth one from the main building and next to the last. Seating himself in a wicker rocker which was there, he once more applied himself to the task of reading the newspaper. The day was Sunday; the paper was a day old. The Sunday papers had not yet reached Grand Isle.[2] He was already acquainted with the market reports, and he glanced restlessly over the editorials and bits of news which he had not had time to read before quitting New Orleans the day before.

Mr. Pontellier wore eye-glasses. He was a man of forty, of medium height and rather slender build; he stooped a little. His hair was brown and straight, parted on one side. His beard was neatly and closely trimmed.

Once in a while he withdrew his glance from the newspaper and

1. "Go away! Go away! For God's sake!"
2. An island fifty miles south of New Orleans, between the Gulf of Mexico and Caminada Bay. The island was famed as the headquarters of Lafitte's pirates in the early nineteenth century, and toward the end of the century became a celebrated Creole resort. In 1893 a hurricane devastated the resort area. This indicates that the novel is set before that date. Chênière Caminada (see below) is an island between Grand Isle and the Louisiana coast.

looked about him. There was more noise than ever over at the house. The main building was called "the house," to distinguish it from the cottages. The chattering and whistling birds were still at it. Two young girls, the Farival twins, were playing a duet from "Zampa"³ upon the piano. Madame Lebrun was bustling in and out, giving orders in a high key to a yard-boy whenever she got inside the house, and directions in an equally high voice to a dining-room servant whenever she got outside. She was a fresh, pretty woman, clad always in white with elbow sleeves. Her starched skirts crinkled as she came and went. Farther down, before one of the cottages, a lady in black was walking demurely up and down, telling her beads. A good many persons of the *pension* had gone over to the *Chênière Caminada* in Beaudelet's lugger to hear mass. Some young people were out under the water-oaks playing croquet. Mr. Pontellier's two children were there—sturdy little fellows of four and five. A quadroon⁴ nurse followed them about with a far-away, meditative air.

Mr. Pontellier finally lit a cigar and began to smoke, letting the paper drag idly from his hand. He fixed his gaze upon a white sunshade that was advancing at snail's pace from the beach. He could see it plainly between the gaunt trunks of the water-oaks and across the stretch of yellow camomile. The gulf looked far away, melting hazily into the blue of the horizon. The sunshade continued to approach slowly. Beneath its pink-lined shelter were his wife, Mrs. Pontellier, and young Robert Lebrun. When they reached the cottage, the two seated themselves with some appearance of fatigue upon the upper step of the porch, facing each other, each leaning against a supporting post.

"What folly! to bathe at such an hour in such heat!" exclaimed Mr. Pontellier. He himself had taken a plunge at daylight. That was why the morning seemed long to him.

"You are burnt beyond recognition," he added, looking at his wife as one looks at a valuable piece of personal property which has suffered some damage. She held up her hands, strong, shapely hands, and surveyed them critically, drawing up her lawn sleeves⁵ above the wrists. Looking at them reminded her of her rings, which she had given to her husband before leaving for the beach. She silently reached out to him, and he, understanding, took the rings from his vest pocket and dropped them into her open palm. She slipped them upon her fingers; then clasping her knees, she looked across at Robert and began to laugh. The rings sparkled upon her fingers. He sent back an answering smile.

---

3. A romantic opera by Louis Hérold. The involved plot includes a lover's death in the sea.
4. A person with one-fourth black ancestry.
5. Sleeves made of lawn, a fine linen or sheer muslin.

"What is it?" asked Pontellier, looking lazily and amused from one to the other. It was some utter nonsense; some adventure out there in the water, and they both tried to relate it at once. It did not seem half so amusing when told. They realized this, and so did Mr. Pontellier. He yawned and stretched himself. Then he got up, saying he had half a mind to go over to Klein's hotel[6] and play a game of billiards.

"Come go along, Lebrun," he proposed to Robert. But Robert admitted quite frankly that he preferred to stay where he was and talk to Mrs. Pontellier.

"Well, send him about his business when he bores you, Edna," instructed her husband as he prepared to leave.

"Here, take the umbrella," she exclaimed, holding it out to him. He accepted the sunshade, and lifting it over his head descended the steps and walked away.

"Coming back to dinner?" his wife called after him. He halted a moment and shrugged his shoulders. He felt in his vest pocket; there was a ten-dollar bill there. He did not know; perhaps he would return for the early dinner and perhaps he would not. It all depended upon the company which he found over at Klein's and the size of "the game." He did not say this, but she understood it, and laughed, nodding good-by to him.

Both children wanted to follow their father when they saw him starting out. He kissed them and promised to bring them back bonbons and peanuts.

II

Mrs. Pontellier's eyes were quick and bright; they were a yellowish brown, about the color of her hair. She had a way of turning them swiftly upon an object and holding them there as if lost in some inward maze of contemplation or thought.

Her eyebrows were a shade darker than her hair. They were thick and almost horizontal, emphasizing the depth of her eyes. She was rather handsome than beautiful. Her face was captivating by reason of a certain frankness of expression and a contradictory subtle play of features. Her manner was engaging.

Robert rolled a cigarette. He smoked cigarettes because he could not afford cigars, he said. He had a cigar in his pocket which Mr. Pontellier had presented him with, and he was saving it for his after-dinner smoke.

This seemed quite proper and natural on his part. In coloring he

6. Probably Kranz's Hotel, described by Catherine Cole in 1892: "An old, popular, well-known resort, built like a plantation quarters in a series of cottages along a grassy street. At one end a ballroom, at the other a dining room . . . out of the sight of the surf and the sea; but three times a day a tram car runs down to the beach where the bathhouses are. In the center of the island, rising above the clustered oaks, are the gray dormer windows of a huge unfinished hotel. . . ." (*The Daily Picayune*, October 5, 1893.)

was not unlike his companion. A clean-shaved face made the resemblance more pronounced than it would otherwise have been.
There rested no shadow of care upon his open countenance. His
eyes gathered in and reflected the light and languor of the summer
day.

Mrs. Pontellier reached over for a palmleaf fan that lay on the
porch and began to fan herself, while Robert sent between his lips
light puffs from his cigarette. They chatted incessantly: about the
things around them; their amusing adventure out in the water—it
had again assumed its entertaining aspect; about the wind, the trees,
the people who had gone to the *Chênière;* about the children playing croquet under the oaks, and the Farival twins, who were now
performing the overture to "The Poet and the Peasant."[7]

Robert talked a good deal about himself. He was very young, and
did not know any better. Mrs. Pontellier talked a little about herself
for the same reason. Each was interested in what the other said.
Robert spoke of his intention to go to Mexico in the autumn, where
fortune awaited him. He was always intending to go to Mexico, but
some way never got there. Meanwhile he held on to his modest
position in a mercantile house in New Orleans, where an equal
familiarity with English, French and Spanish gave him no small
value as a clerk and correspondent.

He was spending his summer vacation, as he always did, with his
mother at Grand Isle. In former times, before Robert could remember, "the house" had been a summer luxury of the Lebruns. Now,
flanked by its dozen or more cottages, which were always filled with
exclusive visitors from the *"Quartier Français,"*[8] it enabled Madame
Lebrun to maintain the easy and comfortable existence which appeared to be her birthright.

Mrs. Pontellier talked about her father's Mississippi plantation
and her girlhood home in the old Kentucky blue-grass country. She
was an American woman, with a small infusion of French which
seemed to have been lost in dilution. She read a letter from her
sister, who was away in the East, and who had engaged herself to be
married. Robert was interested, and wanted to know what manner
of girls the sisters were, what the father was like, and how long the
mother had been dead.

When Mrs. Pontellier folded the letter it was time for her to dress
for the early dinner.

"I see Léonce isn't coming back," she said, with a glance in the
direction whence her husband had disappeared. Robert supposed he

7. An operetta by Franz von Suppé.
8. The French Quarter, or Vieux Carré
—the oldest part of New Orleans—
settled by the French in the early 1700s
and residence of most of the Creole
population in the nineteenth century. See
note 2, p. 11.

was not, as there were a good many New Orleans club men over at Klein's.

When Mrs. Pontellier left him to enter her room, the young man descended the steps and strolled over toward the croquet players, where, during the half-hour before dinner, he amused himself with the little Pontellier children, who were very fond of him.

III

It was eleven o'clock that night when Mr. Pontellier returned from Klein's hotel. He was in an excellent humor, in high spirits, and very talkative. His entrance awoke his wife, who was in bed and fast asleep when he came in. He talked to her while he undressed, telling her anecdotes and bits of news and gossip that he had gathered during the day. From his trousers pockets he took a fistful of crumpled bank notes and a good deal of silver coin, which he piled on the bureau indiscriminately with keys, knife, handkerchief, and whatever else happened to be in his pockets. She was overcome with sleep, and answered him with little half utterances.

He thought it very discouraging that his wife, who was the sole object of his existence, evinced so little interest in things which concerned him and valued so little his conversation.

Mr. Pontellier had forgotten the bonbons and peanuts for the boys. Notwithstanding he loved them very much, and went into the adjoining room where they slept to take a look at them and make sure that they were resting comfortably. The result of his investigation was far from satisfactory. He turned and shifted the youngsters about in bed. One of them began to kick and talk about a basket full of crabs.

Mr. Pontellier returned to his wife with the information that Raoul had a high fever and needed looking after. Then he lit a cigar and went and sat near the open door to smoke it.

Mrs. Pontellier was quite sure Raoul had no fever. He had gone to bed perfectly well, she said, and nothing had ailed him all day. Mr. Pontellier was too well acquainted with fever symptoms to be mistaken. He assured her the child was consuming at that moment in the next room.

He reproached his wife with her inattention, her habitual neglect of the children. If it was not a mother's place to look after children, whose on earth was it? He himself had his hands full with his brokerage business. He could not be in two places at once; making a living for his family on the street, and staying at home to see that no harm befell them. He talked in a monotonous, insistent way.

Mrs. Pontellier sprang out of bed and went into the next room. She soon came back and sat on the edge of the bed, leaning her head down on the pillow. She said nothing, and refused to answer her husband when he questioned her. When his cigar was smoked out he went to bed, and in half a minute he was fast asleep.

Mrs. Pontellier was by that time thoroughly awake. She began to cry a little, and wiped her eyes on the sleeve of her *peignoir*. Blowing out the candle, which her husband had left burning, she slipped her bare feet into a pair of satin *mules* at the foot of the bed and went out on the porch, where she sat down in the wicker chair and began to rock gently to and fro.

It was then past midnight. The cottages were all dark. A single faint light gleamed out from the hallway of the house. There was no sound abroad except the hooting of an old owl in the top of a water-oak, and the everlasting voice of the sea, that was not uplifted at that soft hour. It broke like a mournful lullaby upon the night.

The tears came so fast to Mrs. Pontellier's eyes that the damp sleeve of her *peignoir* no longer served to dry them. She was holding the back of her chair with one hand; her loose sleeve had slipped almost to the shoulder of her uplifted arm. Turning, she thrust her face, steaming and wet, into the bend of her arm, and she went on crying there, not caring any longer to dry her face, her eyes, her arms. She could not have told why she was crying. Such experiences as the foregoing were not uncommon in her married life. They seemed never before to have weighed much against the abundance of her husband's kindness and a uniform devotion which had come to be tacit and self-understood.

An indescribable oppression, which seemed to generate in some unfamiliar part of her consciousness, filled her whole being with a vague anguish. It was like a shadow, like a mist passing across her soul's summer day. It was strange and unfamiliar; it was a mood. She did not sit there inwardly upbraiding her husband, lamenting at Fate, which had directed her footsteps to the path which they had taken. She was just having a good cry all to herself. The mosquitoes made merry over her, biting her firm, round arms and nipping at her bare insteps.

The little stinging, buzzing imps succeeded in dispelling a mood which might have held her there in the darkness half a night longer.

The following morning Mr. Pontellier was up in good time to take the rockaway[9] which was to convey him to the steamer at the wharf. He was returning to the city to his business, and they would not see him again at the Island till the coming Saturday. He had regained his composure, which seemed to have been somewhat im-

9. A four-wheeled carriage with a high top and open sides, named for Rock- away, New Jersey, where it was manu-factured.

paired the night before. He was eager to be gone, as he looked forward to a lively week in Carondelet Street.[1]

Mr. Pontellier gave his wife half the money which he had brought away from Klein's hotel the evening before. She liked money as well as most women, and accepted it with no little satisfaction.

"It will buy a handsome wedding present for Sister Janet!" she exclaimed, smoothing out the bills as she counted them one by one.

"Oh! we'll treat Sister Janet better than that, my dear," he laughed, as he prepared to kiss her good-by.

The boys were tumbling about, clinging to his legs, imploring that numerous things be brought back to them. Mr. Pontellier was a great favorite, and ladies, men, children, even nurses, were always on hand to say good-by to him. His wife stood smiling and waving, the boys shouting, as he disappeared in the old rockaway down the sandy road.

A few days later a box arrived for Mrs. Pontellier from New Orleans. It was from her husband. It was filled with *friandises*, with luscious and toothsome bits—the finest of fruits, *patés*, a rare bottle or two, delicious syrups, and bonbons in abundance.

Mrs. Pontellier was always very generous with the contents of such a box; she was quite used to receiving them when away from home. The *patés* and fruit were brought to the dining-room; the bonbons were passed around. And the ladies, selecting with dainty and discriminating fingers and a little greedily, all declared that Mr. Pontellier was the best husband in the world. Mrs. Pontellier was forced to admit that she knew of none better.

IV

It would have been a difficult matter for Mr. Pontellier to define to his own satisfaction or any one else's wherein his wife failed in her duty toward their children. It was something which he felt rather than perceived, and he never voiced the feeling without subsequent regret and ample atonement.

If one of the little Pontellier boys took a tumble whilst at play, he was not apt to rush crying to his mother's arms for comfort; he would more likely pick himself up, wipe the water out of his eyes and the sand out of his mouth, and go on playing. Tots as they were, they pulled together and stood their ground in childish battles with doubled fists and uplifted voices, which usually prevailed against the other mother-tots. The quadroon nurse was looked upon as a huge encumbrance, only good to button up waists and panties

1. New Orleans' equivalent of Wall Street, and the location of the Cotton Exchange. Chopin's husband, Oscar, a cotton factor (agent, broker, banker) had his office on Carondelet Street.

and to brush and part hair; since it seemed to be a law of society that hair must be parted and brushed.

In short, Mrs. Pontellier was not a mother-woman. The mother-women seemed to prevail that summer at Grand Isle. It was easy to know them, fluttering about with extended, protecting wings when any harm, real or imaginary, threatened their precious brood. They were women who idolized their children, worshiped their husbands, and esteemed it a holy privilege to efface themselves as individuals and grow wings as ministering angels.

Many of them were delicious in the rôle; one of them was the embodiment of every womanly grace and charm. If her husband did not adore her, he was a brute, deserving of death by slow torture. Her name was Adèle Ratignolle. There are no words to describe her save the old ones that have served so often to picture the bygone heroine of romance and the fair lady of our dreams. There was nothing subtle or hidden about her charms; her beauty was all there, flaming and apparent: the spun-gold hair that comb nor confining pin could restrain; the blue eyes that were like nothing but sapphires; two lips that pouted, that were so red one could only think of cherries or some other delicious crimson fruit in looking at them. She was growing a little stout, but it did not seem to detract an iota from the grace of every step, pose, gesture. One would not have wanted her white neck a mite less full or her beautiful arms more slender. Never were hands more exquisite than hers, and it was a joy to look at them when she threaded her needle or adjusted her gold thimble to her taper middle finger as she sewed away on the little night-drawers or fashioned a bodice or a bib.

Madame Ratignolle was very fond of Mrs. Pontellier, and often she took her sewing and went over to sit with her in the afternoons. She was sitting there the afternoon of the day the box arrived from New Orleans. She had possession of the rocker, and she was busily engaged in sewing upon a diminutive pair of night-drawers.

She had brought the pattern of the drawers for Mrs. Pontellier to cut out—a marvel of construction, fashioned to enclose a baby's body so effectually that only two small eyes might look out from the garment, like an Eskimo's. They were designed for winter wear, when treacherous drafts came down chimneys and insidious currents of deadly cold found their way through key-holes.

Mrs. Pontellier's mind was quite at rest concerning the present material needs of her children, and she could not see the use of anticipating and making winter night garments the subject of her summer meditations. But she did not want to appear unamiable and uninterested, so she had brought forth newspapers which she spread upon the floor of the gallery, and under Madame Ratignolle's directions she had cut a pattern of the impervious garment.

Robert was there, seated as he had been the Sunday before, and Mrs. Pontellier also occupied her former position on the upper step, leaning listlessly against the post. Beside her was a box of bonbons, which she held out at intervals to Madame Ratignolle.

That lady seemed at a loss to make a selection, but finally settled upon a stick of nugat, wondering if it were not too rich; whether it could possibly hurt her. Madame Ratignolle had been married seven years. About every two years she had a baby. At that time she had three babies, and was beginning to think of a fourth one. She was always talking about her "condition." Her "condition" was in no way apparent, and no one would have known a thing about it but for her persistence in making it the subject of conversation.

Robert started to reassure her, asserting that he had known a lady who had subsisted upon nugat during the entire—but seeing the color mount into Mrs. Pontellier's face he checked himself and changed the subject.

Mrs. Pontellier, though she had married a Creole,[2] was not thoroughly at home in the society of Creoles; never before had she been thrown so intimately among them. There were only Creoles that summer at Lebrun's. They all knew each other, and felt like one large family, among whom existed the most amicable relations. A characteristic which distinguished them and which impressed Mrs. Pontellier most forcibly was their entire absence of prudery. Their freedom of expression was at first incomprehensible to her, though she had no difficulty in reconciling it with a lofty chastity which in the Creole woman seems to be inborn and unmistakable.

Never would Edna Pontellier forget the shock with which she heard Madame Ratignolle relating to old Monsieur Farival the harrowing story of one of her *accouchements*,[3] withholding no intimate detail. She was growing accustomed to like shocks, but she could not keep the mounting color back from her cheeks. Oftener than once her coming had interrupted the droll story with which Robert was entertaining some amused group of married women.

A book had gone the rounds of the *pension*. When it came her turn to read it, she did so with profound astonishment. She felt moved to read the book in secret and solitude, though none of the others had done so—to hide it from view at the sound of approaching footsteps. It was openly criticised and freely discussed at table. Mrs. Pontellier gave over being astonished, and concluded that wonders would never cease.

---

2. As used in this novel, a person descended from the original French and Spanish settlers of New Orleans, an aristocrat.
3. The birth of one of her children.

V

They formed a congenial group sitting there that summer afternoon—Madame Ratignolle sewing away, often stopping to relate a story or incident with much expressive gesture of her perfect hands; Robert and Mrs. Pontellier sitting idle, exchanging occasional words, glances or smiles which indicated a certain advanced stage of intimacy and *camaraderie*.

He had lived in her shadow during the past month. No one thought anything of it. Many had predicted that Robert would devote himself to Mrs. Pontellier when he arrived. Since the age of fifteen, which was eleven years before, Robert each summer at Grand Isle had constituted himself the devoted attendant of some fair dame or damsel. Sometimes it was a young girl, again a widow; but as often as not it was some interesting married woman.

For two consecutive seasons he lived in the sunlight of Mademoiselle Duvigné's presence. But she died between summers; then Robert posed as an inconsolable, prostrating himself at the feet of Madame Ratignolle for whatever crumbs of sympathy and comfort she might be pleased to vouchsafe.

Mrs. Pontellier liked to sit and gaze at her fair companion as she might look upon a faultless Madonna.

"Could any one fathom the cruelty beneath that fair exterior?" murmured Robert. She knew that I adored her once, and she let me adore her. It was 'Robert, come; go; stand up; sit down; do this; do that; see if the baby sleeps; my thimble, please, that I left God knows where. Come and read Daudet[4] to me while I sew.' "

"*Par exemple!*[5] I never had to ask. You were always there under my feet, like a troublesome cat."

"You mean like an adoring dog. And just as soon as Ratignolle appeared on the scene, then it *was* like a dog. '*Passez! Adieu! Allez vous-en!*' "[6]

"Perhaps I feared to make Alphonse jealous," she interjoined, with excessive naïveté. That made them all laugh. The right hand jealous of the left! The heart jealous of the soul! But for that matter, the Creole husband is never jealous; with him the gangrene passion is one which has become dwarfed by disuse.

Meanwhile Robert, addressing Mrs. Pontellier, continued to tell of his one time hopeless passion for Madame Ratignolle; of sleepless nights, of consuming flames till the very sea sizzled when he took his daily plunge. While the lady at the needle kept up a little running, contemptuous comment:

"*Blagueur—farceur—gros bête, va!*"[7]

---

4. Alphonse Daudet (1840–1887), French novelist of the naturalist school.
5. "For goodness sake!"
6. "Go on! Good-by! Go away!"
7. "Joker—comedian—silly, come off it!"

He never assumed this serio-comic tone when alone with Mrs. Pontellier. She never knew precisely what to make of it; at that moment it was impossible for her to guess how much of it was jest and what proportion was earnest. It was understood that he had often spoken words of love to Madame Ratignolle, without any thought of being taken seriously. Mrs. Pontellier was glad he had not assumed a similar rôle toward herself. It would have been unacceptable and annoying.

Mrs. Pontellier had brought her sketching materials, which she sometimes dabbled with in an unprofessional way. She liked the dabbling. She felt in it satisfaction of a kind which no other employment afforded her.

She had long wished to try herself on Madame Ratignolle. Never had that lady seemed a more tempting subject than at that moment, seated there like some sensuous Madonna, with the gleam of the fading day enriching her splendid color.

Robert crossed over and seated himself upon the step below Mrs. Pontellier, that he might watch her work. She handled her brushes with a certain ease and freedom which came, not from long and close acquaintance with them, but from a natural aptitude. Robert followed her work with close attention, giving forth little ejaculatory expressions of appreciation in French, which he addressed to Madame Ratignolle.

"*Mais ce n'est pas mal! Elle s'y connait, elle a de la force, oui.*"[8]

During his oblivious attention he once quietly rested his head against Mrs. Pontellier's arm. As gently she repulsed him. Once again he repeated the offense. She could not but believe it to be thoughtlessness on his part; yet that was no reason she should submit to it. She did not remonstrate, except again to repulse him quietly but firmly. He offered no apology.

The picture completed bore no resemblance to Madame Ratignolle. She was greatly disappointed to find that it did not look like her. But it was a fair enough piece of work, and in many respects satisfying.

Mrs. Pontellier evidently did not think so. After surveying the sketch critically she drew a broad smudge of paint across its surface, and crumpled the paper between her hands.

The youngsters came tumbling up the steps, the quadroon following at the respectful distance which they required her to observe. Mrs. Pontellier made them carry her paints and things into the house. She sought to detain them for a little talk and some pleasantry. But they were greatly in earnest. They had only come to investigate the contents of the bonbon box. They accepted without murmuring what she chose to give them, each holding out two

8. "Not bad at all! She knows what she's doing, she has talent."

chubby hands scoop-like, in the vain hope that they might be filled; and then away they went.

The sun was low in the west, and the breeze soft and languorous that came up from the south, charged with the seductive odor of the sea. Children, freshly befurbelowed,[9] were gathering for their games under the oaks. Their voices were high and penetrating.

Madame Ratignolle folded her sewing, placing thimble, scissors and thread all neatly together in the roll, which she pinned securely. She complained of faintness. Mrs. Pontellier flew for the cologne water and a fan. She bathed Madame Ratignolle's face with cologne, while Robert plied the fan with unnecessary vigor.

The spell was soon over, and Mrs. Pontellier could not help wondering if there were not a little imagination responsible for its origin, for the rose tint had never faded from her friend's face.

She stood watching the fair woman walk down the long line of galleries with the grace and majesty which queens are sometimes supposed to possess. Her little ones ran to meet her. Two of them clung about her white skirts, the third she took from its nurse and with a thousand endearments bore it along in her own fond, encircling arms. Though, as everybody well knew, the doctor had forbidden her to lift so much as a pin!

"Are you going bathing?" asked Robert of Mrs. Pontellier. It was not so much a question as a reminder.

"Oh, no," she answered, with a tone of indecision. "I'm tired; I think not." Her glance wandered from his face away toward the Gulf, whose sonorous murmur reached her like a loving but imperative entreaty.

"Oh, come!" he insisted. "You mustn't miss your bath. Come on. The water must be delicious; it will not hurt you. Come."

He reached up for her big, rough straw hat that hung on a peg outside the door, and put it on her head. They descended the steps, and walked away together toward the beach. The sun was low in the west and the breeze was soft and warm.

VI

Edna Pontellier could not have told why, wishing to go to the beach with Robert, she should in the first place have declined, and in the second place have followed in obedience to one of the two contradictory impulses which impelled her.

A certain light was beginning to dawn dimly within her,—the light which, showing the way, forbids it.

At that early period it served but to bewilder her. It moved her to dreams, to thoughtfulness, to the shadowy anguish which had overcome her the midnight when she had abandoned herself to tears.

In short, Mrs. Pontellier was beginning to realize her position in

9. Dressed, adorned, especially in petticoats or flounces.

the universe as a human being, and to recognize her relations as an individual to the world within and about her. This may seem like a ponderous weight of wisdom to descend upon the soul of a young woman of twenty-eight—perhaps more wisdom than the Holy Ghost is usually pleased to vouchsafe to any woman.

But the beginning of things, of a world especially, is necessarily vague, tangled, chaotic, and exceedingly disturbing. How few of us ever emerge from such beginning! How many souls perish in its tumult!

The voice of the sea is seductive; never ceasing, whispering, clamoring, murmuring, inviting the soul to wander for a spell in abysses of solitude; to lose itself in mazes of inward contemplation.

The voice of the sea speaks to the soul. The touch of the sea is sensuous, enfolding the body in its soft, close embrace.

VII

Mrs. Pontellier was not a woman given to confidences, a characteristic hitherto contrary to her nature. Even as a child she had lived her own small life all within herself. At a very early period she had apprehended instinctively the dual life—that outward existence which conforms, the inward life which questions.

That summer at Grand Isle she began to loosen a little the mantle of reserve that had always enveloped her. There may have been— there must have been—influences, both subtle and apparent, working in their several ways to induce her to do this; but the most obvious was the influence of Adèle Ratignolle. The excessive physical charm of the Creole had first attracted her, for Edna had a sensuous susceptibility to beauty. Then the candor of the woman's whole existence, which every one might read, and which formed so striking a contrast to her own habitual reserve—this might have furnished a link. Who can tell what metals the gods use in forging the subtle bond which we call sympathy, which we might as well call love.

The two women went away one morning to the beach together, arm in arm, under the huge white sunshade. Edna had prevailed upon Madame Ratignolle` to leave the children behind, though she could not induce her to relinquish a diminutive roll of needlework, which Adèle begged to be allowed to slip into the depths of her pocket. In some unaccountable way they had escaped from Robert.

The walk to the beach was no inconsiderable one, consisting as it did of a long, sandy path, upon which a sporadic and tangled growth that bordered it on either side made frequent and unexpected inroads. There were acres of yellow camomile reaching out on either hand. Further away still, vegetable gardens abounded, with frequent small plantations of orange or lemon trees intervening. The dark green clusters glistened from afar in the sun.

The women were both of goodly height, Madame Ratignolle possessing the more feminine and matronly figure. The charm of Edna Pontellier's physique stole insensibly upon you. The lines of her body were long, clean and symmetrical; it was a body which occasionally fell into splendid poses; there was no suggestion of the trim, stereotyped fashion-plate about it. A casual and indiscriminating observer, in passing, might not cast a second glance upon the figure. But with more feeling and discernment he would have recognized the noble beauty of its modeling, and the graceful severity of poise and movement, which made Edna Pontellier different from the crowd.

She wore a cool muslin that morning—white, with a waving vertical line of brown running through it; also a white linen collar and the big straw hat which she had taken from the peg outside the door. The hat rested any way on her yellow-brown hair, that waved a little, was heavy, and clung close to her head.

Madame Ratignolle, more careful of her complexion, had twined a gauze veil about her head. She wore dogskin gloves, with gauntlets that protected her wrists. She was dressed in pure white, with a fluffiness of ruffles that became her. The draperies and fluttering things which she wore suited her rich, luxuriant beauty as a greater severity of line could not have done.

There were a number of bath-houses along the beach, of rough but solid construction, built with small, protecting galleries facing the water. Each house consisted of two compartments, and each family at Lebrun's possessed a compartment for itself, fitted out with all the essential paraphernalia of the bath and whatever other conveniences the owners might desire. The two women had no intention of bathing; they had just strolled down to the beach for a walk and to be alone and near the water. The Pontellier and Ratignolle compartments adjoined one another under the same roof.

Mrs. Pontellier had brought down her key through force of habit. Unlocking the door of her bath-room she went inside, and soon emerged, bringing a rug, which she spread upon the floor of the gallery, and two huge hair pillows covered with crash,[1] which she placed against the front of the building.

The two seated themselves there in the shade of the porch, side by side, with their backs against the pillows and their feet extended. Madame Ratignolle removed her veil, wiped her face with a rather delicate handkerchief, and fanned herself with the fan which she always carried suspended somewhere about her person by a long, narrow ribbon. Edna removed her collar and opened her dress at the throat. She took the fan from Madame Ratignolle and began to fan both herself and her companion. It was very warm, and for a

1. A heavy linen fabric.

while they did nothing but exchange remarks about the heat, the sun, the glare. But there was a breeze blowing, a choppy stiff wind that whipped the water into froth. It fluttered the skirts of the two women and kept them for a while engaged in adjusting, readjusting, tucking in, securing hair-pins and hat-pins. A few persons were sporting some distance away in the water. The beach was very still of human sound at that hour. The lady in black was reading her morning devotions on the porch of a neighboring bath-house. Two young lovers were exchanging their hearts' yearnings beneath the children's tent, which they had found unoccupied.

Edna Pontellier, casting her eyes about had finally kept them at rest upon the sea. The day was clear and carried the gaze out as far as the blue sky went; there were a few white clouds suspended idly over the horizon. A lateen sail was visible in the direction of Cat Island, and others to the south seemed almost motionless in the far distance.

"Of whom—of what are you thinking?" asked Adèle of her companion, whose countenance she had been watching with a little amused attention, arrested by the absorbed expression which seemed to have seized and fixed every feature into a statuesque repose.

"Nothing," returned Mrs. Pontellier, with a start, adding at once: "How stupid! But it seems to me it is the reply we make instinctively to such a question. Let me see," she went on, throwing back her head and narrowing her fine eyes till they shone like two vivid points of light. "Let me see. I was really not conscious of thinking of anything; but perhaps I can retrace my thoughts."

"Oh! never mind!" laughed Madame Ratignolle. "I am not quite so exacting. I will let you off this time. It is really too hot to think, especially to think about thinking."

"But for the fun of it," persisted Edna. "First of all, the sight of the water stretching so far away, those motionless sails against the blue sky, made a delicious picture that I just wanted to sit and look at. The hot wind beating in my face made me think—without any connection that I can trace—of a summer day in Kentucky, of a meadow that seemed as big as the ocean to the very little girl walking through the grass, which was higher than her waist. She threw out her arms as if swimming when she walked, beating the tall grass as one strikes out in the water. Oh, I see the connection now!"

"Where were you going that day in Kentucky, walking through the grass?"

"I don't remember now. I was just walking diagonally across a big field. My sun-bonnet obstructed the view. I could see only the stretch of green before me, and I felt as if I must walk on forever, without coming to the end of it. I don't remember whether I was frightened or pleased. I must have been entertained.

"Likely as not it was Sunday," she laughed; "and I was running away from prayers, from the Presbyterian service, read in a spirit of gloom by my father that chills me yet to think of."

"And have you been running away from prayers ever since, *ma chère?*" asked Madame Ratignolle, amused.

"No! oh, no!" Edna hastened to say. "I was a little unthinking child in those days, just following a misleading impulse without question. On the contrary, during one period of my life religion took a firm hold upon me; after I was twelve and until—until— why, I suppose until now, though I never though much about it— just driven along by habit. But do you know," she broke off, turning her quick eyes upon Madame Ratignolle and leaning forward a little so as to bring her face quite close to that of her companion, "sometimes I feel this summer as if I were walking through the green meadow again; idly, aimlessly, unthinking and unguided."

Madame Ratignolle laid her hand over that of Mrs. Pontellier, which was near her. Seeing that the hand was not withdrawn, she clasped it firmly and warmly. She even stroked it a little, fondly, with the other hand, murmuring in an undertone, *"Pauvre chérie."*

The action was at first a little confusing to Edna, but she soon lent herself readily to the Creole's gentle caress. She was not accustomed to an outward and spoken expression of affection, either in herself or in others. She and her younger sister, Janet, had quarreled a good deal through force of unfortunate habit. Her older sister, Margaret, was matronly and dignified, probably from having assumed matronly and house-wifely responsibilities too early in life, their mother having died when they were quite young. Margaret was not effusive; she was practical. Edna had had an occasional girl friend, but whether accidentally or not, they seemed to have been all of one type—the self-contained. She never realized that the reserve of her own character had much, perhaps everything, to do with this. Her most intimate friend at school had been one of rather exceptional intellectual gifts, who wrote fine-sounding essays, which Edna admired and strove to imitate; and with her she talked and glowed over the English classics, and sometimes held religious and political controversies.

Edna often wondered at one propensity which sometimes had inwardly disturbed her without causing any outward show or manifestation on her part. At a very early age—perhaps it was when she traversed the ocean of waving grass—she remembered that she had been passionately enamored of a dignified and sad-eyed cavalry officer who visited her father in Kentucky. She could not leave his presence when he was there, nor remove her eyes from his face, which was something like Napoleon's, with a lock of black hair falling across the forehead. But the cavalry officer melted imperceptibly out of her existence.

At another time her affections were deeply engaged by a young gentleman who visited a lady on a neighboring plantation. It was after they went to Mississippi to live. The young man was engaged to be married to the young lady, and they sometimes called upon Margaret, driving over of afternoons in a buggy. Edna was a little miss, just merging into her teens; and the realization that she herself was nothing, nothing, nothing to the engaged young man was a bitter affliction to her. But he, too, went the way of dreams.

She was a grown young woman when she was overtaken by what she supposed to be the climax of her fate. It was when the face and figure of a great tragedian[2] began to haunt her imagination and stir her senses. The persistence of the infatuation lent it an aspect of genuineness. The hopelessness of it colored it with the lofty tones of a great passion.

The picture of the tragedian stood enframed upon her desk. Any one may possess the portrait of a tragedian without exciting suspicion or comment. (This was a sinister reflection which she cherished.) In the presence of others she expressed admiration for his exalted gifts, as she handed the photograph around and dwelt upon the fidelity of the likeness. When alone she sometimes picked it up and kissed the cold glass passionately.

Her marriage to Léonce Pontellier was purely an accident, in this respect resembling many other marriages which masquerade as the decrees of Fate. It was in the midst of her secret great passion that she met him. He fell in love, as men are in the habit of doing, and pressed his suit with an earnestness and an ardor which left nothing to be desired. He pleased her; his absolute devotion flattered her. She fancied there was a sympathy of thought and taste between them, in which fancy she was mistaken. Add to this the violent opposition of her father and her sister Margaret to her marriage with a Catholic, and we need seek no further for the motives which led her to accept Monsieur Pontellier for her husband.

The acme of bliss, which would have been a marriage with the tragedian, was not for her in this world. As the devoted wife of a man who worshiped her, she felt she would take her place with a certain dignity in the world of reality, closing the portals forever behind her upon the realm of romance and dreams.

But it was not long before the tragedian had gone to join the cavalry officer and the engaged young man and a few others; and Edna found herself face to face with the realities. She grew fond of

2. Probably Edwin Booth (1833–1893), the renowned Shakespearean actor par- ticularly acclaimed for his Hamlet.

her husband, realizing with some unaccountable satisfaction that no trace of passion or excessive and fictitious warmth colored her affection, thereby threatening its dissolution.

She was fond of her children in an uneven, impulsive way. She would sometimes gather them passionately to her heart; she would sometimes forget them. The year before they had spent part of the summer with their grandmother Pontellier in Iberville. Feeling secure regarding their happiness and welfare, she did not miss them except with an occasional intense longing. Their absence was a sort of relief, though she did not admit this, even to herself. It seemed to free her of a responsibility which she had blindly assumed and for which Fate had not fitted her.

Edna did not reveal so much as all this to Madame Ratignolle that summer day when they sat with faces turned to the sea. But a good part of it escaped her. She had put her head down on Madame Ratignolle's shoulder. She was flushed and felt intoxicated with the sound of her own voice and the unaccustomed taste of candor. It muddled her like wine, or like a first breath of freedom.

There was the sound of approaching voices. It was Robert, surrounded by a troop of children, searching for them. The two little Pontelliers were with him, and he carried Madame Ratignolle's little girl in his arms. There were other children beside, and two nursemaids followed, looking disagreeable and resigned.

The women at once rose and began to shake out their draperies and relax their muscles. Mrs. Pontellier threw the cushions and rug into the bath-house. The children all scampered off to the awning, and they stood there in a line, gazing upon the intruding lovers, still exchanging their vows and sighs. The lovers got up, with only a silent protest, and walked slowly away somewhere else.

The children possessed themselves of the tent, and Mrs. Pontellier went over to join them.

Madame Ratignolle begged Robert to accompany her to the house; she complained of cramp in her limbs and stiffness of the joints. She leaned draggingly upon his arm as they walked.

VIII

"Do me a favor, Robert," spoke the pretty woman at his side, almost as soon as she and Robert had started on their slow, homeward way. She looked up in his face, leaning on his arm beneath the encircling shadow of the umbrella which he had lifted.

"Granted; as many as you like," he returned, glancing down into her eyes that were full of thoughfulness and some speculation.

"I only ask for one; let Mrs. Pontellier alone."

"*Tiens!*" he exclaimed, with a sudden, boyish laugh. "*Voilà que Madame Ratignolle est jalouse!*"[3]

3. "So! Madame Ratignolle is jealous!"

"Nonsense! I'm in earnest; I mean what I say. Let Mrs. Pontellier alone."

"Why?" he asked; himself growing serious at his companion's solicitation.

"She is not one of us; she is not like us. She might make the unfortunate blunder of taking you seriously."

His face flushed with annoyance, and taking off his soft hat he began to beat it impatiently against his leg as he walked. "Why shouldn't she take me seriously?" he demanded sharply. "Am I a comedian, a clown, a jack-in-the-box? Why shouldn't she? You Creoles! I have no patience with you! Am I always to be regarded as a feature of an amusing programme? I hope Mrs. Pontellier does take me seriously. I hope she has discernment enough to find in me something besides the *blagueur*.[4] If I thought there was any doubt—"

"Oh, enough, Robert!" she broke into his heated outburst. "You are not thinking of what you are saying. You speak with about as little reflection as we might expect from one of those children down there playing in the sand. If your attentions to any married women here were ever offered with any intention of being convincing, you would not be the gentleman we all know you to be, and you would be unfit to associate with the wives and daughters of the people who trust you."

Madame Ratignolle had spoken what she believed to be the law and the gospel. The young man shrugged his shoulders impatiently.

"Oh! well! That isn't it," slamming his hat down vehemently upon his head. "You ought to feel that such things are not flattering to say to a fellow."

"Should our whole intercourse consist of an exchange of compliments? *Ma foi!*"[5]

"It isn't pleasant to have a woman tell you—" he went on, unheedingly, but breaking off suddenly: "Now if I were like Arobin—you remember Alcée Arobin and that story of the consul's wife at Biloxi?"[6] And he related the story of Alcée Arobin and the consul's wife; and another about the tenor of the French Opera,[7] who received letters which should never have been written; and still other stories, grave and gay, till Mrs. Pontellier and her possible propensity for taking young men seriously was apparently forgotten.

Madame Ratignolle, when they had regained her cottage, went in to take the hour's rest which she considered helpful. Before leaving her, Robert begged her pardon for the impatience—he called it rudeness—with which he had received her well-meant caution.

4. Joker, clown.
5. "For heaven's sake!"
6. A Mississippi coastal resort.

7. The French Opera in New Orleans was one of the most distinguished opera companies in nineteenth-century America.

"You made one mistake, Adèle," he said, with a light smile; "there is no earthly possibility of Mrs. Pontellier ever taking me seriously. You should have warned me against taking myself seriously. Your advice might then have carried some weight and given me subject for some reflection. *Au revoir*. But you look tired," he added, solicitously. "Would you like a cup of bouillon? Shall I stir you a toddy? Let me mix you a toddy with a drop of Angostura."

She acceded to the suggestion of bouillon, which was grateful and acceptable. He went himself to the kitchen, which was a building apart from the cottages and lying to the rear of the house. And he himself brought her the golden-brown bouillon, in a dainty Sèvres cup, with a flaky cracker or two on the saucer.

She thrust a bare, white arm from the curtain which shielded her open door, and received the cup from his hands. She told him he was a *bon garçon*,[8] and she meant it. Robert thanked her and turned away toward "the house."

The lovers were just entering the grounds of the *pension*. They were leaning toward each other as the water-oaks bent from the sea. There was not a particle of earth beneath their feet. Their heads might have been turned upside-down, so absolutely did they tread upon blue ether. The lady in black, creeping behind them, looked a trifle paler and more jaded than usual. There was no sign of Mrs. Pontellier and the children. Robert scanned the distance for any such apparition. They would doubtless remain away till the dinner hour. The young man ascended to his mother's room. It was situated at the top of the house, made up of odd angles and a queer, sloping ceiling. Two broad dormer windows looked out toward the Gulf, and as far across it as a man's eye might reach. The furnishings of the room were light, cool, and practical.

Madame Lebrun was busily engaged at the sewing-machine. A little black girl sat on the floor, and with her hands worked the treadle of the machine. The Creole woman does not take any chances which may be avoided of imperiling her health.

Robert went over and seated himself on the broad sill of one of the dormer windows. He took a book from his pocket and began energetically to read it, judging by the precision and frequency with which he turned the leaves. The sewing-machine made a resounding clatter in the room; it was of a ponderous, by-gone make. In the lulls, Robert and his mother exchanged bits of desultory conversation.

"Where is Mrs. Pontellier?"

"Down at the beach with the children."

8. A "nice fellow." Madame is making   means "good waiter."
a pun, as in this context the phrase also

"I promised to lend her the Goncourt.[9] Don't forget to take it down when you go; it's there on the bookshelf over the small table." Clatter, clatter, clatter, bang! for the next five or eight minutes.

"Where is Victor going with the rockaway?"

"The rockaway? Victor?"

"Yes; down there in front. He seems to be getting ready to drive away somewhere."

"Call him." Clatter, clatter!

Robert uttered a shrill, piercing whistle which might have been heard back at the wharf.

"He won't look up."

Madame Lebrun flew to the window. She called "Victor!" She waved a handkerchief and called again. The young fellow below got into the vehicle and started the horse off at a gallop.

Madame Lebrun went back to the machine, crimson with annoyance. Victor was the younger son and brother—a *tête montée*,[1] with a temper which invited violence and a will which no ax could break.

"Whenever you say the word I'm ready to thrash any amount of reason into him that he's able to hold."

"If your father had only lived!" Clatter, clatter, clatter, clatter, bang! It was a fixed belief with Madame Lebrun that the conduct of the universe and all things pertaining thereto would have been manifestly of a more intelligent and higher order had not Monsieur Lebrun been removed to other spheres during the early years of their married life.

"What do you hear from Montel?" Montel was a middle-aged gentleman whose vain ambition and desire for the past twenty years had been to fill the void which Monsieur Lebrun's taking off had left in the Lebrun household. Clatter, clatter, bang, clatter!

"I have a letter somewhere," looking in the machine drawer and finding the letter in the bottom of the work-basket. "He says to tell you he will be in Vera Cruz the beginning of next month"—clatter, clatter!—"and if you still have the intention of joining him"—bang! clatter, clatter, bang!

"Why didn't you tell me so before, mother? You know I wanted—" Clatter, clatter, clatter!

"Do you see Mrs. Pontellier starting back with the children? She will be in late to luncheon again. She never starts to get ready for luncheon till the last minute." Clatter, clatter! "Where are you going?"

"Where did you say the Goncourt was?"

IX

Every light in the hall was ablaze; every lamp turned as high as it could be without smoking the chimney or threatening explosion. The lamps were fixed at intervals against the wall, encircling the whole room. Some one had gathered orange and lemon branches and with these fashioned graceful festoons between. The dark green of the branches stood out and glistened against the white muslin curtains which draped the windows, and which puffed, floated, and flapped at the capricious will of a stiff breeze that swept up from the Gulf.

It was Saturday night a few weeks after the intimate conversation held between Robert and Madame Ratignolle on their way from the beach. An unusual number of husbands, fathers, and friends had come down to stay over Sunday; and they were being suitably entertained by their families, with the material help of Madame Lebrun. The dining tables had all been removed to one end of the hall, and the chairs ranged about in rows and in clusters. Each little family group had had its say and exchanged its domestic gossip earlier in the evening. There was now an apparent disposition to relax; to widen the circle of confidences and give a more general tone to the conversation.

Many of the children had been permitted to sit up beyond their usual bedtime. A small band of them were lying on their stomachs on the floor looking at the colored sheets of the comic papers which Mr. Pontellier had brought down. The little Pontellier boys were permitting them to do so, and making their authority felt.

Music, dancing, and a recitation or two were the entertainments furnished, or rather, offered. But there was nothing systematic about the programme, no appearance of prearrangement nor even premeditation.

At an early hour in the evening the Farival twins were prevailed upon to play the piano. They were girls of fourteen, always clad in the Virgin's colors, blue and white, having been dedicated to the Blessed Virgin at their baptism. They played a duet from "Zampa," and at the earnest solicitation of every one present followed it with the overture to "The Poet and the Peasant."

"*Allez vous-en! Sapristi!*" shrieked the parrot outside the door. He was the only being present who possessed sufficient candor to admit that he was not listening to these gracious performances for the first time that summer. Old Monsieur Farival, grandfather of the twins, grew indignant over the interruption, and insisted upon having the bird removed and consigned to regions of darkness. Victor Lebrun objected; and his decrees were as immutable as those of Fate. The parrot fortunately offered no further interruption to the entertainment, the whole venom of his nature apparently having been cherished up and hurled against the twins in that one impetuous outburst.

Later a young brother and sister gave recitations, which every one present had heard many times at winter evening entertainments in the city.

A little girl performed a skirt dance in the center of the floor. The mother played her accompaniments and at the same time watched her daughter with greedy admiration and nervous apprehension. She need have had no apprehension. The child was mistress of the situation. She had been properly dressed for the occasion in black tulle[2] and black silk tights. Her little neck and arms were bare, and her hair, artificially crimped, stood out like fluffy black plumes over her head. Her poses were full of grace, and her little black-shod toes twinkled as they shot out and upward with a rapidity and suddenness which were bewildering.

But there was no reason why every one should not dance. Madame Ratignolle could not, so it was she who gaily consented to play for the others. She played very well, keeping excellent waltz time and infusing an expression into the strains which was indeed inspiring. She was keeping up her music on account of the children, she said; because she and her husband both considered it a means of brightening the home and making it attractive.

Almost every one danced but the twins, who could not be induced to separate during the brief period when one or the other should be whirling around the room in the arms of a man. They might have danced together, but they did not think of it.

The children were sent to bed. Some went submissively; others with shrieks and protests as they were dragged away. They had been permitted to sit up till after the ice-cream, which naturally marked the limit of human indulgence.

The ice-cream was passed around with cake—gold and silver cake arranged on platters in alternate slices; it had been made and frozen during the afternoon back of the kitchen by two black women, under the supervision of Victor. It was pronounced a great success—excellent if it had only contained a little less vanilla or a little more sugar, if it had been frozen a degree harder, and if the salt might have been kept out of portions of it. Victor was proud of his achievement, and went about recommending it and urging every one to partake of it to excess.

After Mrs. Pontellier had danced twice with her husband, once with Robert, and once with Monsieur Ratignolle, who was thin and tall and swayed like a reed in the wind when he danced, she went out on the gallery and seated herself on the low window-sill, where she commanded a view of all that went on in the hall and could

2. A thin, soft netting, usually silk.

look out toward the Gulf. There was a soft effulgence in the east. The moon was coming up, and its mystic shimmer was casting a million lights across the distant, restless water.

"Would you like to hear Mademoiselle Reisz play?" asked Robert, coming out on the porch where she was. Of course Edna would like to hear Mademoiselle Reisz play; but she feared it would be useless to entreat her.

"I'll ask her," he said. "I'll tell her that you want to hear her. She likes you. She will come." He turned and hurried away to one of the far cottages, where Mademoiselle Reisz was shuffling away. She was dragging a chair in and out of her room, and at intervals objecting to the crying of a baby, which a nurse in the adjoining cottage was endeavoring to put to sleep. She was a disagreeable little woman, no longer young, who had quarreled with almost every one, owing to a temper which was self-assertive and a disposition to trample upon the rights of others. Robert prevailed upon her without any too great difficulty.

She entered the hall with him during a lull in the dance. She made an awkward, imperious little bow as she went in. She was a homely woman, with a small weazened face and body and eyes that glowed. She had absolutely no taste in dress, and wore a batch of rusty black lace with a bunch of artifical violets pinned to the side of her hair.

"Ask Mrs. Pontellier what she would like to hear me play," she requested of Robert. She sat perfectly still before the piano, not touching the keys, while Robert carried her message to Edna at the window. A general air of surprise and genuine satisfaction fell upon every one as they saw the pianist enter. There was a settling down, and a prevailing air of expectancy everywhere. Edna was a trifle embarrassed at being thus signaled out for the imperious little woman's favor. She would not dare to choose, and begged that Mademoiselle Reisz would please herself in her selections.

Edna was what she herself called very fond of music. Musical strains, well rendered, had a way of evoking pictures in her mind. She sometimes liked to sit in the room of mornings when Madame Ratignolle played or practiced. One piece which that lady played Edna had entitled "Solitude."[3] It was a short, plaintive, minor strain. The name of the piece was something else, but she called it "Solitude." When she heard it there came before her imagination the figure of a man standing beside a desolate rock on the seashore.

3. Chopin's first biographer, Daniel Rankin, states that "A Solitary Soul" was the original title of *The Awakening* and that the title may have been changed by her publisher. In her notebook Chopin retained "A Solitary Soul" when she added the present title; and Per Seyersted, her second biographer, suggests she may have wished to retain "A Solitary Soul" as the subtitle. See "Edna Pontellier: A Solitary Soul," p. 224.

He was naked. His attitude was one of hopeless resignation as he looked toward a distant bird winging its flight away from him.

Another piece called to her mind a dainty young woman clad in an Empire gown, taking mincing dancing steps as she came down a long avenue between tall hedges. Again, another reminded her of children at play, and still another of nothing on earth but a demure lady stroking a cat.

The very first chords which Mademoiselle Reisz struck upon the piano sent a keen tremor down Mrs. Pontellier's spinal column. It was not the first time she had heard an artist at the piano. Perhaps it was the first time she was ready, perhaps the first time her being was tempered to take an impress of the abiding truth.

She waited for the material pictures which she thought would gather and blaze before her imagination. She waited in vain. She saw no pictures of solitude, of hope, of longing, or of despair. But the very passions themselves were aroused within her soul, swaying it, lashing it, as the waves daily beat upon her splendid body. She trembled, she was choking, and the tears blinded her.

Mademoiselle had finished. She arose, and bowing her stiff, lofty bow, she went away, stopping for neither thanks nor applause. As she passed along the gallery she patted Edna upon the shoulder.

"Well, how did you like my music?" she asked. The young woman was unable to answer; she pressed the hand of the pianist convulsively. Mademoiselle Reisz perceived her agitation and even her tears. She patted her again upon the shoulder as she said:

"You are the only one worth playing for. Those others? Bah!" and she went shuffling and sidling on down the gallery toward her room.

But she was mistaken about "those others." Her playing had aroused a fever of enthusiasm. "What passion!" "What an artist!" "I have always said no one could play Chopin like Mademoiselle Reisz!" "That last prelude! Bon Dieu! It shakes a man!"

It was growing late, and there was a general disposition to disband. But some one, perhaps it was Robert, thought of a bath at that mystic hour and under that mystic moon.

X

At all events Robert proposed it, and there was not a dissenting voice. There was not one but was ready to follow when he led the way. He did not lead the way, however, he directed the way; and he himself loitered behind with the lovers, who had betrayed a disposition to linger and hold themselves apart. He walked between them, whether with malicious or mischievous intent was not wholly clear, even to himself.

The Pontelliers and Ratignolles walked ahead; the women leaning upon the arms of their husbands. Edna could hear Robert's voice behind them, and could sometimes hear what he said. She wondered why he did not join them. It was unlike him not to. Of late he had sometimes held away from her for an entire day, redoubling his devotion upon the next and the next, as though to make up for hours that had been lost. She missed him the days when some pretext served to take him away from her, just as one misses the sun on a cloudy day without having thought much about the sun when it was shining.

The people walked in little groups toward the beach. They talked and laughed; some of them sang. There was a band playing down at Klein's hotel, and the strains reached them faintly, tempered by the distance. There were strange, rare odors abroad—a tangle of the sea smell and of weeds and damp, new-plowed earth, mingled with the heavy perfume of a field of white blossoms somewhere near. But the night sat lightly upon the sea and the land. There was no weight of darkness; there were no shadows. The white light of the moon had fallen upon the world like the mystery and the softness of sleep.

Most of them walked into the water as though into a native element. The sea was quiet now, and swelled lazily in broad billows that melted into one another and did not break except upon the beach in little foamy crests that coiled back like slow, white serpents.

Edna had attempted all summer to learn to swim. She had received instructions from both the men and women; in some instances from the children. Robert had pursued a system of lessons almost daily; and he was nearly at the point of discouragement in realizing the futility of his efforts. A certain ungovernable dread hung about her when in the water, unless there was a hand near by that might reach out and reassure her.

But that night she was like the little tottering, stumbling, clutching child, who of a sudden realizes it powers, and walks for the first time alone, boldly and with over-confidence. She could have shouted for joy. She did shout for joy, as with a sweeping stroke or two she lifted her body to the surface of the water.

A feeling of exultation overtook her, as if some power of significant import had been given her soul. She grew daring and reckless, overestimating her strength. She wanted to swim far out, where no woman had swum before.

Her unlooked-for achievement was the subject of wonder, applause, and admiration. Each one congratulated himself that his special teachings had accomplished this desired end.

"How easy it is!" she thought. "It is nothing," she said aloud; "why did I not discover before that it was nothing. Think of the time I have lost splashing about like a baby!" She would not join the groups in their sports and bouts, but intoxicated with her newly conquered power, she swam out alone.

She turned her face seaward to gather in an impression of space and solitude, which the vast expanse of water, meeting and melting with the moonlit sky, conveyed to her excited fancy. As she swam she seemed to be reaching out for the unlimited in which to lose herself.

Once she turned and looked toward the shore, toward the people she had left there. She had not gone any great distance—that is, what would have been a great distance for an experienced swimmer. But to her unaccustomed vision the stretch of water behind her assumed the aspect of a barrier which her unaided strength would never be able to overcome.

A quick vision of death smote her soul, and for a second of time appalled and enfeebled her senses. But by an effort she rallied her staggering faculties and managed to regain the land.

She made no mention of her encounter with death and her flash of terror, except to say to her husband, "I thought I should have perished out there alone."

"You were not so very far, my dear; I was watching you," he told her.

Edna went at once to the bath-house, and she had put on her dry clothes and was ready to return home before the others had left the water. She started to walk away alone. They all called to her and shouted to her. She waved a dissenting hand, and went on, paying no further heed to their renewed cries which sought to detain her.

"Sometimes I am tempted to think that Mrs. Pontellier is capricious" said Madame Lebrun, who was amusing herself immensely and feared that Edna's abrupt departure might put an end to the pleasure.

"I know she is," assented Mr. Pontellier; "sometimes, not often."

Edna had not traversed a quarter of the distance on her way home before she was overtaken by Robert.

"Did you think I was afraid?" she asked him, without a shade of annoyance.

"No; I knew you weren't afraid."

"Then why did you come? Why didn't you stay out there with the others?"

"I never thought of it."

"Thought of what?"

"Of anything. What difference does it make?"

"I'm very tired," she uttered, complainingly.

"I know you are."

"You don't know anything about it. Why should you know? I

never was so exhausted in my life. But it isn't unpleasant. A thousand emotions have swept through me to-night. I don't comprehend half of them. Don't mind what I'm saying; I am just thinking aloud. I wonder if I shall ever be stirred again as Mademoiselle Reisz's playing moved me to-night. I wonder if any night on earth will ever again be like this one. It is like a night in a dream. The people about me are like some uncanny, half-human beings. There must be spirits abroad to-night."

"There are," whispered Robert. "Didn't you know this was the twenty-eighth of August?"

"The twenty-eighth of August?"

"Yes. On the twenty-eighth of August, at the hour of midnight, and if the moon is shining—the moon must be shining—a spirit that has haunted these shores for ages rises up from the Gulf. With its own penetrating vision the spirit seeks some one mortal worthy to hold him company, worthy of being exalted for a few hours into realms of the semi-celestials.[4] His search has always hitherto been fruitless, and he has sunk back, disheartened, into the sea. But to-night he found Mrs. Pontellier. Perhaps he will never wholly release her from the spell. Perhaps she will never again suffer a poor, unworthy earthling to walk in the shadow of her divine presence."

"Don't banter me," she said, wounded at what appeared to be his flippancy. He did not mind the entreaty, but the tone with its delicate note of pathos was like a reproach. He could not explain; he could not tell her that he had penetrated her mood and understood. He said nothing except to offer her his arm, for, by her own admission, she was exhausted. She had been walking alone with her arms hanging limp, letting her white skirts trail along the dewy path. She took his arm, but she did not lean upon it. She let her hand lie listlessly, as though her thoughts were elsewhere—somewhere in advance of her body, and she was striving to overtake them.

Robert assisted her into the hammock which swung from the post before her door out to the trunk of a tree.

"Will you stay out here and wait for Mr. Pontellier?" he asked.

"I'll stay out here. Good-night."

"Shall I get you a pillow?"

"There's one here," she said, feeling about, for they were in the shadow.

"It must be soiled; the children have been tumbling it about."

"No matter." And having discovered the pillow, she adjusted it beneath her head. She extended herself in the hammock with a deep breath of relief. She was not a supercilious or an over-dainty woman. She was not much given to reclining in the hammock, and

4. Partly divine.

when she did so it was with no cat-like suggestion of voluptuous ease, but with a beneficent repose which seemed to invade her whole body.

"Shall I stay with you till Mr. Pontellier comes?" asked Robert, seating himself on the outer edge of one of the steps and taking hold of the hammock rope which was fastened to the post.

"If you wish. Don't swing the hammock. Will you get my white shawl which I left on the window-sill over at the house?"

"Are you chilly?"

"No; but I shall be presently."

"Presently?" he laughed. "Do you know what time it is? How long are you going to stay out here?"

"I don't know. Will you get the shawl?"

"Of course I will," he said, rising. He went over to the house, walking along the grass. She watched his figure pass in and out of the strips of moonlight. It was past midnight. It was very quiet.

When he returned with the shawl she took it and kept it in her hand. She did not put it around her.

"Did you say I should stay till Mr. Pontellier came back?"

"I said you might if you wished to."

He seated himself again and rolled a cigarette, which he smoked in silence. Neither did Mrs. Pontellier speak. No multitude of words could have been more significant than those moments of silence, or more pregnant with the first-felt throbbings of desire.

When the voices of the bathers were heard approaching, Robert said good-night. She did not answer him. He thought she was asleep. Again she watched his figure pass in and out of the strips of moonlight as he walked away.

XI

"What are you doing out here, Edna? I thought I should find you in bed," said her husband, when he discovered her lying there. He had walked up with Madame Lebrun and left her at the house. His wife did not reply.

"Are you asleep?" he asked, bending down close to look at her.

"No." Her eyes gleamed bright and intense, with no sleepy shadows, as they looked into his.

"Do you know it is past one o'clock? Come on," and he mounted the steps and went into their room.

"Edna!" called Mr. Pontellier from within, after a few moments had gone by.

"Don't wait for me," she answered. He thrust his head through the door.

"You will take cold out there," he said, irritably. "What folly is this? Why don't you come in?"

"It isn't cold; I have my shawl."

"The mosquitoes will devour you."

"There are no mosquitoes."

She heard him moving about the room; every sound indicating impatience and irritation. Another time she would have gone in at his request. She would, through habit, have yielded to his desire; not with any sense of submission or obedience to his compelling wishes, but unthinkingly, as we walk, move, sit, stand, go through the daily treadmill of the life which has been portioned out to us.

"Edna, dear, are you not coming in soon?" he asked again, this time fondly, with a note of entreaty.

"No; I am going to stay out here."

"This is more than folly," he blurted out. "I can't permit you to stay out there all night. You must come in the house instantly."

With a writhing motion she settled herself more securely in the hammock. She perceived that her will had blazed up, stubborn and resistant. She could not at that moment have done other than denied and resisted. She wondered if her husband had ever spoken to her like that before, and if she had submitted to his command. Of course she had; she remembered that she had. But she could not realize why or how she should have yielded, feeling as she then did.

"Léonce, go to bed," she said. "I mean to stay out here. I don't wish to go in, and I don't intend to. Don't speak to me like that again; I shall not answer you."

Mr. Pontellier had prepared for bed, but he slipped on an extra garment. He opened a bottle of wine, of which he kept a small and select supply in a buffet of his own. He drank a glass of the wine and went out on the gallery and offered a glass to his wife. She did not wish any. He drew up the rocker, hoisted his slippered feet on the rail, and proceeded to smoke a cigar. He smoked two cigars; then he went inside and drank another glass of wine. Mrs. Pontellier again declined to accept a glass when it was offered to her. Mr. Pontellier once more seated himself with elevated feet, and after a reasonable interval of time smoked some more cigars.

Edna began to feel like one who awakens gradually out of a dream, a delicious, grotesque, impossible dream, to feel again the realities pressing into her soul. The physical need for sleep began to overtake her; the exuberance which had sustained and exalted her spirit left her helpless and yielding to the conditions which crowded her in.

The stillest hour of the night had come, the hour before dawn, when the world seems to hold its breath. The moon hung low, and had turned from silver to copper in the sleeping sky. The old owl no longer hooted, and the water-oaks had ceased to moan as they bent their heads.

Edna arose, cramped from lying so long and still in the hammock. She tottered up the steps, clutching feebly at the post before passing into the house.

"Are you coming in, Léonce?" she asked, turning her face toward her husband.

"Yes, dear," he answered, with a glance following a misty puff of smoke. "Just as soon as I have finished my cigar."

XII

She slept but a few hours. They were troubled and feverish hours, disturbed with dreams that were intangible, that eluded her, leaving only an impression upon her half-awakened senses of something unattainable. She was up and dressed in the cool of the early morning. The air was invigorating and steadied somewhat her faculties. However, she was not seeking refreshment or help from any source, either external or from within. She was blindly following whatever impulse moved her, as if she had placed herself in alien hands for direction, and freed her soul of responsibility.

Most of the people at that early hour were still in bed and asleep. A few, who intended to go over to the *Chênière* for mass, were moving about. The lovers, who had laid their plans the night before, were already strolling toward the wharf. The lady in black, with her Sunday prayer book, velvet and gold-clasped, and her Sunday silver beads, was following them at no great distance. Old Monsieur Farival was up, and was more than half inclined to do anything that suggested itself. He put on his big straw hat, and taking his umbrella from the stand in the hall, followed the lady in black, never overtaking her.

The little negro girl who worked Madame Lebrun's sewing-machine was sweeping the galleries with long, absent-minded strokes of the broom. Edna sent her up into the house to awaken Robert.

"Tell him I am going to the *Chênière*. The boat is ready; tell him to hurry."

He had soon joined her. She had never sent for him before. She had never asked for him. She had never seemed to want him before. She did not appear conscious that she had done anything unusual in commanding his presence. He was apparently equally unconscious of anything extraordinary in the situation. But his face was suffused with a quiet glow when he met her.

They went together back to the kitchen to drink coffee. There was no time to wait for any nicety of service. They stood outside the window and the cook passed them their coffee and a roll, which they drank and ate from the window-sill. Edna said it tasted good. She had not thought of coffee nor of anything. He told her he had often noticed that she lacked forethought.

"Wasn't it enough to think of going to the *Chênière* and waking you up?" she laughed. "Do I have to think of everything?—as Léonce says when he's in a bad humor. I don't blame him; he'd never be in a bad humor if it weren't for me."

They took a short cut across the sands. At a distance they could see the curious procession moving toward the wharf—the lovers, shoulder to shoulder, creeping; the lady in black, gaining steadily upon them; old Monsieur Farival, losing ground inch by inch, and a young barefooted Spanish girl, with a red kerchief on her head and a basket on her arm, bringing up the rear.

Robert knew the girl, and he talked to her a little in the boat. No one present understood what they said. Her name was Mariequita. She had a round, sly, piquant face and pretty black eyes. Her hands were small, and she kept them folded over the handle of her basket. Her feet were broad and coarse. She did not strive to hide them. Edna looked at her feet, and noticed the sand and slime between her brown toes.

Beaudelet grumbled because Mariequita was there, taking up so much room. In reality he was annoyed at having old Monsieur Farival, who considered himself the better sailor of the two. But he would not quarrel with so old a man as Monsieur Farival, so he quarreled with Mariequita. The girl was deprecatory at one moment, appealing to Robert. She was saucy the next, moving her head up and down, making "eyes" at Robert and making "mouths" at Beaudelet.

The lovers were all alone. They saw nothing, they heard nothing. The lady in black was counting her beads for the third time. Old Monsieur Farival talked incessantly of what he knew about handling a boat, and of what Beaudelet did not know on the same subject.

Edna liked it all. She looked Mariequita up and down, from her ugly brown toes to her pretty black eyes, and back again.

"Why does she look at me like that?" inquired the girl of Robert.

"Maybe she thinks you are pretty. Shall I ask her?"

"No. Is she your sweetheart?"

"She's a married lady, and has two children."

"Oh! well! Francisco ran away with Sylvano's wife, who had four children. They took all his money and one of the children and stole his boat."

"Shut up!"

"Does she understand?"

"Oh, hush!"

"Are those two married over there—leaning on each other?"

"Of course not," laughed Robert.

"Of course not," echoed Mariequita, with a serious, confirmatory bob of the head.

The sun was high up and beginning to bite. The swift breeze seemed to Edna to bury the sting of it into the pores of her face and hands. Robert held his umbrella over her.

As they went cutting sidewise through the water, the sails bellied taut, with the wind filling and overflowing them. Old Monsieur Farival laughed sardonically at something as he looked at the sails, and Beaudelet swore at the old man under his breath.

Sailing across the bay to the *Chênière Caminada*, Edna felt as if she were being borne away from some anchorage which had held her fast, whose chains had been loosening—had snapped the night before when the mystic spirit was abroad, leaving her free to drift whithersoever she chose to set her sails. Robert spoke to her incessantly; he no longer noticed Mariequita. The girl had shrimps in her bamboo basket. They were covered with Spanish moss. She beat the moss down impatiently, and muttered to herself sullenly.

"Let us go to Grande Terre[5] to-morrow?" said Robert in a low voice.

"What shall we do there?"

"Climb up the hill to the old fort and look at the little wriggling gold snakes, and watch the lizards sun themselves."

She gazed away toward Grande Terre and thought she would like to be alone there with Robert, in the sun, listening to the ocean's roar and watching the slimy lizards writhe in and out among the ruins of the old fort.

"And the next day or the next we can sail to the Bayou Brulow,"[6] he went on.

"What shall we do there?"

"Anything—cast bait for fish."

"No; we'll go back to Grande Terre. Let the fish alone."

"We'll go wherever you like," he said. "I'll have Tonie come over and help me patch and trim my boat. We shall not need Beaudelet nor any one. Are you afraid of the pirogue?"[7]

"Oh, no."

"Then I'll take you some night in the pirogue when the moon shines. Maybe your Gulf spirit will whisper to you in which of these islands the treasures are hidden—direct you to the very spot, perhaps."

"And in a day we should be rich!" she laughed. "I'd give it all to you, the pirate gold and every bit of treasure we could dig up. I

5. An island adjacent to Grand Isle.
6. Bayou Brulow (or Bruleau) was the nearest to Grand Isle of a series of villages built on stilts or platforms in large marshy areas called "bayous."
7. Dugout.

think you would know how to spend it. Pirate gold isn't a thing to be hoarded or utilized. It is something to squander and throw to the four winds, for the fun of seeing the golden specks fly."

"We'd share it, and scatter it together," he said. His face flushed.

They all went together up to the quaint little Gothic church of Our Lady of Lourdes, gleaming all brown and yellow with paint in the sun's glare.

Only Beaudelet remained behind, tinkering at his boat, and Mariequita walked away with her basket of shrimps, casting a look of childish ill-humor and reproach at Robert from the corner of her eye.

XIII

A feeling of oppression and drowsiness overcame Edna during the service. Her head began to ache, and the lights on the altar swayed before her eyes. Another time she might have made an effort to regain her composure; but her one thought was to quit the stifling atmosphere of the church and reach the open air. She arose, climbing over Robert's feet with a muttered apology. Old Monsieur Farival, flurried, curious, stood up, but upon seeing that Robert had followed Mrs. Pontellier, he sank back into his seat. He whispered an anxious inquiry of the lady in black, who did not notice him or reply, but kept her eyes fastened upon the pages of her velvet prayer-book.

"I felt giddy and almost overcome," Edna said, lifting her hands instinctively to her head and pushing her straw hat up from her forehead. "I couldn't have stayed through the service." They were outside in the shadow of the church. Robert was full of solicitude.

"It was folly to have thought of going in the first place, let alone staying. Come over to Madame Antoine's; you can rest there." He took her arm and led her away, looking anxiously and continuously down into her face.

How still it was, with only the voice of the sea whispering through the reeds that grew in the salt-water pools! The long line of little gray, weather-beaten houses nestled peacefully among the orange trees. It must always have been God's day on that low, drowsy island, Edna thought. They stopped, leaning over a jagged fence made of sea-drift, to ask for water. A youth, a mild-faced Acadian,[8] was drawing water from the cistern, which was nothing more than a rusty buoy, with an opening on one side, sunk in the ground. The water which the youth handed to them in a tin pail was not cold to taste, but it was cool to her heated face, and it greatly revived and refreshed her.

8. Descendant of the French Canadians who were expelled from Acadia, or Nova Scotia, by the British in 1755 and who made their way to other French colonies. Their settlements along the Louisiana coast remained French-speaking.

Madame Antoine's cot[9] was at the far end of the village. She welcomed them with all the native hospitality, as she would have opened her door to let the sunlight in. She was fat, and walked heavily and clumsily across the floor. She could speak no English, but when Robert made her understand that the lady who accompanied him was ill and desired to rest, she was all eagerness to make Edna feel at home and to dispose of her comfortably.

The whole place was immaculately clean, and the big, four-posted bed, snow-white, invited one to repose. It stood in a small side room which looked out across a narrow grass plot toward the shed, where there was a disabled boat lying keel upward.

Madame Antoine had not gone to mass. Her son Tonie had, but she supposed he would soon be back, and she invited Robert to be seated and wait for him. But he went and sat outside the door and smoked. Madame Antoine busied herself in the large front room preparing dinner. She was boiling mullets over a few red coals in the huge fireplace.

Edna, left alone in the little side room, loosened her clothes, removing the greater part of them. She bathed her face, her neck and arms in the basin that stood between the windows. She took off her shoes and stockings and stretched herself in the very center of the high, white bed. How luxurious it felt to rest thus in a strange, quaint bed, with its sweet country odor of laurel lingering about the sheets and mattress! She stretched her strong limbs that ached a little. She ran her fingers through her loosened hair for a while. She looked at her round arms as she held them straight up and rubbed them one after the other, observing closely, as if it were something she saw for the first time, the fine, firm quality and texture of her flesh. She clasped her hands easily above her head, and it was thus she fell asleep.

She slept lightly at first, half awake and drowsily attentive to the things about her. She could hear Madame Antoine's heavy, scraping tread as she walked back and forth on the sanded floor. Some chickens were clucking outside the windows, scratching for bits of gravel in the grass. Later she half heard the voices of Robert and Tonie talking under the shed. She did not stir. Even her eyelids rested numb and heavily over her sleepy eyes. The voices went on—Tonie's slow, Acadian drawl, Robert's quick, soft, smooth French. She understood French imperfectly unless directly addressed, and the voices were only part of the other drowsy, muffled sounds lulling her senses.

When Edna awoke it was with the conviction that she had slept long and soundly. The voices were hushed under the shed. Madame Antoine's step was no longer to be heard in the adjoining room.

9. Cottage.

Even the chickens had gone elsewhere to scratch and cluck. The mosquito bar was drawn over her; the old woman had come in while she slept and let down the bar. Edna arose quietly from the bed, and looking between the curtains of the window, she saw by the slanting rays of the sun that the afternoon was far advanced. Robert was out there under the shed, reclining in the shade against the sloping keel of the overturned boat. He was reading from a book. Tonie was no longer with him. She wondered what had become of the rest of the party. She peeped out at him two or three times as she stood washing herself in the little basin between the windows.

Madame Antoine had laid some coarse, clean towels upon a chair, and had placed a box of *poudre de riz* within easy reach. Edna dabbed the powder upon her nose and cheeks as she looked at herself closely in the little distorted mirror which hung on the wall above the basin. Her eyes were bright and wide awake and her face glowed.

When she had completed her toilet she walked into the adjoining room. She was very hungry. No one was there. But there was a cloth spread upon the table that stood against the wall, and a cover was laid for one, with a crusty brown loaf and a bottle of wine beside the plate. Edna bit a piece from the brown loaf, tearing it with her strong, white teeth. She poured some of the wine into the glass and drank it down. Then she went softly out of doors, and plucking an orange from the low-hanging bough of a tree, threw it at Robert, who did not know she was awake and up.

An illumination broke over his whole face when he saw her and joined her under the orange tree.

"How many years have I slept?" she inquired. "The whole island seems changed. A new race of beings must have sprung up, leaving only you and me as past relics. How many ages ago did Madame Antoine and Tonie die? and when did our people from Grand Isle disappear from the earth?"

He familiarly adjusted a ruffle upon her shoulder.

"You have slept precisely one hundred years. I was left here to guard your slumbers; and for one hundred years I have been out under the shed reading a book. The only evil I couldn't prevent was to keep a broiled fowl from drying up."

"If it had turned to stone, still will I eat it," said Edna, moving with him into the house. "But really, what has become of Monsieur Farival and the others?"

"Gone hours ago. When they found that you were sleeping they thought it best not to awake you. Any way, I wouldn't have let them. What was I here for?"

"I wonder if Léonce will be uneasy!" she speculated, as she seated herself at table.

"Of course not; he knows you are with me," Robert replied, as he busied himself among sundry pans and covered dishes which had been left standing on the hearth.

"Where are Madame Antoine and her son?" asked Edna.

"Gone to Vespers,[1] and to visit some friends, I believe. I am to take you back in Tonie's boat whenever you are ready to go."

He stirred the smoldering ashes till the broiled fowl began to sizzle afresh. He served her with no mean repast, dripping the coffee anew and sharing it with her. Madame Antoine had cooked little else than the mullets, but while Edna slept Robert had foraged the island. He was childishly gratified to discover her appetite, and to see the relish with which she ate the food which he had procured for her.

"Shall we go right away?" she asked, after draining her glass and brushing together the crumbs of the crusty loaf.

"The sun isn't as low as it will be in two hours," he answered.

"The sun will be gone in two hours."

"Well, let it go; who cares!"

They waited a good while under the orange trees, till Madame Antoine came back, panting, waddling, with a thousand apologies to explain her absence. Tonie did not dare to return. He was shy, and would not willingly face any woman except his mother.

It was very pleasant to stay there under the orange trees, while the sun dipped lower and lower, turning the western sky to flaming copper and gold. The shadows lengthened and crept out like stealthy, grotesque monsters across the grass.

Edna and Robert both sat upon the ground—that is, he lay upon the ground beside her, occasionally picking at the hem of her muslin gown.

Madame Antoine seated her fat body, broad and squat, upon a bench beside the door. She had been talking all the afternoon, and had wound herself up to the story-telling pitch.

And what stories she told them! But twice in her life she had left the *Chênière Caminada,* and then for the briefest span. All her years she had squatted and waddled there upon the island, gathering legends of the Baratarians[2] and the sea. The night came on, with the moon to lighten it. Edna could hear the whispering voices of dead men and the click of muffled gold.

When she and Robert stepped into Tonie's boat, with the red lateen sail, misty spirit forms were prowling in the shadows and

1. An evening church service.
2. The pirates, especially Jean Lafitte, who operated in the area of Baratria Bay. The area abounded with legends of pirateering, smuggling and buried treasure.

among the reeds, and upon the water were phantom ships, speeding to cover.

XIV

The youngest boy, Etienne, had been very naughty, Madame Ratignolle said, as she delivered him into the hands of his mother. He had been unwilling to go to bed and had made a scene; whereupon she had taken charge of him and pacified him as well as she could. Raoul had been in bed and asleep for two hours.

The youngster was in his long white nightgown, that kept tripping him up as Madame Ratignolle led him along by the hand. With the other chubby fist he rubbed his eyes, which were heavy with sleep and ill humor. Edna took him in her arms, and seating herself in the rocker, began to coddle and caress him, calling him all manner of tender names, soothing him to sleep.

It was not more than nine o'clock. No one had yet gone to bed but the children.

Léonce had been very uneasy at first, Madame Ratignolle said, and had wanted to start at once for the *Chênière*. But Monsieur Farival had assured him that his wife was only overcome with sleep and fatigue, that Tonie would bring her safely back later in the day; and he had thus been dissuaded from crossing the bay. He had gone over to Klein's, looking up some cotton broker whom he wished to see in regard to securities, exchanges, stocks, bonds, or something of the sort, Madame Ratignolle did not remember what. He said he would not remain away late. She herself was suffering from heat and oppression, she said. She carried a bottle of salts and a large fan. She would not consent to remain with Edna, for Monsieur Ratignolle was alone, and he detested above all things to be left alone.

When Etienne had fallen asleep Edna bore him into the back room, and Robert went and lifted the mosquito bar that she might lay the child comfortably in his bed. The quadroon had vanished. When they emerged from the cottage Robert bade Edna goodnight.

"Do you know we have been together the whole livelong day, Robert—since early this morning?" she said at parting.

"All but the hundred years when you were sleeping. Good-night."

He pressed her hand and went away in the direction of the beach. He did not join any of the others, but walked alone toward the Gulf.

Edna stayed outside, awaiting her husband's return. She had no desire to sleep or to retire; nor did she feel like going over to sit with the Ratignolles, or to join Madame Lebrun and a group whose animated voices reached her as they sat in conversation before the house. She let her mind wander back over her stay at Grand Isle;

and she tried to discover wherein this summer had been different from any and every other summer of her life. She could only realize that she herself—her present self—was in some way different from the other self. That she was seeing with different eyes and making the acquaintance of new conditions in herself that colored and changed her environment, she did not yet suspect.

She wondered why Robert had gone away and left her. It did not occur to her to think he might have grown tired of being with her the livelong day. She was not tired, and she felt that he was not. She regretted that he had gone. It was so much more natural to have him stay, when he was not absolutely required to leave her.

As Edna waited for her husband she sang low a little song that Robert had sung as they crossed the bay. It began with "Ah! *Si tu savais*," and every verse ended with "*si tu savais*."[3]

Robert's voice was not pretentious. It was musical and true. The voice, the notes, the whole refrain haunted her memory.

XV

When Edna entered the dining-room one evening a little late, as was her habit, an unusually animated conversation seemed to be going on. Several persons were talking at once, and Victor's voice was predominating, even over that of his mother. Edna had returned late from her bath, had dressed in some haste, and her face was flushed. Her head, set off by her dainty white gown, suggested a rich, rare blossom. She took her seat at table between old Monsieur Farival and Madame Ratignolle.

As she seated herself and was about to begin to eat her soup, which had been served when she entered the room, several persons informed her simultaneously that Robert was going to Mexico. She laid her spoon down and looked about her bewildered. He had been with her, reading to her all the morning, and had never even mentioned such a place as Mexico. She had not seen him during the afternoon; she had heard some one say he was at the house, upstairs with his mother. This she had thought nothing of, though she was surprised when he did not join her later in the afternoon, when she went down to the beach.

She looked across at him, where he sat beside Madame Lebrun, who presided. Edna's face was a blank picture of bewilderment, which she never thought of disguising. He lifted his eyebrows with the pretext of a smile as he returned her glance. He looked embarrassed and uneasy.

"When is he going?" she asked of everybody in general, as if Robert were not there to answer for himself.

"To-night!" "This very evening!" "Did you ever!" "What pos-

3. Refrain from a song by the same title ("Couldst Thou But Know") written by the Irish composer and baritone Michael William Balfe (1808–1870).

sesses him!" were some of the replies she gathered, uttered simultaneously in French and English.

"Impossible!" she exclaimed. "How can a person start off from Grand Isle to Mexico at a moment's notice, as if he were going over to Klein's or to the wharf or down to the beach?"

"I said all along I was going to Mexico; I've been saying so for years!" cried Robert, in an excited and irritable tone, with the air of a man defending himself against a swarm of stinging insects.

Madame Lebrun knocked on the table with her knife handle.

"Please let Robert explain why he is going, and why he is going to-night," she called out. "Really, this table is getting to be more and more like Bedlam[4] every day, with everybody talking at once. Sometimes—I hope God will forgive me—but positively, sometimes I wish Victor would lose the power of speech."

Victor laughed sardonically as he thanked his mother for her holy wish, of which he failed to see the benefit to anybody, except that it might afford her a more ample opportunity and license to talk herself.

Monsieur Farival thought that Victor should have been taken out in mid-ocean in his earliest youth and drowned. Victor thought there would be more logic in thus disposing of old people with an established claim for making themselves universally obnoxious. Madame Lebrun grew a trifle hysterical; Robert called his brother some sharp, hard names.

"There's nothing much to explain, mother," he said; though he explained, nevertheless—looking chiefly at Edna—that he could only meet the gentleman whom he intended to join at Vera Cruz by taking such and such a steamer, which left New Orleans on such a day; that Beaudelet was going out with his lugger-load of vegetables that night, which gave him an opportunity of reaching the city and making his vessel in time.

"But when did you make up your mind to all this?" demanded Monsieur Farival.

"This afternoon," returned Robert, with a shade of annoyance.

"At what time this afternoon?" persisted the old gentleman, with nagging determination, as if he were cross-questioning a criminal in a court of justice.

"At four o'clock this afternoon, Monsieur Farival," Robert replied, in a high voice and with a lofty air, which reminded Edna of some gentleman on the stage.

She had forced herself to eat most of her soup, and now she was picking the flaky bits of a *court bouillon*[5] with her fork.

The lovers were profiting by the general conversation on Mexico to speak in whispers of matters which they rightly considered were

4. An insane asylum.   5. Fish broth.

interesting to no one but themselves. The lady in black had once received a pair of prayer-beads of curious workmanship from Mexico, with very special indulgence attached to them, but she had never been able to ascertain whether the indulgence extended outside the Mexican border. Father Fochel of the Cathedral had attempted to explain it; but he had not done so to her satisfaction. And she begged that Robert would interest himself, and discover, if possible, whether she was entitled to the indulgence accompanying the remarkably curious Mexican prayer-beads.

Madame Ratignolle hoped that Robert would exercise extreme caution in dealing with the Mexicans, who, she considered, were a treacherous people, unscrupulous and revengeful. She trusted she did them no injustice in thus condemning them as a race. She had known personally but one Mexican, who made and sold excellent tamales, and whom she would have trusted implicitly, so softspoken was he. One day he was arrested for stabbing his wife. She never knew whether he had been hanged or not.

Victor had grown hilarious, and was attempting to tell an anecdote about a Mexican girl who served chocolate one winter in a restaurant in Dauphine Street.[6] No one would listen to him but old Monsieur Farival, who went into convulsions over the droll story.

Edna wondered if they had all gone mad, to be talking and clamoring at that rate. She herself could think of nothing to say about Mexico or the Mexicans.

"At what time do you leave?" she asked Robert.

"At ten," he told her. "Beaudelet wants to wait for the moon."

"Are you all ready to go?"

"Quite ready. I shall only take a handbag, and shall pack my trunk in the city."

He turned to answer some question put to him by his mother, and Edna, having finished her black coffee, left the table.

She went directly to her room. The little cottage was close and stuffy after leaving the outer air. But she did not mind; there appeared to be a hundred different things demanding her attention indoors. She began to set the toilet-stand to rights, grumbling at the negligence of the quadroon, who was in the adjoining room putting the children to bed. She gathered together stray garments that were hanging on the backs of chairs, and put each where it belonged in closet or bureau drawer. She changed her gown for a more comfortable and commodious wrapper. She rearranged her hair, combing and brushing it with unusual energy. Then she went in and assisted the quadroon in getting the boys to bed.

They were very playful and inclined to talk—to do anything but lie quiet and go to sleep. Edna sent the quadroon away to her

6. In the French Quarter.

supper and told her she need not return. Then she sat and told the children a story. Instead of soothing it excited them, and added to their wakefulness. She left them in heated argument, speculating about the conclusion of the tale which their mother promised to finish the following night.

The little black girl came in to say that Madame Lebrun would like to have Mrs. Pontellier go and sit with them over at the house till Mr. Robert went away. Edna returned answer that she had already undressed, that she did not feel quite well, but perhaps she would go over to the house later. She started to dress again, and got as far advanced as to remove her *peignoir*. But changing her mind once more she resumed the *peignoir*, and went outside and sat down before her door. She was overheated and irritable, and fanned herself energetically for a while. Madame Ratignolle came down to discover what was the matter.

"All that noise and confusion at the table must have upset me," replied Edna, "and moreover, I hate shocks and surprises. The idea of Robert starting off in such a ridiculously sudden and dramatic way! As if it were a matter of life and death! Never saying a word about it all morning when he was with me."

"Yes," agreed Madame Ratignolle. "I think it was showing us all—you especially—very little consideration. It wouldn't have surprised me in any of the others; those Lebruns are all given to heroics. But I must say I should never have expected such a thing from Robert. Are you not coming down? Come on, dear; it doesn't look friendly."

"No," said Edna, a little sullenly. "I can't go to the trouble of dressing again; I don't feel like it."

"You needn't dress; you look all right; fasten a belt around your waist. Just look at me!"

"No," persisted Edna; "but you go on. Madame Lebrun might be offended if we both stayed away."

Madame Ratignolle kissed Edna good-night, and went away, being in truth rather desirous of joining in the general and animated conversation which was still in progress concerning Mexico and the Mexicans.

Somewhat later Robert came up, carrying his hand-bag.

"Aren't you feeling well?" he asked.

"Oh, well enough. Are you going right away?"

He lit a match and looked at his watch. "In twenty minutes," he said. The sudden and brief flare of the match emphasized the darkness for a while. He sat down upon a stool which the children had left out on the porch.

"Get a chair," said Edna.

"This will do," he replied. He put on his soft hat and nervously took it off again, and wiping his face with his handkerchief, complained of the heat.

"Take the fan," said Edna, offering it to him.

"Oh, no! Thank you. It does no good; you have to stop fanning some time, and feel all the more uncomfortable afterward."

"That's one of the ridiculous things which men always say. I have never known one to speak otherwise of fanning. How long will you be gone?"

"Forever, perhaps. I don't know. It depends upon a good many things."

"Well, in case it shouldn't be forever, how long will it be?"

"I don't know."

"This seems to me perfectly preposterous and uncalled for. I don't like it. I don't understand your motive for silence and mystery, never saying a word to me about it this morning." He remained silent, not offering to defend himself. He only said, after a moment:

"Don't part from me in an ill-humor. I never knew you to be out of patience with me before."

"I don't want to part in any ill-humor," she said. "But can't you understand? I've grown used to seeing you, to having you with me all the time, and your action seems unfriendly, even unkind. You don't even offer an excuse for it. Why, I was planning to be together, thinking of how pleasant it would be to see you in the city next winter."

"So was I," he blurted. "Perhaps that's the—" He stood up suddenly and held out his hand. "Good-by, my dear Mrs. Pontellier; good-by. You won't—I hope you won't completely forget me." She clung to his hand, striving to detain him.

"Write to me when you get there, won't you, Robert?" she entreated.

"I will, thank you. Good-by."

How unlike Robert! The merest acquaintance would have said something more emphatic than "I will, thank you; good-by," to such a request.

He had evidently already taken leave of the people over at the house, for he descended the steps and went to join Beaudelet, who was out there with an oar across his shoulder waiting for Robert. They walked away in the darkness. She could only hear Beaudelet's voice; Robert had apparently not even spoken a word of greeting to his companion.

Edna bit her handkerchief convulsively, striving to hold back and to hide, even from herself as she would have hidden from another, the emotion which was troubling—tearing—her. Her eyes were brimming with tears.

For the first time she recognized anew the symptoms of infatuation which she felt incipiently as a child, as a girl in her earliest teens, and later as a young woman. The recognition did not lessen the reality, the poignancy of the revelation by any suggestion or promise of instability. The past was nothing to her; offered no lesson which she was willing to heed. The future was a mystery which she never attempted to penetrate. The present alone was significant; was hers, to torture her as it was doing then with the biting conviction that she had lost that which she had held, that she had been denied that which her impassioned, newly awakened being demanded.

XVI

"Do you miss your friend greatly?" asked Mademoiselle Reisz one morning as she came creeping up behind Edna, who had just left her cottage on her way to the beach. She spent much of her time in the water since she had acquired finally the art of swimming. As their stay at Grand Isle drew near its close, she felt that she could not give too much time to a diversion which afforded her the only real pleasurable moments that she knew. When Mademoiselle Reisz came and touched her upon the shoulder and spoke to her, the woman seemed to echo the thought which was ever in Edna's mind; or, better, the feeling which constantly possessed her.

Robert's going had some way taken the brightness, the color, the meaning out of everything. The conditions of her life were in no way changed, but her whole existence was dulled, like a faded garment which seems to be no longer worth wearing. She sought him everywhere—in others whom she induced to talk about him. She went up in the mornings to Madame Lebrun's room, braving the clatter of the old sewing-machine. She sat there and chatted at intervals as Robert had done. She gazed around the room at the pictures and photographs hanging upon the wall, and discovered in some corner an old family album, which she examined with the keenest interest, appealing to Madame Lebrun for enlightenment concerning the many figures and faces which she discovered between its pages.

There was a picture of Madame Lebrun with Robert as a baby, seated in her lap, a round-faced infant with a fist in his mouth. The eyes alone in the baby suggested the man. And that was he also in kilts, at the age of five, wearing long curls and holding a whip in his hand. It made Edna laugh, and she laughed, too, at the portrait in his first long trousers; while another interested her, taken when he left for college, looking thin, long-faced, with eyes full of fire, ambition and great intentions. But there was no recent picture, none which suggested the Robert who had gone away five days ago, leaving a void and wilderness behind him.

"Oh, Robert stopped having his pictures taken when he had to pay for them himself! He found wiser use for his money, he says," explained Madame Lebrun. She had a letter from him, written before he left New Orleans. Edna wished to see the letter, and Madame Lebrun told her to look for it either on the table or the dresser, or perhaps it was on the mantelpiece.

The letter was on the bookshelf. It possessed the greatest interest and attraction for Edna; the envelope, its size and shape, the postmark, the handwriting. She examined every detail of the outside before opening it. There were only a few lines, setting forth that he would leave the city that afternoon, that he had packed his trunk in good shape, that he was well, and sent her his love and begged to be affectionately remembered to all. There was no special message to Edna except a postscript saying that if Mrs. Pontellier desired to finish the book which he had been reading to her, his mother would find it in his room, among other books there on the table. Edna experienced a pang of jealousy because he had written to his mother rather than to her.

Every one seemed to take for granted that she missed him. Even her husband, when he came down the Saturday following Robert's departure, expressed regret that he had gone.

"How do you get on without him, Edna?" he asked.

"It's very dull without him," she admitted. Mr. Pontellier had seen Robert in the city, and Edna asked him a dozen questions or more. Where had they met? On Carondelet Street, in the morning. They had gone "in" and had a drink and a cigar together. What had they talked about? Chiefly about his prospects in Mexico, which Mr. Pontellier thought were promising. How did he look? How did he seem—grave, or gay, or how? Quite cheerful, and wholly taken up with the idea of his trip, which Mr. Pontellier found altogether natural in a young fellow about to seek fortune and adventure in a strange, queer country.

Edna tapped her foot impatiently, and wondered why the children persisted in playing in the sun when they might be under the trees. She went down and led them out of the sun, scolding the quadroon for not being more attentive.

It did not strike her as in the least grotesque that she should be making of Robert the object of conversation and leading her husband to speak of him. The sentiment which she entertained for Robert in no way resembled that which she felt for her husband, or had ever felt, or ever expected to feel. She had all her life long been accustomed to harbor thoughts and emotions which never voiced themselves. They had never taken the form of struggles. They belonged to her and were her own, and she entertained the conviction that she had a right to them and that they concerned no one but herself. Edna had once told Madame Ratignolle that she would never sacrifice herself for her children, or for any one. Then had followed a rather heated argument; the two women did not appear to understand each other or to be talking the same language. Edna tried to appease her friend, to explain.

"I would give up the unessential; I would give my money, I would give my life for my children; but I wouldn't give myself. I can't make it more clear; it's only something which I am beginning to comprehend, which is revealing itself to me."

"I don't know what you would call the essential, or what you mean by the unessential," said Madame Ratignolle, cheerfully; "but a woman who would give her life for her children could do no more than that—your Bible tells you so. I'm sure I couldn't do more than that."

"Oh, yes you could!" laughed Edna.

She was not surprised at Mademoiselle Reisz's question the morning that lady, following her to the beach, tapped her on the shoulder and asked if she did not greatly miss her young friend.

"Oh, good morning, Mademoiselle; it is you? Why, of course I miss Robert. Are you going down to bathe?"

"Why should I go down to bathe at the very end of the season when I haven't been in the surf all summer?" replied the woman, disagreeably.

"I beg your pardon," offered Edna, in some embarrassment, for she should have remembered that Mademoiselle Reisz's avoidance of the water had furnished a theme for much pleasantry. Some among them thought it was on account of her false hair, or the dread of getting the violets wet, while others attributed it to the natural aversion for water sometimes believed to accompany the artistic temperament. Mademoiselle offered Edna some chocolates in a paper bag, which she took from her pocket, by way of showing that she bore no ill feeling. She habitually ate chocolates for their sustaining quality; they contained much nutriment in small compass, she said. They saved her from starvation, as Madame Lebrun's table was utterly impossible; and no one save so impertinent a woman as Madame Lebrun could think of offering such food to people and requiring them to pay for it.

"She must feel very lonely without her son," said Edna, desiring to change the subject. "Her favorite son, too. It must have been quite hard to let him go."

Mademoiselle laughed maliciously.

"Her favorite son! Oh, dear! Who could have been imposing such a tale upon you? Aline Lebrun lives for Victor, and for Victor alone. She has spoiled him into the worthless creature he is. She worships him and the ground he walks on. Robert is very well in a way, to give up all the money he can earn to the family, and keep the barest pittance for himself. Favorite son, indeed! I miss the poor fellow myself, my dear. I liked to see him and to hear him about the place—the only Lebrun who is worth a pinch of salt. He comes to see me often in the city. I like to play to him. That Victor! hanging would be too good for him. It's a wonder Robert hasn't beaten him to death long ago."

"I thought he had great patience with his brother," offered Edna, glad to be talking about Robert, no matter what was said.

"Oh! he thrashed him well enough a year or two ago," said Mademoiselle. "It was about a Spanish girl, whom Victor considered that he had some sort of claim upon. He met Robert one day talking to the girl, or walking with her, or bathing with her, or carrying her basket—I don't remember what;—and he became so insulting and abusive that Robert gave him a thrashing on the spot that has kept him comparatively in order for a good while. It's about time he was getting another."

"Was her name Mariequita?" asked Edna.

"Mariequita—yes, that was it; Mariequita. I had forgotten. Oh, she's a sly one, and a bad one, that Mariequita!"

Edna looked down at Mademoiselle Reisz and wondered how she could have listened to her venom so long. For some reason she felt depressed, almost unhappy. She had not intended to go into the water; but she donned her bathing suit, and left Mademoiselle alone, seated under the shade of the children's tent. The water was growing cooler as the season advanced. Edna plunged and swam about with an abandon that thrilled and invigorated her. She remained a long time in the water, half hoping that Mademoiselle Reisz would not wait for her.

But Mademoiselle waited. She was very amiable during the walk back, and raved much over Edna's appearance in her bathing suit. She talked about music. She hoped that Edna would go to see her in the city, and wrote her address with the stub of a pencil on a piece of card which she found in her pocket.

"When do you leave?" asked Edna.

"Next Monday; and you?"

"The following week," answered Edna, adding, "It has been a pleasant summer, hasn't it, Mademoiselle?"

"Well," agreed Mademoiselle Reiz, with a shrug, "rather pleasant, if it hadn't been for the mosquitoes and the Farival twins."

XVII

The Pontelliers possessed a very charming home on Esplanade Street[7] in New Orleans. It was a large, double cottage, with a broad front veranda, whose round, fluted columns supported the sloping roof. The house was painted a dazzling white; the outside shutters, or jalousies, were green. In the yard, which was kept scrupulously neat, were flowers and plants of every description which flourishes in South Louisiana. Within doors the appointments were perfect after the conventional type. The softest carpets and rugs covered the floors; rich and tasteful draperies hung at doors and windows. There were paintings, selected with judgment and discrimination, upon the walls. The cut glass, the silver, the heavy damask which daily appeared upon the table were the envy of many women whose husbands were less generous than Mr. Pontellier.

Mr. Pontellier was very fond of walking about his house examining its various appointments and details, to see that nothing was amiss. He greatly valued his possessions, chiefly because they were his, and derived genuine pleasure from contemplating a painting, a statuette, a rare lace curtain—no matter what—after he had bought it and placed it among his household gods.

On Tuesday afternoons—Tuesday being Mrs. Pontellier's reception day[8]—there was a constant stream of callers—women who came in carriages or in the street cars, or walked when the air was soft and distance permitted. A light-colored mulatto boy, in dress coat and bearing a diminutive silver tray for the reception of cards, admitted them. A maid, in white fluted cap, offered the callers liqueur, coffee, or chocolate, as they might desire. Mrs. Pontellier, attired in a handsome reception gown, remained in the drawing-room the entire afternoon receiving her visitors. Men sometimes called in the evening with their wives.

This had been the programme which Mrs. Pontellier had religiously followed since her marriage, six years before. Certain evenings during the week she and her husband attended the opera or sometimes the play.

Mr. Pontellier left his home in the mornings between nine and ten o'clock, and rarely returned before half-past six or seven in the evening—dinner being served at half-past seven.

He and his wife seated themselves at table on Tuesday evening,

7. The most exclusive address of the Creole aristocracy. Called "Promenade Publique" in the 1830s, it was a street of palatial homes shaded by live oaks, palms, and magnolias.
8. A day once a week when a woman was expected to be "at home" to receive visitors. *The Ladies' Book of Etiquette, and Manual of Politeness* by Frances Hartley (Boston, 1875) instructs: "Let nothing, but the most imperative duty, call you out upon your reception day. Your callers are, in a measure, invited guests, and it will be an insulting mark of rudeness to be out when they call. Neither can you be excused, except in case of sickness" (pp. 76–77).

a few weeks after their return from Grand Isle. They were alone together. The boys were being put to bed; the patter of their bare, escaping feet could be heard occasionally, as well as the pursuing voice of the quadroon, lifted in mild protest and entreaty. Mrs. Pontellier did not wear her usual Tuesday reception gown; she was in ordinary house dress. Mr. Pontellier, who was observant about such things, noticed it, as he served the soup and handed it to the boy in waiting.

"Tired out, Edna? Whom did you have? Many callers?" he asked. He tasted his soup and began to season it with pepper, salt, vinegar, mustard—everything within reach.

"There were a good many," replied Edna, who was eating her soup with evident satisfaction. "I found their cards when I got home; I was out."

"Out!" exclaimed her husband, with something like genuine consternation in his voice as he laid down the vinegar cruet and looked at her through his glasses. "Why, what could have taken you out on Tuesday? What did you have to do?"

"Nothing. I simply felt like going out, and I went out."

"Well, I hope you left some suitable excuse," said her husband, somewhat appeased, as he added a dash of cayenne pepper to the soup.

"No, I left no excuse. I told Joe to say I was out, that was all."

"Why, my dear, I should think you'd understand by this time that people don't do such things; we've got to observe *les convenances*[9] if we ever expect to get on and keep up with the procession. If you felt that you had to leave home this afternoon, you should have left some suitable explanation for your absence.

"This soup is really impossible; it's strange that woman hasn't learned yet to make a decent soup. Any free-lunch stand in town serves a better one. Was Mrs. Belthrop here?"

"Bring the tray with the cards, Joe. I don't remember who was here."

The boy retired and returned after a moment, bringing the tiny silver tray, which was covered with ladies' visiting cards. He handed it to Mrs. Pontellier.

"Give it to Mr. Pontellier," she said.

Joe offered the tray to Mr. Pontellier, and removed the soup.

Mr. Pontellier scanned the names of his wife's callers, reading some of them aloud, with comments as he read.

" 'The Misses Delasidas.' I worked a big deal in futures[1] for their father this morning; nice girls; it's time they were getting married. 'Mrs. Belthrop.' I tell you what it is, Edna; you can't afford to snub

9. Proprieties, social conventions.
1. Items bought and sold for delivery at a future time, a form of speculation in stocks or commodities.

Mrs. Belthrop. Why, Belthrop could buy and sell us ten times over. His business is worth a good, round sum to me. You'd better write her a note. 'Mrs. James Highcamp.' Hugh! the less you have to do with Mrs. Highcamp, the better. 'Madame Laforcé.' Came all the way from Carrolton,[2] too, poor old soul. 'Miss Wiggs,' 'Mrs. Eleanor Boltons.' " He pushed the cards aside.

"Mercy!" exclaimed Edna, who had been fuming. "Why are you taking the thing so seriously and making such a fuss over it?"

"I'm not making any fuss over it. But it's just such seeming trifles that we've got to take seriously; such things count."

The fish was scorched. Mr. Pontellier would not touch it. Edna said she did not mind a little scorched taste. The roast was in some way not to his fancy, and he did not like the manner in which the vegetables were served.

"It seems to me," he said, "we spend money enough in this house to procure at least one meal a day which a man could eat and retain his self-respect."

"You used to think the cook was a treasure," returned Edna, indifferently.

"Perhaps she was when she first came; but cooks are only human. They need looking after, like any other class of persons that you employ. Suppose I didn't look after the clerks in my office, just let them run things their own way; they'd soon make a nice mess of me and my business."

"Where are you going?" asked Edna, seeing that her husband arose from table without having eaten a morsel except a taste of the highly-seasoned soup.

"I'm going to get my dinner at the club. Good night." He went into the hall, took his hat and stick from the stand, and left the house.

She was somewhat familiar with such scenes. They had often made her very unhappy. On a few previous occasions she had been completely deprived of any desire to finish her dinner. Sometimes she had gone into the kitchen to administer a tardy rebuke to the cook. Once she went to her room and studied the cookbook during an entire evening, finally writing out a menu for the week, which left her harassed with a feeling that, after all, she had accomplished no good that was worth the name.

But that evening Edna finished her dinner alone, with forced deliberation. Her face was flushed and her eyes flamed with some inward fire that lighted them. After finishing her dinner she went to her room, having instructed the boy to tell any other callers that she was indisposed.

It was a large, beautiful room, rich and picturesque in the soft,

2. A village to the west of New Orleans later absorbed by the city.

dim light which the maid had turned low. She went and stood at an open window and looked out upon the deep tangle of the garden below. All the mystery and witchery of the night seemed to have gathered there amid the perfumes and the dusky and tortuous outlines of flowers and foliage. She was seeking herself and finding herself in just such sweet, half-darkness which met her moods. But the voices were not soothing that came to her from the darkness and the sky above and the stars. They jeered and sounded mournful notes without promise, devoid even of hope. She turned back into the room and began to walk to and fro down its whole length, without stopping, without resting. She carried in her hands a thin handkerchief, which she tore into ribbons, rolled into a ball, and flung from her. Once she stopped, and taking off her wedding ring, flung it upon the carpet. When she saw it lying there, she stamped her heel upon it, striving to crush it. But her small boot heel did not make an indenture, not a mark upon the little glittering circlet.

In a sweeping passion she seized a glass vase from the table and flung it upon the tiles of the hearth. She wanted to destroy something. The crash and clatter were what she wanted to hear.

A maid, alarmed at the din of breaking glass, entered the room to discover what was the matter.

"A vase fell upon the hearth," said Edna. "Never mind; leave it till morning."

"Oh! you might get some of the glass in your feet, ma'am," insisted the young woman, picking up bits of the broken vase that were scattered upon the carpet. "And here's your ring, ma'am, under the chair."

Edna held out her hand, and taking the ring, slipped it upon her finger.

XVIII

The following morning Mr. Pontellier, upon leaving for his office, asked Edna if she would not meet him in town in order to look at some new fixtures for the library.

"I hardly think we need new fixtures, Léonce. Don't let us get anything new; you are too extravagant. I don't believe you ever think of saving or putting by."

"The way to become rich is to make money, my dear Edna, not to save it," he said. He regretted that she did not feel inclined to go with him and select new fixtures. He kissed her good-by, and told her she was not looking well and must take care of herself. She was unusually pale and very quiet.

She stood on the front veranda as he quitted the house, and absently picked a few sprays of jessamine[3] that grew upon a trellis near by. She inhaled the odor of the blossoms and thrust them into

3. Jasmine.

the bosom of her white morning gown. The boys were dragging along the banquette[4] a small "express wagon," which they had filled with blocks and sticks. The quadroon was following them with little quick steps, having assumed a fictitious animation and alacrity for the occasion. A fruit vender was crying his wares in the street.

Edna looked straight before her with a self-absorbed expression upon her face. She felt no interest in anything about her. The street, the children, the fruit vender, the flowers growing there under her eyes, were all part and parcel of an alien world which had suddenly become antagonistic.

She went back into the house. She had thought of speaking to the cook concerning her blunders of the previous night; but Mr. Pontellier had saved her that disagreeable mission, for which she was so poorly fitted. Mr. Pontellier's arguments were usually convincing with those whom he employed. He left home feeling quite sure that he and Edna would sit down that evening, and possibly a few subsequent evenings, to a dinner deserving of the name.

Edna spent an hour or two in looking over some of her old sketches. She could see their shortcomings and defects, which were glaring in her eyes. She tried to work a little, but found she was not in the humor. Finally she gathered together a few of the sketches— those which she considered the least discreditable; and she carried them with her when, a little later, she dressed and left the house. She looked handsome and distinguished in her street gown. The tan of the seashore had left her face, and her forehead was smooth, white, and polished beneath her heavy, yellow-brown hair. There were a few freckles on her face, and a small, dark mole near the under lip and one on the temple, half-hidden in her hair.

As Edna walked along the street she was thinking of Robert. She was still under the spell of her infatuation. She had tried to forget him, realizing the inutility of remembering. But the thought of him was like an obsession, ever pressing itself upon her. It was not that she dwelt upon details of their acquaintance, or recalled in any special or peculiar way his personality; it was his being, his existence, which dominated her thought, fading sometimes as if it would melt into the mist of the forgotten, reviving again with an intensity which filled her with an incomprehensible longing.

Edna was on her way to Madame Ratignolle's. Their intimacy, begun at Grand Isle, had not declined, and they had seen each other with some frequency since their return to the city. The Ratignolles lived at no great distance from Edna's home, on the corner of a side street, where Monsieur Ratignolle owned and conducted a drug store which enjoyed a steady and prosperous trade. His father had been in the business before him, and Monsieur Ratignolle stood well

4. Sidewalk.

in the community and bore an enviable reputation for integrity and clear-headedness. His family lived in commodious apartments over the store, having an entrance on the side within the *porte cochère*.[5] There was something which Edna thought very French, very foreign, about their whole manner of living. In the large and pleasant salon which extended across the width of the house, the Ratignolles entertained their friends once a fortnight with a *soirée musicale*,[6] sometimes diversified by card-playing. There was a friend who played upon the 'cello. One brought his flute and another his violin, while there were some who sang and a number who performed upon the piano with various degrees of taste and agility. The Ratignolles' *soirées musicales* were widely known, and it was considered a privilege to be invited to them.

Edna found her friend engaged in assorting the clothes which had returned that morning from the laundry. She at once abandoned her occupation upon seeing Edna, who had been ushered without ceremony into her presence.

" 'Cité can do it as well as I; it is really her business," she explained to Edna, who apologized for interrupting her. And she summoned a young black woman, whom she instructed, in French, to be very careful in checking off the list which she handed her. She told her to notice particularly if a fine linen handkerchief of Monsieur Ratignolle's, which was missing last week, had been returned; and to be sure to set to one side such pieces as required mending and darning.

Then placing an arm around Edna's waist, she led her to the front of the house, to the salon, where it was cool and sweet with the odor of great roses that stood upon the hearth in jars.

Madame Ratignolle looked more beautiful than ever there at home, in a negligé which left her arms almost wholly bare and exposed the rich, melting curves of her white throat.

"Perhaps I shall be able to paint your picture some day," said Edna with a smile when they were seated. She produced the roll of sketches and started to unfold them. "I believe I ought to work again. I feel as if I wanted to be doing something. What do you think of them? Do you think it worth while to take it up again and study some more? I might study for a while with Laidpore."[7]

She knew that Madame Ratignolle's opinion in such a matter would be next to valueless, that she herself had not alone decided, but determined; but she sought the words and praise and encouragement that would help her to put heart into her venture.

"Your talent is immense, dear!"

5. In America, a porch under which a carriage is driven in order to protect travelers alighting or boarding.
6. An evening of music.

7. No such painter was known to be active in New Orleans. The name was invented by Chopin, perhaps with satiric intent, as in French *laid* means "ugly."

"Nonsense!" protested Edna, well pleased.

"Immense, I tell you," persisted Madame Ratignolle, surveying the sketches one by one, at close range, then holding them at arm's length, narrowing her eyes, and dropping her head on one side. "Surely, this Bavarian peasant is worthy of framing; and this basket of apples! never have I seen anything more lifelike. One might almost be tempted to reach out a hand and take one."

Edna could not control a feeling which bordered upon complacency at her friend's praise, even realizing, as she did, its true worth. She retained a few of the sketches, and gave all the rest to Madame Ratignolle, who appreciated the gift far beyond its value and proudly exhibited the pictures to her husband when he came up from the store a little later for his midday dinner.

Mr. Ratignolle was one of those men who are called the salt of the earth. His cheerfulness was unbounded, and it was matched by his goodness of heart, his broad charity, and common sense. He and his wife spoke English with an accent which was only discernible through its un-English emphasis and a certain carefulness and deliberation. Edna's husband spoke English with no accent whatever. The Ratignolles understood each other perfectly. If ever the fusion of two human beings into one has been accomplished on this sphere it was surely in their union.

As Edna seated herself at table with them she thought, "Better a dinner of herbs," though it did not take her long to discover that was no dinner of herbs, but a delicious repast, simple, choice, and in every way satisfying.

Monsieur Ratignolle was delighted to see her, though he found her looking not so well as at Grand Isle, and he advised a tonic. He talked a good deal on various topics, a little politics, some city news and neighborhood gossip. He spoke with an animation and earnestness that gave an exaggerated importance to every syllable he uttered. His wife was keenly interested in everything he said, laying down her fork the better to listen, chiming in, taking the words out of his mouth.

Edna felt depressed rather than soothed after leaving them. The little glimpse of domestic harmony which had been offered her, gave her no regret, no longing. It was not a condition of life which fitted her, and she could see in it but an appalling and hopeless ennui. She was moved by a kind of commiseration for Madame Ratignolle,—a pity for that colorless existence which never uplifted its possessor beyond the region of blind contentment, in which no moment of anguish ever visited her soul, in which she would never have the taste of life's delirium. Edna vaguely wondered what she meant by "life's delirium." It had crossed her thought like some unsought, extraneous impression.

XIX

Edna could not help but think that it was very foolish, very childish, to have stamped upon her wedding ring and smashed the crystal vase upon the tiles. She was visited by no more outbursts, moving her to such futile expedients. She began to do as she liked and to feel as she liked. She completely abandoned her Tuesdays at home, and did not return the visits of those who had called upon her. She made no ineffectual efforts to conduct her household *en bonne ménagère*,[8] going and coming as it suited her fancy, and, so far as she was able, lending herself to any passing caprice.

Mr. Pontellier had been a rather courteous husband so long as he met a certain tacit submissiveness in his wife. But her new and unexpected line of conduct completely bewildered him. It shocked him. Then her absolute disregard for her duties as a wife angered him. When Mr. Pontellier became rude, Edna grew insolent. She had resolved never to take another step backward.

"It seems to me the utmost folly for a woman at the head of a household, and the mother of children, to spend in an atelier[9] days which would be better employed contriving for the comfort of her family."

"I feel like painting," answered Edna. "Perhaps I shan't always feel like it."

"Then in God's name paint! but don't let the family go to the devil. There's Madame Ratignolle; because she keeps up her music, she doesn't let everything else go to chaos. And she's more of a musician than you are a painter."

"She isn't a musician, and I'm not a painter. It isn't on account of painting that I let things go."

"On account of what, then?"

"Oh! I don't know. Let me alone; you bother me."

It sometimes entered Mr. Pontellier's mind to wonder if his wife were not growing a little unbalanced mentally. He could see plainly that she was not herself. That is, he could not see that she was becoming herself and daily casting aside that fictitious self which we assume like a garment with which to appear before the world.

Her husband let her alone as she requested, and went away to his office. Edna went up to her atelier—a bright room in the top of the house. She was working with great energy and interest, without accomplishing anything, however, which satisfied her even in the smallest degree. For a time she had the whole household enrolled in the service of art. The boys posed for her. They thought it amusing at first, but the occupation soon lost its attractiveness when they discovered that it was not a game arranged especially for their entertainment. The quadroon sat for hours before Edna's palette,

8. As a good housewife.　　　9. Studio.

patient as a savage, while the housemaid took charge of the children, and the drawing-room went undusted. But the house-maid, too, served her term as model when Edna perceived that the young woman's back and shoulders were molded on classic lines, and that her hair, loosened from its confining cap, became an inspiration. While Edna worked she sometimes sang low the little air, "*Ah! si tu savais!*"

It moved her with recollections. She could hear again the ripple of the water, the flapping sail. She could see the glint of the moon upon the bay, and could feel the soft, gusty beating of the hot south wind. A subtle current of desire passed through her body, weakening her hold upon the brushes and making her eyes burn.

There were days when she was very happy without knowing why. She was happy to be alive and breathing, when her whole being seemed to be one with the sunlight, the color, the odors, the luxuriant warmth of some perfect Southern day. She liked then to wander alone into strange and unfamiliar places. She discovered many a sunny, sleepy corner, fashioned to dream in. And she found it good to dream and to be alone and unmolested.

There were days when she was unhappy, she did not know why, —when it did not seem worth while to be glad or sorry, to be alive or dead; when life appeared to her like a grotesque pandemonium and humanity like worms struggling blindly toward inevitable annihilation. She could not work on such a day, nor weave fancies to stir her pulses and warm her blood.

XX

It was during such a mood that Edna hunted up Mademoiselle Reisz. She had not forgotten the rather disagreeable impression left upon her by their last interview; but she nevertheless felt a desire to see her—above all, to listen while she played upon the piano. Quite early in the afternoon she started upon her quest for the pianist. Unfortunately she had mislaid or lost Mademoiselle Reisz's card, and looking up her address in the city directory, she found that the woman lived on Bienvilles Street,[1] some distance away. The directory which fell into her hands was a year or more old, however, and upon reaching the number indicated, Edna discovered that the house was occupied by a respectable family of mulattoes who had *chambres garnies*[2] to let. They had been living there for six months, and knew absolutely nothing of a Mademoiselle Reisz. In fact, they knew nothing of any of their neighbors; their lodgers were all people of the highest distinction, they assured Edna. She did not linger to discuss class distinctions with Madame Pouponne, but hastened

1. On the opposite side of the French Quarter from the Pontellier's house, the street runs down to the shipyards.
2. Furnished rooms.

to a neighboring grocery store, feeling sure that Mademoiselle would have left her address with the proprietor.

He knew Mademoiselle Reisz a good deal better than he wanted to know her, he informed his questioner. In truth, he did not want to know her at all, anything concerning her—the most disagreeable and unpopular woman who ever lived in Bienville Street. He thanked heaven she had left the neighborhood, and was equally thankful that he did not know where she had gone.

Edna's desire to see Mademoiselle Reisz had increased tenfold since these unlooked-for obstacles had arisen to thwart it. She was wondering who could give her the information she sought, when it suddenly occurred to her that Madame Lebrun would be the one most likely to do so. She knew it was useless to ask Madame Ratignolle, who was on the most distant terms with the musician, and preferred to know nothing concerning her. She had once been almost as emphatic in expressing herself upon the subject as the corner grocer.

Edna knew that Madame Lebrun had returned to the city, for it was the middle of November. And she also knew where the Lebruns lived, on Chartres Street.[3]

Their home from the outside looked like a prison, with iron bars before the door and lower windows. The iron bars were a relic of the old *régime*,[4] and no one had ever thought of dislodging them. At the side was a high fence enclosing the garden. A gate or door opening upon the street was locked. Edna rang the bell at this side garden gate, and stood upon the banquette, waiting to be admitted.

It was Victor who opened the gate for her. A black woman, wiping her hands upon her apron, was close at his heels. Before she saw them Edna could hear them in altercation, the woman—plainly an anomaly—claiming the right to be allowed to perform her duties, one of which was to answer the bell.

Victor was surprised and delighted to see Mrs. Pontellier, and he made no attempt to conceal either his astonishment or his delight. He was a dark-browed, good-looking youngster of nineteen, greatly resembling his mother, but with ten times her impetuosity. He instructed the black woman to go at once and inform Madame Lebrun that Mrs. Pontellier desired to see her. The woman grumbled a refusal to do part of her duty when she had not been permitted to do it all, and started back to her interrupted task of weeding the garden. Whereupon Victor administered a rebuke in the form of a volley of abuse, which owing to its rapidity and incoherence, was all but incomprehensible to Edna. Whatever it was, the rebuke was convincing, for the woman dropped her hoe and went mumbling into the house.

3. In the heart of the French Quarter.   4. The Spanish regime (1766–1803).

Edna did not wish to enter. It was very pleasant there on the side porch, where there were chairs, a wicker lounge, and a small table. She seated herself, for she was tired from her long tramp; and she began to rock gently and smooth out the folds of her silk parasol. Victor drew up his chair beside her. He at once explained that the black woman's offensive conduct was all due to imperfect training, as he was not there to take her in hand. He had only come up from the island the morning before, and expected to return next day. He stayed all winter at the island; he lived there, and kept the place in order and got things ready for the summer visitors.

But a man needed occasional relaxation, he informed Mrs. Pontellier, and every now and again he drummed up a pretext to bring him to the city. My! but he had had a time of it the evening before! He wouldn't want his mother to know, and he began to talk in a whisper. He was scintillant with recollections. Of course, he couldn't think of telling Mrs. Pontellier all about it, she being a woman and not comprehending such things. But it all began with a girl peeping and smiling at him through the shutters as he passed by. Oh! but she was a beauty! Certainly he smiled back, and went up and talked to her. Mrs. Pontellier did not know him if she supposed he was one to let an opportunity like that escape him. Despite herself, the youngster amused her. She must have betrayed in her look some degree of interest or entertainment. The boy grew more daring, and Mrs. Pontellier might have found herself, in a little while, listening to a highly colored story but for the timely appearance of Madame Lebrun.

That lady was still clad in white, according to her custom of the summer. Her eyes beamed an effusive welcome. Would not Mrs. Pontellier go inside? Would she partake of some refreshment? Why had she not been there before? How was that dear Mr. Pontellier and how were those sweet children? Has Mrs. Pontellier ever known such a warm November?

Victor went and reclined on the wicker lounge behind his mother's chair, where he commanded a view of Edna's face. He had taken her parasol from her hands while he spoke to her, and he now lifted it and twirled it above him as he lay on his back. When Madame Lebrun complained that it was *so* dull coming back to the city; that she saw *so* few people now; that even Victor, when he came up from the island for a day or two, had *so* much to occupy him and engage his time; then it was that the youth went into contortions on the lounge and winked mischievously at Edna. She somehow felt like a confederate in crime, and tried to look severe and disapproving.

There had been but two letters from Robert, with little in them, they told her. Victor said it was really not worth while to go inside for the letters, when his mother entreated him to go in search of them. He remembered the contents, which in truth he rattled off very glibly when put to the test.

One letter was written from Vera Cruz and the other from the City of Mexico. He had met Montel, who was doing everything toward his advancement. So far, the financial situation was no improvement over the one he had left in New Orleans, but of course the prospects were vastly better. He wrote of the City of Mexico, the buildings, the people and their habits, the conditions of life which he found there. He sent his love to the family. He inclosed a check to his mother, and hoped she would affectionately remember him to all his friends. That was about the substance of the two letters. Edna felt that if there had been a message for her, she would have received it. The despondent frame of mind in which she had left home began again to overtake her, and she remembered that she wished to find Mademoiselle Reisz.

Madame Lebrun knew where Mademoiselle Reisz lived. She gave Edna the address, regretting that she would not consent to stay and spend the remainder of the afternoon, and pay a visit to Mademoiselle Reisz some other day. The afternoon was already well advanced.

Victor escorted her out upon the banquette, lifted her parasol, and held it over her while he walked to the car with her. He entreated her to bear in mind that the disclosures of the afternoon were strictly confidential. She laughed and bantered him a little, remembering too late that she should have been dignified and reserved.

"How handsome Mrs. Pontellier looked!" said Madame Lebrun to her son.

"Ravishing!" he admitted. "The city atmosphere has improved her. Some way she doesn't seem like the same woman."

XXI

Some people contended that the reason Mademoiselle Reisz always chose apartments up under the roof was to discourage the approach of beggars, peddlars and callers. There were plenty of windows in her little front room. They were for the most part dingy, but as they were nearly always open it did not make so much difference. They often admitted into the room a good deal of smoke and soot; but at the same time all the light and air that there was came through them. From her windows could be seen the crescent of the river, the masts of ships and the big chimneys of the Mississippi steamers. A magnificent piano crowded the apartment. In the next room she slept, and in the third and last she harbored a gasoline stove on which she cooked her meals when disinclined to descend to the neighboring restaurant. It was there also that she ate, keeping her belongings in a rare old buffet, dingy and battered from a hundred years of use.

When Edna knocked at Mademoiselle Reisz's front room door and entered, she discovered that person standing beside the window, engaged in mending or patching an old prunella gaiter.[5] The little musician laughed all over when she saw Edna. Her laugh consisted of a contortion of the face and all the muscles of the body. She seemed strikingly homely, standing there in the afternoon light. She still wore the shabby lace and the artificial bunch of violets on the side of her head.

"So you remembered me at last," said Mademoiselle. "I had said to myself, 'Ah, bah! she will never come.'"

"Did you want me to come?" asked Edna with a smile.

"I had not thought much about it," answered Mademoiselle. The two had seated themselves on a little bumpy sofa which stood against the wall. "I am glad, however, that you came. I have the water boiling back there, and was just about to make some coffee. You will drink a cup with me. And how is *la belle dame?*[6] Always handsome! always healthy! always contented!" She took Edna's hand between her strong wiry fingers, holding it loosely without warmth, and executing a sort of double theme upon the back and palm.

"Yes," she went on; "I sometimes thought: 'She will never come. She promised as those women in society always do, without meaning it. She will not come.' For I really don't believe you like me, Mrs. Pontellier."

"I don't know whether I like you or not," replied Edna, gazing down at the little woman with a quizzical look.

The candor of Mrs. Pontellier's admission greatly pleased Mademoiselle Reisz. She expressed her gratification by repairing forthwith to the region of the gasoline stove and rewarding her guest with the promised cup of coffee. The coffee and the biscuit accompanying it proved very acceptable to Edna, who had declined refreshment at Madame Lebrun's and was now beginning to feel hungry. Mademoiselle set the tray which she brought in upon a small table near at hand, and seated herself once again on the lumpy sofa.

"I have had a letter from your friend," she remarked, as she poured a little cream into Edna's cup and handed it to her.

"My friend?"

"Yes, your friend Robert. He wrote to me from the City of Mexico."

5. A button shoe with a cloth upper   6. "My elegant friend."
section.

"Wrote to *you?*" repeated Edna in amazement, stirring her coffee absently.

"Yes, to me. Why not? Don't stir all the warmth out of your coffee; drink it. Though the letter might as well have been sent to you; it was nothing but Mrs. Pontellier from beginning to end."

"Let me see it," requested the young woman, entreatingly.

"No; a letter concerns no one but the person who writes it and the one to whom it is written."

"Haven't you just said it concerned me from beginning to end?"

"It was written about you, not to you. 'Have you seen Mrs. Pontellier? How is she looking?' he asks. 'As Mrs. Pontellier says,' or 'as Mrs. Pontellier once said.' 'If Mrs. Pontellier should call upon you, play for her that Impromptu of Chopin's, my favorite. I heard it here a day or two ago, but not as you play it. I should like to know how it affects her,' and so on, as if he supposed we were constantly in each other's society."

"Let me see the letter."

"Oh, no."

"Have you answered it?"

"No."

"Let me see the letter."

"No, and again, no."

"Then play the Impromptu for me."

"It is growing late; what time do you have to be home?"

"Time doesn't concern me. Your question seems a little rude. Play the Impromptu."

"But you have told me nothing of yourself. What are you doing?"

"Painting!" laughed Edna. "I am becoming an artist. Think of it!"

"Ah! an artist! You have pretensions, Madame."

"Why pretensions? Do you think I could not become an artist?"

"I do not know you well enough to say. I do not know your talent or your temperament. To be an artist includes much; one must possess many gifts—absolute gifts—which have not been acquired by one's own effort. And, moreover, to succeed, the artist must possess the courageous soul."

"What do you mean by the courageous soul?"

"Courageous, *ma foi!* The brave soul. The soul that dares and defies."

"Show me the letter and play for me the Impromptu. You see that I have persistence. Does that quality count for anything in art?"

"It counts with a foolish old woman whom you have captivated," replied Mademoiselle, with her wriggling laugh.

The letter was right there at hand in the drawer of the little table upon which Edna had just placed her coffee cup. Mademoiselle opened the drawer and drew forth the letter, the topmost one. She placed it in Edna's hands, and without further comment arose and went to the piano.

Mademoiselle played a soft interlude. It was an improvisation. She sat low at the instrument, and the lines of her body settled into ungraceful curves and angles that gave it an appearance of deformity. Gradually and imperceptibly the interlude melted into the soft opening minor chords of the Chopin Impromptu.

Edna did not know when the Impromptu began or ended. She sat in the sofa corner reading Robert's letter by the fading light. Mademoiselle had glided from the Chopin into the quivering love-notes of Isolde's song,[7] and back again to the Impromptu with its soulful and poignant longing.

The shadows deepened in the little room. The music grew strange and fantastic—turbulent, insistent, plaintive and soft with entreaty. The shadows grew deeper. The music filled the room. It floated out upon the night, over the housetops, the crescent of the river, losing itself in the silence of the upper air.

Edna was sobbing, just as she had wept one midnight at Grand Isle when strange, new voices awoke in her. She arose in some agitation to take her departure. "May I come again, Mademoiselle?" she asked at the threshold.

"Come whenever you feel like it. Be careful; the stairs and landings are dark; don't stumble."

Mademoiselle reëntered and lit a candle. Robert's letter was on the floor. She stooped and picked it up. It was crumpled and damp with tears. Mademoiselle smoothed the letter out, restored it to the envelope, and replaced it in the table drawer.

XXII

One morning on his way into town Mr. Pontellier stopped at the house of his old friend and family physician, Doctor Mandelet. The Doctor was a semi-retired physician, resting, as the saying is, upon his laurels. He bore a reputation for wisdom rather than skill—leaving the active practice of medicine to his assistants and younger comtemporaries—and was much sought for in matters of consultation. A few families, united to him by bonds of friendship, he still attended when they required the services of a physician. The Pontelliers were among these.

Mr. Pontellier found the Doctor reading at the open window of

---

7. From Wagner's opera *Tristan und Isolde*, based on a medieval legend of ill-fated love. Isolde's song, known as her *Liebestod* ("Love-death"), is sung as she bids her dead lover farewell and falls dead herself in his arms.

his study. His house stood rather far back from the street, in the center of a delightful garden, so that it was quiet and peaceful at the old gentleman's study window. He was a great reader. He stared up disapprovingly over his eye-glasses as Mr. Pontellier entered, wondering who had the temerity to disturb him at that hour of the morning.

"Ah, Pontellier! Not sick, I hope. Come and have a seat. What news do you bring this morning?" He was quite portly, with a profusion of gray hair, and small blue eyes which age had robbed of much of their brightness but none of their penetration.

"Oh! I'm never sick, Doctor. You know that I come of tough fiber—of that old Creole race of Pontelliers that dry up and finally blow away. I came to consult—no, not precisely to consult—to talk to you about Edna. I don't know what ails her."

"Madame Pontellier not well?" marveled the Doctor. "Why, I saw her—I think it was a week ago—walking along Canal Street,[8] the picture of health, it seemed to me."

"Yes, yes; she seems quite well," said Mr. Pontellier, leaning forward and whirling his stick between his two hands; "but she doesn't act well. She's odd, she's not like herself. I can't make her out, and I thought perhaps you'd help me."

"How does she act?" inquired the doctor.

"Well, it isn't easy to explain," said Mr. Pontellier, throwing himself back in his chair. "She lets the housekeeping go to the dickens."

"Well, well; women are not all alike, my dear Pontellier. We've got to consider—"

"I know that; I told you I couldn't explain. Her whole attitude—toward me and everbody and everything—has changed. You know I have a quick temper, but I don't want to quarrel or be rude to a woman, especially my wife; yet I'm driven to it, and feel like ten thousand devils after I've made a fool of myself. She's making it devilishly uncomfortable for me," he went on nervously. "She's got some sort of notion in her head concerning the eternal rights of women; and—you understand—we meet in the morning at the breakfast table."

The old gentleman lifted his shaggy eyebrows, protruded his thick nether lip, and tapped the arms of his chair with his cushioned finger-tips.

"What have you been doing to her, Pontellier?"

"Doing! *Parbleu!*"

"Has she," asked the Doctor, with a smile, "has she been associat-

8. The main street of downtown New Orleans, separating the old French city from the newer American section.

ing of late with a circle of pseudo-intellectual women[9]—super-spiritual superior beings? My wife has been telling me about them."

"That's the trouble," broke in Mr. Pontellier, "she hasn't been associating with any one. She has abandoned her Tuesdays at home, has thrown over all her acquaintances, and goes tramping about by herself, moping in the street-cars, getting in after dark. I tell you she's peculiar. I don't like it; I feel a little worried over it."

This was a new aspect for the Doctor. "Nothing hereditary?" he asked, seriously. "Nothing peculiar about her family antecedents, is there?"

"Oh, no, indeed! She comes of sound old Presbyterian Kentucky stock. The old gentleman, her father, I have heard, used to atone for his week-day sins with his Sunday devotions. I know for a fact, that his race horses literally ran away with the prettiest bit of Kentucky farming land I ever laid eyes upon. Margaret—you know Margaret—she has all the Presbyterianism undiluted. And the youngest is something of a vixen. By the way, she gets married in a couple of weeks from now."

"Send your wife up to the wedding," exclaimed the Doctor, foreseeing a happy solution. "Let her stay among her own people for a while; it will do her good."

"That's what I want her to do. She won't go to the marriage. She says a wedding is one of the most lamentable spectacles on earth. Nice thing for a woman to say to her husband!" exclaimed Mr. Pontellier, fuming anew at the recollection.

"Pontellier," said the Doctor, after a moment's reflection, "let your wife alone for a while. Don't bother her, and don't let her bother you. Woman, my dear friend, is a very peculiar and delicate organism—a sensitive and highly organized woman, such as I know Mrs. Pontellier to be, is especially peculiar. It would require an inspired psychologist to deal successfully with them. And when ordinary fellows like you and me attempt to cope with their idiosyncrasies the result is bungling. Most women are moody and whimsical. This is some passing whim of your wife, due to some cause or causes which you and I needn't try to fathom. But it will pass happily over, especially if you let her alone. Send her around to see me."[1]

"Oh! I couldn't do that; there'd be no reason for it," objected Mr. Pontellier.

9. Women's clubs flourished during the late nineteenth century in America. They were a source of education for women as well as an arena for political organization. As the Doctor's remark indicates, the club movement was met with scorn in some quarters.

1. See Ann Douglas Wood, "The Fashionable Diseases: Women's Complaints and Their Treatment in Nineteenth-Century America," *Journal of Interdisciplinary History*, IV (Summer 1973), 25–52, for a discussion of upper-class women's "nervous" disorders.

"Then I'll go around and see her," said the Doctor. "I'll drop in to dinner some evening *en bon ami.*"[2]

"Do! by all means," urged Mr. Pontellier. "What evening will you come? Say Thursday. Will you come Thursday?" he asked, rising to take his leave.

"Very well; Thursday. My wife may possibly have some engagement for me Thursday. In case she has, I shall let you know. Otherwise, you may expect me."

Mr. Pontellier turned before leaving to say:

"I am going to New York on business very soon. I have a big scheme on hand, and want to be on the field proper to pull the ropes and handle the ribbons.[3] We'll let you in on the inside if you say so, Doctor," he laughed.

"No, I thank you, my dear sir," returned the Doctor. "I leave such ventures to you younger men with the fever of life still in your blood."

"What I wanted to say," continued Mr. Pontellier, with his hand on the knob; "I may have to be absent a good while. Would you advise me to take Edna along?"

"By all means, if she wishes to go. If not, leave her here. Don't contradict her. The mood will pass, I assure you. It may take a month, two, three months—possibly longer, but it will pass; have patience."

"Well, good-by, *à jeudi,*"[4] said Mr. Pontellier, as he let himself out.

The Doctor would have liked during the course of conversation to ask, "Is there any man in the case?" but he knew his Creole too well to make such a blunder as that.

He did not resume his book immediately, but sat for a while meditatively looking out into the garden.

XXIII

Edna's father was in the city, and had been with them several days. She was not very warmly or deeply attached to him, but they had certain tastes in common, and when together they were companionable. His coming was in the nature of a welcome disturbance; it seemed to furnish a new direction for her emotions.

He had come to purchase a wedding gift for his daughter, Janet, and an outfit for himself in which he might make a creditable appearance at her marriage. Mr. Pontellier had selected the bridal gift, as every one immediately connected with him always deferred to his taste in such matters. And his suggestions on the question of dress—which too often assumes the nature of a problem—were of inestimable value to his father-in-law. But for the past few days the

2. "As a friend."
3. Handle the reins—that is, to be in charge.
4. "Until Thursday."

old gentleman had been upon Edna's hands, and in his society she was becoming acquainted with a new set of sensations. He had been a colonel in the Confederate army, and still maintained, with the title, the military bearing which had always accompanied it. His hair and mustache were white and silky, emphasizing the rugged bronze of his face. He was tall and thin, and wore his coats padded, which gave a fictitious breadth and depth to his shoulders and chest. Edna and her father looked very distinguished together, and excited a good deal of notice during their perambulations. Upon his arrival she began by introducing him to her atelier and making a sketch of him. He took the whole matter very seriously. If her talent had been ten-fold greater than it was, it would not have surprised him, convinced as he was that he had bequeathed to all of his daughters the germs of a masterful capability, which only depended upon their own efforts to be directed toward successful achievement.

Before her pencil he sat rigid and unflinching, as he had faced the cannon's mouth in days gone by. He resented the intrusion of the children, who gaped with wondering eyes at him, sitting so stiff up there in their mother's bright atelier. When they drew near he motioned them away with an expressive action of the foot, loath to disturb the fixed lines of his countenance, his arms, or his rigid shoulders.

Edna, anxious to entertain him, invited Mademoiselle Reisz to meet him, having promised him a treat in her piano playing; but Mademoiselle declined the invitation. So together they attended a *soirée musicale* at the Ratignolle's. Monsieur and Madame Ratignolle made much of the Colonel, installing him as the guest of honor and engaging him at once to dine with them the following Sunday, or any day which he might select. Madame coquetted with him in the most captivating and naïve manner, with eyes, gestures, and a profusion of compliments, till the Colonel's old head felt thirty years younger on his padded shoulders. Edna marveled, not comprehending. She herself was almost devoid of coquetry.

There were one or two men whom she observed at the *soirée musicale*; but she would never have felt moved to any kittenish display to attract their notice—to any feline or feminine wiles to express herself toward them. Their personality attracted her in an agreeable way. Her fancy selected them, and she was glad when a lull in the music gave them an opportunity to meet her and talk with her. Often on the street the glance of strange eyes had lingered in her memory, and sometimes had disturbed her.

Mr. Pontellier did not attend these *soirées musicales*. He considered them *bourgeois*,[5] and found more diversion at the club. To Madame Ratignolle he said the music dispensed at her *soirées* was

5. Middle-class, common.

too "heavy," too far beyond his untrained comprehension. His excuse flattered her. But she disapproved of Mr. Pontellier's club, and she was frank enough to tell Edna so.

"It's a pity Mr. Pontellier doesn't stay home more in the evenings. I think you would be more—well, if you don't mind my saying it—more united, if he did."

"Oh! dear no!" said Edna, with a blank look in her eyes. "What should I do if he stayed home? We wouldn't have anything to say to each other."

She had not much of anything to say to her father, for that matter; but he did not antagonize her. She discovered that he interested her, though she realized that he might not interest her long; and for the first time in her life she felt as if she were thoroughly acquainted with him. He kept her busy serving him and ministering to his wants. It amused her to do so. She would not permit a servant or one of the children to do anything for him which she might do herself. Her husband noticed, and thought it was the expression of a deep filial attachment which he had never suspected.

The Colonel drank numerous "toddies" during the course of the day, which left him, however, imperturbed. He was an expert at concocting strong drinks. He had even invented some, to which he had given fantastic names, and for whose manufacture he required diverse ingredients that it devolved upon Edna to procure for him.

When Doctor Mandelet dined with the Pontelliers on Thursday he could discern in Mrs. Pontellier no trace of that morbid condition which her husband had reported to him. She was excited and in a manner radiant. She and her father had been to the race course, and their thoughts when they seated themselves at table were still occupied with the events of the afternoon, and their talk was still of the track. The Doctor had not kept pace with turf affairs. He had certain recollections of racing in what he called "the good old times" when the Lecompte stables[6] flourished, and he drew upon this fund of memories so that he might not be left out and seem wholly devoid of the modern spirit. But he failed to impose upon the Colonel, and was even far from impressing him with this trumped-up knowledge of bygone days. Edna had staked her father on his last venture, with the most gratifying results to both of them. Besides, they had met some very charming people, according to the Colonel's impressions. Mrs. Mortimer Merriman and Mrs. James Highcamp, who were there with Alcée Arobin, had joined them and had enlivened the hours in a fashion that warmed him to think of.

Mr. Pontellier himself had no particular leaning toward horse-

6. New Orleans was a celebrated racing center before the Civil War, boasting four race tracks. The Lecompte stables were owned by a famous Creole racing family.

racing, and was even rather inclined to discourage it as a pastime, especially when he considered the fate of that blue-grass farm in Kentucky. He endeavored, in a general way, to express a particular disapproval, and only succeeded in arousing the ire and opposition of his father-in-law. A pretty dispute followed, in which Edna warmly espoused her father's cause and the Doctor remained neutral.

He observed his hostess attentively from under his shaggy brows, and noted a subtle change which had transformed her from the listless woman he had known into a being who, for the moment, seemed palpitant with the forces of life. Her speech was warm and energetic. There was no repression in her glance or gesture. She reminded him of some beautiful, sleek animal waking up in the sun.

The dinner was excellent. The claret was warm and the champagne was cold, and under their beneficent influence the threatened unpleasantness melted and vanished with the fumes of the wine.

Mr. Pontellier warmed up and grew reminiscent. He told some amusing plantation experiences, recollections of old Iberville and his youth, when he hunted 'possum in company with some friendly darky; thrashed the pecan trees, shot the grosbec,[7] and roamed the woods and fields in mischievous idleness.

The Colonel, with little sense of humor and of the fitness of things, related a somber episode of those dark and bitter days, in which he had acted a conspicuous part and always formed a central figure. Nor was the Doctor happier in his selection, when he told the old, ever new and curious story of the waning of a woman's love, seeking strange, new channels, only to return to its legitimate source after days of fierce unrest. It was one of the many little human documents which had been unfolded to him during his long career as a physician. The story did not seem especially to impress Edna. She had one of her own to tell, of a woman who paddled away with her lover one night in a pirogue and never came back. They were lost amid the Baratarian Islands, and no one ever heard of them or found trace of them from that day to this. It was a pure invention. She said that Madame Antoine had related it to her. That, also, was an invention. Perhaps it was a dream she had had. But every glowing word seemed real to those who listened. They could feel the hot breath of the Southern night; they could hear the long sweep of the pirogue through the glistening moonlit water, the beating of birds' wings, rising startled from among the reeds in the salt-water pools; they could see the faces of the lovers, pale, close together, rapt in oblivious forgetfulness, drifting into the unknown.

7. Grosbeak, game birds distinguished by their large bills.

The champagne was cold, and its subtle fumes played fantastic tricks with Edna's memory that night.

Outside, away from the glow of the fire and the soft lamplight, the night was chill and murky. The Doctor doubled his old-fashioned cloak across his breast as he strode home through the darkness. He knew his fellow-creatures better than most men; knew that inner life which so seldom unfolds itself to unanointed eyes. He was sorry he had accepted Pontellier's invitation. He was growing old, and beginning to need rest and an imperturbed spirit. He did not want the secrets of other lives thrust upon him.

"I hope it isn't Arobin," he muttered to himself as he walked. "I hope to heaven it isn't Alcée Arobin."

XXIV

Edna and her father had a warm, and almost violent dispute upon the subject of her refusal to attend her sister's wedding. Mr. Pontellier declined to interfere, to interpose either his influence or his authority. He was following Doctor Mandelet's advice, and letting her do as she liked. The Colonel reproached his daughter for her lack of filial kindness and respect, her want of sisterly affection and womanly consideration. His arguments were labored and unconvincing. He doubted if Janet would accept any excuse—forgetting that Edna had offered none. He doubted if Janet would ever speak to her again, and he was sure Margaret would not.

Edna was glad to be rid of her father when he finally took himself off with his wedding garments and his bridal gifts, with his padded shoulders, his Bible reading, his "toddies" and ponderous oaths.

Mr. Pontellier followed him closely. He meant to stop at the wedding on his way to New York and endeavor by every means which money and love could devise to atone somewhat for Edna's incomprehensible action.

"You are too lenient, too lenient by far, Léonce," asserted the Colonel. "Authority, coercion are what is needed. Put your foot down good and hard; the only way to manage a wife. Take my word for it."

The Colonel was perhaps unaware that he had coerced his own wife into her grave. Mr. Pontellier had a vague suspicion of it which he thought it needless to mention at that late day.

Edna was not so consciously gratified at her husband's leaving home as she had been over the departure of her father. As the day approached when he was to leave her for a comparatively long stay, she grew melting and affectionate, remembering his many acts of consideration and his repeated expressions of an ardent attachment. She was solicitous about his health and his welfare. She bustled around, looking after his clothing, thinking about heavy underwear,

quite as Madame Ratignolle would have done under similar circumstances. She cried when he went away, calling him her dear, good
friend, and she was quite certain she would grow lonely before very
long and go to join him in New York.

But after all, a radiant peace settled upon her when she at last
found herself alone. Even the children were gone. Old Madame
Pontellier had come herself and carried them off to Iberville with
their quadroon. The old madame did not venture to say she was
afraid they would be neglected during Léonce's absence; she hardly
ventured to think so. She was hungry for them—even a little fierce
in her attachment. She did not want them to be wholly "children of
the pavement," she always said when begging to have them for a
space. She wished them to know the country, with its streams, its
fields, its woods, its freedom, so delicious to the young. She wished
them to taste something of the life their father had lived and known
and loved when he, too, was a little child.

When Edna was at last alone, she breathed a big, genuine sigh of
relief. A feeling that was unfamiliar but very delicious came over
her. She walked all through the house, from one room to another,
as if inspecting it for the first time. She tried the various chairs and
lounges, as if she had never sat and reclined upon them before. And
she perambulated around the outside of the house, investigating,
looking to see if windows and shutters were secure and in order.
The flowers were like new acquaintances; she approached them in a
familiar spirit, and made herself at home among them. The garden
walks were damp, and Edna called to the maid to bring out her
rubber sandals. And there she stayed, and stooped, and digging around
the plants, trimming, picking dead, dry leaves. The children's little
dog came out, interfering, getting in her way. She scolded him,
laughing at him, played with him. The garden smelled so good and
looked so pretty in the afternoon sunlight. Edna plucked all the
bright flowers she could find, and went into the house with them,
she and the little dog.

Even the kitchen assumed a sudden interesting character which
she had never before perceived. She went in to give directions to the
cook, to say that the butcher would have to bring much less meat,
that they would require only half their usual quantity of bread, of
milk and groceries. She told the cook that she herself would be
greatly occupied during Mr. Pontellier's absence, and she begged
her to take all thought and responsibility of the larder upon her own
shoulders.

That night Edna dined alone. The candelabra, with a few candles
in the center of the table, gave all the light she needed. Outside the
circle of light in which she sat, the large dining-room looked solemn
and shadowy. The cook, placed upon her mettle, served a delicious

repast—a luscious tenderloin broiled à point. The wine tasted good; the marron glacé[8] seemed to be just what she wanted. It was so pleasant, too, to dine in a comfortable peignoir.

She thought a little sentimentally about Léonce and the children, and wondered what they were doing. As she gave a dainty scrap or two to the doggie, she talked intimately to him about Etienne and Raoul. He was beside himself with astonishment and delight over these companionable advances, and showed his appreciation by his little quick, snappy barks and a lively agitation.

Then Edna sat in the library after dinner and read Emerson[9] until she grew sleepy. She realized that she had neglected her reading, and determined to start anew upon a course of improving studies, now that her time was completely her own to do with as she liked.

After a refreshing bath, Edna went to bed. And as she snuggled comfortably beneath the eiderdown a sense of restfulness invaded her, such as she had not known before.

XXV

When the weather was dark and cloudy Edna could not work. She needed the sun to mellow and temper her mood to the sticking point. She had reached a stage when she seemed to be no longer feeling her way, working, when in the humor, with sureness and ease. And being devoid of ambition, and striving not toward accomplishment, she drew satisfaction from the work in itself.

On rainy or melancholy days Edna went out and sought the society of the friends she had made at Grand Isle. Or else she stayed indoors and nursed a mood with which she was becoming too familiar for her own comfort and peace of mind. It was not despair; but it seemed to her as if life were passing by, leaving its promise broken and unfulfilled. Yet there were other days when she listened, was led on and deceived by fresh promises which her youth held out to her.

She went again to the races, and again. Alcée Arobin and Mrs. Highcamp called for her one bright afternoon in Arobin's drag.[1] Mrs. Highcamp was a worldly but unaffected, intelligent, slim, tall blonde woman in the forties, with an indifferent manner and blue eyes that stared. She had a daughter who served her as a pretext for cultivating the society of young men of fashion. Alcée Arobin was one of them. He was a familiar figure at the race course, the opera, the fashionable clubs. There was a perpetual smile in his eyes,

8. Chestnuts glazed with sugar.
9. Ralph Waldo Emerson (1803–1882), American philosopher, essayist and poet of the transcendental school. Critics have interpreted this single reference to an American author variously. Ringe uses the allusion as a bit of evidence that the novel is in the romantic tradition, while Arms notes that Emerson is putting Edna to sleep.
1. A heavy coach with seats on top drawn by four horses.

which seldom failed to awaken a corresponding cheerfulness in any one who looked into them and listened to his good-humored voice. His manner was quiet, and at times a little insolent. He possessed a good figure, a pleasing face, not overburdened with depth of thought or feeling; and his dress was that of the conventional man of fashion.

He admired Edna extravagantly, after meeting her at the races with her father. He had met her before on other occasions, but she had seemed to him unapproachable until that day. It was at his instigation that Mrs. Highcamp called to ask her to go with them to the Jockey Club[2] to witness the turf event of the season.

There were possibly a few track men out there who knew the race horse as well as Edna, but there was certainly none who knew it better. She sat between her two companions as one having authority to speak. She laughed at Arobin's pretensions, and deplored Mrs. Highcamp's ignorance. The race horse was a friend and intimate associate of her childhood. The atmosphere of the stables and the breath of the blue grass paddock revived in her memory and lingered in her nostrils. She did not perceive that she was talking like her father as the sleek geldings ambled in review before them. She played for very high stakes, and fortune favored her. The fever of the game flamed in her cheeks and eyes, and it got into her blood and into her brain like an intoxicant. People turned their heads to look at her, and more than one lent an attentive ear to her utterances, hoping thereby to secure the elusive but ever-desired "tip." Arobin caught the contagion of excitement which drew him to Edna like a magnet. Mrs. Highcamp remained, as usual, unmoved, with her indifferent stare and uplifted eyebrows.

Edna stayed and dined with Mrs. Highcamp upon being urged to do so. Arobin also remained and sent away his drag.

The dinner was quiet and uninteresting, save for the cheerful efforts of Arobin to enliven things. Mrs. Highcamp deplored the absence of her daughter from the races, and tried to convey to her what she had missed by going to the "Dante[3] reading" instead of joining them. The girl held a geranium leaf up to her nose and said nothing, but looked knowing and noncommittal. Mr. Highcamp was a plain, bald-headed man, who only talked under compulsion. He was unresponsive. Mrs. Highcamp was full of delicate courtesy and consideration toward her husband. She addressed most of her conversation to him at table. They sat in the library after dinner and read the evening papers together under the drop-light;[4] while the

---

2. The New Louisiana Jockey Club, a social club with membership limited to several hundred of the most prominent and wealthy citizens of New Orleans.

3. Dante Alighieri (1265–1321) Italian poet, author of The Divine Comedy.
4. Portable gas lamp attached to chandelier or wall fixture.

younger people went into the drawing-room near by and talked. Miss Highcamp played some selections from Grieg upon the piano. She seemed to have apprehended all of the composer's coldness and none of his poetry. While Edna listened she could not help wondering if she had lost her taste for music.

When the time came for her to go home, Mr. Highcamp grunted a lame offer to escort her, looking down at his slippered feet with tactless concern. It was Arobin who took her home. The car ride was long, and it was late when they reached Esplanade Street. Arobin asked permission to enter for a second to light his cigarette —his match safe[5] was empty. He filled his match safe, but did not light his cigarette until he left her, after she had expressed her willingness to go to the races with him again.

Edna was neither tired nor sleepy. She was hungry again, for the Highcamp dinner, though of excellent quality, had lacked abundance. She rummaged in the larder and brought forth a slice of "Gruyère"[6] and some crackers. She opened a bottle of beer which she found in the ice-box. Edna felt extremely restless and excited. She vacantly hummed a fantastic tune as she poked at the wood embers on the hearth and munched a cracker.

She wanted something to happen—something, anything; she did not know what. She regretted that she had not made Arobin stay a half hour to talk over the horses with her. She counted the money she had won. But there was nothing else to do, so she went to bed, and tossed there for hours in a sort of monotonous agitation.

In the middle of the night she remembered that she had forgotten to write her regular letter to her husband; and she decided to do so next day and tell him about her afternoon at the Jockey Club. She lay wide awake composing a letter which was nothing like the one which she wrote next day. When the maid awoke her in the morning Edna was dreaming of Mr. Highcamp playing the piano at the entrance of a music store on Canal Street, while his wife was saying to Alcée Arobin, as they boarded an Esplanade Street car:

"What a pity that so much talent has been neglected! but I must go."

When, a few days later, Alcée Arobin again called for Edna in his drag, Mrs. Highcamp was not with him. He said they would pick her up. But as that lady had not been apprised of his intention of picking her up, she was not at home. The daughter was just leaving the house to attend the meeting of a branch Folk Lore Society,[7] and regretted that she could not accompany them. Arobin

---

5. Box of noncombustible material made for holding friction matches.
6. Cheese originally made in Gruyère, Switzerland.

7. The New Orleans Association of the American Folklore Society, founded in 1892 by Alcée Fortier of Tulane University, was very active from 1892–1895.

appeared nonplused, and asked Edna if there were any one else she cared to ask.

She did not deem it worth while to go in search of any of the fashionable acquaintances from whom she had withdrawn herself. She thought of Madame Ratignolle, but knew that her fair friend did not leave the house, except to take a languid walk around the block with her husband after nightfall. Mademoiselle Reisz would have laughed at such a request from Edna. Madame Lebrun might have enjoyed the outing, but for some reason Edna did not want her. So they went alone, she and Arobin.

The afternoon was intensely interesting to her. The excitement came back upon her like a remittent fever. Her talk grew familiar and confidential. It was no labor to become intimate with Arobin. His manner invited easy confidence. The preliminary stage of becoming acquainted was one which he always endeavored to ignore when a pretty and engaging woman was concerned.

He stayed and dined with Edna. He stayed and sat beside the wood fire. They laughed and talked; and before it was time to go he was telling her how different life might have been if he had known her years before. With ingenuous frankness he spoke of what a wicked, ill-disciplined boy he had been, and impulsively drew up his cuff to exhibit upon his wrist the scar from a saber cut which he had received in a duel outside of Paris when he was nineteen. She touched his hand as she scanned the red cicatrice[8] on the inside of his white wrist. A quick impulse that was somewhat spasmodic impelled her fingers to close in a sort of clutch upon his hand. He felt the pressure of her pointed nails in the flesh of his palm.

She arose hastily and walked toward the mantel.

"The sight of a wound or scar always agitates and sickens me," she said. "I shouldn't have looked at it."

"I beg your pardon," he entreated, following her; "it never occurred to me that it might be repulsive."

He stood close to her, and the effrontery in his eyes repelled the old, vanishing self in her, yet drew all her awakening sensuousness. He saw enough in her face to impel him to take her hand and hold it while he said his lingering good night.

"Will you go to the races again?" he asked.

"No," she said. "I've had enough of the races. I don't want to lose all the money I've won, and I've got to work when the weather is bright, instead of—"

"Yes; work; to be sure. You promised to show me your work. What morning may I come up to your atelier? To-morrow?"

"No!"

"Day after?"

8. Scar.

"No, no."

"Oh, please don't refuse me! I know something of such things. I might help you with a stray suggestion or two."

"No. Good night. Why don't you go after you have said good night? I don't like you," she went on in a high, excited pitch, attempting to draw away her hand. She felt that her words lacked dignity and sincerity, and she knew that he felt it.

"I'm sorry you don't like me. I'm sorry I offended you. How have I offended you? What have I done? Can't you forgive me?" And he bent and pressed his lips upon her hand as if he wished never more to withdraw them.

"Mr. Arobin," she complained, "I'm greatly upset by the excitement of the afternoon; I'm not myself. My manner must have misled you in some way. I wish you to go, please." She spoke in a monotonous, dull tone. He took his hat from the table, and stood with eyes turned from her, looking into the dying fire. For a moment or two he kept an impressive silence.

"Your manner has not misled me, Mrs. Pontellier," he said finally. "My own emotions have done that. I couldn't help it. When I'm near you, how could I help it? Don't think anything of it, don't bother, please. You see, I go when you command me. If you wish me to stay away, I shall do so. If you let me come back, I—oh! you will let me come back?"

He cast one appealing glance at her, to which she made no response. Alcée Arobin's manner was so genuine that it often deceived even himself.

Edna did not care or think whether it were genuine or not. When she was alone she looked mechanically at the back of her hand which he had kissed so warmly. Then she leaned her head down on the mantelpiece. She felt somewhat like a woman who in a moment of passion is betrayed into an act of infidelity, and realizes the significance of the act without being wholly awakened from its glamour. The thought was passing vaguely through her mind, "What would he think?"

She did not mean her husband; she was thinking of Robert Lebrun. Her husband seemed to her now like a person whom she had married without love as an excuse.

She lit a candle and went up to her room. Alcée Arobin was absolutely nothing to her. Yet his presence, his manners, the warmth of his glances, and above all the touch of his lips upon her hand had acted like a narcotic upon her.

She slept a languorous sleep, interwoven with vanishing dreams.

XXVI

Alcée Arobin wrote Edna an elaborate note of apology, palpitant with sincerity. It embarrassed her; for in a cooler, quieter moment it appeared to her absurd that she should have taken his action so seriously, so dramatically. She felt sure that the significance of the whole occurrence had lain in her own self-consciousness. If she ignored his note it would give undue importance to a trivial affair. If she replied to it in a serious spirit it would still leave in his mind the impression that she had in a susceptible moment yielded to his influence. After all, it was no great matter to have one's hand kissed. She was provoked at his having written the apology. She answered in as light and bantering a spirit as she fancied it deserved, and said she would be glad to have him look in upon her at work whenever he felt the inclination and his business gave him the opportunity.

He responded at once by presenting himself at her home with all his disarming naïveté. And then there was scarcely a day which followed that she did not see him or was not reminded of him. He was prolific in pretexts. His attitude became one of good-humored subservience and tacit adoration. He was ready at all times to submit to her moods, which were as often kind as they were cold. She grew accustomed to him. They became intimate and friendly by imperceptible degrees, and then by leaps. He sometimes talked in a way that astonished her at first and brought the crimson into her face; in a way that pleased her at last, appealing to the animalism that stirred impatiently within her.

There was nothing which so quieted the turmoil of Edna's senses as a visit to Mademoiselle Reisz. It was then, in the presence of that personality which was offensive to her, that the woman, by her divine art, seemed to reach Edna's spirit and set it free.

It was misty, with heavy, lowering atmosphere, one afternoon, when Edna climbed the stairs to the pianist's apartments under the roof. Her clothes were dripping with moisture. She felt chilled and pinched as she entered the room. Mademoiselle was poking at a rusty stove that smoked a little and warmed the room indifferently. She was endeavoring to heat a pot of chocolate on the stove. The room looked cheerless and dingy to Edna as she entered. A bust of Beethoven, covered with a hood of dust, scowled at her from the mantelpiece.

"Ah! here comes the sunlight!" exclaimed Mademoiselle, rising from her knees before the stove. "Now it will be warm and bright enough; I can let the fire alone."

She closed the stove door with a bang, and approaching, assisted in removing Edna's dripping mackintosh.

"You are cold; you look miserable. The chocolate will soon be hot. But would you rather have a taste of brandy? I have scarcely touched the bottle which you brought me for my cold." A piece of red flannel was wrapped around Mademoiselle's throat; a stiff neck compelled her to hold her head on one side.

"I will take some brandy," said Edna, shivering as she removed her gloves and overshoes. She drank the liquor from the glass as a man would have done. Then flinging herself upon the uncomfortable sofa she said, "Mademoiselle, I am going to move away from my house on Esplanade Street."

"Ah!" ejaculated the musician, neither surprised nor especially interested. Nothing ever seemed to astonish her very much. She was endeavoring to adjust the bunch of violets which had become loose from its fastening in her hair. Edna drew her down upon the sofa, and taking a pin from her own hair, secured the shabby artificial flowers in their accustomed place.

"Aren't you astonished?"

"Passably. Where are you going? To New York? to Iberville? to your father in Mississippi? where?"

"Just two steps away," laughed Edna, "in a little four-room house around the corner. It looks so cozy, so inviting and restful, whenever I pass by; and it's for rent. I'm tired looking after that big house. It never seemed like mine, anyway—like home. It's too much trouble. I have to keep too many servants. I am tired bothering with them."

"That is not your true reason, *ma belle*. There is no use in telling me lies. I don't know your reason, but you have not told me the truth." Edna did not protest or endeavor to justify herself.

"The house, the money that provides for it, are not mine. Isn't that enough reason?"

"They are your husband's," returned Mademoiselle, with a shrug and a malicious elevation of the eyebrows.

"Oh! I see there is no deceiving you. Then let me tell you: It is a caprice. I have a little money of my own from my mother's estate, which my father sends me by driblets. I won a large sum this winter on the races, and I am beginning to sell my sketches. Laidpore is more and more pleased with my work; he says it grows in force and individuality. I cannot judge of that myself, but I feel that I have gained in ease and confidence. However, as I said, I have sold a good many through Laidpore. I can live in the tiny house for little or nothing, with one servant. Old Celestine, who works occasionally for me, says she will come stay with me and do my work. I know I shall like it, like the feeling of freedom and independence."

"What does your husband say?"

"I have not told him yet. I only thought of it this morning. He will think I am demented, no doubt. Perhaps you think so."

Mademoiselle shook her head slowly. "Your reason is not yet clear to me," she said.

Neither was it quite clear to Edna herself; but it unfolded itself as she sat for a while in silence. Instinct had prompted her to put away her husband's bounty in casting off her allegiance. She did not know how it would be when he returned. There would have to be an understanding, an explanation. Conditions would some way adjust themselves, she felt; but whatever came, she had resolved never again to belong to another than herself.

"I shall give a grand dinner before I leave the old house!" Edna exclaimed. "You will have to come to it, Mademoiselle. I will give you everything that you like to eat and to drink. We shall sing and laugh and be merry for once." And she uttered a sigh that came from the very depths of her being.

If Mademoiselle happened to have received a letter from Robert during the interval of Edna's visits, she would give her the letter unsolicited. And she would seat herself at the piano and play as her humor prompted her while the young woman read the letter.

The little stove was roaring; it was red-hot, and the chocolate in the tin sizzled and sputtered. Edna went forward and opened the stove door, and Mademoiselle rising, took a letter from under the bust of Beethoven and handed it to Edna.

"Another! so soon!" she exclaimed, her eyes filled with delight. "Tell me, Mademoiselle, does he knew that I see his letters?"

"Never in the world! He would be angry and would never write to me again if he thought so. Does he write to you? Never a line. Does he send you a message? Never a word. It is because he loves you, poor fool, and is trying to forget you, since you are not free to listen to him or to belong to him."

"Why do you show me his letters, then?"

"Haven't you begged for them? Can I refuse you anything? Oh! you cannot deceive me," and Mademoiselle approached her beloved instrument and began to play. Edna did not at once read the letter. She sat holding it in her hand, while the music penetrated her whole being like an effulgence, warming and brightening the dark places of her soul. It prepared her for joy and exultation.

"Oh!" she exclaimed, letting the letter fall to the floor. "Why did you not tell me?" She went and grasped Mademoiselle's hands up from the keys. "Oh! unkind! malicious! Why did you not tell me?"

"That he was coming back? No great news, *ma foi*.[9] I wonder he did not come long ago."

"But when, when?" cried Edna, impatiently. "He does not say when."

"He says 'very soon.' You know as much about it as I do; it is all in the letter."

9. "In fact."

"But why? Why is he coming? Oh, if I thought—" and she snatched the letter from the floor and turned the pages this way and that way, looking for the reason, which was left untold.

"If I were young and in love with a man," said Mademoiselle, turning on the stool and pressing her wiry hands between her knees as she looked down at Edna, who sat on the floor holding the letter, "it seems to me he would have to be some *grand esprit*; a man with lofty aims and ability to reach them; one who stood high enough to attract the notice of his fellow-men. It seems to me if I were young and in love I should never deem a man of ordinary caliber worthy of my devotion."

"Now it is you who are telling lies and seeking to deceive me, Mademoiselle; or else you have never been in love, and know nothing about it. Why," went on Edna, clasping her knees and looking up into Mademoiselle's twisted face, "do you suppose a woman knows why she loves? Does she select? Does she say to herself: 'Go to! Here is a distinguished statesman with presidential possibilities; I shall proceed to fall in love with him.' Or, 'I shall set my heart upon this musician, whose fame is on every tongue?' Or, 'This financier, who controls the world's money markets?' "

"You are purposely misunderstanding me, *ma reine*.[1] Are you in love with Robert?"

"Yes," said Edna. It was the first time she had admitted it, and a glow overspread her face, blotching it with red spots.

"Why?" asked her companion. "Why do you love him when you ought not to?"

Edna, with a motion or two, dragged herself on her knees before Mademoiselle Reisz, who took the glowing face between her two hands.

"Why? Because his hair is brown and grows away from his temples; because he opens and shuts his eyes, and his nose is a little out of drawing; because he has two lips and a square chin, and a little finger which he can't straighten from having played baseball too energetically in his youth. Because—"

"Because you do, in short," laughed Mademoiselle. "What will you do when he comes back?" she asked.

"Do? Nothing, except feel glad and happy to be alive."

She was already glad and happy to be alive at the mere thought of his return. The murky, lowering sky, which had depressed her a few hours before, seemed bracing and invigorating as she splashed through the streets on her way home.

She stopped at a confectioner's and ordered a huge box of bon-bons for the children in Iberville. She slipped a card in the box, on

1. "My love" (literally, "my queen").

which she scribbled a tender message and sent an abundance of kisses.

Before dinner in the evening Edna wrote a charming letter to her husband, telling him of her intention to move for a while into the little house around the block, and to give a farewell dinner before leaving, regretting that he was not there to share it, to help her out with the menu and assist her in entertaining the guests. Her letter was brilliant and brimming with cheerfulness.

XXVII

"What is the matter with you?" asked Arobin that evening. "I never found you in such a happy mood." Edna was tired by that time, and was reclining on the lounge before the fire.

"Don't you know the weather prophet has told us we shall see the sun pretty soon?"

"Well, that ought to be reason enough," he acquiesced. "You wouldn't give me another if I sat here all night imploring you." He sat close to her on a low tabouret, and as he spoke his fingers lightly touched the hair that fell a little over her forehead. She liked the touch of his fingers through her hair, and closed her eyes sensitively.

"One of these days," she said, "I'm going to pull myself together for a while and think—try to determine what character of a woman I am; for, candidly, I don't know. By all the codes which I am acquainted with, I am a devilishly wicked specimen of the sex. But some way I can't convince myself that I am. I must think about it."

"Don't. What's the use? Why should you bother thinking about it when I can tell you what manner of woman you are." His fingers strayed occasionally down to her warm, smooth cheeks and firm chin, which was growing a little full and double.

"Oh, yes! You will tell me that I am adorable; everything that is captivating. Spare yourself the effort."

"No; I shan't tell you anything of the sort, though I shouldn't be lying if I did."

"Do you know Mademoiselle Reisz?" she asked irrelevantly.

"The pianist? I know her by sight. I've heard her play."

"She says queer things sometimes in a bantering way that you don't notice at the time and you find yourself thinking about afterward."

"For instance?"

"Well, for instance, when I left her today, she put her arms around me and felt my shoulder blades, to see if my wings were strong, she said. 'The bird that would soar above the level plain of tradition and prejudice must have strong wings. It is a sad spectacle to see the weaklings bruised, exhausted, fluttering back to earth.'"

"Whither would you soar?"

"I'm not thinking of any extraordinary flights. I only half comprehend her."

"I've heard she's partially demented," said Arobin.

"She seems to me wonderfully sane," Edna replied.

"I'm told she's extremely disagreeable and unpleasant. Why have you introduced her at a moment when I desired to talk of you?"

"Oh! talk of me if you like," cried Edna, clasping her hands beneath her head; "but let me think of something else while you do."

"I'm jealous of your thoughts to-night. They're making you a little kinder than usual; but some way I feel as if they were wandering, as if they were not here with me." She only looked at him and smiled. His eyes were very near. He leaned upon the lounge with an arm extended across her, while the other hand still rested upon her hair. They continued silently to look into each other's eyes. When he leaned forward and kissed her, she clasped his head, holding his lips to hers.

It was the first kiss of her life to which her nature had really responded. It was a flaming torch that kindled desire.

XXVIII

Edna cried a little that night after Arobin left her. It was only one phase of the multitudinous emotions which had assailed her. There was with her an overwhelming feeling of irresponsibility. There was the shock of the unexpected and the unaccustomed. There was her husband's reproach looking at her from the external things around her which he had provided for her external existence. There was Robert's reproach making itself felt by a quicker, fiercer, more overpowering love, which had awakened within her toward him. Above all, there was understanding. She felt as if a mist had been lifted from her eyes, enabling her to look upon and comprehend the significance of life, that monster made up of beauty and brutality. But among the conflicting sensations which assailed her, there was neither shame nor remorse. There was a dull pang of regret because it was not the kiss of love which had inflamed her, because it was not love which had held this cup of life to her lips.

XXIX

Without even waiting for an answer from her husband regarding his opinion or wishes in the matter, Edna hastened her preparations for quitting her home on Esplanade Street and moving into the little house around the block. A feverish anxiety attended her every action in that direction. There was no moment of deliberation, no interval of repose between the thought and its fulfillment. Early upon the morning following those hours passed in Arobin's society, Edna set about securing her new abode and hurrying her arrangements for occupying it. Within the precincts of her home she felt

like one who has entered and lingered within the portals of some
forbidden temple in which a thousand muffled voices bade her be-
gone.

Whatever was her own in the house, everything which she had
acquired aside from her husband's bounty, she caused to be trans-
ported to the other house, supplying simple and meager deficiencies
from her own resources.

Arobin found her with rolled sleeves, working in company with
the house-maid when he looked in during the afternoon. She was
splendid and robust, and had never appeared handsomer than in the
old blue gown, with a red silk handkerchief knotted at random
around her head to protect her hair from the dust. She was mounted
upon a high step-ladder, unhooking a picture from the wall when he
entered. He had found the front door open, and had followed his
ring by walking in unceremoniously.

"Come down!" he said. "Do you want to kill yourself?" She
greeted him with affected carelesness, and appeared absorbed in her
occupation.

If he had expected to find her languishing, reproachful, or indulging in sentimental tears, he must have been greatly surprised.

He was no doubt prepared for any emergency, ready for any one
of the foregoing attitudes, just as he bent himself easily and naturally to the situation which confronted him.

"Please come down," he insisted, holding the ladder and looking
up at her.

"No," she answered; "Ellen is afraid to mount the ladder. Joe is
working over at the 'pigeon house'—that's the name Ellen gives it,
because it's so small and looks like a pigeon house[2]—and some one
has to do this."

Arobin pulled off his coat, and expressed himself ready and willing to tempt fate in her place. Ellen brought him one of her dust-
caps, and went into contortions of mirth, which she found it impossible to control, when she saw him put it on before the mirror as
grotesquely as he could. Edna herself could not refrain from smiling
when she fastened it at his request. So it was he who in turn
mounted the ladder, unhooking pictures and curtains, and dislodging ornaments as Edna directed. When he had finished he took off
his dust-cap and went out to wash his hands.

Edna was sitting on the tabouret, idly brushing the tips of a
feather duster along the carpet when he came in again.

"Is there anything more you will let me do?" he asked.

"That is all," she answered. "Ellen can manage the rest." She kept

2. A house or dovecot for the domesticated birds kept for show or sport. The
breeds kept by these fashionable hobby-
ists were elegantly colored, little resembling the drab street pigeon.

the young woman occupied in the drawing-room, unwilling to be left alone with Arobin.

"What about the dinner?" he asked; "the grand event, the *coup d'état?*"

"It will be day after to-morrow. Why do you call it the '*coup d'état?*' Oh! it will be very fine; all my best of everything—crystal, silver and gold, Sèvres, flowers, music, and champagne to swim in. I'll let Léonce pay the bills. I wonder what he'll say when he sees the bills."

"And you ask me why I call it a *coup d'état?*" Arobin had put on his coat, and he stood before her and asked if his cravat was plumb. She told him it was, looking no higher than the tip of his collar.

"When do you go to the 'pigeon house?'—with all due acknowledgment to Ellen."

"Day after to-morrow, after the dinner. I shall sleep there."

"Ellen, will you very kindly get me a glass of water?" asked Arobin. "The dust in the curtains, if you will pardon me for hinting such a thing, has parched my throat to a crisp."

"While Ellen gets the water," said Edna, rising, "I will say good-by and let you go. I must get rid of this grime, and I have a million things to do and think of."

"When shall I see you?" asked Arobin, seeking to detain her, the maid having left the room.

"At the dinner, of course. You are invited."

"Not before?—not to-night or to-morrow morning or to-morrow noon or night? or the day after morning or noon? Can't you see yourself, without my telling you, what an eternity it is?"

He had followed her into the hall and to the foot of the stairway, looking up at her as she mounted with her face half turned to him.

"Not an instant sooner," she said. But she laughed and looked at him with eyes that at once gave him courage to wait and made it torture to wait.

XXX

Though Edna had spoken of the dinner as a very grand affair, it was in truth a very small affair and very select, in so much as the guests invited were few and were selected with discrimination. She had counted upon an even dozen seating themselves at her round mahogany board, forgetting for the moment that Madame Ratignolle was to the last degree *souffrante*[3] and unpresentable, and not foreseeing that Madame Lebrun would send a thousand regrets at the last moment. So there were only ten, after all, which made a cozy, comfortable number.

There were Mr. and Mrs. Merriman, a pretty, vivacious little

3. III.

woman in the thirties; her husband, a jovial fellow, something of a shallow-pate, who laughed a good deal at other people's witticisms, and had thereby made himself extremely popular. Mrs. Highcamp had accompanied them. Of course, there was Alcée Arobin; and Mademoiselle Reisz had consented to come. Edna had sent her a fresh bunch of violets with black lace trimmings for her hair. Monsieur Ratignolle brought himself and his wife's excuses. Victor Lebrun, who happened to be in the city, bent upon relaxation, had accepted with alacrity. There was a Miss Mayblunt, no longer in her teens, who looked at the world through lorgnettes and with the keenest interest. It was thought and said that she was intellectual; it was suspected of her that she wrote under a *nom de guerre*.[4] She had come with a gentleman by the name of Gouvernail, connected with one of the daily papers, of whom nothing special could be said, except that he was observant and seemed quiet and inoffensive. Edna herself made the tenth, and at half-past eight they seated themselves at table, Arobin and Monsieur Ratignolle on either side of their hostess.

Mrs. Highcamp sat between Arobin and Victor Lebrun. Then came Mrs. Merriman, Mr. Gouvernail, Miss Mayblunt, Mr. Merriman, and Mademoiselle Reisz next to Monsieur Ratignolle.

There was something extremely gorgeous about the appearance of the table, an effect of splendor conveyed by a cover of pale yellow satin under strips of lace-work. There were wax candles in massive brass candelabra, burning softly under yellow silk shades; full, fragrant roses, yellow and red, abounded. There were silver and gold, as she had said there would be, and crystal which glittered like the gems which the women wore.

The ordinary stiff dining chairs had been discarded for the occasion and replaced by the most commodious and luxurious which could be collected throughout the house. Mademoiselle Reisz, being exceedingly diminutive, was elevated upon cushions, as small children are sometimes hoisted at table upon bulky volumes.

"Something new, Edna?" exclaimed Miss Mayblunt, with lorgnette directed toward a magnificent cluster of diamonds that sparkled, that almost sputtered, in Edna's hair, just over the center of her forehead.

"Quite new; 'brand' new, in fact; a present from my husband. It arrived this morning from New York. I may as well admit that this is my birthday, and that I am twenty-nine. In good time I expect you to drink my health. Meanwhile, I shall ask you to begin with this cocktail, composed—would you say 'composed?' " with an appeal to Miss Mayblunt—"composed by my father in honor of Sister Janet's wedding."

4. Pseudonym.

Before each guest stood a tiny glass that looked and sparkled like a garnet gem.

"Then, all things considered," spoke Arobin, "it might not be amiss to start out by drinking the Colonel's health in the cocktail which he composed, on the birthday of the most charming of women—the daughter whom he invented."

Mr. Merriman's laugh at this sally was such a genuine outburst and so contagious that it started the dinner with an agreeable swing that never slackened.

Miss Mayblunt begged to be allowed to keep her cocktail untouched before her, just to look at. The color was marvelous! She could compare it to nothing she had ever seen, and the garnet lights which it emitted were unspeakably rare. She pronounced the Colonel an artist, and stuck to it.

Monsieur Ratignolle was prepared to take things seriously; the *mets*, the *entre-mets*,[5] the service, the decorations, even the people. He looked up from his pompono and inquired of Arobin if he were related to the gentleman of that name who formed one of the firm of Laitner and Arobin, lawyers. The young man admitted that Laitner was a warm personal friend, who permitted Arobin's name to decorate the firm's letterheads and to appear upon a shingle that graced Perdido Street.[6]

"There are so many inquisitive people and institutions abounding," said Arobin, "that one is really forced as a matter of convenience these days to assume the virtue of an occupation if he has it not."

Monsieur Ratignolle stared a little, and turned to ask Mademoiselle Reisz if she considered the symphony concerts up to the standard which had been set the previous winter. Mademoiselle Reisz answered Monsieur Ratignolle in French, which Edna thought a little rude, under the circumstances, but characteristic. Mademoiselle had only disagreeable things to say of the symphony concerts, and insulting remarks to make of all the musicians of New Orleans, singly and collectively. All her interest seemed to be centered upon the delicacies placed before her.

Mr. Merriman said that Mr. Arobin's remark about inquisitive people reminded him of a man from Waco[7] the other day at the St. Charles Hotel—but as Mr. Merriman's stories were always lame and lacking point, his wife seldom permitted him to complete them. She interrupted him to ask if he remembered the name of the author whose book she had bought the week before to send to a friend in Geneva. She was talking "books" with Mr. Gouvernail

5. The main courses, the side dishes.
6. From *perdido*, the Spanish word for "lost," because the street ends in a cypress swamp where by legend travelers have strayed.
7. Waco, Texas.

and trying to draw from him his opinion upon current literary topics. Her husband told the story of the Waco man privately to Miss Mayblunt, who pretended to be greatly amused and to think it extremely clever.

Mrs. Highcamp hung with languid but unaffected interest upon the warm and impetuous volubility of her left-hand neighbor, Victor Lebrun. Her attention was never for a moment withdrawn from him after seating herself at table; and when he turned to Mrs. Merriman, who was prettier and more vivacious than Mrs. Highcamp, she waited with easy indifference for an opportunity to reclaim his attention. There was the occasional sound of music, of mandolins, sufficiently removed to be an agreeable accompaniment rather than an interruption to the conversation. Outside the soft, monotonous splash of a fountain could be heard; the sound penetrated into the room with the heavy odor of jessamine that came through the open windows.

The golden shimmer of Edna's satin gown spread in rich folds on either side of her. There was a soft fall of lace encircling her shoulders. It was the color of her skin, without the glow, the myriad living tints that one may sometimes discover in vibrant flesh. There was something in her attitude, in her whole appearance when she leaned her head against the high-backed chair and spread her arms, which suggested the regal woman, the one who rules, who looks on, who stands alone.

But as she sat there amid her guests, she felt the old ennui overtaking her; the hopelessness which so often assailed her, which came upon her like an obsession, like something extraneous, independent of volition. It was something which announced itself; a chill breath that seemed to issue from some vast cavern wherein discords wailed. There came over her the acute longing which always summoned into her spiritual vision the presence of the beloved one, overpowering her at once with a sense of the unattainable.

The moments glided on, while a feeling of good fellowship passed around the circle like a mystic cord, holding and binding these people together with jest and laughter. Monsieur Ratignolle was the first to break the pleasant charm. At ten o'clock he excused himself. Madame Ratignolle was waiting for him at home. She was *bien souffrante*,[8] and she was filled with vague dread, which only her husband's presence could allay.

Mademoiselle Reisz arose with Monsieur Ratignolle, who offered to escort her to the car. She had eaten well; she had tasted the good, rich wines, and they must have turned her head, for she bowed pleasantly to all as she withdrew from table. She kissed Edna upon the shoulder, and whispered: "*Bonne nuit, ma reine; soyez sage.*"[9]

8. Very ill.   9. "Good night, my love; be good."

She had been a little bewildered upon rising, or rather, descending from her cushions, and Monsieur Ratignolle gallantly took her arm and led her away.

Mrs. Highcamp was weaving a garland of roses, yellow and red. When she had finished the garland, she laid it lightly upon Victor's black curls. He was reclining far back in the luxurious chair, holding a glass of champagne to the light.

As if a magician's wand had touched him, the garland of roses transformed him into a vision of Oriental beauty. His cheeks were the color of crushed grapes, and his dusky eyes glowed with a languishing fire.

"*Sapristi!*" exclaimed Arobin.

But Mrs. Highcamp had one more touch to add to the picture. She took from the back of her chair a white silken scarf, with which she had covered her shoulders in the early part of the evening. She draped it across the boy in graceful folds, and in a way to conceal his black, conventional evening dress. He did not seem to mind what she did to him, only smiled, showing a faint gleam of white teeth, while he continued to gaze with narrowing eyes at the light through his glass of champagne.

"Oh! to be able to paint in color rather than in words!" exclaimed Miss Mayblunt, losing herself in a rhapsodic dream as she looked at him.

> " 'There was a graven image of Desire
> Painted with red blood on a ground of gold.' "[1]

murmured Gouvernail, under his breath.

The effect of the wine upon Victor was, to change his accustomed volubility into silence. He seemed to have abandoned himself to a reverie, and to be seeing pleasing visions in the amber bead.

"Sing," entreated Mrs. Highcamp. "Won't you sing to us?"

"Let him alone," said Arobin.

"He's posing," offered Mr. Merriman; "let him have it out."

"I believe he's paralyzed," laughed Mrs. Merriman. And leaning over the youth's chair, she took the glass from his hand and held it to his lips. He sipped the wine slowly, and when he had drained the glass she laid it upon the table and wiped his lips with her little filmy handkerchief.

"Yes, I'll sing for you," he said, turning in his chair toward Mrs. Highcamp. He clasped his hands behind his head, and looking up at the ceiling began to hum a little, trying his voice like a musician tuning an instrument. Then, looking at Edna, he began to sing:

"Ah! si tu savais!"

1. Lines from a sonnet by A. C. Swinburne (1837–1909) called "A Cameo." See p. 227.

"Stop!" she cried, "don't sing that. I don't want you to sing it," and she laid her glass so impetuously and blindly upon the table as to shatter it against a caraffe. The wine spilled over Arobin's legs and some of it trickled down upon Mrs. Highcamp's black gauze gown. Victor had lost all idea of courtesy, or else he thought his hostess was not in earnest, for he laughed and went on:

"Ah! si tu savais
Ce que tes yeux me disent"—

"Oh! you mustn't! you mustn't," exclaimed Edna, and pushing back her chair she got up, and going behind him placed her hand over his mouth. He kissed the soft palm that pressed upon his lips.

"No, no, I won't, Mrs. Pontellier. I didn't know you meant it," looking up at her with caressing eyes. The touch of his lips was like a pleasing sting to her hand. She lifted the garland of roses from his head and flung it across the room.

"Come, Victor; you've posed long enough. Give Mrs. Highcamp her scarf."

Mrs. Highcamp undraped the scarf from about him with her own hands. Miss Mayblunt and Mr. Gouvernail suddenly conceived the notion that it was time to say good night. And Mr. and Mrs. Merriman wondered how it could be so late.

Before parting from Victor, Mrs. Highcamp invited him to call upon her daughter, who she knew would be charmed to meet him and talk French and sing French songs with him. Victor expressed his desire and intention to call upon Miss Highcamp at the first opportunity which presented itself. He asked if Arobin were going his way. Arobin was not.

The mandolin players had long since stolen away. A profound stillness had fallen upon the broad, beautiful street. The voices of Edna's disbanding guests jarred like a discordant note upon the quiet harmony of the night.

XXXI

"Well?" questioned Arobin, who had remained with Edna after the others had departed.

"Well," she reiterated, and stood up, stretching her arms, and feeling the need to relax her muscles after having been so long seated.

"What next?" he asked.

"The servants are all gone. They left when the musicians did. I have dismissed them. The house has to be closed and locked, and I shall trot around to the pigeon house, and shall send Celestine over in the morning to straighten things up."

He looked around, and began to turn out some of the lights.

"What about upstairs?" he inquired.

"I think it is all right; but there may be a window or two unlatched. We had better look; you might take a candle and see. And bring me my wrap and hat on the foot of the bed in the middle room."

He went up with the light, and Edna began closing doors and windows. She hated to shut in the smoke and the fumes of the wine. Arobin found her cape and hat, which he brought down and helped her to put on.

When everything was secured and the lights put out, they left through the front door, Arobin locking it and taking the key, which he carried for Edna. He helped her down the steps.

"Will you have a spray of jessamine?" he asked, breaking off a few blossoms as he passed.

"No; I don't want anything."

She seemed disheartened, and had nothing to say. She took his arm, which he offered her, holding up the weight of her satin train with the other hand. She looked down, noticing the black line of his leg moving in and out so close to her against the yellow shimmer of her gown. There was the whistle of a railway train somewhere in the distance, and the midnight bells were ringing. They met no one in their short walk.

The "pigeon-house" stood behind a locked gate, and a shallow *parterre*[2] that had been somewhat neglected. There was a small front porch, upon which a long window and the front door opened. The door opened directly into the parlor; there was no side entry. Back in the yard was a room for servants, in which old Celestine had been ensconced.

Edna had left a lamp burning low upon the table. She had succeeded in making the room look habitable and homelike. There were some books on the table and a lounge near at hand. On the floor was a fresh matting, covered with a rug or two; and on the walls hung a few tasteful pictures. But the room was filled with flowers. These were a surprise to her. Arobin had sent them, and had had Celestine distribute them during Edna's absence. Her bedroom was adjoining, and across a small passage were the dining-room and kitchen.

Edna seated herself with every appearance of discomfort.

"Are you tired?" he asked.

"Yes, and chilled, and miserable. I feel as if I had been wound up to a certain pitch—too tight—and something inside of me had snapped." She rested her head against the table upon her bare arm.

"You want to rest," he said, "and to be quiet. I'll go; I'll leave you and let you rest."

2. Garden.

"Yes," she replied.

He stood up beside her and smoothed her hair with his soft, magnetic hand. His touch conveyed to her a certain physical comfort. She could have fallen quietly asleep there if he had continued to pass his hand over her hair. He brushed the hair upward from the nape of her neck.

"I hope you will feel better and happier in the morning," he said. "You have tried to do too much in the past few days. The dinner was the last straw; you might have dispensed with it."

"Yes," she admitted; "it was stupid."

"No, it was delightful; but it has worn you out." His hand had strayed to her beautiful shoulders, and he could feel the response of her flesh to his touch. He seated himself beside her and kissed her lightly upon the shoulder.

"I thought you were going away," she said, in an uneven voice.

"I am, after I have said good night."

"Good night," she murmured.

He did not answer, except to continue to caress her. He did not say good night until she had become supple to his gentle, seductive entreaties.

XXXII

When Mr. Pontellier learned of his wife's intention to abandon her home and take up her residence elsewhere, he immediately wrote her a letter of unqualified disapproval and remonstrance. She had given reasons which he was unwilling to acknowledge as adequate. He hoped she had not acted upon her rash impulse; and he begged her to consider first, foremost, and above all else, what people would say. He was not dreaming of scandal when he uttered this warning; that was a thing which would never have entered into his mind to consider in connection with his wife's name or his own. He was simply thinking of his financial integrity. It might get noised about that the Pontelliers had met with reverses, and were forced to conduct their *ménage*[3] on a humbler scale than heretofore. It might do incalculable mischief to his business prospects.

But remembering Edna's whimsical turn of mind of late, and foreseeing that she had immediately acted upon her impetuous determination, he grasped the situation with his usual promptness and handled it with his well-known business tact and cleverness.

The same mail which brought to Edna his letter of disapproval carried instructions—the most minute instructions—to a well-known architect concerning the remodeling of his home, changes which he had long contemplated, and which he desired carried forward during his temporary absence.

Expert and reliable packers and movers were engaged to convey

3. Household.

the furniture, carpets, pictures—everything movable, in short—to places of security. And in an incredibly short time the Pontellier house was turned over to the artisans. There was to be an addition —a small snuggery; there was to be frescoing, and hardwood flooring was to be put into such rooms as had not yet been subjected to this improvement.

Furthermore, in one of the daily papers appeared a brief notice to the effect that Mr. and Mrs. Pontellier were contemplating a summer sojourn abroad, and that their handsome residence on Esplanade Street was undergoing sumptuous alterations, and would not be ready for occupancy until their return. Mr. Pontellier had saved appearances!

Edna admired the skill of his maneuver, and avoided any occasion to balk his intentions. When the situation as set forth by Mr. Pontellier was accepted and taken for granted, she was apparently satisfied that it should be so.

The pigeon-house pleased her. It at once assumed the intimate character of a home, while she herself invested it with a charm which it reflected like a warm glow. There was with her a feeling of having descended in the social scale, with a corresponding sense of having risen in the spiritual. Every step which she took toward relieving herself from obligations added to her strength and expansion as an individual. She began to look with her own eyes; to see and to apprehend the deeper undercurrents of life. No longer was she content to "feed upon opinion" when her own soul had invited her.

After a little while, a few days, in fact, Edna went up and spent a week with her children in Iberville. They were delicious February days, with all the summer's promise hovering in the air.

How glad she was to see the children! She wept for very pleasure when she felt their little arms clasping her; their hard, ruddy cheeks pressed against her own glowing cheeks. She looked into their faces with hungry eyes that could not be satisfied with looking. And what stories they had to tell their mother! About the pigs, the cows, the mules! About riding to the mill behind Gluglu; fishing back in the lake with their Uncle Jasper; picking pecans with Lidie's little black brood, and hauling chips in their express wagon. It was a thousand times more fun to haul real chips for old lame Susie's real fire than to drag painted blocks along the banquette on Esplanade Street!

She went with them herself to see the pigs and the cows, to look at the darkies laying the cane, to thrash the pecan trees, and catch fish in the back lake. She lived with them a whole week long, giving them all of herself, and gathering and filling herself with their young existence. They listened, breathless, when she told them the house in Esplanade Street was crowded with workmen, hammering, nailing, sawing, and filling the place with clatter. They wanted to know where their bed was; what had been done with their rocking-horse; and where did Joe sleep, and where had Ellen gone, and the cook? But, above all, they were fired with a desire to see the little house around the block. Was there any place to play? Were there any boys next door? Raoul, with pessimistic foreboding, was convinced that there were only girls next door. Where would they sleep, and where would papa sleep? She told them the fairies would fix it all right.

The old Madame was charmed with Edna's visit, and showered all manner of delicate attentions upon her. She was delighted to know that the Esplanade Street house was in a dismantled condition. It gave her the promise and pretext to keep the children indefinitely.

It was with a wrench and a pang that Edna left her children. She carried away with her the sound of their voices and the touch of their cheeks. All along the journey homeward their presence lingered with her like the memory of a delicious song. But by the time she had regained the city the song no longer echoed in her soul. She was again alone.

XXXIII

It happened sometimes when Edna went to see Mademoiselle Reisz that the little musician was absent, giving a lesson or making some small necessary household purchase. The key was always left in a secret hiding-place in the entry, which Edna knew. If Mademoiselle happened to be away, Edna would usually enter and wait for her return.

When she knocked at Mademoiselle Reisz's door one afternoon there was no response; so unlocking the door, as usual, she entered and found the apartment deserted, as she had expected. Her day had been quite filled up, and it was for a rest, for a refuge, and to talk about Robert, that she sought out her friend.

She had worked at her canvas—a young Italian character study —all the morning, completing the work without the model; but there had been many interruptions, some incident to her modest housekeeping, and others of a social nature.

Madame Ratignolle had dragged herself over, avoiding the too public thoroughfares, she said. She complained that Edna had neglected her much of late. Besides, she was consumed with curiosity to see the little house and the manner in which it was conducted. She wanted to hear all about the dinner party; Monsieur Ratignolle had left *so* early. What had happened after he left? The champagne and grapes which Edna sent over were *too* delicious. She had so little appetite; they had refreshed and toned her stomach. Where on earth was she going to put Mr. Pontellier in that little house, and the boys? And then she made Edna promise to go to her when her hour of trial overtook her.

"At any time—any time of the day or night, dear," Edna assured her.

Before leaving Madame Ratignolle said:

"In some way you seem to me like a child, Edna. You seem to act without a certain amount of reflection which is necessary in this life. That is the reason I want to say you mustn't mind if I advise you to be a little careful while you are living here alone. Why don't you have some one come and stay with you? Wouldn't Mademoiselle Reisz come?"

"No; she wouldn't wish to come, and I shouldn't want her always with me."

"Well, the reason—you know how evil-minded the world is— some one was talking of Alcée Arobin visiting you. Of course, it wouldn't matter if Mr. Arobin had not such a dreadful reputation. Monsieur Ratignolle was telling me that his attentions alone are considered enough to ruin a woman's name."

"Does he boast of his successes?" asked Edna, indifferently, squinting at her picture.

"No, I think not. I believe he is a decent fellow as far as that goes. But his character is so well known among the men. I shan't be able to come back and see you; it was very, very imprudent to-day."

"Mind the step!" cried Edna.

"Don't neglect me," entreated Madame Ratignolle; "and don't mind what I said about Arobin, or having some one to stay with you."

"Of course not," Edna laughed. "You may say anything you like to me." They kissed each other good-bye. Madame Ratignolle had not far to go, and Edna stood on the porch a while watching her walk down the street.

Then in the afternoon Mrs. Merriman and Mrs. Highcamp had made their "party call." Edna felt that they might have dispensed with the formality. They had also come to invite her to play *vingt-et-un*[4] one evening at Mrs. Merriman's. She was asked to go early, to dinner, and Mr. Merriman or Mr. Arobin would take her home. Edna accepted in a half-hearted way. She sometimes felt very tired of Mrs. Highcamp and Mrs. Merriman.

Late in the afternoon she sought refuge with Mademoiselle Reisz, and stayed there alone, waiting for her, feeling a kind of repose invade her with the very atmosphere of the shabby, unpretentious little room.

Edna sat at the window, which looked out over the house-tops

4. Twenty-one: a card game.

and across the river. The window frame was filled with pots of flowers, and she sat and picked the dry leaves from a rose geranium. The day was warm, and the breeze which blew from the river was very pleasant. She removed her hat and laid it on the piano. She went on picking the leaves and digging around the plants with her hat pin. Once she thought she heard Mademoiselle Reisz approaching. But it was a young black girl, who came in, bringing a small bundle of laundry, which she deposited in the adjoining room, and went away.

Edna seated herself at the piano, and softly picked out with one hand the bars of a piece of music which lay open before her. A half-hour went by. There was the occasional sound of people going and coming in the lower hall. She was growing interested in her occupation of picking out the aria, when there was a second rap at the door. She vaguely wondered what these people did when they found Mademoiselle's door locked.

"Come in," she called, turning her face toward the door. And this time it was Robert Lebrun who presented himself. She attempted to rise; she could not have done so without betraying the agitation which mastered her at sight of him, so she fell back upon the stool, only exclaiming, "Why, Robert!"

He came and clasped her hand, seemingly without knowing what he was saying or doing.

"Mrs. Pontellier! How do you happen—oh! how well you look! Is Mademoiselle Reisz not here? I never expected to see you."

"When did you come back?" asked Edna in an unsteady voice, wiping her face with her handkerchief. She seemed ill at ease on the piano stool, and he begged her to take the chair by the window. She did so, mechanically, while he seated himself on the stool.

"I returned day before yesterday," he answered, while he leaned his arm on the keys, bringing forth a crash of discordant sound.

"Day before yesterday!" she repeated, aloud; and went on thinking to herself, "day before yesterday," in a sort of an uncomprehending way . She had pictured him seeking her at the very first hour, and he had lived under the same sky since day before yesterday; while only by accident had he stumbled upon her. Mademoiselle must have lied when she said, "Poor fool, he loves you."

"Day before yesterday," she repeated, breaking off a spray of Mademoiselle's geranium; "then if you had not met me here to-day you wouldn't—when—that is, didn't you mean to come and see me?"

"Of course, I should have gone to see you. There have been so many things—" he turned the leaves of Mademoiselle's music nervously. "I started in at once yesterday with the old firm. After all there is as much chance for me here as there was there—that is, I might find it profitable some day. The Mexicans were not very congenial."

So he had come back because the Mexicans were not congenial; because business was as profitable here as there; because of any reason, and not because he cared to be near her. She remembered the day she sat on the floor, turning the pages of his letter, seeking the reason which was left untold.

She had not noticed how he looked—only feeling his presence; but she turned deliberately and observed him. After all, he had been absent but a few months, and was not changed. His hair—the color of hers—waved back from his temples in the same way as before. His skin was not more burned than it had been at Grand Isle. She found in his eyes, when he looked at her for one silent moment, the same tender caress, with an added warmth and entreaty which had not been there before—the same glance which had penetrated to the sleeping places of her soul and awakened them.

A hundred times Edna had pictured Robert's return, and imagined their first meeting. It was usually at her home, whither he had sought her out at once. She always fancied him expressing or betraying in some way his love for her. And here, the reality was that they sat ten feet apart, she at the window, crushing geranium leaves in her hand and smelling them, he twirling around on the piano stool, saying:

"I was very much surprised to hear of Mr. Pontellier's absence; it's a wonder Mademoiselle Reisz did not tell me; and your moving —mother told me yesterday. I should think you would have gone to New York with him, or to Iberville with the children, rather than be bothered here with housekeeping. And you are going abroad, too, I hear. We shan't have you at Grand Isle next summer; it won't seem—do you see much of Mademoiselle Reisz? She often spoke of you in the few letters she wrote."

"Do you remember that you promised to write to me when you went away?" A flush overspread his whole face.

"I couldn't believe that my letters would be of any interest to you."

"That is an excuse; it isn't the truth." Edna reached for her hat on the piano. She adjusted it, sticking the hat pin through the heavy coil of hair with some deliberation.

"Are you not going to wait for Mademoiselle Reisz?" asked Robert.

"No; I have found when she is absent this long, she is liable not to come back till late." She drew on her gloves, and Robert picked up his hat.

"Won't you wait for her?" asked Edna.

"Not if you think she will not be back till late," adding, as if suddenly aware of some discourtesy in his speech, "and I should miss the pleasure of walking home with you." Edna locked the door and put the key back in its hiding-place.

They went together, picking their way across muddy streets and sidewalks encumbered with the cheap display of small tradesmen. Part of the distance they rode in the car, and after disembarking, passed the Pontellier mansion, which looked broken and half torn asunder. Robert had never known the house, and looked at it with interest.

"I never knew you in your home," he remarked.

"I am glad you did not."

"Why?" She did not answer. They went on around the corner, and it seemed as if her dreams were coming true after all, when he followed her into the little house.

"You must stay and dine with me, Robert. You see I am all alone, and it is so long since I have seen you. There is so much I want to ask you."

She took off her hat and gloves. He stood irresolute, making some excuse about his mother who expected him; he even muttered something about an engagement. She struck a match and lit the lamp on the table; it was growing dusk. When he saw her face in the lamp-light, looking pained, with all the soft lines gone out of it, he threw his hat aside and seated himself.

"Oh! you know I want to stay if you will let me!" he exclaimed. All the softness came back. She laughed, and went and put her hand on his shoulder.

"This is the first moment you have seemed like the old Robert. I'll go tell Celestine." She hurried away to tell Celestine to set an extra place. She even sent her off in search of some added delicacy which she had not thought of for herself. And she recommended great care in dripping the coffee and having the omelet done to a proper turn.

When she reëntered, Robert was turning over magazines, sketches, and things that lay upon the table in great disorder. He picked up a photograph, and exclaimed:

"Alcée Arobin! What on earth is his picture doing here?"

"I tried to make a sketch of his head one day," answered Edna, "and he thought the photograph might help me. It was at the other house. I thought it had been left there. I must have packed it up with my drawing materials."

"I should think you would give it back to him if you have finished with it."

"Oh! I have a great many such photographs. I never think of returning them. They don't amount to anything." Robert kept on looking at the picture.

"It seems to me—do you think his head worth drawing? Is he a friend of Mr. Pontellier's? You never said you knew him."

"He isn't a friend of Mr. Pontellier's; he's a friend of mine. I always knew him—that is, it is only of late that I know him pretty well. But I'd rather talk about you, and know what you have been seeing and doing and feeling out there in Mexico." Robert threw aside the picture.

"I've been seeing the waves and the white beach of Grand Isle; the quiet, grassy street of the *Chênière*; the old fort at Grande Terre. I've been working like a machine, and feeling like a lost soul. There was nothing interesting."

She leaned her head upon her hand to shade her eyes from the light.

"And what have you been seeing and doing and feeling all these days?" he asked.

"I've been seeing the waves and the white beach of Grand Isle; the quiet, grassy street of the *Chênière Caminada*; the old sunny fort at Grande Terre. I've been working with little more comprehension than a machine, and still feeling like a lost soul. There was nothing interesting."

"Mrs. Pontellier, you are cruel," he said, with feeling, closing his eyes and resting his head back in his chair. They remained in silence till old Celestine announced dinner.

XXXIV

The dining-room was very small. Edna's round mahogany would have almost filled it. As it was there was but a step or two from the little table to the kitchen, to the mantel, the small buffet, and the side door that opened out on the narrow brick-paved yard.

A certain degree of ceremony settled upon them with the announcement of dinner. There was no return to personalities. Robert related incidents of his sojourn in Mexico, and Edna talked of events likely to interest him, which had occurred during his absence. The dinner was of ordinary quality, except for the few delicacies which she had sent out to purchase. Old Celestine, with a bandana *tignon*[5] twisted about her head, hobbled in and out, taking a personal interest in everything; and she lingered occasionally to talk patois[6] with Robert, whom she had known as a boy.

He went out to a neighboring cigar stand to purchase cigarette papers, and when he came back he found that Celestine had served the black coffee in the parlor.

"Perhaps I shouldn't have come back," he said. "When you are tired of me, tell me to go."

5. Archaic form of the word *chignon*, a "coil of hair," a "bun." She has her hair tied up with a scarf.
6. A dialect of archaic French mixed with English, Spanish, German, and American Indian words spoken by the descendants of the Acadians.

"You never tire me. You must have forgotten the hours and hours at Grand Isle in which we grew accustomed to each other and used to being together."

"I have forgotten nothing at Grand Isle," he said, not looking at her, but rolling a cigarette. His tobacco pouch, which he laid upon the table, was a fantastic embroidered silk affair, evidently the handiwork of a woman.

"You used to carry your tobacco in a rubber pouch," said Edna, picking up the pouch and examining the needlework.

"Yes; it was lost."

"Where did you buy this one? In Mexico?"

"It was given to me by a Vera Cruz girl; they are very generous," he replied, striking a match and lighting his cigarette.

"They are very handsome, I suppose, those Mexican women; very picturesque, with their black eyes and their lace scarfs."

"Some are; others are hideous. Just as you find women everywhere."

"What was she like—the one who gave you the pouch? You must have known her very well."

"She was very ordinary. She wasn't of the slightest importance. I knew her well enough."

"Did you visit at her house? Was it interesting? I should like to know and hear about the people you met, and the impressions they made on you."

"There are some people who leave impressions not so lasting as the imprint of an oar upon the water."

"Was she such a one?"

"It would be ungenerous for me to admit that she was of that order and kind." He thrust the pouch back in his pocket, as if to put away the subject with the trifle which had brought it up.

Arobin dropped in with a message from Mrs. Merriman, to say that the card party was postponed on account of the illness of one of her children.

"How do you do, Arobin?" said Robert, rising from the obscurity.

"Oh! Lebrun. To be sure! I heard yesterday you were back. How did they treat you down in Mexique?"

"Fairly well."

"But not well enough to keep you there. Stunning girls, though, in Mexico. I thought I should never get away from Vera Cruz when I was down there a couple of years ago."

"Did they embroider slippers and tobacco pouches and hat-bands and things for you?" asked Edna.

"Oh! my! no! I didn't get so deep in their regard. I fear they made more impression on me than I made on them."

"You were less fortunate than Robert, then."

"I am always less fortunate than Robert. Has he been imparting tender confidences?"

"I've been imposing myself long enough," said Robert, rising, and shaking hands with Edna. "Please convey my regards to Mr. Pontellier when you write."

He shook hands with Arobin and went away.

"Fine fellow, that Lebrun," said Arobin when Robert had gone. "I never heard you speak of him."

"I knew him last summer at Grand Isle," she replied. "Here is that photograph of yours. Don't you want it?"

"What do I want with it? Throw it away." She threw it back on the table.

"I'm not going to Mrs. Merriman's," she said. "If you see her, tell her so. But perhaps I had better write. I think I shall write now, and say that I am sorry her child is sick, and tell her not to count on me."

"It would be a good scheme," acquiesced Arobin. "I don't blame you; stupid lot!"

Edna opened the blotter, and having procured paper and pen, began to write the note. Arobin lit a cigar and read the evening paper, which he had in his pocket.

"What is the date?" she asked. He told her.

"Will you mail this for me when you go out?"

"Certainly." He read to her little bits out of the newspaper, while she straightened things on the table.

"What do you want to do?" he asked, throwing aside the paper. "Do you want to go out for a walk or a drive or anything? It would be a fine night to drive."

"No; I don't want to do anything but just be quiet. You go away and amuse yourself. Don't stay."

"I'll go away if I must; but I shan't amuse myself. You know that I only live when I am near you."

He stood up to bid her good night.

"Is that one of the things you always say to women?"

"I have said it before, but I don't think I ever came so near meaning it," he answered with a smile. There were no warm lights in her eyes; only a dreamy, absent look.

"Good night. I adore you. Sleep well," he said, and he kissed her hand and went away.

She stayed alone in a kind of reverie—a sort of stupor. Step by step she lived over every instant of the time she had been with Robert after he had entered Mademoiselle Reisz's door. She recalled his words, his looks. How few and meager they had been for her hungry heart! A vision—a transcendently seductive vision of a Mexican girl arose before her. She writhed with a jealous pang. She wondered when he would come back. He had not said he would come back. She had been with him, had heard his voice and touched his hand. But some way he had seemed nearer to her off there in Mexico.

XXXV

The morning was full of sunlight and hope. Edna could see before her no denial—only the promise of excessive joy. She lay in bed awake, with bright eyes full of speculation. "He loves you, poor fool." If she could but get that conviction firmly fixed in her mind, what mattered about the rest? She felt she had been childish and unwise the night before in giving herself over to despondency. She recapitulated the motives which no doubt explained Robert's reserve. They were not insurmountable; they would not hold if he really loved her; they could not hold against her own passion, which he must come to realize in time. She pictured him going to his business that morning. She even saw how he was dressed; how he walked down one street, and turned the corner of another; saw him bending over his desk, talking to people who entered the office, going to his lunch, and perhaps watching for her on the street. He would come to her in the afternoon or evening, sit and roll his cigarette, talk a little, and go away as he had done the night before. But how delicious it would be to have him there with her! She would have no regrets, nor seek to penetrate his reserve if he still chose to wear it.

Edna ate her breakfast only half dressed. The maid brought her a delicious printed scrawl from Raoul, expressing his love, asking her to send him some bonbons, and telling her they had found that morning ten tiny white pigs all lying in a row beside Lidie's big white pig.

A letter also came from her husband, saying he hoped to be back early in March, and then they would get ready for that journey abroad which he had promised her so long, which he felt now fully able to afford; he felt able to travel as people should, without any thought of small economies—thanks to his recent speculations in Wall Street.

Much to her surprise she received a note from Arobin, written at midnight from the club. It was to say good morning to her, to hope that she had slept well, to assure her of his devotion, which he trusted she in some faintest manner returned.

All these letters were pleasing to her. She answered the children in a cheerful frame of mind, promising them bonbons, and congratulating them upon their happy find of the little pigs.

She answered her husband with friendly evasiveness,—not with any fixed design to mislead him, only because all sense of reality had gone out of her life; she had abandoned herself to Fate, and awaited the consequences with indifference.

To Arobin's note she made no reply. She put it under Celestine's stove-lid.

Edna worked several hours with much spirit. She saw no one but a picture dealer, who asked her if it were true that she was going abroad to study in Paris.

She said possibly she might, and he negotiated with her for some Parisian studies to reach him in time for the holiday trade in December.

Robert did not come that day. She was keenly disappointed. He did not come the following day, nor the next. Each morning she awoke with hope, and each night she was a prey to despondency. She was tempted to seek him out. But far from yielding to the impulse, she avoided any occasion which might throw her in his way. She did not go to Mademoiselle Reisz's nor pass by Madame Lebrun's, as she might have done if he had still been in Mexico.

When Arobin, one night, urged her to drive with him, she went— out to the lake, on the Shell Road.[7] His horses were full of mettle, and even a little unmanageable. She liked the rapid gait at which they spun along, and the quick, sharp sound of the horses' hoofs on the hard road. They did not stop anywhere to eat or to drink. Arobin was not needlessly imprudent. But they ate and they drank when they regained Edna's little dining-room—which was comparatively early in the evening.

It was late when he left her. It was getting to be more than a passing whim with Arobin to see her and be with her. He had detected the latent sensuality, which unfolded under his delicate sense of her nature's requirements like a torpid, torrid, sensitive blossom.

There was no despondency when she fell asleep that night; nor was there hope when she awoke in the morning.

XXXVI

There was a garden out in the suburbs; a small, leafy corner, with a few green tables under the orange trees. An old cat slept all day on the stone step in the sun, and an old *mulatresse*[8] slept her idle hours away in her chair at the open window, till some one happened to knock on one of the green tables. She had milk and cream cheese to sell, and bread and butter. There was no one who could make such excellent coffee or fry a chicken so golden brown as she.

The place was too modest to attract the attention of people of

---

7. Bordering Lake Pontchartrain, the road was a favorite to test the speed of one's horses.

8. Mulatto woman—a woman of mixed blood, black and white.

fashion, and so quiet as to have escaped the notice of those in search of pleasure and dissipation. Edna had discovered it accidentally one day when the high-board gate stood ajar. She caught sight of a little green table, blotched with the checkered sunlight that filtered through the quivering leaves overhead. Within she had found the slumbering *mulatresse*, the drowsy cat, and a glass of milk which reminded her of the milk she had tasted in Iberville.

She often stopped there during her perambulations; sometimes taking a book with her, and sitting an hour or two under the trees when she found the place deserted. Once or twice she took a quiet dinner there alone, having instructed Celestine beforehand to prepare no dinner at home. It was the last place in the city where she would have expected to meet any one she knew.

Still she was not astonished when, as she was partaking of a modest dinner late in the afternoon, looking into an open book, stroking the cat, which had made friends with her—she was not greatly astonished to see Robert come in at the tall garden gate.

"I am destined to see you only by accident," she said, shoving the cat off the chair beside her. He was surprised, ill at ease, almost embarrassed at meeting her thus so unexpectedly.

"Do you come here often?" he asked.

"I almost live here," she said.

"I used to drop in very often for a cup of Catiche's good coffee. This is the first time since I came back."

"She'll bring you a plate, and you will share my dinner. There's always enough for two—even three." Edna had intended to be indifferent and as reserved as he when she met him; she had reached the determination by a laborious train of reasoning, incident to one of her despondent moods. But her resolve melted when she saw him before her, seated there beside her in the little garden, as if a designing Providence had led him into her path.

"Why have you kept away from me, Robert?" she asked, closing the book that lay open upon the table.

"Why are you so personal, Mrs. Pontellier? Why do you force me to idiotic subterfuges?" he exclaimed with sudden warmth. "I suppose there's no use telling you I've been very busy, or that I've been sick, or that I've been to see you and not found you at home. Please let me off with any one of these excuses."

"You are the embodiment of selfishness," she said. "You save yourself something—I don't know what—but there is some selfish motive, and in sparing yourself you never consider for a moment what I think, or how I feel your neglect and indifference. I suppose this is what you would call unwomanly; but I have got into a habit of expressing myself. It doesn't matter to me, and you may think me unwomanly if you like."

"No; I only think you cruel, as I said the other day. Maybe not intentionally cruel; but you seem to be forcing me into disclosures which can result in nothing; as if you would have me bare a wound for the pleasure of looking at it, without the intention or power of healing it."

"I'm spoiling your dinner, Robert; never mind what I say. You haven't eaten a morsel."

"I only came in for a cup of coffee." His sensitive face was all disfigured with excitement.

"Isn't this a delightful place?" she remarked. "I am so glad it has never actually been discovered. It is so quiet, so sweet, here. Do you notice there is scarcely a sound to be heard? It's so out of the way; and a good walk from the car. However, I don't mind walking. I always feel so sorry for women who don't like to walk; they miss so much—so many rare little glimpses of life; and we women learn so little of life on the whole.

"Catiche's coffee is always hot. I don't know how she manages it, here in the open air. Celestine's coffee gets cold bringing it from the kitchen to the dining-room. Three lumps! How can you drink it so sweet? Take some of the cress with your chop; it's so biting and crisp. Then there's the advantage of being able to smoke with your coffee out here. Now, in the city—aren't you going to smoke?"

"After a while," he said, laying a cigar on the table.

"Who gave it to you?" she laughed.

"I bought it. I suppose I'm getting reckless; I bought a whole box." She was determined not to be personal again and make him uncomfortable.

The cat made friends with him, and climbed into his lap when he smoked his cigar. He stroked her silky fur, and talked a little about her. He looked at Edna's book, which he had read; and he told her the end, to save her the trouble of wading through it, he said.

Again he accompanied her back to her home; and it was after dusk when they reached the little "pigeon-house." She did not ask him to remain, which he was grateful for, as it permitted him to stay without the discomfort of blundering through an excuse which he had no intention of considering. He helped her to light the lamp; then she went into her room to take off her hat and to bathe her face and hands.

When she came back Robert was not examining the pictures and magazines as before; he sat off in the shadow, leaning his head back on the chair as if in a reverie. Edna lingered a moment beside the table, arranging the books there. Then she went across the room to where he sat. She bent over the arm of his chair and called his name.

"Robert," she said, "are you asleep?"

"No," he answered, looking up at her.

She leaned over and kissed him—a soft, cool, delicate kiss, whose voluptuous sting penetrated his whole being—then she moved away from him. He followed, and took her in his arms, just holding her close to him. She put her hand up to his face and pressed his cheek against her own. The action was full of love and tenderness. He sought her lips again. Then he drew her down upon the sofa beside him and held her hand in both of his.

"Now you know," he said, "now you know what I have been fighting against since last summer at Grand Isle; what drove me away and drove me back again."

"Why have you been fighting against it?" she asked. Her face glowed with soft lights.

"Why? Because you were not free; you were Léonce Pontellier's wife. I couldn't help loving you if you were ten times his wife; but so long as I went away from you and kept away I could help telling you so." She put her free hand up to his shoulder, and then against his cheek, rubbing it softly. He kissed her again. His face was warm and flushed.

"There in Mexico I was thinking of you all the time, and longing for you."

"But not writing to me," she interrupted.

"Something put into my head that you cared for me; and I lost my senses. I forgot everything but a wild dream of your some way becoming my wife."

"Your wife!"

"Religion, loyalty, everything would give way if only you cared."

"Then you must have forgotten that I was Léonce Pontellier's wife."

"Oh! I was demented, dreaming of wild, impossible things, recalling men who had set their wives free, we have heard of such things."

"Yes, we have heard of such things."

"I came back full of vague, mad intentions. And when I got here—"

"When you got here you never came near me!" She was still caressing his cheek.

"I realized what a cur I was to dream of such a thing, even if you had been willing."

She took his face between her hands and looked into it as if she would never withdraw her eyes more. She kissed him on the forehead, the eyes, the cheeks, and the lips.

"You have been a very, very foolish boy, wasting your time dreaming of impossible things when you speak of Mr. Pontellier setting me free! I am no longer one of Mr. Pontellier's possessions to dispose of or not. I give myself where I choose. If he were to say, 'Here, Robert, take her and be happy; she is yours,' I should laugh at you both."

His face grew a little white. "What do you mean?" he asked.

There was a knock at the door. Old Celestine came in to say that Madame Ratignolle's servant had come around the back way with a message that Madame had been taken sick and begged Mrs. Pontellier to go to her immediately.

"Yes, yes," said Edna, rising; "I promised. Tell her yes—to wait for me. I'll go back with her."

"Let me walk over with you," offered Robert.

"No," she said; "I will go with the servant." She went into her room to put on her hat, and when she came in again she sat once more upon the sofa beside him. He had not stirred. She put her arms about his neck.

"Good-by, my sweet Robert. Tell me good-by." He kissed her with a degree of passion which had not before entered into his caress, and strained her to him.

"I love you," she whispered, "only you; no one but you. It was you who awoke me last summer out of a life-long, stupid dream. Oh! you have made me so unhappy with your indifference. Oh! I have suffered, suffered! Now you are here we shall love each other, my Robert. We shall be everything to each other. Nothing else in the world is of any consequence. I must go to my friend; but you will wait for me? No matter how late; you will wait for me, Robert?"

"Don't go; don't go! Oh! Edna, stay with me," he pleaded. "Why should you go? Stay with me, stay with me."

"I shall come back as soon as I can; I shall find you here." She buried her face in his neck, and said good-by again. Her seductive voice, together with his great love for her, had enthralled his senses, had deprived him of every impulse but the longing to hold her and keep her.

XXXVII

Edna looked in at the drug store. Monsieur Ratignolle was putting up a mixture himself, very carefully, dropping a red liquid into a tiny glass. He was grateful to Edna for having come; her presence would be a comfort to his wife. Madame Ratignolle's sister, who had always been with her at such trying times, had not been able to come up from the plantation, and Adèle had been inconsolable until Mrs. Pontellier so kindly promised to come to her. The nurse had been with them at night for the past week, as she lived a great distance away. And Dr. Mandelet had been coming and going all the afternoon. They were then looking for him any moment.

Edna hastened upstairs by a private stairway that led from the rear of the store to the apartments above. The children were all sleeping in a back room. Madame Ratignolle was in the salon, whither she had strayed in her suffering impatience. She sat on the sofa, clad in an ample white *peignoir*, holding a handkerchief tight in her hand with a nervous clutch. Her face was drawn and pinched, her sweet blue eyes haggard and unnatural. All her beautiful hair had been drawn back and plaited. It lay in a long braid on the sofa pillow, coiled like a golden serpent. The nurse, a comfortable looking *Griffe* woman[9] in white apron and cap, was urging her to return to her bedroom.

"There is no use, there is no use," she said at once to Edna. "We must get rid of Mandelet; he is getting too old and careless. He said he would be here at half-past seven; now it must be eight. See what time it is, Joséphine."

The woman was possessed of a cheerful nature, and refused to take any situation too seriously, especially a situation with which she was so familiar. She urged Madame to have courage and patience. But Madame only set her teeth hard into her under lip, and Edna saw the sweat gather in beads on her white forehead. After a moment or two she uttered a profound sigh and wiped her face with the handkerchief rolled in a ball. She appeared exhausted. The nurse gave her a fresh handkerchief, sprinkled with cologne water.

"This is too much!" she cried. "Mandelet ought to be killed! Where is Alphonse? Is it possible I am to be abandoned like this— neglected by every one?"

"Neglected, indeed!" exclaimed the nurse. Wasn't she there? And here was Mrs. Pontellier leaving, no doubt, a pleasant evening at home to devote to her? And wasn't Monsieur Ratignolle coming that very instant through the hall? And Joséphine was quite sure she had heard Doctor Mandelet's coupé. Yes, there it was, down at the door.

Adèle consented to go back to her room. She sat on the edge of a little low couch next to her bed.

Doctor Mandelet paid no attention to Madame Ratignolle's upbraidings. He was accustomed to them at such times, and was too well convinced of her loyalty to doubt it.

He was glad to see Edna, and wanted her to go with him into the salon and entertain him. But Madame Ratignolle would not consent that Edna should leave her for an instant. Between agonizing moments, she chatted a little, and said it took her mind off her sufferings.

Edna began to feel uneasy. She was seized with a vague dread. Her own like experiences seemed far away, unreal, and only half remembered. She recalled faintly an ecstasy of pain, the heavy odor

9. The daughter of a mulatto and a black, or a mulatto and an American Indian.

of chloroform, a stupor which had deadened sensation, and an awakening to find a little new life to which she had given being, added to the great unnumbered multitude of souls that come and go.

She began to wish she had not come; her presence was not necessary. She might have invented a pretext for staying away; she might even invent a pretext now for going. But Edna did not go. With an inward agony, with a flaming, outspoken revolt against the ways of Nature, she witnessed the scene [of] torture.

She was still stunned and speechless with emotion when later she leaned over her friend to kiss her and softly say good-by. Adèle, pressing her cheek, whispered in an exhausted voice: "Think of the children, Edna. Oh think of the children! Remember them!"

XXXVIII

Edna still felt dazed when she got outside in the open air. The Doctor's coupé had returned for him and stood before the *porte cochère*. She did not wish to enter the coupé, and told Doctor Mandelet she would walk; she was not afraid, and would go alone. He directed his carriage to meet him at Mrs. Pontellier's, and he started to walk home with her.

Up—away up, over the narrow street between the tall houses, the stars were blazing. The air was mild and caressing, but cool with the breath of spring and the night. They walked slowly, the Doctor with a heavy, measured tread and his hands behind him; Edna, in an absent-minded way, as she had walked one night at Grand Isle, as if her thoughts had gone ahead of her and she was striving to overtake them.

"You shouldn't have been there, Mrs. Pontellier," he said. "That was no place for you. Adèle is full of whims at such times. There were a dozen women she might have had with her, unimpressionable women. I felt that it was cruel, cruel. You shouldn't have gone."

"Oh, well!" she answered, indifferently. "I don't know that it matters after all. One has to think of the children some time or other; the sooner the better."

"When is Léonce coming back?"

"Quite soon. Some time in March."

"And you are going abroad?"

"Perhaps—no, I am not going. I'm not going to be forced into doing things. I don't want to go abroad. I want to be let alone. Nobody has any right—except children, perhaps—and even then, it seems to me—or it did seem—" She felt that her speech was voicing the incoherency of her thoughts, and stopped abruptly.

"The trouble is," sighed the Doctor, grasping her meaning intuitively, "that youth is given up to illusions. It seems to be a provision of Nature; a decoy to secure mothers for the race. And Nature takes no account of moral consequences, of arbitrary conditions which we create, and which we feel obliged to maintain at any cost."

"Yes," she said. "The years that are gone seem like dreams—if one might go on sleeping and dreaming—but to wake up and find— oh! well! perhaps it is better to wake up after all, even to suffer, rather than to remain a dupe to illusions all one's life."

"It seems to me, my dear child," said the Doctor at parting, holding her hand, "you seem to me to be in trouble. I am not going to ask for your confidence. I will only say that if ever you feel moved to give it to me, perhaps I might help you. I know I would understand, and I tell you there are not many who would—not many, my dear."

"Some way I don't feel moved to speak of things that trouble me. Don't think I am ungrateful or that I don't appreciate your sympathy. There are periods of despondency and suffering which take possession of me. But I don't want anything but my own way. That is wanting a good deal, of course, when you have to trample upon the lives, the hearts, the prejudices of others—but no matter—still, I shouldn't want to trample upon the little lives. Oh! I don't know what I'm saying, Doctor. Good night. Don't blame me for anything."

"Yes, I will blame you if you don't come and see me soon. We will talk of things you never have dreamt of talking about before. It will do us both good. I don't want you to blame yourself, whatever comes. Good night, my child."

She let herself in at the gate, but instead of entering she sat upon the step of the porch. The night was quiet and soothing. All the tearing emotion of the last few hours seemed to fall away from her like a somber, uncomfortable garment, which she had but to loosen to be rid of. She went back to that hour before Adèle had sent for her; and her senses kindled afresh in thinking of Robert's words, the pressure of his arms, and the feeling of his lips upon her own. She could picture at that moment no greater bliss on earth than possession of the beloved one. His expression of love had already given him to her in part. When she thought that he was there at hand, waiting for her, she grew numb with the intoxication of expectancy. It was so late; he would be asleep perhaps. She would awaken him with a kiss. She hoped he would be asleep that she might arouse him with her caresses.

Still, she remembered Adèle's voice whispering, "Think of the children; think of them." She meant to think of them; that determination had driven into her soul like a death wound—but not tonight. To-morrow would be time to think of everything.

Robert was not waiting for her in the little parlor. He was no-where at hand. The house was empty. But he had scrawled on a piece of paper that lay in the lamplight:

"I love you. Good-by—because I love you."

Edna grew faint when she read the words. She went and sat on the sofa. Then she stretched herself out there, never uttering a sound. She did not sleep. She did not go to bed. The lamp sputtered and went out. She was still awake in the morning, when Celestine unlocked the kitchen door and came in to light the fire.

XXXIX

Victor, with hammer and nails and scraps of scantling, was patching a corner of one of the galleries. Mariequita sat near by, dangling her legs, watching him work, and handing him nails from the tool-box. The sun was beating down upon them. The girl had covered her head with her apron folded into a square pad. They had been talking for an hour or more. She was never tired of hearing Victor describe the dinner at Mrs. Pontellier's. He exaggerated every detail, making it appear a veritable Lucillean[1] feast. The flowers were in tubs, he said. The champagne was quaffed from huge golden goblets. Venus rising from the foam[2] could have presented no more entrancing a spectacle than Mrs. Pontellier, blazing with beauty and diamonds at the head of the board, while the other women were all of them youthful houris[3] possessed of incom-parable charms.

She got it into her head that Victor was in love with Mrs. Pontel-lier, and he gave her evasive answers, framed so as to confirm her belief. She grew sullen and cried a little, threatening to go off and leave him to his fine ladies. There were a dozen men crazy about her at the *Chênière*; and since it was the fashion to be in love with married people, why, she could run away any time she liked to New Orleans with Célina's husband.

Célina's husband was a fool, a coward, and a pig, and to prove it to her, Victor intended to hammer his head into a jelly the next time he encountered him. This assurance was very consoling to Marie-quita. She dried her eyes, and grew cheerful at the prospect.

They were still talking of the dinner and the allurements of city life when Mrs. Pontellier herself slipped around the corner of the house. The two youngsters stayed dumb with amazement before what they considered to be an apparition. But it was really she in flesh and blood, looking tired and a little travel-stained.

1. After the Roman satirist Gaius Lucilius (180–103 B.C.) who ridiculed the indulgences of his society.
2. Roman goddess of love and beauty, daughter of Jupiter and Dione, sprung from the foam at birth. In a version of the myth about Aphrodite, her Greek counterpart, she attempts to drown her-self, ashamed of her love affair with a beautiful young man, but she is changed instead into a fish with a human face.
3. Virgin nymphs, everlastingly young and beautiful.

"I walked up from the wharf," she said, "and heard the hammering. I supposed it was you, mending the porch. It's a good thing. I was always tripping over those loose planks last summer. How dreary and deserted everything looks!"

It took Victor some little time to comprehend that she had come in Beaudelet's lugger, that she had come alone, and for no purpose but to rest.

"There's nothing fixed up yet, you see. I'll give you my room; it's the only place."

"Any corner will do," she assured him.

"And if you can stand Philomel's cooking," he went on, "though I might try to get her mother while you are here. Do you think she would come?" turning to Mariequita.

Mariequita thought that perhaps Philomel's mother might come for a few days, and money enough.

Beholding Mrs. Pontellier make her appearance, the girl had at once suspected a lovers' rendezvous. But Victor's astonishment was so genuine, and Mrs. Pontellier's indifference so apparent, that the disturbing notion did not lodge long in her brain. She contemplated with the greatest interest this woman who gave the most sumptuous dinners in America, and who had all the men in New Orleans at her feet.

"What time will you have dinner?" asked Edna. "I'm very hungry; but don't get anything extra."

"I'll have it ready in little or no time," he said, bustling and packing away his tools. "You may go to my room to brush up and rest yourself. Mariequita will show you."

"Thank you," said Edna. "But, do you know, I have a notion to go down to the beach and take a good wash and even a little swim, before dinner?"

"The water is too cold!" they both exclaimed. "Don't think of it."

"Well, I might go down and try—dip my toes in. Why, it seems to me the sun is hot enough to have warmed the very depths of the ocean. Could you get me a couple of towels? I'd better go right away, so as to be back in time. It would be a little too chilly if I waited till this afternoon."

Mariequita ran over to Victor's room, and returned with some towels, which she gave to Edna.

"I hope you have fish for dinner," said Edna, as she started to walk away; "but don't do anything extra if you haven't."

"Run and find Philomel's mother," Victor instructed the girl. "I'll go to the kitchen and see what I can do. By Gimminy! Women have no consideration! She might have sent me word."

Edna walked on down to the beach rather mechanically, not

noticing anything special except that the sun was hot. She was not dwelling upon any particular train of thought. She had done all the thinking which was necessary after Robert went away, when she lay awake upon the sofa till morning.

She had said over and over to herself: "To-day it is Arobin; to-morrow it will be some one else. It makes no difference to me, it doesn't matter about Léonce Pontellier—but Raoul and Etienne!" She understood now clearly what she had meant long ago when she said to Adèle Ratignolle that she would give up the unessential, but she would never sacrifice herself for her children.

Despondency had come upon her there in the wakeful night, and had never lifted. There was no one thing in the world that she desired. There was no human being whom she wanted near her except Robert; and she even realized that the day would come when he, too, and the thought of him would melt out of her existence, leaving her alone. The children appeared before her like antagonists who had overcome her; who had overpowered and sought to drag her into the soul's slavery for the rest of her days. But she knew a way to elude them. She was not thinking of these things when she walked down to the beach.

The water of the Gulf stretched out before her, gleaming with the million lights of the sun. The voice of the sea is seductive, never ceasing, whispering, clamoring, murmuring, inviting the soul to wander in abysses of solitude. All along the white beach, up and down, there was no living thing in sight. A bird with a broken wing was beating the air above, reeling, fluttering, circling disabled down, down to the water.

Edna had found her old bathing suit still hanging, faded, upon its accustomed peg.

She put it on, leaving her clothing in the bath-house. But when she was there beside the sea, absolutely alone, she cast the unpleasant, pricking garments from her, and for the first time in her life she stood naked in the open air, at the mercy of the sun, the breeze that beat upon her, and the waves that invited her.

How strange and awful it seemed to stand naked under the sky! how delicious! She felt like some new-born creature, opening its eyes in a familiar world that it had never known.

The foamy wavelets curled up to her white feet, and coiled like serpents about her ankles. She walked out. The water was chill, but she walked on. The water was deep, but she lifted her white body and reached out with a long, sweeping stroke. The touch of the sea is sensuous, enfolding the body in its soft, close embrace.

She went on and on. She remembered the night she swam far out, and recalled the terror that seized her at the fear of being unable to regain the shore. She did not look back now, but went on and on, thinking of the blue-grass meadow that she had traversed when a little child, believing that it had no beginning and no end.

Her arms and legs were growing tired.

She thought of Léonce and the children. They were a part of her life. But they need not have thought that they could possess her, body and soul. How Mademoiselle Reisz would have laughed, perhaps sneered, if she knew! "And you call yourself an artist! What pretensions, Madame! The artist must possess the courageous soul that dares and defies."

Exhaustion was pressing upon and over-powering her.

"Good-by—because, I love you." He did not know; he did not understand. He would never understand. Perhaps Doctor Mandelet would have understood if she had seen him—but it was too late; the shore was far behind her, and her strength was gone.

She looked into the distance, and the old terror flamed up for an instant, then sank again. Edna heard her father's voice and her sister Margaret's. She heard the barking of an old dog that was chained to the sycamore tree. The spurs of the cavalry officer clanged as he walked across the porch. There was the hum of bees, and the musky odor of pinks filled the air.

Contexts

MARGARET CULLEY

The Context of *The Awakening*

The 1890s in America were a decade of social tension. The depression of 1893–1896 accentuated class divisions, and urbanization and industrialization were beginning to change traditional ways of life. The World's Columbian Exposition in Chicago in 1893 announced the fact of the machine age in a dramatic, public fashion. Darwinism and higher criticism of the Bible were threatening traditional ways of thinking about human origins and destiny. It is not surprising that in such a period the particular Puritan-American brand of Victorian morality became an especially rigidified stronghold against social and intellectual ferment.

By 1890 "the woman question" had been a matter of public discussion for over fifty years. In that year the two national suffrage organizations merged for the final push for the vote—which would not come, however, for another thirty years. Upper-class women were attending college in record numbers, entering professions previously barred to them, and beginning to reap the benefits of improved medical care and dress reform. They belonged to innumerable women's organizations: social, intellectual, political, and philanthropic. Lower-class women came together to work long hours for low wages, and what organizing they did was into unions to combat the working conditions in the textile mills and other factories where they were employed. Women at all levels of society were active in attempts to better their lot, and the "New Woman," the late nineteenth-century equivalent of the "liberated woman," was much on the public mind.

Upper-class southern women, raised with a special sense of "woman's place" derived from some mythic age of chivalry, and then drawn by the Civil War into arenas of activity previously unknown and forbidden to them, seemed comparatively little interested in ideology. Kate Chopin was never a feminist or a suffragist; in fact, she was suspicious of any ideology. She was committed to personal freedom and defied social convention in a number of ways, including smoking cigarettes and walking out alone. Her diary records that she met one of the Claflin sisters while on her honeymoon and assured her that she would not fall into "the useless degrading life of most married ladies."[1]

1. Per Seyersted, *Kate Chopin: A Critical Biography* (Baton Rouge: Louisiana State University Press, 1969), p. 33. Tennessee Claflin (1845–1923) and Victoria Claflin Woodhull (1838–1927) were flamboyant advocates of women's rights who in their political, financial, and private involvements constantly offended Victorian sensibilities. Chopin does not record which woman she met.

Most married ladies in New Orleans, where the novel is set, were the property of their husbands. The Napoleonic Code was still the basis of the laws governing the marriage contract. All of a wife's "accumulations" after marriage were the property of her husband, including money she might earn and the clothes she wore. The husband was the legal guardian of the children, and until 1888 was granted custody of the children in the event of a divorce. The wife was "bound to live with her husband, and follow him wherever he [chose] to reside." A wife could not sign any legal contract (with the exception of her will) without the consent of her husband, nor could she institute a lawsuit, appear in court, hold public office, or make a donation to a living person. The woman's position in the eyes of the law was conveyed by the language of Article 1591 of the laws of Louisiana: "The following persons are absolutely incapable of being witness to testaments: 1. Women of any age soever. 2. Male children who have not attained the age of sixteen years complete. 3. Persons who are insane, deaf, dumb or blind. 4. Persons whom the criminal laws declare incapable of exercising civil functions." Though divorce laws in the state were somewhat more liberal than those in other parts of the country—divorce could be granted on the grounds of abandonment after one year of separation—divorce rates were much lower than in other states. Louisiana was a largely Catholic state and divorce was a scandalous and rather rare occurrence (29 divorces granted per 100,000 members of the population in 1890). In any case, Edna Pontellier had no grounds for divorce, though her husband undoubtedly did.

Despite, or perhaps because of, the repressive legal condition, the 1890s brought the first stirrings of the women's movement to New Orleans. In 1892 the first suffrage organization, the Portia Club, was formed. In 1895 Susan B. Anthony visited the city. In 1896 a second suffrage organization, the Era Club (Equal Rights Association), joined efforts with the Portia Club. Before the end of the decade women had won the right to vote on matters of local taxation. Though this concession was undoubtedly in part to insure white supremacy in the state, the women's political power was felt in two important reform efforts: the anti-lottery campaign of 1891 —before the vote was won—and later a major campaign for adequate sewage and drainage in a city especially subject to epidemic disease.

The New Orleans *Daily Picayune* was the first major American newspaper edited by a woman, and its pages supported a variety of women's causes in the 1890s. A June 1897 article recounts the occupations women in the city were pursuing: "Among other things gleaned from [the city directory] of our own city, is the fact that there are two women barbers, following the hirsute tradition in the

Crescent City. There are also importers of cigars among the fair sex, six women undertakers, one embalmer, a real estate agent, an insurance agent (it is true in partnership with a man), insurance solicitors, several practicing physicians, a box manufacturer, three drummers, a steamboat captain, several florists and a number of liquor dealers." The national census of 1890 showed that in only 9 of the 369 professions listed were women not represented.

Despite social and political advances, women in the 1890s still encountered disadvantages in almost every aspect of their lives, and a majority of the populace still believed that a woman's most sacred duty was to be "the angel in the house."

Though Kate Chopin was not a feminist, and *The Awakening* is not a political novel in the narrow sense of the term, it is important to understand the political and social context in which it appeared. A novel exploring the consequences of personal—particularly sexual—freedom for the married woman, appearing as it did in a decade much preoccupied with the New Woman in its midst, was certain to provoke strong reactions.

MARY L. SHAFFTER

Creole Women†

Creoles are the descendants of French or Spanish, born in Louisiana. Incorrectly the term is applied to any one born and living in New Orleans or its vicinity. Indeed there is a broader misapplication common in some parts of the state, where fresh eggs, Louisiana cows, horses, and chickens are called creole eggs, creole ponies, etc.

New Orleans, in reality, is two cities, the dividing line being a broad, tree-bordered avenue, running east and west from Lake Pontchartrain to the Mississippi River. "Up town," or the south side of this avenue, which is called Canal Street, is the home of the American population, while "down town," the north side, is the French or Creole Quarter. Up town the streets and the houses and many of the residents are new. It is a progressive, a self-made, a new city. Down town is the old town, with little improvement since the days when the houses were first built. Occasionally a creole family crosses the line, as it were, and goes to live up town, but they rarely become Americanized, for, above all things the creole is conservative.

† Originally appeared in *The Chautauquan*, VX (June 1892), 346–7. Footnotes are by the editor.

To-day the wealth of the city is in the American portion: thirty or forty years ago its wealth and refinement were centered in the French Quarter. Not much wealth remains there, but the people still possess what money cannot buy—the chivalry of their men and the grace and beauty of their women.

The women are called beautiful, and justly so. It is true that as the years creep on apace, they incline to *embonpoint*[1] and the down on their upper lips often darkens and deepens into a very perceptible line. Despite these facts, a creole woman grows old gracefully, she never becomes coarse looking, and her hands never lose their distinctive marks of refinement.

There live no lovelier girls than those one meets in creole society in New Orleans. Such figures, lithe yet full, such shapely heads, with crowns of glossy black hair, such a clear olive complexion, and great dark eyes, which speak before the arched red lips,—who can condemn the heart that is taken captive by the bewitching beauty of *la belle creole?*[2]

Creole women are artistic by nature; they paint and play and sing. They talk well and are good at repartee. They usually speak several languages, French being their mother tongue. They emphasize with gesture, and occasionally surprise the listener with a *Mondieu!* or *O ciel!*[3] which, with them, is no profanity.

As wives, creole women are without superiors; loving and true, they seldom figure in domestic scandals.

The creole woman entertains beautifully. Her salon, her toilet, show the refinement of her taste. In her manner there is none of the American "gush"; she receives with unaffected cordiality, which has the true ring. She is careful in the selection of her friends, for down in the *vieux carré*[4] of New Orleans money cannot purchase an entrance into society.

Creole women, as a rule, are good housekeepers, are economical and industrious. When one pauses to think that these women were reared as princesses, with slaves at their command, one realizes that noble blood has made noble women. They never speak of their poverty, or proclaim their ingenuity in supplying a dainty table from a slender larder. They have accepted their lot, they attend to their homes, they make their cheap dresses with their French taste and wear them with the grace of a *grande dame*[5]. There are many creole women who have striven hard with pride, and have wished to die rather than to acknowledge their poverty, but whose better nature conquered, and they now hold honored places among the bread winners of to-day.

1. Stoutness, plumpness.
2. The beautiful creole.
3. "My God!" or "Heavens!"
4. The French Quarter or "old city." See note 8, page 6.
5. Great lady.

Creole women have large families. This they do not regard as a misfortune, after the manner of some of their more progressive sisters. Their babies are made welcome and tenderly reared. Especially are the girls the object of much solicitude. Above all their beauty must be preserved, their hands and feet, their glossy hair and white teeth must be cared for. They must learn to dance, to sing, and to embroider. Their religion, too, must not be neglected. At ten or twelve they must go, arrayed as brides, to take their first communion. The next few years are spent at a convent, and at sixteen or seventeen the girl is ready for society. She receives with *maman*, visits with *maman*, shops with *maman*, goes to balls, the opera, and to church with *maman*. Sometimes it happens that a gentleman visits the house say five or six times; if so *papa* asks his intentions. If he expresses friendship only, he is then requested to discontinue his coming; but if, on the other hand, he declares his love, all things being desirable, the visitor becomes a suitor, the engagement is announced, the girl wears the honors as a *fiancée* but a short time, and then becomes a wife.

While there is about creole women that refinement that one admires, a *noblesse oblige* that one respects, a dependence that attracts love, it must be acknowledged that as a class they are not progressive. They are tender, loving mothers, they care for the health and beauty of their children, but they know nothing of the beauty and development that come from physical culture. They train the little feet to dance bewitchingly, but are horrified at the suggestion of a thick-soled, broad-heeled boot and a five-mile walk.

They are accomplished rather than intellectual. Women's rights, for them, are the right to love and be loved, and to name the babies rather than the next president or city officials.

Musically gifted, they prefer a gay *chansonette* to the intricate passages of one of Bach's fugues, and they would rather wander through the realms of poesie than to venture into the shadowy region of metaphysical laws.

They are not club women, they do not aspire to fame, and it is true that the average creole woman cannot compete, in some respects, with her American sisters.

When the pictures in books do not make creole women proud and pure and loving, capable of great development morally and mentally, women of whom Louisiana should be proud, then it is simply because the painters painted without a model and the writers never knew the password by which to gain admittance into the society of creole women.

WILBUR FISK TILLETT

[Southern Womanhood]†

Among the many changes that have taken place in the Southern States and among Southern people within the past thirty years, some of which are the direct result of war, and others the simple and natural development of the times, there is none more significant and worthy of notice than the change that has taken place in the condition, the life and the labor of Southern women.

* * *

We might conveniently divide our subject into these three heads: (1) the Southern woman before the war; (2) the Southern woman during the war; (3) the Southern woman since the war. Were this our mode of presenting the subject, it would be to give three pictures of the same woman, and not of three different women. The virtues that adorn and ennoble the Southern woman of to-day find their explanation and origin largely in that womanhood which for the last fifty years and more has been the product and the pride of the Southern people. No matter what may be one's sympathy with or prejudice against the institution of slavery, there is no denying the fact that American civilization has nowhere produced a purer and loftier type of refined and cultured womanhood than existed in the South before the war. Nowhere else in America have hospitality and social intercourse among the better classes been so cultivated or have constituted so large a part of life as in what is called the old South. These large and constant social demands upon Southern women, growing out of the hospitable customs of the old plantation life, made the existing conditions very favorable for developing women of rare social gifts and accomplishments. In native womanly modesty, in neatness, grace, and beauty of person, in ease and freedom without boldness of manner, in refined and cultivated minds, in gifts and qualities that shone brilliantly in the social circle, in spotless purity of thought and character, in laudable pride of family and devotion to home, kindred, and loved ones—these were the qualities for which Southern women were noted and in which they excelled. That the Southern woman of ante-bellum times lacked those stronger qualities of character and mind that are

---

† From "Southern Womanhood as Affected by the Civil War," *The Century Magazine*, XLIII (November 1891), 5–16. For more recent discussion of southern womanhood see Anne Firor Scott, *The Southern Lady: From Pedestal to Politics 1830–1930* (Chicago: The University of Chicago Press, 1970).

Kate O'Flaherty was ten years old when the Civil War broke out. She lost a beloved stepbrother who died of disease when returning from the Confederate Army. The O'Flaherty and the Chopin family were staunchly anti-Union. [*Editor.*]

born only of trials and hardships and poverty and adversity may be granted. That she contributed less in labor, especially manual labor, to the support and economy of the household than women in like financial condition elsewhere may also be granted. But this was not because she was unable or unwilling to work, but simply because it was unnecessary. Before the Southern woman had passed through the four years' fiery ordeal of war, the virtues of character, of head and heart, that are born of adversity were all richly hers.

But the Southern woman's most trying period came only after the war, terminating as it did in the loss of nearly all property, in the entire breaking up of the old home life, and in the emancipation of the slaves, who had always relieved white women of the more unpleasant duties that would otherwise have long fallen to their lot in the economy of domestic life. Thousands upon thousands of delicate and cultivated women who had never done any of the harder and more disagreeable duties of domestic and home life, universally performed by the slaves, were now compelled to enter upon a life of drudgery and hardship for which nothing in their previous training had prepared them. If in prosperity, wealth, and luxury woman is weaker and frailer than man, when adversity comes she is stronger than man, stronger in heart and purpose, stronger to adapt herself to unfortunate circumstances and to make the best of them. Indeed, it is not until adversity comes that we know how strong a creature woman is. Many a trouble that utterly crushes strong man transforms weak woman into a tower of strength. Never did woman have a better opportunity to show this strength than at the close of the war, and right nobly did she meet the emergency and set herself to her work, encouraging and inspiring with hope Southern men, too many of whom had lost heart with their lost cause. It was the heart, the hope, the faith of Southern womanhood that set Southern men to working when the war was over, and in this work they led the way, filling the stronger sex with utter amazement at the readiness and power with which they began to perform duties to which they had never been used before. The wonderful recuperative energies of the Southern people since the war, as manifested in the present wide-spread prosperity of the Southern States, is recognized and admired by all; but who can tell how largely this is due to Southern womanhood? Was it not the brave-hearted wife that inspired the despairing husband when the war had ended to go to work and redeem his lost fortune, happy enough herself that she had a living husband to work with her, since so many of her sisters had to fight the battle with labor and poverty alone, while their husbands slept in the soldier's grave? Was it not the ambitious and hopeful sister that inspired her soldier brother, the unconquered and unconquerable maiden that inspired her dis-

heartened lover, when the war was over? And was not this womanly
inspiration the most potent factor that entered the problem of the
white man's immediate future in the South? Nor has woman's part
in the up-building of the South been one of inspiration simply. It is
the work which her own head and hands have accomplished that we
wish to speak of more particularly in this paper; not her influence
upon other things, but the influence upon her of the changes of the
last thirty years. How then has Southern womanhood been affected
by these great changes?

* * *

[The author then puts this question to a number of his women corres-
pondents, whose answers follow.]

There is no point perhaps wherein the Southern ideal of woman
has changed so much as in the nobility of helplessness in woman.
Before the war, so far as I have been able to learn from contact and
conversation with those whose knowledge and experience antedate
my own by many years, self-support was a last resort with respectable women in the South, and such a thought was never entertained
so long as there was any male relative to look to for support, and
men felt responsible for the support of even remote female relatives.
So deeply embedded in Southern ideas and feeling was this sentiment of the nobility of dependence and helplessness in woman, and
the degradation of labor, even for self-support, in the sex, that I
have heard of instances where refined and able-bodied women
would allow themselves to be supported by the charity of their
friends rather than resort to work for self-support—and this not
because they had any reluctance to work, but because livelihood by
charity seemed to them to be the more respectable and honorable
alternative of the two. Such instances may not have been very
numerous, but they were at least of frequent enough occurrence to
show the strong prejudice that existed in the South before the war
with reference to white women working. Of course this does not
mean that the thousands of wives, mothers, and housekeepers
throughout the South did not perform the duties incident to their
situation. It was single ladies, and those who had no means of
support within their own homes, whom public sentiment forbade to
work for self-support; or if they did, it was at the expense of
injuring or entirely forfeiting their social standing, and hence was to
compromise themselves and their families. Now, on the contrary, a
woman is respected and honored in the South for earning her own
living, and would lose respect if, as an able-bodied woman, she
settled herself as a burden on a brother, or even on a father, working hard for a living, while looking to more-distant male relatives
for support is now quite out of the question. As a woman is now

respected and honored, rather than discounted socially, for earning her own living when necessary, the field of labor for women is constantly widening. While she would not injure her social position by earning a living at any calling open to her sex, yet, socially, teaching and other forms of literary work have the advantage, and are to be preferred. Other callings, though not exactly tabooed by the sex, yet have such objections to them as would cause a young woman's friends to ask, "What makes her do that? Couldn't she get a place to teach?" This increasing tendency among women to earn their own living by teaching has raised the standard of thoroughness in female education to some extent, though much is still to be desired, especially in the larger schools, where girls are too often sent to be "graduated" rather than to be educated. Southern people, having passed through the financial reverses of the war, now realize as never before that a daughter's bread may some day depend upon herself, and so they want her well educated. And as a thorough knowledge of a few things is a better foundation for self-support than a mere smattering of many accomplishments, there is more tendency toward specialties in woman's education than before the war.

* * *

Woman's opportunities for work have increased. The number of single women who support themselves, and of married women who help their husbands in supporting their families, is much larger than before the war, and this class of women is more respected than in ante-bellum times. The number of vocations open to women is of course much larger than before the war, but the value in money of woman's work is shamefully depreciated. No matter what work a woman does, men will not pay her its full value, not half what they would pay a man for the very same work. There is proof of this unjust discrimination in almost every female college in the South where men and women are employed to do the same or equal work as teachers, not to speak of other callings where they are performing exactly the same work for very unequal wages.

If then we look at this question concerning Southern womanhood in the light of the present and of the more hopeful future, rather than of the past succeeding the war, I can say that in my judgment the freeing of the slaves and the changed conditions of life resulting from the war have proved a blessing to the white women of the South. It has taught them the value of actual labor with their own hands; it has taught them that the hardships and trials of life teach useful lessons, and have their rewards. It has proved to them that poverty does not necessarily degrade, that culture and refinement may preside in the kitchen, mold the biscuit and watch the griddle, turn the steak and bake the cake, but that wisdom and economy must be constantly exercised or there will be little time for anything but these homely duties.

* * *

The growing respectability of self-support in woman is everywhere recognized as one of the healthiest signs of the times. The number of vocations open to women is constantly on the increase. Some modes of self-support are, and always will be, socially more respectable than others. In the report for 1888 of the Commissioner of Labor concerning the number and condition of working-women in the large cities is the following concerning Charleston, South Carolina:

> In no other Southern city has the exclusion of women from business been so rigid and the tradition that respectability is forfeited by manual labor so influential and powerful. Proud and well-born women have practised great self-denial at ill-paid conventional pursuits in preference to independence in untrodden paths. The embargo against self-support, however, has to some extent been lifted, and were there a larger number of remunerative occupations open to women, the rush to avail of them would show how ineffectual the old traditions have become.

A similar report of 1890 would show rapid changes and advances in public sentiment concerning the respectability of self-support in women, and would reveal that the "embargo" had, in most parts of the South at least, been entirely removed.

If we look at the South as a whole, and not at individual portions of it, it is unquestionably true that the great changes which the past thirty years have witnessed have wrought most favorably upon the intellectual life of Southern womanhood. The conditions under which Southern women now live are far more favorable for developing literary women than those existing in the days of slavery. In 1869 a volume was published by Mr. James Wood Davidson entitled "The Living Writers of the South," in which 241 writers are noticed, of which number 75 are women and 166 are men. Of the 241 named, 40 had written only for newspapers and magazines, while 201 had published one or more volumes, aggregating 739 in all. Although this book was published only four years after the close of the war, it was even then true that from two thirds to three fourths of the volumes mentioned in it as having been published by women—not to speak of the others—had been written and published after the opening of the war. They had been called forth by the war and the trying experiences following it. Whether the changed conditions under which we live have anything to do with it, it is nevertheless certainly true that there have been more literary women developed in the South in the thirty years since the war than in all our previous history.

* * *

It is Victor Hugo who has called this "the century of woman." It is certainly an age that has witnessed great changes in the life, education, and labor of women everywhere; and these changes have all been in the direction of enlarging the sphere of woman's activities, increasing her liberties, and opening up possibilities to her life hitherto retricted to man. It is a movement limited to no land and to no race. So far as this movement may have any tendency to take woman out of her true place in the home, to give her man's work to do and to develop masculine qualities in her, it finds no sympathy in the South. The Southern woman loves the retirement of home, and shrinks from everything that would tend to bring her into the public gaze.

DOROTHY DIX[†]

Are Women Growing Selfish?[1]

Women have been extolled for their unselfishness so long that it comes with a shock of surprise to learn that their pet virtue has at last been called into question. Nay, it has been more than questioned. It has been positively asserted that woman is the very quintessence of selfishness. It is boldly charged that she thinks of nothing but her own pleasures, amusements and interest. She is accused of belonging to clubs that are neither more nor less than mutual admiration societies, where women meet together to glorify their own sex and formulate plans for its advancement. Worse than that, she goes off in summer to the mountains or seaside, leaving her poor down-trodden husband to swelter in the city, without even the reward of a cool smile or a frozen glance when he returns home at night after his arduous day's work. If this is not ingrained, hopeless, conscienceless selfishness, the critics would just like to know what is, that's all.

From time immemorial it has been the custom of woman to sacrifice herself whenever she got a chance, and any deflection from the course she was expected to pursue must necessarily occasion a deal of comment. Unselfishness with her has been a cult. She has

† Dorothy Dix (Elizabeth Gilmer, 1861–1951) was the first advice-to-women columnist in America. Beginning in 1895 she wrote for the major newspaper in New Orleans, *The Daily Picayune*. The items here are from her column, which was entitled "Dorothy Dix Speaks."
1. *The Daily Picayune*, August 15, 1897.

worn it ostentatiously, and flaunted it in the face of the world with a feeling that it would make good any other deficiencies or short-comings. She has courted persecution, and gone out of her way to become a martyr. She has accounted it unto herself for righteous-ness to do those things she did not wish to do, and to leave undone those things she was dying to do. On the platform of pure and unadulterated unselfishness she has taken a stand, and defied com-petition, and now when she wishes to climb down and off, and give other people a chance to practice the virtue they admire so much, she is cruelly misjudged and assailed.

It must be admitted in all fairness that this attitude of perfect self-abnegation is one which men have never failed to praise, but seldom emulated. Men have always taken a saner view of life than women. A woman sacrifices herself in a thousand needless little ways which do no one any good, but when a man makes a sacrifice it is big with heroism, and counts. A woman thinks she is being good when she is uncomfortable. A man knows people are much more apt to be good when they are comfortable. No man with a full purse and a full stomach was ever an anarchist.

The truth of the matter simply is that women have awakened to the fact that they have been overdoing the self-sacrifice business. A reasonable amount of unselfishness is all right. It is the sense of justice with which we recognize other people's rights; it is the love that makes us prefer another to ourselves; it is the adorable grace and sweetness that softens a strong and independent character, and is as far different as possible from the lack of backbone that weakly gives away before everything and everybody.

* * *

The same thing may be said of the attitude of one's husband. The woman who makes a slave of herself, gets a slave's pay in con-temptuous indifference. No man ever cared for the thing that grov-eled at his feet, and those women have been best loved who have stood up for their rights, and at every stage of the matrimonial journey have demanded upon courteous treatment, and a fair divide of the pleasures and perquisites of their joint partnership. It is a theory of the perfectly unselfish woman that she must bear every-thing without complaint. She must put up with drunkenness, and ill-temper, and abuse, and not a murmur must cross her lips. I have often wondered how much these evils were encouraged by this supineness, and that if women had the courage to kick, like men would, if they couldn't remedy them. You never catch a man bear-ing a thing until he has made a vigorous protest against it. A drunken woman, reeling home, is no more disgusting than a drunken man, yet nobody would expect a man to put up with such a state of affairs for a moment. A woman knows very well she isn't going to be pitied and forgiven, and the result is she keeps sober. I have known a man who browbeat and bullied a meek, little, self-sacrificing wife into the grave, called down and terrorized into a decent and considerate husband by a determined second wife. Undoubtedly the woman who is imposed upon has only herself to blame.

Are women growing selfish? I answer, no. They are beginning to realize that there is a middle ground between being a monster of selfishness and a door mat for everybody to walk over and on that middle ground they propose to take their stand. But wherever there is a clarion call to duty, wherever love lies wounded and bleeding, and in want of succor, wherever there is need of tender nursing or pitying tears, there in the future, as in the past, will women be found, last at the cross, and earliest at the tomb.

The American Wife[2]

* * * It always seems to the American woman that the wives of other countries, who are held up for her admiration and imitation, have rather the easiest time of it. It would be comparatively simple to make yourself a decorative object to adorn a man's house, if that were all that was expected of you. It would be simple enough to accomplish marvels of cooking and housekeeping if that were the chief end of life. It is when one attempts to combine the useful and the ornamental—to be a Dresden statuette in the parlor and a reliable range in the kitchen—that the situation becomes trying, and calls for genuine ability. Yet this is what we expect of the average American wife, merely as a matter of course. She must be a paragon of domesticity, an ornament in society, a wonder in finance and a light in the literary circle to which she belongs.

In our curious social system, many things are left to her that the men attend to in other countries. For one thing, her husband expects her to assume all authority and management of the home and family. He doesn't want to be bothered about it. When he makes the money he feels he has done his whole duty, and he leaves the rest to her. When he comes home, tired out, after a day's work, he wants to rest, to read his paper, to think out some scheme in which he is interested. If his wife has any idea of leaning on his superior judgment and asking his advice about domestic problems she is very soon undeceived. "Great Scotts, Mary," is the impatient reply, "can't you manage your own affairs? I haven't got time to see about it. Settle it yourself."

It is the same way about the children. The American father is generally a devoted parent, but he wants his wife to do the manag-

2. *The Daily Picayune*, January 23, 1898.

ing and disciplining. In the brief hours he is at home, the little ones are his playthings, and he spoils them, and indulges them with a happy sense that he has no responsibility about it and that their mother will have to do the subsequent disciplining. She is responsible for their mental and physical well-being. She decides on the schools, and what they shall study, what colleges they shall attend, and all the rest of it. The average American John has a well-founded belief that his Mary is the smartest woman in the world, and knows what she is about, and so, at last, when she announces that the children need to go to Europe to study this or that, he consents through mere force of habit. He is so much in the way of letting her decide things it doesn't occur to him he could raise a dissenting voice.

To her, too, he leaves the matter of society. She dominates it, and runs it, and an American married man's social position depends entirely on his wife. If she is ambitious he climbs meekly up the social ladder in her wake; if she is not ambitious, they sit comfortably and contentedly down on the lower rungs, and stay there. He feels that he would be a bungler in the game of society, and he simply backs her hand for all it is worth. He pays for the house in the fashionable neighborhood of her choice, and for her entertainments, but he leaves all the rest to "mother and the girls." They must attend to the intricate social machinery, that he admits is a necessity, and is perfectly willing to support with anything but his own presence.* * *

Summer Flirtations[3]

* * * But did you ever think that among all the inexplicable vagaries of human nature there is none so peculiar as the latitude we lend ourselves in the summer? Is dignity, common sense and even plain decency a matter of the thermometer? You see women such prudes they will hardly raise their frocks two inches to keep them out of the mud in the winter, posing around on the beach at the seaside in summer in clothes that would bring a blush to the cheek of a wooden Indian. You see women who are the pink of propriety at home drinking mixed drinks in public places that are none too proper, and you see women noted for exclusiveness, recklessly making acquaintances with strangers of whose antecedents they know absolutely nothing. What, one might ask, has brought about such a revolution? Nothing at all. It is merely summer, and we have let ourselves go. With the first cold weather madame will resume her stiff tailor-made frock, and with it her perfectly correct ideas of deportment. She will also resume her previous attitude towards the

3. *The Daily Picayune*, August 13, 1899.

church and society, and when she meets the pleasant, though socially undesirable men and women with whom she was on such delightful terms of bon commaradie during the summer, she will simply look through them as if she was gazing at vacancy, with nothing to intercept her view. We have all seen it a hundred times, and we will see it again as long as summer follies and winter repentance continue to follow each other.

But by far the most amazing part of the whole thing is the summer flirtation. Why summer should be given over to sentiment more than other seasons of the year is one of the things nobody understands. That it is, is a fact no one will deny, and it is probably the reason that we call the summer season the silly season. The summer flirtation, at any rate, is a recognized institution, and an accessory just as much as the hop and tennis courts, and golf links, and no matter what other diversions a girl had during her summer outing she would consider the whole thing a dead failure if it did not include a flirtation. It is this that makes the presence of man such an event. Of course, we all recognize that at times everywhere man is a necessity, and at all seasons a convenience to have about the house, but at a summer resort he becomes a gilt-edged luxury.

* * *

The married flirt—the woman who has achieved a kind of temporary widowhood by going off for the summer—is even more dangerous. Like the widow, she knows all the ropes and possesses all the advantage that the professional always has over the amateur, with this further point in her favor, that there is a definite time limit to the flirtation. She knows, and the man knows, that when the vacation is over and the time comes to part, he will look down upon her and sigh, and she will look up and sigh, and both will murmur, "If we had only met sooner," and that will end it. No tears, no future making good of reckless promises and vows, no scenes, nothing more expected of either one, nothing to sneak out of and feel mean about, which men hate. It was a game played on top of the table between evenly matched players, and it ends in a draw.* * *

A Strike for Liberty[4]

There comes a time in the life of almost every woman when she has to choose between a species of slavery and freedom, and when, if she ever expects to enjoy any future liberty, she must hoist the red flag of revolt and make a fight for her rights. It counts for nothing that the oppressor is generally of her own household and is blissfully unconscious of being a tyrant. One may be bound just as securely and as fatally with silken cords as with iron fetters, and the

4. *The Daily Picayune*, October 29, 1899.

fact that our jailer happens to love us does not offer adequate compensation for being in prison. No amount of gilding ever made a cage attractive to the poor wretch within.

All of us have sufficient spirit to repel the attacks of the enemy from without. We are armed and prepared for them, and their first act of aggression rouses our fighting blood, but there is nothing else on earth that takes so much cool nerve and determination and courage as to make a stand against those we love and whom we dread to wound. The thought that we will hurt them or anger them, makes cowards of us, and we keep giving in, and giving in, to their demands and whims and caprices until some fine day we find out that we have not a vestige of personal liberty left, and are nothing more than bond slaves to the tyrant on our hearth.

Chief and foremost among these oppressors are children. In her desire to be a good mother, and to do everything possible for her child's welfare, the average mother permits herself to be made a martyr before she realizes it. It doesn't take a baby but three days to develop all the amiable traits and the despotic power of a Nero and a Caligula,[5] and there are plenty of women who never draw a single breath of freedom after their first child is born. They may have the very best of nurses, but angel Freddy howls like a Commanche unless his mother sits by his side and holds his hand until he goes to sleep, or darling Mary won't let the nurse undress her, and so no matter how interesting the conversation downstairs, or how important the guest, the poor mother has to leave it all, and spend her evening in solitary confinement in a dark room to gratify the whims of a selfish and unreasonable little creature.

* * *

Sometimes—and it is one of the cruelest situations of untoward fate—it is against her husband that a woman must make a stand, unless her whole married life is to degenerate into a kind of purgatory. She loves him and is sure of his affection for her. She respects all the sterling worth of his character, his honor, his honesty, his truth and goodness. She appreciates all his hard work and his sacrifices to support his family in comfort. For a long time it has made her bear many things with patience. She has made the excuse of "overwork" and "nerves," those convenient packhorses on which we lay to much ill-temper and brutality, hoping that time would cure the fault. It may be that he has fallen into a way of petty nagging. She cannot express an opinion without having him sneer it down. He ridicules her efforts at self-improvement, and derides her church and clubs, and she feels insulted and outraged before her children and servants; or he flashes out impatient speeches that sear her

5. Emperors of Rome: Nero from 54 to 68 A.D., Caligula from 37 to 41 A.D. [*Editor*.]

heart like a redhot iron. Often and often it is the money question. He doles out a quarter here and there, and grumbles over the bills until she feels herself as much a mendicant as the very beggar that asks alms on the street corner.

A woman in such a position, and her name is Mrs. Legion, feels that she is the most helpless creature living. There's no question of divorce for her. With all his faults she loves her tyrant still for the good and the lovableness that is in him. She wouldn't leave him if she could, but none the less the bitterness of death is in her soul, all the crueler and more desperate that she sees nothing for it but endurance. My dear sisters, if you have got the courage to make a fight, you can conquer. Make your stand on your right to be treated with the courtesy your husband would show a lady, and you take an unassailable position. Assert your right to a share in the finances of the partnership of matrimony. Refuse to be any longer a beggar. Ninety-nine times out of a hundred a woman has only to make one stand against oppression to gain a victory that lasts a life time, and she not only wins for herself decent treatment, but respect and admiration, for it is one of the unalterable principles of human nature that we despise those who permit us to impose on them. Contemporary history does not show one single meek woman whose husband treated her with ordinary civility.* * *

Women and Suicide[6]

The claim recently put boldly forth by a distinguished lawyer that a person has a right to die, when by means of disease or misfortune life becomes a burden, has provoked renewed discussion of the suicide question, and it is interesting, in this connection, to note that by far the larger number of suicides are among men. Women seldom take their own lives, and so we have the curious and contradictory spectacle of the sex that is universally accounted the braver and stronger, flinging themselves out of the world to avoid its troubles, while the weaklings patiently bear theirs on to the bitter end.

Nothing is more common than for the man who has speculated with other people's money and lost, and so brought ruin and disgrace on his family, to commit suicide. In fact, after reading of the trusted cashier going wrong, in one column, we almost expect to read in the next that he shot himself. No thought apparently comes to him of having any duty to stay and help lift the misery he brought on innocent people. In times of great financial stress, when a rich man has everything swept away, he, too, often solves the

6. *The Daily Picayune*, October 8, 1899. Appeared unsigned on the woman's page, which was under the editorship of Dorothy Dix.

question of the future for himself by suicide, leaving his wife and little children to face a situation for which they are wholly unprepared. You never hear of a woman committing suicide and leaving her little children to the cruel mercies of the world, because she has lost her property. Instead, she feels more than ever that they need her care, and her help, and that she would be incapable of the unmentionable baseness of deserting them in such a crisis.

Yet if suicide is ever justifiable, it is for woman far more than men. She is always handicapped in the race of life. Sometimes with bodily infirmities, sometimes with mental idiosyncrasies, always by lack of training and business experience. Hard as poverty is for a man, it is harder still for a woman. Desperate as the struggle for existence is for him, it is still more desperate for her, limited by narrower opportunities, and rewarded with lesser pay. Terrible as are the tortures suffered by many a poor wretch, they are no worse than the life-long martyrdom that many a woman endures with never a thought of doing anything but bearing them with Christian fortitude and resignation until God's own hand sets her free.

There are many reasons why this state of affairs should exist. Woman's whole life is one long lesson in patience and submission. She must always give in. Men feel that they are born to command, to force circumstances to their will, and when circumstances can no longer be forced or bent, and they must yield to untoward fate, too many yield to the desire to avoid the misery they see before them by sneaking out of life. It is always a coward's deed. The babe salutes life with a wail, and the dying man takes leave of it with a groan. Between there is no time that has not its own troubles, and cares, and sorrows, and it is our part to bear them with courage, and it should be part of our pride in our sex that so many women sustain this brave attitude towards life under circumstances that might well tempt them to play the coward's part.

CHARLOTTE PERKINS STETSON (GILMAN)

From *Women and Economics*†

* * * Our thrones have been emptied, and turned into mere chairs for passing presidents. Our churches have been opened to the light of modern life, and the odor of sanctity has been freshened with sweet sunny air. We can see room for change in these old sanctuaries, but none in the sanctuary of the home. And this temple,

---

† From *Women and Economics: A Study of the Economic Relation Between Men and Women as a Factor in Social Evolution* (Boston: Small, Maynard, 1899).

with its rights, is so closely interwound with the services of subject woman, its altar so demands her ceaseless sacrifices, that we find it impossible to conceive of any other basis of human living. We are chilled to the heart's core by the fear of losing any of these ancient and hallowed associations. Without this blessed background of all our memories and foreground of all our hopes, life seems empty indeed. In homes we were all born. In homes we all die or hope to die. In homes we all live or want to live. For homes we all labor, in them or out of them. The home is the centre and circumference, the start and the finish, of most of our lives. We love it with a love older than the human race. We reverence it with the blind obeisance of those crouching centuries when its cult began. We cling to it with the tenacity of every inmost, oldest instinct of our animal natures, and with the enthusiasm of every latest word in the unbroken chant of adoration which we have sung to it since first we learned to praise.

And since we hold that our home life, just as we have it, is the best thing on earth, and that our home life plainly demands one whole woman at the least to each home, and usually more, it follows that anything which offers to change the position of woman threatens to "undermine the home," "strikes at the root of the family," and we will none of it. If, in honest endeavor to keep up to the modern standard of free thought and free speech, we do listen, —turning from our idol for a moment, and saying to the daring iconoclast, "Come, show us anything better!"—with what unlimited derision do we greet his proposed substitute! Yet everywhere about us to-day this inner tower, this castle keep of vanishing tradition, is becoming more difficult to defend or even to keep in repair. We buttress it anew with every generation; we love its very cracks and crumbling corners; we hang and drape it with endless decorations; we hide the looming dangers overhead with fresh clouds of incense; and we demand of the would-be repairers and rebuilders that they prove to us the desirability of their wild plans before they lift a hammer. But, when they show their plans, we laugh them to scorn.

* * *

Worse than the check set upon the physical activities of women has been the restriction of their power to think and judge for themselves. The extended use of the human will and its decisions is conditioned upon free, voluntary action. In her rudimentary position, woman was denied the physical freedom which underlies all knowledge, she was denied the mental freedom which is the path to further wisdom, she was denied the moral freedom of being mistress of her own action and of learning by the merciful law of consequences what was right and what was wrong; and she has remained, perforce, undeveloped in the larger judgment of ethics.

Her moral sense is large enough, morbidly large, because in this tutelage she is always being praised or blamed for her conduct. She lives in a forcing-bed of sensitiveness to moral distinctions, but the broad judgment that alone can guide and govern this sensitiveness she has not. Her contribution to moral progress has added to the anguish of the world the fierce sense of sin and shame, the desperate desire to do right, the fear of wrong; without giving it the essential help of a practical wisdom and a regulated will. Inheriting with each generation the accumulating forces of our social nature, set back in each generation by the conditions of the primitive human female, women have become vividly self-conscious centres of moral impulse, but poor guides as to the conduct which alone can make that impulse useful and build the habit of morality into the constitution of the race.

Recognizing her intense feeling on moral lines, and seeing in her the rigidly preserved virtues of faith, submission, and self-sacrifice, —qualities which in the Dark Ages were held to be the first of virtues,—we have agreed of late years to call woman the moral superior of man. But the ceaseless growth of human life, social life, has developed in him new virtues, later, higher, more needful; and the moral nature of woman, as maintained in this rudimentary stage by her economic dependence, is a continual check to the progress of the human soul. The main feature of her life—the restriction of her range of duty to the love and service of her own immediate family —acts upon us continually as a retarding influence, hindering the expansion of the spirit of social love and service on which our very lives depend. It keeps the moral standard of the patriarchal era still before us, and blinds our eyes to the full duty of man.

An intense self-consciousness, born of the ceaseless contact of close personal relation; an inordinate self-interest, bred by the constant personal attention and service of this relation; a feverish, torturing, moral sensitiveness, without the width and clarity of vision of a full-grown moral sense; a thwarted will, used to meek surrender, cunning evasion, or futile rebellion; a childish, wavering, short-range judgment, handicapped by emotion; a measureless devotion to one's own sex relatives, and a maternal passion swollen with the full strength of the great social heart, but denied social expression,—such psychic qualities as these, born in us all, are the inevitable result of the sexuo-economic relation.

It is not alone upon woman, and, through her, upon the race, that the ill-effects may be observed. Man, as master, has suffered from his position also. The lust for power and conquest, natural to the male of any species, has been fostered in him to an enormous degree by this cheap and easy lordship. His dominance is not that of one chosen as best fitted to rule or of one ruling by successful competition with "foemen worthy of his steel"; but it is a sovereignty based on the accident of sex, and holding over such helpless and inferior dependants as could not question or oppose. The easy superiority that needs no striving to maintain it; the temptation to cruelty always begotten by irresponsible power; the pride and self-will which surely accompany it,—these qualities have been bred into the souls of men by their side of the relation. When man's place was maintained by brute force, it made him more brutal: when his place was maintained by purchase, by the power of economic necessity, then he grew into the merciless use of such power as distinguishes him to-day.

Another giant evil engendered by this relation is what we call selfishness. Social life tends to reduce this feeling, which is but a belated individualism; but the sexuo-economic relation fosters and developes it. To have a whole human creature consecrated to his direct personal service, to pleasing and satisfying him in every way possible,—this has kept man selfish beyond the degree incidental to our stage of social growth. Even in our artificial society life men are more forbearing and considerate, more polite and kind, than they are at home. Pride, cruelty, and selfishness are the vices of the master; and these have been kept strong in the bosom of the family through the false position of woman. And every human soul is born, an impressionable child, into the close presence of these conditions. Our men must live in the ethics of a civilized, free, industrial, democratic age; but they are born and trained in the moral atmosphere of a primitive patriarchate. No wonder that we are all somewhat slow to rise to the full powers and privileges of democracy, to feel full social honor and social duty, while every soul of us is reared in this stronghold of ancient and outgrown emotions,—the economically related family.

So we may trace from the sexuo-economic relation of our species not only definite evils in psychic development, bred severally in men and women, and transmitted indifferently to their offspring, but the innate perversion of character resultant from the moral miscegenation of two so diverse souls,—the unfailing shadow and distortion which has darkened and twisted the spirit of man from its beginnings. We have been injured in body and in mind by the too dissimilar traits inherited from our widely separated parents, but nowhere is the injury more apparent than in its ill effects upon the moral nature of the race.

Yet here, as in the other evil results of the sexuo-economic relation, we can see the accompanying good that made the condition necessary in its time; and we can follow the beautiful results of our present changes with comforting assurance. A healthy, normal moral sense will be ours, freed from its exaggerations and contradictions; and, with that clear perception, we shall no longer conceive of the ethical process as something outside of and against nature, but as the most natural thing in the world.

Where now we strive and agonize after impossible virtues, we shall then grow naturally and easily into those very qualities; and we shall not even think of them as especially commendable. Where our progress hitherto has been warped and hindered by the retarding influence of surviving rudimentary forces, it will flow on smoothly and rapidly when both men and women stand equal in economic relation. When the mother of the race is free, we shall have a better world, by the easy right of birth and by the calm, slow, friendly forces of social evolution. * * *

THORSTEIN VEBLEN

[Conspicuous Consumption and the Servant-Wife]†

* * * In what has been said of the evolution of the vicarious leisure class and its differentiation from the general body of the working classes, reference has been made to a further division of labour,—that between different servant classes. One portion of the servant class, chiefly those persons whose occupation is vicarious leisure, come to undertake a new, subsidiary range of duties—the vicarious consumption of goods. The most obvious form in which this consumption occurs is seen in the wearing of liveries and the occupation of spacious servants' quarters. Another, scarcely less obtrusive or less effective form of viracious consumption, and a much more widely prevalent one, is the consumption of food, clothing, dwelling, and furniture by the lady and the rest of the domestic establishment.

* * *

With the disappearance of servitude, the number of vicarious consumers attached to any one gentleman tends, on the whole, to decrease. The like is of course true, and perhaps in a still higher degree, of the number of dependents who perform vicarious leisure for him. In a general way, though not wholly nor consistently, these two groups coincide. The dependent who was first delegated for these duties was the wife, or the chief wife; and, as would be expected, in the later development of the institution, when the number of persons by whom these duties are customarily performed

† From *The Theory of the Leisure Class: An Economic Study in the Evolution of* *Institutions* (New York and London: Macmillan, 1899).

gradually narrows, the wife remains the last. In the higher grades of society a large volume of both these kinds of service is required; and here the wife is of course still assisted in the work by a more or less numerous corps of menials. But as we descend the social scale, the point is presently reached where the duties of vicarious leisure and consumption devolve upon the wife alone. In the communities of the Western culture, this point is at present found among the lower middle class.

And here occurs a curious inversion. It is a fact of common observation that in this lower middle class there is no pretence of leisure on the part of the head of the household. Through force of circumstances it has fallen into disuse. But the middle-class wife still carries on the business of vicarious leisure, for the good name of the household and its master. In descending the social scale in any modern industrial community, the primary fact—the conspicuous leisure of the master of the household—disappears at a relatively high point. The head of the middle-class household has been reduced by economic circumstances to turn his hand to gaining a livelihood by occupations which often partake largely of the character of industry, as in the case of the ordinary business man of to-day. But the derivative fact—the vicarious leisure and consumption rendered by the wife, and the auxiliary vicarious performance of leisure by menials—remains in vogue as a conventionality which the demands of reputability will not suffer to be slighted. It is by no means an uncommon spectacle to find a man applying himself to work with the utmost assiduity, in order that his wife may in due form render for him that degree of vicarious leisure which the common sense of the time demands.

The leisure rendered by the wife in such cases is, of course, not a simple manifestation of idleness or indolence. It almost invariably occurs disguised under some form of work or household duties or social amenities, which prove on analysis to serve little or no ulterior end beyond showing that she does not and need not occupy herself with anything that is gainful or that is of substantial use. As has already been noticed under the head of manners, the greater part of the customary round of domestic cares to which the middle-class housewife gives her time and effort is of this character. Not that the results of her attention to household matters, of a decorative and mundificatory character, are not pleasing to the sense of men trained in middle-class proprieties; but the taste to which these effects of household adornment and tidiness appeal is a taste which has been formed under the selective guidance of a canon of propriety that demands just these evidences of wasted effort. The effects are pleasing to us chiefly because we have been taught to find them pleasing. There goes into these domestic duties much solicitude for a proper combination of form and colour, and for other ends that are to be classed as æsthetic in the proper sense of the term; and it is not denied that effects having some substantial æsthetic value are sometimes attained. Pretty much all that is here insisted on is that, as regards these amenities of life, the housewife's efforts are under the guidance of traditions that have been shaped by the law of conspicuously wasteful expenditure of time and substance. If beauty or comfort is achieved,—and it is a more or less fortuitous circumstance if they are,—they must be achieved by means and methods that commend themselves to the great economic law of wasted effort. The more reputable, "presentable" portion of middle-class household paraphernalia are, on the one hand, items of conspicuous consumption, and on the other hand, apparatus for putting in evidence the vicarious leisure rendered by the housewife.

The requirement of vicarious consumption at the hands of the wife continues in force even at a lower point in the pecuniary scale than the requirement of vicarious leisure. At a point below which little if any pretence of wasted effort, in ceremonial cleanness and the like, is observable, and where there is assuredly no conscious attempt at ostensible leisure, decency still requires the wife to consume some goods conspicuously for the reputability of the household and its head. So that, as the latter-day outcome of this evolution of an archaic institution, the wife, who was at the outset the drudge and chattel of the man, both in fact and in theory,—the producer of goods for him to consume,—has become the ceremonial consumer of goods which he produces. But she still quite unmistakably remains his chattel in theory; for the habitual rendering of vicarious leisure and consumption is the abiding mark of the unfree servant. * * *

Criticism

Editor's Note

Early reviewers of *The Awakening* whose moral sensibilities were affronted by the novel's themes of sex and suicide gave testimony to the power of the novel in their vigorous condemnations of it. C. L. Deyo wrote: "It is sad and mad and bad, but it is all consummate art." The power of the novel is precisely what made it such a dangerous book in the opinions of most early reviewers; Kate Chopin did not seem to use her power to condemn the actions of Edna Pontellier as Flaubert condemned Emma Bovary in the novel to which it is most often compared. The first to pursue this comparison was Willa Cather, whose review—along with that of C. L. Deyo, who was a friend of Chopin—was the most perceptive and provocative of the early reviews.

Hostile reactions to the novel, combined with the fact that it was written by a woman who was considered a regional writer ("regionalism" is nothing a Hawthorne or a Faulkner is ever accused of), contributed to the half-century of neglect which the novel endured and which it has survived. Revival of interest in the book in this country began slowly in the late 1950s, with the promptings of a French critic, Cyrille Arnavon. American critics and literary historians who had for decades omitted even mention of the novel[1] now began to take notice. In 1952 Van Wyck Brooks wrote "But there was one novel of the nineties in the South that should have been remembered, one small perfect book that mattered more than the whole life-work of many a prolific writer."[2] In 1956 Robert Cantwell and Kenneth Eble, who gave the novel the first extended attention it had received in this country since its publication, wrote appreciative essays; and in 1962 Edmund Wilson assured the book a place in the American canon when he wrote of a novel "quite uninhibited and beautifully written, which anticipates D. H. Lawrence in its treatment of infidelity."[3]

Critics of the sixties were first concerned with identifying the tradition with which the novel is most closely associated. Is Chopin a realist or a romantic? Does she most resemble Flaubert or Tolstoy, or Emerson or Whitman, or Dreiser or Mary Wilkins Freeman? They then turned new critical attention to the details of her artistry, particularly her imagery.

Critics of the seventies have become interested in the problems of the ending and the narrative posture, and are using psychology, ideology, and Chopin's sources to illuminate the work. The novel continues to generate widespread interest, particularly among those re-evaluating the lost work of women in America. It is currently being adapted by Julia Demmin and Patsie Rodgers into a three-act opera to be performed professionally.

---

1. See, for example, Robert Spiller, et al, *Literary History of the United States*, III (New York: Macmillan, 1948). The 1953 and 1963 editions do not mention *The Awakening*, either.

2. Van Wyck Brooks, *The Confident Years 1885–1915* (New York: Dutton, 1952), p. 341.

3. Edmund Wilson, *Patriotic Gore: Studies in the Literature of the American Civil War* (New York: Oxford University Press, 1962), p. 590.

Whatever one may think of the moralistic tone of the early reviewers of *The Awakening*, who are responsible in part for the half-century neglect of the novel, one must conclude that they were correct in their basic perception: The novel is a powerful one about female sexuality. It may still be a dangerous book.

Contemporary Reviews

From *The Mirror*†

[*". . . what an ugly, cruel, loathsome monster*
Passion can be . . ."]

Of an already successful writer's first novel one should not write,
perhaps, while the spell of the book is upon one; it is something to
be "dreamed upon," like a piece of wedding-cake for luck on one's
first marriage-proposal, or anything upon which hangs some importance of decision. And so, because we admire Kate Chopin's
other work immensely and delight in her evergrowing fame and are
proud that she is "one-of-us St. Louisans," one dislikes to acknowledge a wish that she had not written her novel.

Not because it is not bright with her own peculiar charm of style,
not because there is missing any touch of effect or lacking any
beauty of description—but—well, it is one of the books of which
we feel *"cui bono?"*[1] It absorbs and interests, then makes one
wonder, for the moment, with a little sick feeling, if all women are
like the one, and that isn't a pleasant reflection after you have
thoroughly taken in this character study whose "awakening" gives
title to Mrs. Chopin's novel.

One would fain beg the gods, in pure cowardice, for sleep unend-
ing rather than to know what an ugly, cruel, loathsome monster
Passion can be when, like a tiger, it slowly stretches its graceful
length and yawns and finally awakens. This is the kind of an awakening that impresses the reader in Mrs. Chopin's heroine. I do not
believe it impressed the heroine herself that way. I think, like the
tiger, she hated to be balked of her desire and that was about the
worst of it to her.

* * *

It is not a pleasant picture of soul-dissection, take it anyway you
like; and so, though she finally kills herself, or rather lets herself
drown to death, one feels that it is not in the desperation born of an
over-burdened heart, torn by complicating duties but rather because
she realizes that something is due to her children, that she cannot
get away from, and she is too weak to face the issue. Besides which,
and this is the stronger feeling, she has offered herself wholly to the

---

† Frances Porcher, "Kate Chopin's
Novel," *The Mirror* IX (May 4, 1899),
6. This review set the tone for the many
negative ones that followed it. [*Editor.*]
1. "What's the use?" [*Editor.*]

man, who loves her too well to take her at her word; "she realizes that the day would come when he, too, and the thought of him, would melt out of her existence," she has awakened to know the shifting, treacherous, fickle deeps of her own soul in which lies, alert and strong and cruel, the fiend called Passion that is all animal and all of the earth, earthy. It is better to lie down in the green waves and sink down in close embraces of old ocean, and so she does.

There is no fault to find with the telling of the story, there are no blemishes in its art, but it leaves one sick of human nature and so one feels—*cui bono!*

From the St. Louis *Daily Globe-Democrat*†

["*It is not a healthy book* . . ."]

The appearance of a new novel by Kate Chopin, of St. Louis, is an event of interest to St. Louisans. The appearance of a book such as "The Awakening" by this St. Louis lady, is fraught with especial interest, and that interest carries with it surprise. Whether that surprise is pleasant or the reverse depends largely on the view point of the reader. It is hardly the kind of a book some people would look for from her. It is pre-eminently a romance of to-day—a love story with one woman as the central figure, around which several male characters revolve; and thoughts of the proverbial moth and the traditional candle force themselves on the reader in almost every chapter. At the very outset of the story one feels that the heroine should pray for deliverance from temptation, and in the very closing paragraph, when, having removed every vestige of clothes she "stands naked in the sun" and then walks out into the water until she can walk no farther, and then swims on into eternity, one thinks that her very suicide is in itself a prayer for deliverance from the evils that beset her, all of her own creating.

It is not a healthy book; if it points any particular moral or teaches any lesson, the fact is not apparent. But there is no denying the fact that it deals with existent conditions, and without attempting a solution, handles a problem that obtrudes itself only too frequently in the social life of people with whom the question of food and clothing is not the all absorbing one.

* * *

There are some pretty bits of description of Louisiana Creole life, and there are two or three minor characters in the book that are drawn with a deft hand. After reading the whole story, it can not be

† From "Notes from Bookland," St. Louis *Daily Globe-Democrat*, May 13, 1899, p. 5.

said that either of the principal characters claims admiration or sympathy. It is a morbid book, and the thought suggests itself that the author herself would probably like nothing better than to "tear it to pieces" by criticism if only some other person had written it.

From the St. Louis *Post-Dispatch*†

["*. . . flawless art.*"]

There may be many opinions touching other aspects of Mrs. Chopin's novel "The Awakening," but all must concede its flawless art. The delicacy of touch of rare skill in construction, the subtle understanding of motive, the searching vision into the recesses of the heart—these are known to readers of "Bayou Folk" and "A Night in Acadie." But in this new work power appears, power born of confidence. There is no uncertainty in the lines, so surely and firmly drawn. Complete mastery is apparent on every page. Nothing is wanting to make a complete artistic whole. In delicious English, quick with life, never a word too much, simple and pure, the story proceeds with classic severity through a labyrinth of doubt and temptation and dumb despair.

It is not a tragedy, for it lacks the high motive of tragedy. The woman, not quite brave enough, declines to a lower plane and does not commit a sin ennobled by love. But it is terribly tragic. Compassion, not pity, is excited, for pity is for those who sin, and Edna Pontellier only offended—weakly, passively, vainly offended.

"The Awakening" is not for the young person; not because the young person would be harmed by reading it, but because the young person wouldn't understand it, and everybody knows that the young person's understanding should be scrupulously respected. It is for seasoned souls, for those who have lived, who have ripened under the gracious or ungracious sun of experience and learned that realities do not show themselves on the outside of things where they can be seen and heard, weighed, measured and valued like the sugar of commerce, but treasured within the heart, hidden away, never to be known perhaps save when exposed by temptation or called out by occasions of great pith and moment. No, the book is not for the young person, nor, indeed, for the old person who has no relish for unpleasant truths. For such there is much that is very improper in it, not to say positively unseemly. A fact, no matter how essential, which we have all agreed shall not be acknowledged, is as good as no fact at all. And it is disturbing—even indelicate—to mention it

† "The Newest Books," by C. L. Deyo, St. Louis *Post-Dispatch*, May 20, 1899, p. 4.

This, the most favorable of the early reviews, was written by a journalist friend of Chopin. [*Editor.*]

as something which, perhaps, does play an important part in the life behind the mask.

It is the life and not the mask that is the subject of the story. One day Edna Pontellier, whose husband has vaguely held her dear as a bit of decorative furniture, a valuable piece of personal property, suddenly becomes aware she is a human being. It was her husband's misfortune that he did not make this interesting discovery himself, but he had his brokerage business to think about and brokers deal in stocks, not hearts. It was Mrs. Pontellier's misfortune that another man revealed her to herself, and when the knowledge came it produced profound dissatisfaction, as often happens when love is born in a cage not of its own building. In the beginning she had no thought of wrong-doing, but resentment was hot and made her sullen. Robert Lebrun, whose heart was ensnared before he realized it, went away to Mexico to make money, which was quite the proper thing to do. It would have been the right thing had he gone before it was too late, for then he might have been only a shadowy dream in Edna's life, instead of a consuming reality. This made the poor woman still more discontented. She took to all sorts of foolish fancies to divert her mind. Her children did not help her, for she was not a mother woman and didn't feel that loving babies was the whole duty of a woman. She loved them, but said that while she was willing to die for them she couldn't give up anything essential for them. This sounded clever because it was paradoxical, but she didn't quite know what it meant. She dabbled with brush and canvas. Mademoiselle Reisz told her that to be an artist one must be courageous, to dare and defy. But, unhappily, Mrs. Pontellier was not courageous. So she was not an artist. Mademoiselle Reisz, who was a witch, and knew Robert and Edna better than they knew themselves, did not add, what was really in her mind, that to be a great sinner a woman must be courageous, for great sinners are those who sin for a pure, howbeit unlawful, motive. Edna was not courageous. So she was not a great sinner, but by and by she became a poor, helpless offender, which is the way of such persons—not good enough for heaven, not wicked enough for hell.

Mrs. Pontellier was prepared by unlawful love for unholy passion. Her husband was extinct so far as she was concerned, and the man she loved was beyond her power. She had no anchor and no harbor was in sight. She was a derelict in a moral ocean, whose chart she had never studied, and one of the pirates who cruise in that sea made her his prize. Robert might have saved her from ignoble temptation by supplying a motive for a robust sin, but he was in Mexico and the thought of him only deepened her discontent. The moment came and with it the man. There is always a man for the moment, sometimes two or three. So thought Mrs. Pontellier, and she grew dull with despair. Passion without love was not to her liking and she feared the future. If she had been a courageous woman she would have put away passion and waited for love, but she was not courageous. She let sensation occupy a vacant life, knowing the while that it only made it emptier and more hopeless.

So because she could not forget her womanhood, and to save the remnants of it, she swam out into the sunkissed gulf and did not come back.

It is sad and mad and bad, but it is all consummate art. The theme is difficult, but it is handled with a cunning craft. The work is more than unusual. It is unique. The integrity of its art is that of well-knit individuality at one with itself, with nothing superfluous to weaken the impression of a perfect whole.

From the Chicago *Times-Herald*†

[*". . . sex fiction."*]

Kate Chopin, author of those delightful sketches, "A Night in Acadie," has made a new departure in her long story, "The Awakening." The many admirers whom she has won by her earlier work will be surprised—perhaps disagreeably—by this latest venture. That the book is strong and that Miss Chopin has a keen knowledge of certain phases of feminine character will not be denied. But it was not necessary for a writer of so great refinement and poetic grace to enter the overworked field of sex fiction. * * *

From the Providence *Sunday Journal*‡

[*"The purport of the story can hardly be described in language fit for publication."*]

* * * Miss Kate Chopin is another clever woman, but she has put her cleverness to a very bad use in writing "The Awakening." The purport of the story can hardly be described in language fit for publication. We are fain to believe that Miss Chopin did not herself realize what she was doing when she wrote it. With a bald realism that fairly out Zolas Zola,[1] she describes the result upon a married woman who lives amiably with her husband without caring for him, of a slowly growing admiration for another man. He is too honorable to speak and goes away; but her life is spoiled already, and she falls with a merely animal instinct into the arms of the first man she

† From "Books of the Day," Chicago *Times-Herald*, June 1, 1899, p. 9.
‡ From "Books of the Week," Providence *Sunday Journal*, June 4, 1899, p. 15.

1. Émile Zola (1840–1902), French naturalistic novelist whose work is known for its frank, realistic detail. [*Editor.*]

meets. The worst of such stories is that they will fall into the hands of youth, leading them to dwell on things that only matured persons can understand, and promoting unholy imaginations and unclean desires. It is nauseating to remember that those who object to the bluntness of our older writers will excuse and justify the gilded dirt of these latter days. * * *

From the New Orleans *Times-Democrat*†

[". . . *an undercurrent of sympathy for Edna* . . ."]

* * * By the way, "The Awakening" does not strike one as a very happy title for the story Mrs. Chopin tells. A woman of twenty-eight, a wife and twice a mother who in pondering upon her relations to the world about her, fails to perceive that the relation of a mother to her children is far more important than the gratification of a passion which experience has taught her is, by its very nature, evanescent, can hardly be said to be fully awake. This unhappy Edna's awakening seems to have been confined entirely to the senses, while reason, judgment, and all the higher faculties and perceptions, whose office it is to weigh and criticise, impulse and govern conduct, fell into slumber deep as that of the seven sleepers. It gives one a distinct shock to see Edna's crude mental operations, of which we are compelled to judge chiefly by results—character-ized as "perhaps more wisdom than the Holy Ghost is usually pleased to vouchsafe to any woman." The assumption that such a course as that pursued by Edna has any sort of divine sanction cannot be too strongly protested against. In a civilized society the right of the individual to indulge all his caprices is, and must be, subject to many restrictive clauses, and it cannot for a moment be admitted that a woman who has willingly accepted the love and devotion of a man, even without an equal love on her part—who has become his wife and the mother of his children—has not in-curred a moral obligation which peremptorily forbids her from wantonly severing her relations with him, and entering openly upon the independent existence of an unmarried woman. It is not alto-gether clear that this is the doctrine Mrs. Chopin intends to teach, but neither is it clear that it is not. Certainly there is throughout the story an undercurrent of sympathy for Edna, and nowhere a single note of censure of her totally unjustifiable conduct.

† "New Publications," New Orleans *Times-Democrat*, June 18, 1899, p. 15.

From *Public Opinion*†

["... *we are well satisfied when Mrs. Pontellier deliberately swims out to her death* ..."]

* * * "The Awakening," by Kate Chopin, is a feeble reflection of Bourget,[1] theme and manner of treatment both suggesting the French novelist. We very much doubt the possibility of a woman of "solid old Presbyterian Kentucky stock" being at all like Mrs. Edna Pontellier who has a long list of lesser loves, and one absorbing passion, but gives herself only to the man for whom she did not feel the least affection. If the author had secured our sympathy for this unpleasant person it would not have been a small victory, but we are well satisfied when Mrs. Pontellier deliberately swims out to her death in the waters of the gulf. * * *

From *Literature*‡

["... *an essentially vulgar story*."]

* * * One cannot refrain from regret that so beautiful a style and so much refinement of taste have been spent by Miss Chopin on an essentially vulgar story. The peculiarities of Creole life and temperament, and the sensuous atmosphere of life in New Orleans and at summer resorts on the Gulf, are happily sketched and outlined in this dramatic tale, and emphasis is laid upon the freedom of the Creole from false modesty and the pleasant social relations which inhere among Creole circles. A Creole husband as a rule entirely trusts his wife and is incapable of jealousy, for the reason that the right hand is not jealous of the left nor the head of the heart. Nevertheless, Léonce Pontellier, the Creole husband in the story, having married a beautiful Kentuckian, is less fortunate than most of his compatriots in having excellent reason for jealousy. His wife, having married him in a reaction from a fancied love affair of her girlhood, does not find marriage and motherhood a cable strong enough to keep her from forming other attachments, and the story of these and of her final awakening has little to redeem it from the commonplace, nor is it strong enough to condone the character of its revelations. The awakening itself is tragic, as might have been anticipated, and the waters of the gulf close appropriately over one

† From "Book Reviews," *Public Opinion*, XXVI (June 22, 1899), 794.
1. Paul Charles Joseph Bourget (1852– 1935), French novelist and critic whose work examines moral complexities in the relationships between men and women of the upper class. [*Editor.*]
‡ From "Fiction," *Literature*, IV (June 23, 1899), 570.

who has drifted from all right moorings, and has not the grace to repent. * * *

From the Los Angeles *Sunday Times*†

[". . . *unhealthily introspective and morbid* . . ."]

It is rather difficult to decide whether Mrs. Kate Chopin, the author of "The Awakening," tried in that novel merely to make an intimate, analytical study of the character of a selfish, capricious woman, or whether she wanted to preach the doctrine of the right of the individual to have what he wants, no matter whether or not it may be good for him. It is true that the woman in the book who wanted her own way comes to an untimely end in the effort to get what she wants, or rather, in the effort to gratify every whim that moves her capricious soul, but there are sentences here and there through the book that indicate the author's desire to hint her belief that her heroine had the right of the matter and that if the woman had only been able to make other people "understand" things as she did she would not have had to drown herself in the blue waters of the Mexican Gulf. The scene of the story is laid in New Orleans and in a summer resort on the coast of the Gulf, and the book is concerned mainly with the mental and moral development of Edna, wife of Leonce Pontellier, a Kentucky woman, married to a creole, after she discovers that she has fallen in love with Robert Lebrun, another creole. And as the biography of one individual out of that large section of femininity which may be classified as "fool women," the book is a strong and graceful piece of work. It is like one of Aubrey Beardsley's[1] hideous but haunting pictures with their disfiguring leer of sensuality, but yet carrying a distinguishing strength and grace and individuality. The book shows a searching insight into the motives of the "fool woman" order of being, the woman who learns nothing by experience and has not a large enough circle of vision to see beyond her own immediate desires. In many ways, it is unhealthily introspective and morbid in feeling, as the story of that sort of woman must inevitably be. The evident powers of the author are employed on a subject that is unworthy of them, and when she writes another book it is to be hoped that she will choose a theme more healthful and sweeter of smell.

† From "Fresh Literature," Los Angeles *Sunday Times*, June 25, 1899, p. 12.
1. Aubrey Vincent Beardsley (1872–1898), English artist whose black and white line compositions were widely criticized in the 1890s as gloomy and unwholesome. [*Editor.*]

From the Pittsburgh *Leader*†

["A Creole *Bovary* . . ."]

A Creole *Bovary* is this little novel of Miss Chopin's.[1] Not that the heroine is a Creole exactly, or that Miss Chopin is a Flaubert—save the mark!—but the theme is similar to that which occupied Flaubert. There was, indeed, no need that a second *Madame Bovary* should be written, but an author's choice of themes is frequently as inexplicable as his choice of a wife. It is governed by some innate temperamental bias that cannot be diagrammed. This is particularly so in women who write, and I shall not attempt to say why Miss Chopin has devoted so exquisite and sensitive, well-governed a style to so trite and sordid a theme. She writes much better than it is ever given to most people to write, and hers is a genuinely literary style; of no great elegance or solidity; but light, flexible, subtle, and capable of producing telling effects directly and simply. The story she has to tell in the present instance is new neither in matter nor treatment. Edna Pontellier, a Kentucky girl, who, like Emma Bovary, had been in love with innumerable dream heroes before she was out of short skirts, married Leonce Pontellier as a sort of reaction from a vague and visionary passion for a tragedian whose unresponsive picture she used to kiss. She acquired the habit of liking her husband in time, and even of liking her children. Though we are not justified in presuming that she ever threw articles from her dressing table at them, as the charming Emma had a winsome habit of doing. We are told that "she would sometimes gather them passionately to her heart; she would sometimes forget them." At a Creole watering place, which is admirably and deftly sketched by Miss Chopin, Edna met Robert Lebrun, son of the landlady, who dreamed of a fortune awaiting him in Mexico while he occupied a petty clerical position in New Orleans. Robert made it his business to be agreeable to his mother's boarders, and Edna, not being a Creole, much against his wish and will, took him seriously. . . . The lover of course disappointed her, was a coward and ran away from his responsibilities before they began. He was afraid to begin a chapter with so serious and limited a woman. She remembered the sea where she had first met Robert. Perhaps from the same motive which threw Anna Karenina under the engine wheels,[2] she threw herself into the sea, swam until she was tired and then let go. . . .

† From "Books and Magazines," Pittsburgh *Leader* (July 8, 1899), p. 6. Signed "Sibert" [Willa Cather]. Footnotes are by the editor.
1. Cather is the first of a number of critics to compare the novel to *Madame Bovary* (1856) by Gustave Flaubert (1821–1880).
2. A reference to the ending of Leo Tolstoy's (1828–1910) *Anna Karenina* (1875–76).

Edna Pontellier and Emma Bovary are studies in the same feminine type; one a finished and complete portrayal, the other a hasty
sketch, but the theme is essentially the same. Both women belong to
a class, not large, but forever clamoring in our ears, that demands
more romance out of life than God put into it. Mr. G. Bernard
Shaw would say that they are the victims of the over-idealization of
love.[3] They are the spoil of the poets, the Iphigenias of sentiment.[4]
The unfortunate feature of their disease is that it attacks only
women of brains, at least of rudimentary brains, but whose development is one-sided; women of strong and fine intuitions, but without the faculty of observation, comparison, reasoning about things.
Probably, for emotional people, the most convenient thing about
being able to think is that it occasionally gives them a rest from
feeling. Now with women of the Bovary type, this relaxation and
recreation is impossible. They are not critics of life, but, in the most
personal sense, partakers of life. They receive impressions through
the fancy. With them everything begins with fancy, and passions
rise in the brain rather than in the blood, the poor, neglected,
limited one-sided brain that might do so much better things than
badgering itself into frantic endeavors to love. For these are the
people who pay with their blood for the fine ideals of the poets, as
Marie Delclasse paid for Dumas' great creation, Marguerite
Gauthier.[5] These people really expect the passion of love to fill and
gratify every need of life, whereas nature only intended that it
should meet one of many demands. They insist upon making it
stand for all the emotional pleasures of life and art; expecting an
individual and self-limited passion to yield infinite variety, pleasure,
and distraction, to contribute to their lives what the arts and the
pleasurable exercise of the intellect gives to less limited and less
intense idealists. So this passion, when set up against Shakespeare,
Balzac, Wagner, Raphael, fails them. They have staked everything
on one hand, and they lose. They have driven the blood until it will
drive no further, they have played their nerves up to the point where
any relaxation short of absolute annihilation is impossible. Every
idealist abuses his nerves, and every sentimentalist brutally abuses
them. And in the end, the nerves get even. Nobody ever cheats
them, really. Then "the awakening" comes. Sometimes it comes in
the form of arsenic, as it came to Emma Bovary, sometimes it is
carbolic acid taken covertly in the police station, a goal to which

---

3. George Bernard Shaw (1856–1950),
Irish playwright, known for his satiric
criticism of romantic love which he
later embodied in several plays, among
them *Man and Superman* (1903).
4. Sacrificial victims. Iphigenia, daughter
of Agamemnon, was sacrificed to the
gods in order to obtain favorable winds

for the Greek fleet on its way to Troy.
5. Cather means Marie Duplessis, a Paris
courtesan with whom Alexander Dumas,
the younger (1824–1895), lived for one
year before she died of consumption.
Marguerite Gauthier is the main character in Dumas's *Camille* (1848), based on
the life of Marie Duplessis.

unbalanced idealism not infrequently leads. Edna Pontellier, fanciful and romantic to the last, chose the sea on a summer night and went down with the sound of her first lover's spurs in her ears, and the scent of pinks about her. And next time I hope that Miss Chopin will devote that flexible iridescent style of hers to a better cause.

Letters from "Lady Janet Scammon Young" and "Dr. Dunrobin Thomson"†

8 *Newman Street*
Oxford St. W.
London

"Kate Chopin":

I feel sure I ought to send you the enclosed letter from the great consulting physician of England, who is also one of the purest and best of men, and who has been said by a great editor to be "the soundest critic since Matthew Arnold."[1]

Your book has deeply stirred some other noble souls to whom I have lent it. Like Doctor T—— I assume that it is to be republished over here. Maarten Maartens,[2] who was here last week, said *The Awakening* ought to be translated into Dutch, Scandinavian, and Russian.

But great as is my interest in this book I confess to a still deeper interest in one which you ought to write—which you alone among living novelists *could* write. Evidently like all of us you believe *Edna* to have been worth saving—believe her to have been too noble to go to her death as she did. I quite bow to Doctor T's better sense of art. The conventions required her to die. But suppose her husband had been conceived on higher lines? Suppose Dr. Mandelet had said other things to him—had said, for example: "Pontellier, like most men you fancy that because you have possessed your wife hundreds of times she necessarily long ago came to entire womanly self knowledge—that your embraces have as a matter of course aroused whatever of passion she may be endowed with. You are mistaken. She is just becoming conscious of sex—is just finding herself compelled to take account of masculinity *as such*. You cannot *arrest* that process whatever you do; you should not wish to do so. Assist this birth of your wife's deeper womanliness. Be tender, let her

† One of the mysteries of Chopin scholarship is the origin of these letters. The existence of the persons who wrote them has never been established, and it is possible that they are not genuine. The original letters are in the collection of Chopin papers at the Missouri Histori- cal Society. Footnotes are by the editor. 1. Prodigious and prolific critic and poet of Victorian England. 2. Pen name of J. M. W. van der Poorten Schwarz (1858–1915), Anglo-Dutch novelist.

know that you see how *Robert, Arobin* affect her. Laugh with her over the evident influence of her womanhood over them. Tell her how, *in itself* it is *natural*, that it is divinely made & therefore innocent and pure and the very basis of social life—else why is true society absolutely non-existent without both sexes. There is no *society* in Turkey. Show her the nonsense of ascribing all this interinfluence to 'the feminine mind acting upon the masculine mind'—a saying that so severe a thinker as Herbert Spencer[3] ridicules. Above all *trust* her, let her see that you do. Only the inherently base woman betrays a *trust*. Leave her with *Robert*, with *Arobin*. *Trusted* she will never fail you—distrusted, ignored, left in ignorance of what her new unrest really means she will fall. Follow my advice and in a year you will have a new wife with whom you will fall in love again; & you will be a new husband, manlier, more virile and impassioned with whom she will fall in love again."

Suppose *Dr. Mandelet* had thus spoken, and *Pontellier* had thus acted?

Of course in its brutal literal significance we wholly reject and loathe the French maxim: "The lover completes the wife," yet if we know the true facts of nature we must confess that there is a profound inner truth in it. No woman comes to her full womanly empire and charm who has not felt in what Dr. T—— calls "her passional nature" the arousing power of more than one man. But oh how important to her purity, her honor, her inner self-respect that she (again quoting Dr. T——) "distinguish between passion and love." So that instead of guiltily saying, "I fear I love that man" she shall say within herself with *no* sense of guilt—"How that man's masculinity stirs me"—say it above all to *her husband*. Now all this, which I am saying so clumsily needs saying powerfully; needs to be taught by that most potent method of expression open to man—a great novel. *You* can write it. You alone. You are free from decadency. Your mind and heart are beautiful, free, clean, sympathetic. Give us a great hearted manly *man*—give us a great natured woman for his wife. Give us the awakening of her whole nature, let her go to the *utmost* short of *actual* adultery—show that her danger is in her ignorance of the great distinctions of which Dr. T—— speaks. Show us how such a husband can save such a wife and turn the influence of sex to its intended beneficent end. I trust I need not say that my suggestion that she go *very very* far is not for the sake of scenes of passion, but that readers may be helped whose self respect is shipwrecked or near it because *they* have gone far and are saying "I might as well go all the way. . . ."

If I can do anything for you pray command me. I know publish-

---

3. English philosopher of evolutionary theory (1820–1903).

ers, translators, &c, &c. I shall go to Montreux in December at latest, but the address at the beginning will always find me.

With every best wish,

JANET SCAMMON YOUNG

Langham Hotel
London
5. Oct. 99

My dear Lady Janet:

It is commonplace to say that I am indebted to you for a great pleasure in the loan of that remarkable book *The Awakening*. I have read it twice—once at a sitting when I ought to have been asleep, and again more deliberately in my brougham. Doubtless it will be published over here, but I am having my bookseller get two copies of the American edition—one for Crestwood and one for town. It is easily the book of the year. The ending reminds one of *The Open Question*,[4] but how vastly superior in power, ethic and wit is this newer novel.

You accuse "Kate Chopin" (a pen name I suppose) of an unnecessary tragedy. My dear Lady Janet, the authoress took the world as it is, as all art must—and 'twas inevitable that poor dear *Edna*, being noble, and having Pontellier for husband, and Arobin for lover, and average women for friends, should die.

My wrath is not toward "Kate Chopin" at all. That which makes *The Awakening* legitimate is that the author deals with the commonest of human experiences. You fancy *Edna's* case exceptional? Trust an old doctor—most common. It is only that *Edna* was nobler, and took that last clean swim. The others live. Not all meet *Arobin* or *Robert*. The essence of the matter lies in the accursed stupidity of men. They marry a girl, she becomes a mother. They imagine she has sounded the heights and depths of womanhood. Poor fools! She is not even awakened. She, on her part is a victim of the abominable prudishness which masquerades as modesty or virtue. Every great and beautiful fact of nature has a vile counterfeit. The counterfeit of goodness is self-righteousness—of true modesty, prudishness. The law, spoken or implied, which governs the upbringing of girls is that passion is disgraceful. It is to be assumed that a self respecting female has it not. In so far as normally constituted womanhood *must* take account of *something* sexual, it is called "love." It was inevitable, therefore, that *Edna* should call her feeling for *Robert* love. It was as simply & purely passion as her

---

4. *The Open Question: A Tale of Two Temperaments*, by C. E. Raimond, pseudonym for Elizabeth Robbins, American actress who was famed for her portrayal of Ibsen's roles in London during the 1890s. (New York and London: Harper, 1899).

feeling for *Arobin*. "Kate Chopin" would not admit that. Being (I assume) a woman, she too would reserve the word love for *Edna's* feeling for *Robert*.

The especial point of a wife's danger when her beautiful, God given womanhood awakes, is that she will save her self-respect by imagining herself in love with the awakener. She should be taught by her husband to distinguish between passion and love. Then she is safe, invulnerable. Even if, at the worst she "falls"—she will rise again.

It is inevitable, natural, and therefore clean and harmless, that a normal, beautifully constituted married woman will be stirred in her passional being by the men between whom and herself there is that mysterious affinity of the real nature of which we know nothing. If she calls that stirring of her nature "love" she is lost. If she knows perfectly well that it is passion; if she esteems and respects her passional capacity as she does her capacity to be moved by a song or a sonnet, or a great poem, or a word nobly said—she is safe. She knows that that thing *is*. She is no more ashamed of it than of her responsiveness to any other great appeal. She knows that it does not touch her wife-life, her mother-life, her self-hood. It is not "naughty."

A wise husband (there are some) is at no point so loving and tenderly wise at this point. A cad or a cur is (God save the mark) *jealous*. If his wife is weak she quails, and hides from men or shelters herself in a pretended indifference. If she is strong she resents the monstrous insult of his suspicion. I am happier over nothing in my professional life than that I have helped many *men* at this point—many men, many women. I have said to more than one man: "Your wife's nature is stirring; lovingly help her. Let her see that you know it and like it; and that you distinguish perfectly between her *heart*, her wifely loyalty, and her body—make her distinguish it too."

But I weary you. This book has stirred me to the soul. *Edna* is like a personal friend. She is not impure. The art, the local colour, the distinctness of characterisation of even the minor personages are something wonderful.

Thanking you again, dear Lady Janet,

I am as ever yours faithfully

DUNROBIN THOMSON

Chopin's "Retraction"†

The Awakening

BY KATE CHOPIN

Having a group of people at my disposal, I thought it might be entertaining (to myself) to throw them together and see what would happen. I never dreamed of Mrs. Pontellier making such a mess of things and working out her own damnation as she did. If I had had the slightest intimation of such a thing I would have excluded her from the company. But when I found out what she was up to, the play was half over and it was then too late.

St. Louis, Mo.,
May 28, 1899

KATE CHOPIN

† From "Aims and Autographs of Authors," *Book News*, XVII (July, 1899), 612.

In response to adverse criticism of the novel, Chopin published this "tongue-in-cheek" note. [*Editor.*]

Essays in Criticism

PERCIVAL POLLARD

[The Unlikely Awakening of a Married Woman] †

* * * "The Awakening" asked us to believe that a young woman who had been several years married, and had borne children, had never, in all that time, been properly "awake." It would be an arresting question for students of sleep-walking; but one must not venture down that bypath now. Her name was Edna Pontellier. She was married to a man who had Creole blood in him; yet the marrying, and the having children, and all the rest of it, had left her still slumbrous, still as innocent of her physical self, as the young girl who graduates in the early summer would have us believe she is. She was almost at the age that Balzac[1] held so dangerous—almost she was the Woman of Thirty—yet she had not properly tasted the apple of knowledge. She had to wait until she met a young man who was not her husband, was destined to tarry until she was under the influence of a Southern moonlight and the whispers of the Gulf and many other passionate things, before there began in her the first faint flushings of desire. So, at any rate, Kate Chopin asked us to believe.

The cynic was forced to observe that simply because a young woman showed interest in a man who was not her husband, especially at a fashionable watering-place, in a month when the blood was hottest, there was no need to argue the aforesaid fair female had lain coldly dormant all her life. There are women in the world quite as versatile as the butterfly, and a sprouting of the physical today need not mean that yesterday was all spiritual.

However, taking Kate Chopin's word for it that Edna had been asleep, her awakening was a most champagne-like performance. After she met Robert Lebrun the awakening stirred in her, to use a rough simile, after the manner of ferment in new wine. Robert would, I fancy, at any Northern summer resort have been sure of a lynching; for, after a trifling encounter with him, Edna became utterly unmanageable. She neglected her house; she tried to paint—

† From Percival Pollard, *Their Day in Court* (New York and Washington: Neale Publishing, 1909), pp. 41–45. Footnotes are by the editor.

1. Honoré de Balzac (1799–1850), a master of the French novel. In 1841 he published a novel called *La Femme de Trente Ans* [The Woman of Thirty].

always a bad sign, that, when women want to paint, or act, or sing, or write!—and the while she painted there was "a subtle current of desire passing through her body, weakening her hold upon the brushes and making her eyes burn."

* * *

All this, mind you, with Robert merely a reminiscence. If the mere memory of him made her weak, what must the touch of him have done? Fancy shrinks at so volcanic a scene. Ah, these sudden awakenings of women, of women who prefer the dead husband to the quick,[2] of women who accept the croupier's[3] caresses while waiting for hubby to come up for the week-end, and of women who have been in a trance, though married! Especially the awakenings of women like Edna!

We were asked to believe that Edna was devoid of coquetry; that she did not know the cheap delights of promiscuous conquests; though sometimes on the street glances from strange eyes lingered in her memory, disturbing her. Well, then those are the women to look out for—those women so easily disturbed by the unfamiliar eye. Those women do not seem to care, once they are awake, so much for the individual as for what he represents. Consider Edna. It was Robert who awoke her. But, when he went away, it was another who continued the arousal. Do you think Edna cared whether it was Robert or Arobin? Not a bit. Arobin's kiss upon her hand acted on her like a narcotic, causing her to sleep "a languorous sleep, interwoven with vanishing dreams." You see, she was something of a quick-change sleep-artist: first she slept; a look at Robert awakened her; Arobin's kiss sent her off into dreamland again; a versatile somnambulist, this. Yet she must have been embarrassing; you could never have known just when you had her in a trance or out of it.

How wonderful, how magical those Creole kisses of Arobin's must have been, if one of them, upon the hand, could send Edna to sleep! What might another sort of kiss have done? One shivers thinking of it; one has uncanny visions of a beautiful young woman all ablaze with passion as with a robe of fire. Arobin, however, had no such fears. He continued gaily to awake Edna—or to send her to sleep; our author was never clear which was which!—and it was not long before he was allowed to talk to her in a way that pleased her, "appealing to the animalism that stirred impatiently within her." One wonders what he said! It was not long before a kiss was permitted Arobin. "She clasped his head, holding his lips to hers. It was the first kiss of her life to which her nature had really responded. It was a flaming torch that kindled desire."

2. The living.
3. Croupier: one who stands second, usually used in reference to one who runs a gambling table.

Ah, these married women, who have never, by some strange
chance, had the flaming torch applied, how they do flash out when
the right moment comes! This heroine, after that first flaming torch,
went to her finish with lightning speed. She took a walk with
Arobin, and paused, mentally, to notice "the black line of his leg
moving in and out so close to her against the yellow shimmer of her
gown." She let the young man sit down beside her, let him caress
her, and they did not "say good-night until she had become supple
to his gentle seductive entreaties."

To think of Kate Chopin, who once contented herself with mild
yarns about genteel Creole life—pages almost clean enough to put
into the Sunday school library, abreast of Geo. W. Cable's stories[4]
—blowing us a hot blast like that! Well, San Francisco, and Paris,
and London, and New York had furnished Women Who Did; why
not New Orleans?

*   *   *

It may seem indelicate, in view of where we left Edna, to return
to her at once; we must let some little time elapse. Imagine, then,
that time elapsed, and Robert returned. He did not know that
Arobin had been taking a hand in Edna's awakening. Robert had
gone away, it seems, because he scrupled to love Edna, she being
married. But Edna had no scruples left; she hastened to intimate to
Robert that she loved him, that her husband meant nothing to her.
Never, by any chance, did she mention Arobin. But, dear me,
Arobin, to a woman like that, had been merely an incident; he
merely happened to hold the torch. Now, what in the world do you
suppose that Robert did? Went away—pouff!—like that! Went
away, saying he loved Edna too well to—well, to partake of the fire
the other youth had lit. Think of it! Edna finally awake—
completely, fiercely awake—and the man she had waked up for
goes away!

Of course, she went and drowned herself. She realised that you
can only put out fire with water, if all other chemical engines go
away. She realised that the awakening was too great; that she was
too aflame; that it was now merely Man, not Robert or Arobin, that
she desired. So she took an infinite dip in the passionate Gulf.

Ah, what a hiss, what a fiery splash, there must have been in
those warm waters of the South! But—what a pity that poor Pontellier, Edna's husband, never knew that his wife was in a trance all
their wedded days, and that he was away at the moment of her
awakening! *   *   *

---

4. Contemporary of Kate Chopin who wrote novels and stories of Creole life.

DANIEL S. RANKIN

[Influences Upon the Novel] †

* * * What is most curious and valuable to consider, is the relationship between Kate Chopin's life and her study of the feminine mind in *The Awakening*. The author's imagination, as a very young girl, through the zeal and the story-telling propensity of her great-grandmother, had been saturated with a keen interest in woman's nature, and its mysterious vagaries. This curiosity never dimmed.

I believe *The Awakening* had its origin in these story-telling days of impressionable youth. I have no doubt Kate Chopin's sympathies in the stories told her by Madame Victoria Charleville were with Madame Chouteau.[1] One review suggested that her sympathies in *The Awakening* were with Edna (*The Los Angeles Times*, June 25, 1899). I believe they were.

More important than the consideration of the influence of curiosity aroused in youth, is the endeavor to discriminate and discover the literary influences that engendered *The Awakening*. The novel may be similar to D'Annunzio's *Triumph of Death*,[2] Edna may be "la femme de trente ans" whose dangerous attractions Marcel Proust admirably displayed,[3] but it is also possible to decide that Kate Chopin was influenced by Beardsley's hideous and haunting pictures, with their disfiguring leer of sensuality,[4] yet carrying a distinguishing strength and grace and individuality.

An exposition of an author as nothing but a synthesis of influences, strong and sharply defined as links in a chain, does more credit to an investigator's industry and intimate acquaintance with fiction than to a sense of perspective, and to what I must call, for want of a more comprehensive phrase, a knowledge of literary

† From Daniel S. Rankin, *Kate Chopin and Her Creole Stories* (Philadelphia: University of Pennsylvania Press, 1932), pp. 173–175.
This first biography of Chopin, though containing a number of inaccuracies, is invaluable in its collection of remembrances from Chopin contemporaries. The footnotes are by the editor.
1. Victoria Verdon Charleville (1780–1863), Kate O'Flaherty's maternal great-grandmother, was a contemporary of the first settlers of St. Louis and delighted in telling the young Kate stories and legends about the founding of the city. Marie Thérèse Chouteau, the subject of one of these stories, left her husband after the birth of their son Auguste and formed an unsanctioned but

widely approved union with Pierre Laclède, the founder of St. Louis, by whom she had four children.
2. Gabriele D'Annunzio (1863–1938), Italian novelist, author of *Triumph of Death*, a novel about extramarital love which ends with the death of the lovers in the sea.
3. "The woman of thirty." Odette de Crecy Swan in *Remembrance of Things Past*, by Marcel Proust (1871–1922), may be the woman alluded to. More likely is that Rankin took the idea from Pollard, who more precisely attributes the phrase to Balzac. See note 1, p. 160.
4. Rankin is incorporating the idea and the phraseology of the review which appeared in the Los Angeles *Sunday Times*. See p. 152.

psychology. Kate Chopin was an original genius. Her story may be similar to any number of novels, but all suggestion of direct literary descent in method or manner of treatment is false. Literary influences are deceptive at best, and in the case of Kate Chopin no single author can be said to have contributed the weightiest influential impetus to *The Awakening*. She was a great reader, a contemporary mind. She absorbed the atmosphere and the mood of the ending of the century, as that ending is reflected in Continental European art and literature. Perhaps in St. Louis she was closest in touch with the tendencies of the century's ending—in music, poetry, fiction. She was not imitative in the narrow sense of being completely under the sway of any one writer, but the range of her debts is wide: Flaubert, Tolstoi, Turgénieff, D'Annunzio, Bourget, especially de Maupassant, all contributed to her broad and diverse culture.[5]

The Awakening follows the current of erotic morbidity that flowed strongly through the literature of the last two decades of the nineteenth century. The end of the century became a momentary dizziness over an abyss of voluptuousness, and Kate Chopin in St. Louis experienced a partial attack of the prevailing artistic vertigo. The philosophy of Schopenhauer, the music of Wagner, the Russian novel, Maeterlinck's plays—all this she absorbed.[6] *The Awakening* in her case is the result—an impression of life as a delicious agony of longing.

In *The Awakening* under her touch the Creole life of Louisiana glowed with a rich exotic beauty. The very atmosphere of the book is voluptuous, the atmosphere of the Gulf Coast, a place of strange and passionate moods.

The mania for the exotic that fed upon evocations of a barbaric past—Salome's dance, Cleopatra's luxury, the splendor and cruelty of Salammbo's Carthage[7]—gave energy to the creation in this coun-

5. Gustave Flaubert (1828–1880), French novelist whose *Madame Bovary* has been thought by a number of critics, the first of whom was Willa Cather, to be the model for Chopin's novel. Leo Tolstoy (1828–1910), Russian novelist best known for his *War and Peace* and *Anna Karenina*. He wrote a novel originally entitled *The Awakening* which was published serially in *The Cosmopolitan*; the title was changed to *The Resurrection* when it was published in book form (Rankin, p. 177). Ivan Turgénieff (Turgenev), Russian novelist (1818–1883) best known for his *Fathers and Children*. Paul Bourget (1852–1935), French psychological novelist. Guy de Maupassant (1850–1893), French writer whom Chopin particularly admired; she translated four of his short pieces. He wrote a short sketch also entitled "The Awakening."
6. Arthur Schopenhauer (1788–1860), German philosopher known for his dark vision of the human condition. Richard Wagner (1813–1883), German composer of elaborate operas based on Nordic and Teutonic mythology. Maurice Maeterlinck (1862–1949), Belgian writer best known for his symbolic dramas. Rankin is not suggesting any specific influence, but rather the excesses which were thought to be characteristic of the end of the century.
7. Salome, a Biblical figure who danced for Herod and demanded the head of John the Baptist as a reward. Oscar Wilde's play (1894) on the subject suggests Salome's romantic attachment to the Baptist. Cleopatra, queen of Egypt from 69 b.c. to 30 b.c., figures in plays by Shakespeare and Dryden and in George Bernard Shaw's *Caesar and Cleopatra* (1900). *Salammbo* (1862) is a novel by Flaubert set in ancient Carthage.

try of two works dealing with southern Louisiana, Lafcadio Hearn's *Chita*[8] and Kate Chopin's *The Awakening*. These books owe nothing to each other. They are derived from a common source.

The Awakening is exotic in setting, morbid in theme, erotic in motivation.

Kate Chopin felt most profoundly and expressed most poignantly in *The Awakening* facts about life which to her were important, facts which easily might be overlooked, she thought. Being a woman she saw life instinctively in terms of the individual. She took a direct, personal, immediate interest in the intimate personal affairs of Edna's daily life and changing moods. But the questions arise, "Is it at all important? Did Kate Chopin by her art reveal a fresh beauty or vision or aspiration?" In all earnestness she meant *The Awakening* to be something more than literature, more than the mere art of writing, more than a pleasant help for the passing of leisure hours!

The reader, following Edna as she walks for the last time down to the beach at Grand Isle—well, what does he feel? Merely that human nature can be a sickening reality. Then the insistent query comes—*cui bono?*[9]

KENNETH EBLE

A Forgotten Novel†

* * * The claim of the book upon the reader's attention is simple. It is a first-rate novel. The justification for urging its importance is that we have few enough novels of its stature. One could add that it is advanced in theme and technique over the novels of its day, and that it anticipates in many respects the modern novel. It could be claimed that it adds to American fiction an example of what Gide called the *roman pur*,[1] a kind of novel not characteristic of American writing. One could offer the book as evidence that the regional writer can go beyond the limitations of regional material. But these matters aside, what recommends the novel is its general excellence.

It is surprising that the book has not been picked up today by

8. Lafcadio Hearn (1850–1904), American journalist and novelist whose *Chita* (1887) concerns a young Creole girl who survives a mid-century hurricane on Grand Isle.
9. The expression, meaning "what's the use?", was first used in relation to the novel by Frances Porcher. See note 1, p. 145.
† From Kenneth Eble, "A Forgotten

Novel: Kate Chopin's *The Awakening*," *Western Humanities Review*, X (Summer 1956), 261–269. Footnotes are by the editor.
1. Andre Gide (1869–1951), French writer and critic. The phrase *roman pur*, the "pure novel," distinguishes the work from other forms of the genre such as *roman à thèse*, the "novel with a purpose."

reprint houses long on lurid covers and short on new talent. The nature of its theme, which had much to do with its adverse reception in 1899, would offer little offense today. In a way, the novel is an American *Bovary*, though such a designation is not precisely accurate. Its central character is similar: the married woman who seeks love outside a stuffy, middle-class marriage. It is similar too in the definitive way it portrays the mind of a woman trapped in marriage and seeking fulfillment of what she vaguely recognizes as her essential nature. The husband, Léonce Pontellier, is a businessman whose nature and preoccupations are not far different from those of Charles Bovary. There is a Léon Dupuis in Robert Lebrun, a Rodolphe Boulanger in Alcée Arobin. And too, like *Madame Bovary*, the novel handles its material superbly well. Kate Chopin herself was probably more than any other American writer of her time under French influence. Her background was French-Irish; she married a Creole; she read and spoke French and knew contemporary French literature well; she associated both in St. Louis and Louisiana with families of French ancestry and disposition. But despite the similarities and the possible influences, the novel, chiefly because of the independent character of its heroine, Edna Pontellier, and because of the intensity of the focus upon her, is not simply a good but derivative work. It has a manner and matter of its own.

Quite frankly, the book is about sex. Not only is it about sex, but the very texture of the writing is sensuous, if not sensual, from the first to the last. Even as late as 1932, Chopin's biographer, Daniel Rankin, seemed somewhat shocked by it. He paid his respects to the artistic excellence of the book, but he was troubled by "that insistent query—*cui bono?*" He called the novel "exotic in setting, morbid in theme, erotic in motivation." One questions the accuracy of these terms, and even more the moral disapproval implied in their usage. One regrets that Mr. Rankin did not emphasize that the book was amazingly honest, perceptive and moving.

* * *

Kate Chopin, almost from her first story, had the ability to capture character, to put the right word in the mouth, to impart the exact gesture, to select the characteristic action. An illustration of her deftness in handling even minor characters is her treatment of Edna's father. When he leaves the Pontelliers' after a short visit, Edna is glad to be rid of him and "his padded shoulders, his Bible reading, his 'toddies,' and ponderous oaths." A moment later, it is a side of Edna's nature which is revealed. She felt a sense of relief at her father's absence; "she read Emerson until she grew sleepy."

Characterization was always Mrs. Chopin's talent. Structure was not. Those who knew her working habits say that she seldom revised, and she herself mentions that she did not like reworking her stories. Though her reputation rests upon her short narratives, her collected stories give abundant evidence of the sketch, the outlines of stories which remain unformed. And when she did attempt a tightly organized story, she often turned to Maupassant and was as likely as not to effect a contrived symmetry. Her early novel *At Fault* suffers most from her inability to control her material. In *The Awakening* she is in complete command of structure. She seems to have grasped instinctively the use of the unifying symbol—there the sea, sky and sand—and with it the power of individual images to bind the story together.

The sea, the sand, the sun and sky of the Gulf Coast become almost a presence themselves in the novel. Much of the sensuousness of the book comes from the way the reader is never allowed to stray far from the water's edge. A refrain beginning "The voice of the sea is seductive, never ceasing, clamoring, murmuring, . . ." is used throughout the novel. It appears first at the beginning of Edna Pontellier's awakening, and it appears at the end as the introduction to the long final scene, previously quoted. Looking closely at the final form of this refrain, one can notice the care with which Mrs. Chopin composed this theme and variation. In the initial statement, the sentence does not end with "solitude," but goes on, as it should, "to lose itself in mazes of inward contemplation." Nor is the image of the bird with the broken wing in the earlier passage; rather there is a prefiguring of the final tragedy: "The voice of the sea speaks to the soul. The touch of the sea is sensuous, enfolding the body in its soft close embrace." The way scene, mood, action and character are fused reminds one not so much of literature as of an impressionist painting, of a Renoir[2] with much of the sweetness missing. Only Stephen Crane,[3] among her American contemporaries, had an equal sensitivity to light and shadow, color and texture, had the painter's eye matched with the writer's perception of character and incident.

The best example of Mrs. Chopin's use of a visual image which is also highly symbolic is the lady in black and the two nameless lovers. They are seen as touches of paint upon the canvas and as indistinct yet evocative figures which accompany Mrs. Pontellier and Robert Lebrun during the course of their intimacy. They appear first early in the novel. "The lady in black was reading her morning devotions on the porch of a neighboring bath house. Two young lovers were exchanging their heart's yearning beneath the

---

2. Pierre-Auguste Renoir (1841–1919), French impressionist painter.
3. Stephen Crane (1871–1900), American novelist and short-story writer whose *The Red Badge of Courage* introduced the "stream of consciousness" novel to America in 1895.

children's tent which they had found unoccupied." Throughout the course of Edna's awakening, these figures appear and reappear, the lovers entering the pension, leaning toward each other as the water-oaks bent from the sea, the lady in black, creeping behind them. They accompany Edna and Robert when they first go to the Chêni-ère, "the lovers, shoulder to shoulder, creeping, the lady in black, gaining steadily upon them." When Robert departs from Mexico, the picture changes. Lady and lovers depart together, and Edna finds herself back from the sea and shore, and set among her human acquaintances, her husband; her father; Mme. Reisz, the musician, "a homely woman with a small wizened face and body, and eyes that glowed"; Alcée Arobin; Mme. Ragtinolle; and others. One brief scene from this milieu will further illustrate Mrs. Chopin's conscious or unconscious symbolism.

The climax of Edna's relationship with Arobin is the dinner which is to celebrate her last night in her and her husband's house. Edna is ready to move to a small place around the corner where she can escape (though she does not phrase it this way) the feeling that she is one more of Léonce Pontellier's possessions. At the dinner Victor Lebrun, Robert's brother, begins singing, "Ah! si tu savais!" a song which brings back all her memories of Robert. She sets her glass so blindly down that she shatters it against the carafe. "The wine spilled over Arobin's legs and some of it trickled down upon Mrs. Highcamp's black gauze gown." After the other guests have gone, Edna and Arobin walk to the new house. Mrs. Chopin writes of Edna, "She looked down, noticing the black line of his leg moving in and out so close to her against the yellow shimmer of her gown." The chapter concludes:

> His hand had strayed to her beautiful shoulders, and he could feel the response of her flesh to his touch. He seated himself beside her and kissed her lightly upon the shoulder.
> "I thought you were going away," she said, in an uneven voice.
> "I am, after I have said good night."
> "Good night," she murmured.
> He did not answer, except to continue to caress her. He did not say good night until she had become supple to his gentle, seductive entreaties.

It is not surprising that the sensuous quality of the book, both from the incidents of the novel and the symbolic implications, would have offended contemporary reviewers. What convinced many critics of the indecency of the book, however, was not simply the sensuous scenes, but rather that the author obviously sympathized with Mrs. Pontellier. More than that, the readers probably found that she aroused their own sympathies.

It is a letter from an English reader which states most clearly, in a matter-of-fact way, the importance of Edna Pontellier. The letter was to Kate Chopin from Lady Janet Scammon Young, and included a more interesting analysis of the novel by Dr. Dunrobin Thomson, a London physician whom Lady Janet said a great editor had called "the soundest critic since Matthew Arnold."[4] "That which makes *The Awakening* legitimate," Dr. Thomson wrote, "is that the author deals with the commonest of human experiences. You fancy *Edna's* case exceptional? Trust an old doctor—most common." He goes on to speak of the "abominable prudishness" masquerading as "modesty or virtue," which makes the woman who marries a victim. For passion is regarded as disgraceful and the self-respecting female assumes she does not possess passion. "In so far as normally constituted womanhood *must* take account of something *sexual*," he points out, "it is called love." But marital love and passion may not be one. The wise husband, Dr. Thomson advises, seeing within his wife the "mysterious affinity" between a married woman and a man who stirs her passions, will help her see the distinction between her heart and her love, which wifely loyalty owes to the husband, and her body, which yearns for awakening. But more than clinically analyzing the discrepancy between Victorian morals and woman's nature, Dr. Thomson testifies that Mrs. Chopin has not been false or sensational to no purpose. He does not feel that she has corrupted, nor does he regard the warring within Edna's self as insignificant.

Greek tragedy—to remove ourselves from Victorian morals—knew well *eros*[5] was not the kind of *love* which can be easily prettified and sentimentalized. Phaedra's struggle with elemental passion in the *Hippolytus*[6] is not generally regarded as being either morally offensive or insignificant. Mrs. Pontellier, too, has the power, the dignity, the self-possession of a tragic heroine. She is not an Emma Bovary, deluded by ideas of "romance," nor is she the sensuous but guilt-ridden woman of the sensational novel. We can find only partial reason for her affair in the kind of romantic desire to escape a middle-class existence which animates Emma Bovary. Edna Pontellier is neither deluded nor deludes. She is woman, the physical woman who, despite her Kentucky Presbyterian upbringing and a comfortable marriage, must struggle with the sensual appeal of physical ripeness itself, with passion of which she is only dimly aware. Her struggle is not melodramatic, nor is it artificial, nor vapid. It is objective, real and moving. And when she walks into the sea, it does not leave a reader with the sense of sin punished, but

4. See page 155 for the complete letters.
5. Passionate love, after the Greek god Eros.
6. Euripides' play *Hippolytus*, in which

Phaedra, wife of Theseus, is made to fall passionately in love with Hippolytus by Aphrodite, who is angry because Hippolytus has scorned the love of women.

rather with the sense evoked by Edwin Arlington Robinson's *Eros Turannos:*[7]

> . . . for they
> That with a god have striven
> Not hearing much of what we say,
> Take what the god has given;
> Though like waves breaking it may be,
> Or like a changed familiar tree,
> Or like a stairway to the sea
> Where down the blind are driven.

How wrong to call Edna, as Daniel Rankin does, "a selfish, capricious" woman. Rather, Edna's struggle, the struggle with *eros* itself, is farthest removed from capriciousness. It is her self-awareness, and her awakening into a greater degree of self-awareness than those around her can comprehend, which gives her story dignity and significance.

Our advocacy of the novel is not meant to obscure its faults. It is not perfect art, but in total effect it provokes few dissatisfactions. A sophisticated modern reader might find something of the derivative about it. Kate Chopin read widely, and a list of novelists she found interesting would include Flaubert, Tolstoy, Turgenev, D'Annunzio, Bourget, Goncourt and Zola. It is doubtful, however, that there was any direct borrowing, and *The Awakening* exists, as do most good novels, as a product of the author's literary, real, and imagined life.

How Mrs. Chopin managed to create in ten years the substantial body of work she achieved is no less a mystery than the excellence of *The Awakening* itself. But, having added to American literature a novel uncommon in its kind as in its excellence, she deserves not to be forgotten. *The Awakening* deserves to be restored and to be given its place among novels worthy of preservation.

MARIE FLETCHER

[The Southern Woman in Fiction][†]

* * * Kate Chopin's most ambitious work is *The Awakening*, a novel which tells of the awakening of Edna Pontellier from the easy comfort of a marriage of convenience to a realization of what she

---

7. Edwin Arlington Robinson (1869–1935), American poet. His "Eros Turannos," about a woman's life-experience with *eros*, is from his volume *The Man Against the Sky* (1916).

† From Marie Fletcher, "The Southern Woman in the Fiction of Kate Chopin," *Louisiana History*, VII (Spring 1966), 117–32. Author's footnotes deleted.

considers to be the deeper needs of her soul. Edna, a Kentucky Presbyterian, has impetuously and somewhat rebelliously married the Louisiana Creole, Léonce Pontellier. It is suggested that the marriage was purely an accident, a decree of Fate, for it is "his absolute devotion" and "the violent opposition of her father and her sister Margaret to her marriage with a Catholic" that led Edna to accept Léonce. But as subsequent developments in the novel reveal, Edna's first "rebellion" was only one of many. Indeed, her entire life is a flight from one kind of confinement after another.

In an account of a summer vacation on Grand Isle, Mrs. Pontellier is sharply contrasted with the other New Orleans matrons so that the qualities of Creole wives and mothers are emphasized. She is definitely not one of the "mother women" who prevail on the island:

> It was easy to know them, fluttering about with extended, protecting wings when any harm, real or imaginary, threatened their brood. They were women who idolized their children, worshiped their husbands, and esteemed it a holy privilege to efface themselves as individuals and grow wings as ministering angels.

One of these mothers, Adele Ratignolle, is "the embodiment of every womanly grace and charm." With her beauty "flaming and apparent," she is like "the bygone heroines of romance and the fair lady of our dreams." She has spun-gold hair hanging loose, sapphire blue eyes, lips like cherries or other delicious crimson fruit, soft white skin, slender hands and arms. The fact that she is growing a little stout does not detract from her poise and grace. Her exquisite hands draw attention as she threads her needle or adjusts her gold thimble to sew on night-drawers for her children. Even when she visits, Adele takes her sewing with her; and though Edna is not concerned about winter garments for her sons, in order not to appear unamiable, she cuts a pattern for their drawers. Unlike the French ladies, she cannot devote herself exclusively to her husband and children. She hugs her sons passionately one moment and then forgets them the next; she is even gratified by their occasional absence. Edna is willing to give her time and her money but not her inner self to her family.

Mrs. Pontellier, intimately associated with a group of Creoles for the first time, is impressed forcibly by their "entire absence of prudery. Their freedom of expression was at first incomprehensible to her, though she had no difficulty in reconciling it with a lofty chastity which in the Creole woman seems to be inborn and unmistakable." A book openly read and discussed by the others, Edna feels compelled to read only in secret. Like most Creole women, Madame Ratignolle has a baby about every two years. During this summer she talks constantly about her "condition," though her pregnancy—her fourth in seven years—is in no way apparent and no one would have known about it had she not persisted in making it a topic of conversation. Even the young Creole Robert Lebrun joins in until he notices the color mount into Mrs. Pontellier's face. After that, when she arrives, he even stops the amusing stories he often tells the married women.

Always "self-contained," Edna "was not accustomed to an outward and spoken expression of affection, either in herself or in others," and hardly knows how to accept the spontaneous caresses of her French associates. In fact, one reason she grew fond of her husband was her "realizing with some unaccountable satisfaction that no trace of passion or excessive and fictitious warmth colored her affection, thereby threatening its dissolution."

* * *

She is not like the Creole women in being able to continue as a long-suffering, self-sacrificing, faithful, and loyal wife and mother when love is gone. She is also unable—perhaps because of her Protestant rigidity, anarchic individualism, pride, and conscience— to live on and enjoy the fuller, happier life of which her "awakening" has made her aware. For love, of which she is now capable, is also a threat to selfhood, which she still cannot surrender. The easy-going, relaxed Creole women, with their South European Catholic background, function as norms against which to contrast Edna's little drama of revolt first against the life for which her ancestry and rearing designed her and then her final escape from the consequences of repudiating this life and learning about a more complete existence. Her suicide is the last in a series of rebellions which structure her life, give it pathos, and make of the novel a study in contrasting cultures (as well as an interpretation of the "new woman").

* * * the Creole girl lives to become a Creole wife; she should marry once, and, once married, she should be a devoted and dutiful wife even though her husband and her life in general may prove anything but ideal. With their assumption that marriage is of supreme importance, these women see no happiness, actually no real existence, without marriage; and most of them are wed young. To satisfy her strong maternal instinct, it was assumed that a women should by all means have children to complete the family. If she is unable to marry or if she marries and has no children, she feels the lack very deeply.

Though the heroines of Kate Chopin's local color fiction have some of the characteristics of the traditional lady, changes are already appearing. However, Edna Pontellier, a Southerner, though a

Kentucky Protestant rather than a Creole Roman Catholic, is the only one of the heroines who finds and likes personal independence. The irony is that to keep from relinquishing it she has to commit suicide. Sexually awakened as she is, she cannot bear to live on as the wife of Léonce Pontellier; Robert Leburn does not really want her; and with Alcée Arobin there is no feeling of companionship, only sexual satisfaction about which she has a sense of guilt because of her feeling that she has betrayed Robert.

The most unchanging quality in Southern heroines is the ideal of chastity. In spite of her realism, or perhaps because if it, Kate Chopin, throughout her work, upholds the Creole belief in the purity of womanhood and those other aspects of the feminine mystique and Southern cult of family which follow from it. There is "modern" honesty in her treatment of human situations, such as Edna Pontellier's awakening, her need for fulfillment, and her inability to live on with her husband in a hypocritical relationship. Emotional realism notwithstanding, Mrs. Chopin's fictional treatment of French Louisiana is illustrative of the truth of the old adage, well known amongst them, that the more some things change, the more they stay the same.

LARZER ZIFF

From *The American 1890s*†

* * * The community about which she wrote was one in which respectable women took wine with their dinner and brandy after it, smoked cigarettes, played Chopin sonatas, and listened to the men tell risqué stories. It was, in short, far more French than American, and Mrs. Chopin reproduced this little world with no specific intent to shock or make a point, as did, for instance, Frederic, who was straining after a specific effect when he posed his Celia Madden at the piano with a cigarette.[1] Rather, these were for Mrs. Chopin the conditions of civility, and, since they were so French, a magazine public accustomed to accepting naughtiness from that quarter and taking pleasure in it on those terms raised no protest. But for Mrs. Chopin they were only outward signs of a culture that was hers and had its inner effects in the moral make-up of her characters. Though she seldom turned her plot on these facts, she showed that her

† From Larzer Ziff, *The American 1890s: Life and Times of a Lost Generation* (New York: Viking Press, 1966), pp. 297–305. Author's footnotes have been renumbered.

1. Celia Madden is an innocent Irish-Catholic girl in the 1896 novel *The Damnation of Theron Ware*, written by Harold Frederic (1856–1898). [*Editor.*]

women were capable of loving more than one man at a time and were not only attractive but sexually attracted also.

The quality of daily life in Kate Chopin's Nachitoches[2] is genial and kind. People openly like one another, enjoy life, and savor its sensual riches. Their likes and their dislikes are held passionately, so that action bears a close and apparent relation to feeling. In setting a character, Mrs. Chopin writes, "Grégoire loved women. He liked their nearness, their atmosphere; the tones of their voices and the things they said; their ways of moving and turning about; the brushing of their garments when they passed him by pleased him."[3] This open delight in the difference between the sexes was not a mentionable feeling until Mrs. Chopin brought to American literature a setting in which it could be demonstrated with an open geniality.

* * *

Like *Madame Bovary*, *The Awakening* is about the adulterous experiments of a married woman, and while Mrs. Chopin did not have to go to Flaubert for the theme, she obviously was indebted to him for it as well as for the masterful economy of setting and character and the precision of style which she here achieved. Sarah Orne Jewett had also been an admirer of *Madame Bovary* and had defended Flaubert's theme by saying that "a master writer gives everything weight."[4] But she had drawn quite a different moral from the novel. Miss Jewett wrote of Emma Bovary: "She is such a lesson to dwellers in country towns, who drift out of relation to their surroundings, not only social, but the very companionship of nature, unknown to them."[5] Emma Bovary is a foolish, bored woman, while Mrs. Chopin's Edna Pontellier is an intelligent, nervous woman, but Edna's salvation is not to be found in drifting back into relation with her environment. Rather, the questions Mrs. Chopin raises through her are what sort of nature she, twenty-eight years of age, married to a rich man and the mother of two children, possesses, and how her life is related to the dynamics of her inner self. Sarah Jewett counseled sublimation; Kate Chopin pursued self-discovery and counseled not at all.

* * *

The Awakening was the most important piece of fiction about the sexual life of a woman written to date in America, and the first fully to face the fact that marriage, whether in point of fact it closed the range of a woman's sexual experiences or not, was but an episode in

2. Oldest town in Louisiana, in the parish of the same name located in the central part of the state. Chopin lived with her husband in Cloutierville, Natchitoches Parish, from 1879 until his death. Many of her short stories are set here. [*Editor.*]

3. *Bayou Folk* (Boston: Houghton

Mifflin, 1894), p. 86.

4. Sarah Orne Jewett, *Letters*, ed. by Annie Fields (Boston, 1911), p. 86. [Jewett (1849–1909) wrote short stories set in Maine, the best-known volume of which is *The Country of the Pointed Firs* (1896).—*Editor.*]

5. Ibid., pp. 82–3.

her continuous growth. It did not attack the institution of the family, but it rejected the family as the automatic equivalent of feminine self-fulfillment, and on the very eve of the twentieth century it raised the question of what woman was to do with the freedom she struggled toward. The Creole woman's acceptance of maternity as totally adequate to the capacities of her nature carried with it the complements of a fierce chastity, a frankness of speech on sexual matters, a mature ease among men, and a frank and unguilty pleasure in sensual indulgence. But this was not, ultimately, Edna Pontellier's birthright, and she knew it. She was an American woman, raised in the Protestant mistrust of the senses and in the detestation of sexual desire as the root of evil. As a result, the hidden act came for her to be equivalent to the hidden and true self, once her nature awakened in the open surroundings of Creole Louisiana. The new century was to provide just such an awakening for countless American women, and *The Awakening* spoke of painful times ahead on the road to fulfillment.

Kate Chopin sympathized with Edna, but she did not pity her. She rendered her story with a detachment akin to Flaubert's. At one point Edna's doctor says, "Youth is given up to illusions. It seems to be a provision of Nature; a decoy to secure mothers for the race. And Nature takes no account of moral consequences, of arbitrary conditions which we create, and which we feel obliged to maintain at any cost." These appear to be the author's sentiments. Edna Pontellier is trapped between her illusions and the conditions which society arbitrarily establishes to maintain itself, and she is made to pay. Whether girls should be educated free of illusions, if possible, whether society should change the conditions it imposes on women, or whether both are needed, the author does not say; the novel is about what happened to Edna Pontellier. * * *

GEORGE ARMS

[Contrasting Forces in the Novel] †

* * * Basically she [Chopin] writes as a non-intrusive author but principally presents her material with a sense of constant contrast, partly in the whole social situation, partly in Edna, but essentially as the author's way of looking at life. In the first of her two editorializing chapters she speaks of this contrast: "In short, Mrs.

† From George Arms, "Kate Chopin's *The Awakening* in the Perspective of Her Literary Career," in *Essays on American Literature in Honor of Jay B.* *Hubbell*, Clarence Gohdes, ed. (Durham: Duke University Press, 1967), pp. 215–28.

Pontellier was beginning to realize her position in the universe as a human being, and to recognize her relations as an individual to the world within and about her." Into the next chapter she extends this observation by remarking, "At a very early period she had apprehended instinctively the dual life—that outward existence which conforms, the inward life which questions." Yet Mrs. Chopin is unwilling to present Edna as simply struggling between two opposites, later remarking that her emotions "had never taken the form of struggles." On occasion the polarity reappears, as when the author writes that the husband could not see that his wife "was becoming herself and daily casting aside that fictitious self which we assume like a garment with which to appear before the world." In a much more adolescent fashion Edna speaks: "By all the codes which I am acquainted with, I am a devilishly wicked specimen of the sex. But some way I can't convince myself that I am."

On the whole, as she reveals herself, her aimlessness impresses us more than her sense of conflict. Early in the novel, recalling an incident from her childhood, Edna first interprets it as running away from the gloomy Presbyterianism of her father, but then goes on to say that her walk on that Sunday morning was "idly, aimlessly, unthinking and unguided." Thus Edna appears not so much as a woman who is aware of the opposition of two ideals but rather as one who drifts—who finally, even in death, is drifting when she again recalls having wandered on the blue-green meadow as a little girl. In the second editorial chapter, the author again considers the conflicts in Edna's life, but at this stage the contrasts have become a series of "multitudinous emotions." Edna is sensitive to many states of mind as the author describes her after the consummation of her affair with Arobin: irresponsibility, shock, her husband's and Robert's reproach, but not shame and not remorse, though regret that she has yielded from erotic longing rather than from love. Still, there is an "understanding" that hints of a polarity: "She felt as if a mist had been lifted from her eyes, enabling her to look upon and comprehend the significance of life, that monster made up of beauty and brutality."

At the time of Edna's suicide she thinks of many things, yet in the final paragraph the images that come to her are all those of her childhood. One is that of a cavalry officer whom she had romantically loved when he visited her father. When she married, the author observes that "she felt she would take her place with a certain dignity in the world of reality, closing the portals forever behind her upon the realm of romance and dreams." And upon Robert's leaving for Mexico, "she recognized anew the symptoms of infatuation" of her earlier life, but the recognition "did not lessen the reality, the poignancy of the revelation by any suggestion or promise of instability." Thus one of the oppositions which the author develops throughout the novel is that of romance and reality, and she suggests that Edna remains a figure of romantic ideals in spite of her acting with a sexual freedom that the common reader would call realistic or even naturalistic. Part of Edna's romanticism derives from a sense of fate, as the comment late in the book suggests: "She answered her husband with friendly evasiveness,—not with any fixed design to mislead him, only because all sense of reality had gone out of her life; she had abandoned herself to Fate, and awaited the consequences with indifference." As so often in the novel, Mrs. Chopin made specific preparation by noting that marriages "masquerade as the decrees of Fate." So one can summarize that instead of identifying herself with Edna's actions, Mrs. Chopin tends to regard them as romantically motivated rather than as realistically considered. Yet, as if to say that there are other kinds of romanticism, the author introduces Adele Ratignolle, Edna's friend who is completely in love with her husband, in this fashion: "There are no words to describe her save the old ones that have served so often to picture the bygone heroine of romance and the fair lady of our dreams."

In all, the author presents these contrasts suggestively rather than systematically. Perhaps if she takes any stand at all it is to favor individualism against social obligation, for she writes of Edna, "Every step which she took toward relieving herself from obligations added to her strength and expansion as an individual." Yet even here she leaves the question open. What does the author mean when she writes that after her father and husband leave on trips, "Then Edna sat in the library after dinner and read Emerson until she grew sleepy"? Eble interprets this as a reaction against the father's Presbyterianism, and such it may be; but to grow sleepy over a Transcendental individualist also hints that Edna's individualism lacks philosophical grounding.

This sleepiness from reading Emerson leads to the contrast, implicit in the title. In treating Edna's awakening, the author shows irony and even deviousness. We look upon Edna's awakening as archetypal in marking her passage from death to rebirth, but we may also look upon her awakening as not a rebirth but as another kind of death that is self-sought. Amusingly enough, the author, quite consciously I am sure, allows Edna to do an inordinate amount of sleeping throughout the novel, in spite of her underlying vitality. She first appears "with some appearance of fatigue" (admittedly after she has been swimming); that night she is "fast asleep," and her weariness is noted many times, especially when she falls in love with Robert, though at one time she only sleeps fitfully. When she first openly seeks out Robert and takes him—again amusingly—to Sunday morning mass, she is so drowsy at the service that she has to leave, and sleeps the whole of the rest of the morning and afternoon at a nearby house, with Robert remarking at the end, "You have slept precisely one hundred years." Again, when she celebrates her decision to break with her husband at a dinner party, "the old ennui" overtakes her. It is almost as if the author were saying: here is my heroine who at the critical points of her progress toward an awakening constantly falls asleep.

An even grimmer irony, of course, is in her awakening to an erotic life not through Robert, whom she truly loves, but through Alcée, whom she uses merely as a convenience. Though Edna recognizes this, she hardly does so in the sense that the novel does. We are told that "Alcée Arobin's manner was so genuine that it often deceived even himself," but also that "Edna did not care or think whether it were genuine or not." We cannot help suspecting that Edna simplifies and melodramatizes her view of herself far more than the author does. After Robert's return, she exclaims to him, "It was you who awoke me last summer out of a life-long, stupid dream. Oh! you have made me so unhappy with your indifference. Oh! I have suffered, suffered!" Almost compulsively she is soon saying the same thing to the family doctor, who earlier had seen her as an "animal waking up in the sun" and now cautions her about the illusions of youth:

> "Yes," she said. "The years that are gone seem like dreams—if one might go on sleeping and dreaming—but to wake up and find—oh! well! perhaps it is better to wake up after all, even to suffer, rather than to remain a dupe to illusions all one's life."

Finally, the underlying awareness of contrasting forces in the novel is exhibited in its use of children. Edna has two boys of four and five. With them she has little intimacy, and her husband accuses her of neglecting them, as does her mother-in-law—an accusation endorsed by the author, who early in the story announces, "In short, Mrs. Pontellier was not a mother-woman." Again we are somewhat perplexed as to whether or not the author approves of Edna's attitude toward her children. I suppose that those who look upon the novel as a defense of the New Woman would feel that Mrs. Chopin regards freedom from children as a necessary basis for complete freedom. But again I am doubtful, for Mrs. Chopin delights in the contraries which are present in Edna's response toward her boys.

Perhaps Edna most fully expresses her attitude in a conversation with Madame Ratignolle midway in the book:

"I would give up the unessential; I would give my money, I would give my life for my children; but I wouldn't give myself. I can't make it more clear; it's only something which I am beginning to comprehend, which is revealing itself to me."

This passage will be recalled for us at the time of Edna's death, but in the meantime we observe her constantly returning to her children as a kind of penance whenever she displays most markedly her love outside of marriage. When she suspects that Robert goes to Mexico to avoid her, she shows an unusual intimacy with her children by telling them a bedtime story. She had already coddled and caressed one of her sons immediately after her day spent with Robert. After her second night with Alcée she visits her children in the country— one would think more as an act of penance than of affection. Just after Edna had fully admitted her love for Robert to a friend, she sent her children "a huge box of bonbons."

When Robert finally returns to New Orleans and Edna declares her love for him, she is called away from their reunion to attend the birth of another child of Adele Ratignolle. After the birth, which is not an easy one, Adele's parting injunction is: "Think of the children, Edna. Oh think of the children! Remember them!" From this scene she returns to discover that Robert has not waited for her, but instead has left a note, bidding her "Good-by—because I love you." The next day she goes to Grand Isle to drown herself, saying in the meanwhile again and again: "To-day it is Arobin; to-morrow it will be some one else. It makes no difference to me, it doesn't matter about Léonce Pontellier—but Raoul and Etienne!" Immediately afterward, she thinks back to her earlier conversation with Adele in which she had declared that she would give up everything for her children, including her life, but not "herself." This final opposition then leads directly to her death: "The children appeared before her like antagonists who had overcome her; who had overpowered and sought to drag her into the soul's slavery for the rest of her days. But she knew a way to elude them." Though she does not think of these things, the author tells us, when she walks toward the beach, her thoughts revert to the children and her husband as she tires in her swim toward death: "They were a part of her life. But they need not have thought that they could possess her, body and soul."

While the motivation from the children has been amply anticipated, its final realization produces something of a shift. Perhaps one might go so far as to say that the children, used in this way, somewhat flaw the novel. We recall that many of Mrs. Chopin's short stories first appeared in *Harper's Young People's Magazine*, the *Youth's Companion*, and also in *Vogue*, with the uneasy feeling that the author is still writing in a juvenile vein or from the conventional angle of a woman's magazine. Yet this difficulty might be answered by recognizing that the children stand for a stable society and the permanency of an unbroken home. Perhaps it would even be better to treat them as bringing another contrast into the story. Like those contrasts of purpose and aimlessness, of romance and realism, and of sleep and awakening, this one is not of absolute opposition but is complex and even blurred. As my argument has suggested, precisely this complexity may be what Mrs. Chopin is trying to achieve. She presents a series of events in which the truth is present, but with a philosophical pragmatism she is unwilling to extract a final truth. Rather, she sees truth as constantly re-forming itself and as so much a part of the context of what happens that it can never be final or for that matter abstractly stated. * * *

PER SEYERSTED

[Kate Chopin and the American Realists] †

* * * Cyrille Arnavon is thus no longer alone in elevating Kate Chopin from the group of local colorists to that of the American pioneer writers of the 1890's, the group which comprises such authors as Crane, Garland, Norris, and Dreiser.[1] It is therefore fitting to look at works like *Maggie, Rose of Dutcher's Coolly, McTeague,* and *Sister Carrie,* all written in that formative decade of American literature, and compare their approach to certain fundamental issues with that of *The Awakening.*

If we turn to the treatment of sexuality in Garland's novel, for example, we find that his Rose, a farmer's daughter, views all aspects of animal reproduction as natural matters. We might then perhaps expect her to see sex in humans as equally natural, a view undoubtedly held by Edna. But though she is courted by "wholesome," "clean" men—one of them observes that human procreation is "not as yet a noble business"—she feels "revulsion" when she realizes how their presence stirs up desire in her "pure wholesome

† From Per Seyersted, *Kate Chopin: A Critical Biography* (Baton Rouge: Louisiana State University Press, 1969), pp. 190–96. Except as noted, all footnotes are by the editor; those by the author have been renumbered.
1. Hamlin Garland (1860–1940) wrote novels depicting the hardships of farm life in the Middle West. Frank Norris (1870–1902) is best known for his *The Octopus* (1901), one of a number of novels examining economic and social realities. Theodore Dreiser (1871–1945),

prolific naturalist novelist, best known for his *Sister Carrie* (1900) and *An American Tragedy* (1925). See also p. 167, note 3.
See also Cyrille Arnavon, "Les Débuts du Roman Réaliste American et l'Influence Française," in *Romanciers Américains Contemporains* Henri Kerst, ed. (*Cahiers des Langues Modernes,* I Paris, 1946), pp. 9–35; and the introduction to Arnavon's French translation of the novel: *Edna* (Paris, 1953), pp. 1–22.

awakening womanhood." While men are "sordid and vicious, . . . polygamous by instinct, insatiable as animals," women are virtuous by nature, Garland declares, and Rose sublimates her "brute passion" into a desire to become a great poet.[2]

That man's erotic and other drives are brutal is of course one of the tenets of naturalism, and Garland's illustration of it is mild compared to that of the others of the quartet. Norris, for example, whose theme in *McTeague* is how greed leads to murder, compares his hero to an evil beast who takes a "panther leap" and kisses Trina, the heroine, "grossly, full on the mouth," and who delights his wife and himself with biting and beating her.[3] Though Kate Chopin saw brute selfishness as the dominant principle of the world, she rarely used the imagery of man as a warring animal, and, more specifically, she never attached anything brutish to physical passion. Moreover, she lets Edna make absolutely no attempt to suppress her amatory impulses.

In fact, not only does Mrs. Chopin treat sex at least as amorally as any of the other four writers, but she also describes it more openly than they do. Their heroines—Maggie, Rose, Trina, and Carrie—are all rather sexless compared to Edna, and their descriptions of sexual matters in general are tame. This is perhaps most surprising in Dreiser, who is otherwise so elaborate and who wants us to believe that Carrie is dangerously attractive to men, and in Norris, who had made sex the main theme of his unfinished *Vandover and the Brute*. Garland is comparatively daring when he lets Rose feel desire and when he speaks of her "splendid curve of bust," but he allows her no more than a kiss on the hand.[4] It is hard to understand that this book was locally banned; yet this reaction frightened the author, who thereafter fully adhered to R. W. Gilder's genteel literary code.[5] *The Awakening*, meanwhile, is suffused with sex, and we witness how Alcée arouses Edna and how she in turn sets Robert on fire with a voluptuous kiss. On this point of physical attraction and contact, Kate Chopin gave not only a fuller, but also a more convincing picture than any other serious American novelist had done.

A fact which significantly sets off *The Awakening* from *Maggie, Rose, McTeague,* and *Sister Carrie,* is that Edna has children and the other heroines do not. This points to a fundamental difference in emphasis: Kate Chopin concentrates mainly on the biological aspects of woman's situation, while the other writers are more con-

2. Hamlin Garland, *Rose of Dutcher's Coolly* (Chicago, 1895), pp. 59, 62, 121, 147, 288, 294, 364. [*Author.*]
3. Frank Norris, *McTeague* (New York, 1899), pp. 30–31, 300, 310. [*Author.*]
4. Garland, *Rose*, p. 245. [*Author.*]
5. R. W. Gilder, editor of *Scribner's Monthly* (1870–1881) and *The Century Magazine* (1881–1909), was a strong influence in establishing what he considered standards of moral wholesomeness in the popular and literary magazines at the end of the century.

cerned with the socio-economic forces shaping her life. Where Edna stands back from society and questions its rules for woman's existence, the other women move with the procession in their fight for wealth, rank, or physical survival.

Common to all Edna's four counterparts is their admiration of those who are well dressed. Maggie and Carrie are more easily seduced because of their suitors' stylishness, which they equate with power and standing. Both Rose and Carrie[6] are allured by the life of the rich, and their "imagination," as it is called, represents a desire to succeed and move up in the world. Dreiser speaks in one breath of Carrie's "emancipation" and her "more showy life." For Edna, who is the only one of these five women to start near the top, emancipation means something quite different; as she moves to a smaller house, she has "a feeling of having descended in the social scale, with a corresponding sense of having risen in the spiritual."

When Carrie leaves Hurstwood, on the other hand, it is not her inner integrity she is thinking of, but her outer or material progress. She arrives at the attitude which long dominates Rose, that is, she does not want a husband and children to impede her climb on the ladder. As the two women rise, both judge themselves against their betters in society. Rose is particularly influenced by a woman doctor who tells her to think first of her career. Garland, who had once let a heroine demand "the right to be an individual human being first and a woman afterwards," is ostensibly in favor of female emancipation; the doctor leaves out the promise of obedience in her marriage ceremony, and Rose is told by her suitor that he expects her to be as "free and as sovereign" as himself and to follow her profession. But the author could not quite free himself from accepted ideas: The doctor insists that though she is ambitious in her career, she "could bear to give it all up a hundred times over, rather than [her] hope of being a mother," and Rose revels in "doing wifely things" for her friend the moment he has proposed, just as she suddenly finds it much more important that he appreciates her as a woman than that he praises her poetry.[7]

In Crane's version of the relationship between man and woman, Maggie's swaggering seducer asserts his "reassuring proprietorship" while she shows a dependent air: "Her life was Pete's." Norris' view is also uncomplicated when he lets Trina be subdued and conquered by McTeague's "sheer brute force" and declares that she "belongs" to him, body and soul, "forever and forever," because "the woman

6. Garland, *Rose*, p. 299; Theodore Dreiser, *Sister Carrie* (New York, 1900), pp. 58, 126. Jessie Ogden of Henry B. Fuller's *The Cliff-Dwellers* (New York, 1893) is an example of a contemporary American heroine who has a child; when she neglects it, it is in order to rise socially, not spiritually. [*Author.*]

7. Hamlin Garland, "A Spoil of Office" in *Arena*, V (March, 1892), 515; *Rose*, pp. 330, 380, 395. [*Author.*]

[worships] the man for that which she yields up to him." Norris
here seems to have been influenced by the Darwinian idea of the
female selecting the strongest suitor (which fits in with general male
conceptions), and he also accepts the concomitant unromantic view
of the love of an aroused heroine when he writes: "The Woman is
awakened, and, starting from her sleep, catches blindly at what first
her newly opened eyes light upon. It is a spell, a witchery, ruled by
chance. . . ." *McTeague* thus for a moment parallels *The Awakening,* but Trina's "love of submission," on the other hand, is utterly
unthinkable in the self-asserting Edna.[8]

Kate Chopin's novel stands up well when compared to these four
important works in the canon of early American realism or naturalism. *Maggie* is a stereotype seduction-story which is only saved by
Crane's irony and general artistic mastery; *Rose* has much of a
moralistic, sentimental romance in spite of Garland's attempts to
make it into a serious *Bildungsroman*,[9] and *McTeague* has not a
little of the melodramatic, particularly in the conclusion of its
Zolaesque motif. *The Awakening,* on the other hand, has a fundamental seriousness which goes beyond that of these three works,
and this and other qualities unite it more closely with *Sister Carrie*
than with any of the other books.

Kate Chopin and Theodore Dreiser have in common a directness
and a complete honesty in their descriptions of Edna's and Carrie's
violations of what both writers considered society's "arbitrary scale"
of morals. Unable to see their heroines as sinners, they braved
public opinion by refusing to let the two repent, and they had the
further audacity to present their stories with no trace of moralism
and without apology. There are no villains in the two works. A
seducer like Arobin appeals to the reader; Hurstwood achieves a
certain dignity even in his downfall, and Adèle, who represents
everything that Edna opposes, is portrayed with sympathy and
understanding.

We have here two unillusioned authors each writing about a
heroine pursuing a chimera; the magnet drawing Carrie is the
golden radiance on the distant hill tops, and the illusion firing Edna
is the idea that she can achieve the ecstasy of an all-encompassing
love. Both writers see their protagonists as wisps in the wind among
the forces that move us, but with a difference. Though Dreiser at
one point speaks in terms of evolutionary optimism and Kate
Chopin sees man as basically unimprovable, there are greater
changes, certainly a greater spiritual evolution, in Edna than in
Carrie.

8. Stephen Crane, *Maggie: A Girl of the
Streets* (New York, 1893), pp. 106, 107;
Norris, *McTeague,* pp. 84, 88, 89, 183,
309. [*Author.*]
9. A novel of "education," usually of a
young boy arriving at manhood.

The reason is that Dreiser, reflecting a mostly socio-economic determinism, endows Carrie with less free will than that found in Edna. What freedom Carrie has she uses to act out the changing roles which she copies from those one step ahead of her. True, she achieves outer independence, but she is unthinkable without the society which provides her with models. As symbolized by the rocking-chair, she has scarcely moved at the end of the novel; she is basically unchanged, ever looking to the next hill, her eyes still largely unopened to the real emptiness of her longings.

Edna, meanwhile, is awakened to a spiritual independence in general and to a realization of the nature of reality in particular. Of these two solitary souls, the outwardly successful Carrie gains little more than the finery without which she, like her first lover, is merely "nothing";[1] when the apparently defeated Edna takes off her clothes, on the other hand, it symbolizes a victory of self-knowledge and authenticity as she fully becomes herself.

Carrie's blind, irresistible fight to get ahead has an unquestionable universality, and there is a similar quality in Edna's open-eyed choice to defy illusions and conventions. Different as these two novels are in form and theme—one terse in its concentration on inner reality, the other full of details on the outer show—both give a sense of tragic life, conveying something of the human condition.

What unites these five works from the 1890's is that they all, in one way or another, represent their authors' will to renew American literature. In subject matter or approach, they had enough of the new realism or naturalism to shock the Iron Madonnas.[2] Refusing to idealize life in the old manner, these writers all took a step forward in what Howells[3] called truthful treatment of material.

Kate Chopin parallels the naturalists in her view of basic urges as imperative, but differs from them in that she lets Edna decide her own destiny in an existentialist way. *The Awakening* also differs from *Maggie* and *McTeague* in that there is nothing of the sordid in it. Yet we note that while Norris and Crane became less iconoclastic in their subsequent work, Mrs. Chopin moved on to the increased openness of "The Storm."[4] After science had robbed her of some of her early beliefs, she may at times have wanted to join one of her heroines who decided to "go back into the dark to think" because "the sight of things" confused her. However, whereas Maupassant's reaction to the new knowledge was sadness rather than exhilaration

1. Dreiser, *Sister Carrie*, p. 4. [*Author*.]
2. A phrase widely used to describe the female audience of late-century fiction.
3. William Dean Howells (1837–1920), very influential critic and novelist, proponent of literary realism. Edited *The Atlantic Monthly* from 1871–1881, served on the editorial board of *Harper's*. His best-known novel is *The Rise of Silas Lapham* (1885).
4. See Per Seyersted, ed. *The Complete Works of Kate Chopin* (Baton Rouge: Louisiana State University Press, 1969), II, 592–6.

—"tous ces voiles levés m'attristent," as he expressed it[5]—Kate Chopin was sad only at the thought of woman's position, while being exhilarated at the opportunity of portraying life truthfully. Though she did not aim at exposing false respectability, her work is in certain respects a forerunner of such later eye-openers as *Spoon River Anthology, Winesburg, Ohio,* and *Main Street.*[6]

Mrs. Chopin was at least a decade ahead of her time. During the years following America's silencing of her, "Edith Wharton's genteel satire and Ellen Glasgow's moral searchings were the strongest fare that it could take," as Robert E. Spiller has observed.[7] Kate Chopin can be seen not only as one of the American realists of the 1890's, but also as a link in the tradition formed by such distinguished American women authors as Sarah Orne Jewett, Mary E. Wilkins Freeman, Willa Cather,[8] and the two just mentioned. One factor uniting these writers is their emphasis on female characters. Another is their concern with values, but here we see a difference between the St. Louisian and the others in that she is less interested than they are in preserving these values. As exemplified in Mrs. Todd of *The Country of the Pointed Firs,* for instance, woman is a rock guarding the old qualities, the men being either weak or dead. To Mrs. Chopin, woman is no more of a rock than is man, being neither better nor worse than he. Mrs. Wharton and Miss Glasgow may have attacked certain aspects of the aristocracies they sprang from, but they also wanted to preserve some of their values. Kate Chopin, on the other hand, was no celebrant of the aristocratic qualities of her own distinguished background.

The one value that really counted with her was woman's opportunity for self-expression. She knew that there are many *Woman's Kingdoms.*[9] She was sensitive, intelligent, and broad enough in her outlook to see the different basic needs of the female and the various sides of her existence and to represent them with impartiality. Her work is thus no feminist plea in the usual sense, but an il-

5. Maupassant, as quoted in Edward D. Sullivan, *Maupassant: The Short Stories* (London, 1962), p. 57. [*Author.*] "All these lifted veils sadden me." [*Editor.*]
6. Edgar Lee Masters's *Spoon River Anthology* (1915), Sherwood Anderson's *Winesburg Ohio* (1919), and Sinclair Lewis's *Main Street* are all works of realism with a satiric edge which made them controversial books, especially in the locales they depict.
7. Robert E. Spiller, et al, eds. *Literary History of the United States*, II (New York, 1948), 1197. [*Author*] Edith Wharton (1862–1937), American novelist of manners and morals in New York society. Ellen Glasgow (1847–1945), American author of nineteen novels,

many of which are set in Virginia.
8. See page 174, note 4; Mary Wilkins Freeman (1852–1930) wrote short stories and a novel of life in New England; Willa Cather (1876–1947), best known for her *Death Comes for the Archbishop* (1927), wrote a number of studies of southwest immigrant settlers. Seyersted shows an appreciation of the great women writers of America which is not often shown by native critics.
9. The title of a novel by Dinah Maria Muluck Craik, published in New York in 1869, from which Chopin copied an antifeminist passage into her diary. See Seyersted, *Kate Chopin*, p. 29.

lustration—rather than an assertion—of woman's right to be herself, to be individual and independent whether she wants to be weak or strong, a nest-maker or a soaring bird.

GEORGE M. SPANGLER

[The Ending of the Novel]†

* * * one can easily and happily join in the praise that in recent years has been given to *The Awakening*—one can, that is, until one reaches the conclusion of the novel, which is unsatisfactory because it is fundamentally evasive. Other commentators, it should be noted here, have been as affirmative about the conclusion as they have been about the novel as a whole. Though Edmund Wilson merely notes that the ending has "the same sensuous beauty as all the rest," other writers have not confined their praise to the esthetic. Berthoff, for example, finds Edna's suicide "psychologically, sensually, convincing," "matter-of-course, unarguable"; and Kauffmann sees it as "the confrontation of resultant consequences without plot contrivance or escape."[1] Ziff, in some detail, argues for the psychological coherence and, by implication, the rightness of the suicide; and Eble comments on Mrs. Chopin's "complete command of structure," including, presumably, the conclusion. What, in the narrowest sense, happens in the final pages, which seem so right to five readers and so unsatisfactory to at least one?

After finding Robert's farewell note and spending a sleepless night in her home, Edna takes a boat to the resort, now in its off-season, where the novel and her attraction to Robert began. She arranges with the caretaker for a room and for dinner in the evening, and then, deciding to go swimming, borrows some towels. There is no hint that suicide is her intention. As she walks toward the beach thinking of nothing in particular, the reader learns of her thoughts during the previous night. Primary was her fear of a succession of lovers and the effect such a future would have on her children: "To-day it is Arobin; tomorrow it will be some one else. It makes no difference to me, it doesn't matter about Léonce Pontellier —but Raoul and Etienne!" In her despondency (which "had never lifted"), her children "appeared before her like antagonists who had

† From George M. Spangler, "Kate Chopin's *The Awakening:* A Partial Dissent," *Novel*, III (Spring 1970), 249–55. Footnotes are by the editor.
1. Edmund Wilson, *Patriotic Gore: Studies in the Literature of the American Civil War* (New York: Oxford University Press, 1962), p. 151. Warner Berthoff, *The Ferment of Realism* (New York: Free Press, 1965), p. 89. Stanley Kauffmann, "The Really Lost Generation," *New Republic* CLV (December 3, 1966), 38. Other essays noted are included in part in this collection.

overcome her; who had overpowered and sought to drag her into the soul's slavery for the rest of her days. But she knew a way to elude them." However, "she was not thinking of these things" as she walks to the beach, decides against a bathing suit ("How strange and awful it seemed to stand naked under the sky! How delicious!"), and begins her walk into the sea. As she goes farther and farther out, "her arms and legs growing tired," she thinks again of her husband and children ("they need not have thought that they could possess her, body and soul"); of Robert ("He did not know; he did not understand. He would never understand"); and, in the final lines, of her childhood in Kentucky.

And what is wrong with this conclusion? Its great fault is inconsistent characterization, which asks the reader to accept a different and diminished Edna from the one developed so impressively before. Throughout the novel the most striking feature of Edna's character has been her strength of will, her ruthless determination to go her own way. In thought and act she has rejected unequivocally the restraints of conventional morality, social custom and personal obligation to her husband and children (through most of the novel the children are visiting their grandmother). Yet in the final pages, Mrs. Chopin asks her reader to believe in an Edna who is completely defeated by the loss of Robert, to believe in the paradox of a woman who has awakened to passional life and yet quietly, almost thoughtlessly, chooses death. Having overcome so much in the way of frustration, Edna is destroyed by so little. As well, the reasonings and feelings attributed to her as motivation at the end do not bear scrutiny. Her brief affair with Arobin hardly proves the certainty of a host of future lovers, but it has clearly shown her what is missing from her life; and since she has long been indifferent to convention and domestic ties, she could well expect to find someone less shoddy than Arobin and less scrupulous than Robert. Equally perplexing is her sudden concern for her children, who previously have seemed to matter little as long as they were out of the way. Increasingly strong, practical and sure of herself and her needs through most of the novel, Edna suddenly collapses, and what the reader gets in the way of explanation does not follow from what he has witnessed before. Once capable of leaving her husband, relegating her children, establishing her own home, earning money with her painting, accepting one lover, pursuing another—at the end she is unable to endure Robert's tender note of rejection.

What happened was that Mrs. Chopin provided a conclusion for a novel other than the one she wrote, a conclusion for a novel much more conventional and much less interesting than *The Awakening*. Specifically it is a conclusion for an ordinary sentimental novel, not for a subtle psychological treatment of female sexuality. If the rest of the novel existed only at the sentimental, romantic level, then Edna's suicide would be conventionally appropriate and acceptable: a woman surrenders her chastity and death is the consequence. In such a novel Robert would be the single great love of her life, a great romantic passion, finally doomed and destructive. But despite its conclusion *The Awakening* is not such a novel; indeed its relation to the conventional sentimental novel is not apparent until the final pages. For Mrs. Chopin was concerned not with seduction and retribution, but with woman's passional nature and its relation to self, marriage and society. Yet at the end she transformed a character who has embodied these complex issues into one who simply dies from disappointed, illicit love. In a word, a complex psychological novel is converted into a commonplace sentimental one.

Possible reasons for such an unfortunate change, which also mars a number of Mrs. Chopin's short stories, are not difficult to discover. With her conclusion the author managed to provide both pathos and poetic justice, pathos to please her sentimental readers and justice to satisfy her moralistic ones. The shift toward the sentimental and pathetic is implicit in the image of "a bird with a broken wing" which Edna, just before her death, sees "reeling, fluttering, circling, disabled down, down to the water." Nearly a hundred pages before, Edna's confidant used the image of the crippled bird to suggest what happens to those who, lacking great strength, would "soar above the level plain of tradition and prejudice." When the image recurs at the end, the reader no doubt is expected to see Edna as such a person. But of course she is not: whatever destroys Edna, it is not tradition and prejudice, not environmental pressure—except, perhaps, that of the tradition of the sentimental novel. The sentimental is also present in a different and rather special form. Just as the reader of Mrs. Wharton's *House of Mirth* may well conclude that Lily Bart's death is the result of Selden's conventionality[2] so he can hardly avoid the suggestion in *The Awakening* that Edna dies because Robert is so foolishly scrupulous—the conventionality of both men of course being a mask to hide a severe deficiency of masculine force. The result in both novels is, unfortunately, the special pathos, the feminine self-pity, expressed in the words of the ballad, "hard is the lot of all womankind," and of course in countless magazine stories aimed at a feminine audience.

The moralistic explanation for the conclusion is just as obvious, though far less evident in the tone and diction of the concluding

---

2. Edith Wharton (1862–1937), whose *House of Mirth* (1905) ends with the suicide of Lily Bart. See Cynthia Griffin Wolff, "Lily Bart and the Beautiful Death," *American Literature* XLV (May 1974), 16–41.

pages: Edna has sinned in thought and deed against accepted sexual morality, and for the average reader in 1899, her sin required that she suffer and die. But if Mrs. Chopin had hoped to avoid the kind of trouble Dreiser was soon to have with *Sister Carrie*, she was to be disappointed.[3] The reviewers were hostile to her subject, the book was withdrawn from the libraries in St. Louis, her native city, and she was denied membership in the St. Louis Fine Arts Club because of the scandal.

If then, the conclusion Mrs. Chopin chose for *The Awakening* allows for pathos and poetic justice to please the sentimental and moralistic—a dubious accomplishment indeed—it also leads to a painful reduction in Edna's character. For in the final pages Edna is different and diminished: she is no longer purposeful, merely willful; no longer liberated, merely perverse; no longer justified, merely spiteful. And the painful failure of vision (or, more likely, of nerve) implicit in the change prevents a very good, very interesting novel from being the extraordinary masterpiece some commentators have claimed it is.

JOHN R. MAY

Local Color in *The Awakening*†

Kate Chopin appeals subtly to all of the reader's senses, and her descriptions are delicate impressionistic touches on her canvas of New Orleans and Grand Isle. In her use of color she is similar to Stephen Crane, yet somehow the strokes of her brush are less jarring. Leonce Pontellier watches his wife and Robert Lebrun approach the cottage: "He fixed his gaze upon a white sunshade that was advancing at a snail's pace from the beach. He could see it plainly between the gaunt trunks of the water-oaks and across the stretch of yellow camomile. The gulf looked far away, melting hazily into the blue of the horizon." When Edna goes with Arobin to the "pigeon-house" after her farewell party, she notices "the black line of his leg moving in and out so close to her against the yellow shimmer of her gown." The garden that Edna visits in the suburbs of New Orleans is "a small, leafy corner, with a few green tables under the orange trees."

The Gulf breeze that reaches the Lebrun cottages is "soft and

---

3. Theodore Dreiser (1871–1945), whose frank study of a "fallen woman"—*Sister Carrie* (1900)—met with adverse criticism.

† From John R. May, "Local Color in *The Awakening*," *The Southern Review*, VI (Fall 1970), 1031–1040. Author's footnotes have been renumbered.

languorous . . . , charged with the seductive odor of the sea." After the Lebrun party, as the guests leave for the beach, there are "strange, rare odors abroad—a tangle of the sea smell and of weeds and damp, new-plowed earth, mingled with the heavy perfume of a field of white blossoms somewhere near." "The everlasting voice of the sea" breaks "like a mournful lullaby upon the night."

As the story progresses there is an increasing emphasis on tactile imagery. When Victor ceremoniously apologizes for offending Edna, the touch of his lips is "like a pleasing sting to her hand." During her reunion with Robert, Edna notices the "same tender caress" of his eyes. Edna's "soft, cool, delicate kiss" is a "voluptuous sting," penetrating Robert's whole being. When Edna leaves Adele after the birth of her child, the air is "mild and caressing, but cool with the breath of spring and the night."

It is the personification of the sea, though, that dominates all the imagery. The sea is undoubtedly the central symbol of the novel; like all natural symbols it is basically ambiguous. Initially, though, it embodies for Edna all of the sensuousness of her new environment. The early passage describing the voice and touch of the sea becomes a poetic refrain when repeated at the close of the story. The sea presides over the dawn of Edna's awakening as it does over the night of her fate; but it is not just another sea, as Seyersted seems to imply.[1] The images attempt to capture the mystery and enchantment of the semitropical summer Gulf: "The voice of the sea is seductive; never ceasing, whispering, clamoring, murmuring, inviting the soul to wander for a spell in abysses of solitude; to lose itself in mazes of inward contemplation. The voice of the sea speaks to the soul. The touch of the sea is sensuous, enfolding the body in its soft, close embrace."

When the description appears again in the final chapter, the words "for a spell" have been dropped and the first sentence ends with "solitude." The second sentence is not repeated. The effect of the repetition is to suggest that the end for Edna was indeed the beginning of her awakening. The omissions emphasize the finality of her solitude; she gives herself to the sea only because she has already lost herself in a maze of self-contemplation.

The full symbolism of the novel is complex, yet Kate Chopin proves herself at all times to be the master of it. Supporting the rhythmic movement of the narrative from Grand Isle to the Creole quarter of New Orleans and back to Grand Isle are the basic symbols of sea and city. Even though the Lebrun cottages at Grand Isle the summer the novel begins are occupied exclusively by Creoles, there is a more relaxed atmosphere at the beach than in the winter

---

1. *Kate Chopin: A Critical Biography* (Baton Rouge: Louisiana State Univer- sity Press, 1969), p. 151.

of the city—because there one must "observe *les convenances*." The
tension between freedom and restraint is evident in the use of the
symbols.

Paralleling the significance of sea and city in the temporal sequence of the narrative is Edna's remembrance of the contrast
between the Kentucky meadow and the Presbyterian household of
her youth. She recalls the summer day when as a child she ran from
the Sunday prayer service that her father always conducted "in a
spirit of gloom." The meadow seemed like an ocean to her as she
walked through it, "beating the tall grass as one strikes out in the
water." "My sunbonnet obstructed the view," she tells Adele; "I
could see only the stretch of green before me, and I felt as if I must
walk on forever, without coming to an end of it. . . . Sometimes I
feel this summer as if I were walking through the green meadow
again; idly, aimlessly, unthinking and unguided."

The lady in black, the young lovers, and the mother-women
represent the actual limits imposed by the Creole environment; as
symbols they specify the restraint of the city. The lady in black is
either "walking demurely up and down, telling her beads," or "reading her morning devotions." The young lovers lean upon each other
like "water-oaks bent from the sea," "exchanging their vows and
sighs" and showing an inclination "to linger and hold themselves
apart." Yet it is the mother-women who seem to prevail: "It was
easy to know them, fluttering about with extended, protecting wings
when any harm, real or imaginary, threatened their precious brood.
They were women who idolized their children, worshipped their
husbands, and esteemed it a holy privilege to efface themselves as
individuals and grow wings as ministering angels." By reason of her
marriage and children, Edna rightfully belongs to this group; but
she is not and cannot be a mother-woman.

In the criticism of the novel to date, no one has commented on
the symbolic stages of Edna's rebellion against the restraints of
Creole society—a withdrawal into solitude that poses as a quest for
freedom. The sequence also adds irony to the final meaning of the
sea. I refer here to the significance of the home on Esplanade Street,
the "pigeon-house" around the corner, the garden in the suburbs,
and finally the sea. The Pontellier home on Esplanade is a perfect
microcosm of the restraints of the Creole city. There Edna must be
mistress of the household, receive callers on Tuesday afternoons,
and be the perfect mother-woman. Yet, even while still there, Edna
stops receiving callers, abandons the household to the erratic performance of the servants, and severs ties with her family. She refuses to attend her sister's wedding; and when her father terminates
his shopping trip to New Orleans, which is also an abortive mission
of persuasion, Edna is "glad to be rid of . . . his wedding garments

and his bridal gifts, . . . his padded shoulders, his Bible reading, his 'toddies' and his ponderous oaths." At the farewell party, Edna's appearance suggests "the regal woman, the one who rules, who looks on, *who stands alone*" (my emphasis). The "pigeon-house," which Edna moves into in her husband's absence, the first stage of her actual physical withdrawal from Creole society, is just large enough to satisfy her needs. She knows that she will "like the feeling of freedom and independence." Seyersted's preoccupation with sexual freedom leads him at this point to ignore the obvious reference to the size of the place in relation to the home on Esplanade and to suggest that "it is to be a place of cooing love."[2]

After her disappointing reunion with Robert, Edna becomes the prey of alternating moods of hope and despondency. Robert does not return to see her during the days that follow. "Each morning she awoke with hope, and each night she was a prey to despondency." Then one night Arobin asks her to drive with him out to the lake. Her realization that it has become "more than a passing whim with Arobin to see her and be with her" leads to a second and more significant stage in her withdrawal. We are told that "there was no despondency when she fell asleep that night; nor was there hope when she awoke in the morning." Significantly, the very next scene takes place in a garden in the suburbs—a place "too modest to attract the attention of the people of fashion, and so quiet as to have escaped the notice of those in search of pleasure and dissipation."

The final stage of Edna's withdrawal is, of course, the return to Grand Isle and the sea. It is the day after Robert has left her the note which says: "I love you. Good-bye—because I love you." Despondency has returned to her and has not left. Now, at the beach, there is "no living thing in sight." "Absolutely alone," Edna removes her "unpleasant, pricking garments" and swims out into the water. The sea which at first spoke sensuously to Edna of freedom has become finally the symbol of her liberation—but, also, ironically, of her complete withdrawal from society, her total isolation. It is curious that, as she swims on, Edna is drawn back in her memory to the days of her youth. She hears the voices of her father and sister, the barking of a chained dog, the clanging spur of the cavalry officer, and the hum of the bees. Seyersted, consistent as always with his critical motif, sees these final lines as "a parable on the female condition."[3] He ignores the voices and the barking dog to note the symbol of male dominance in the clanging spurs and the generative symbolism of the bees. The meaning of Edna's recollections is, at best, ambiguous. Although the sea and the meadow were associated

2. Ibid., p. 159.   3. Ibid., p. 160.

earlier, she remembers now instead the sounds of her Presbyterian home. The gradual diminution of sound may indicate simply that her strength is gone, but it may also suggest ironically that Edna is returning home—defeated.

In what sense, then, has Edna been awakened by the alien Creole environment? I have already suggested that an explanation of her awakening simply in terms of a growing awareness of her sexual needs is too facile an interpretation of this rather complex novel. On a much deeper level Edna awakens to the reality of her own nature in relation to life. In seeking to possess Robert and be possessed by him, she has allowed herself to be duped by the sensuous freedom of the environment into thinking that she can satisfy her deepest human longings. Robert himself represents the unattainable, the possibilities that life offers, but never actualizes. During her farewell party on Esplanade Street, Edna experiences "the acute longing which always summoned into her spiritual vision the presence of the beloved one, overpowering her at once with a sense of the unattainable." It is longing which summons Robert as its symbol.

While still at Grand Isle, where her "awakening" begins, Edna is disturbed by dreams that leave "only an impression on her half-awakened senses of something unattainable." She pities Adele Ratignolle because of the "colorless existence" that Adele leads as a mother-woman, one "in which she would never have the taste of life's delirium," although Edna wonders at the time what she means by "life's delirium." The irony here, and Edna clearly awakens to this realization, is that life's delirium is never attainable. There are days when she feels as if life is passing her by, "leaving its promise broken and unfulfilled," yet others when she is "led on and *deceived* by fresh promises" (my emphasis). Once when Edna is with Robert at Grand Isle and again when she returns from Adele's at the end of the novel, she has the sensation of striving to overtake her thoughts.

Life itself creates the longing within her, but it never fulfills its promise. Edna is not simply a dreamer, a romantic, because it was life that offered her the promise of the sad-eyed cavalry officer, the engaged young men, and the great tragedian. The fulfillment though was only the frustration of Leonce Pontellier, Alcée Arobin, and Robert Lebrun. Life among the Creoles promised familiarity, open expression of affection, and freedom from moral rigor, but then only as a mother-woman, a lady in black, or an innocent young lover.

It is nature and man that conspire to frustrate human longing. "As if a mist had been lifted from her eyes," Edna awakens to "the significance of life, that monster made up of beauty and brutality." Clearly, beauty and brutality correspond to vision and reality, promise and fulfillment. When, finally, Edna assists Adele in childbirth, it is "with an inward agony, with a flaming, outspoken revolt against the ways of Nature." Doctor Mandelet, sensing the honest questions that Edna wants to ask, attempts an answer: "The trouble is . . . that youth is given up to illusions. It seems to be a provision of Nature; a decoy to secure mothers for the race. And Nature takes no account of moral consequences, of arbitrary conditions which we create, and which we feel obliged to maintain at any cost."

If Edna opens her eyes to the tyranny of life, she also becomes aware of her own nature. She is "a solitary soul," as Kate Chopin's original title for the novel indicated.[4] Nature has made her independent, willful, and selfish. When she moves from the home on Esplanade, she resolves "never again to belong to another than herself." She assures Robert, "I give myself where I choose." And when Doctor Mandelet asks if she is going abroad with her husband, Edna answers: "I'm not going to be forced into doing things. . . . I want to be let alone." Realizing that she is "wanting a good deal," she adds, "I don't want anything but my own way."

In reality, the Creole setting has simply provided a climate of psychological relaxation sufficient to allow Edna's true nature to reveal itself. Thus, because Edna is what she is, the longing for freedom has become the assertion of independence. The possibility of an open break with tradition has led simply to withdrawal from life. And the atmosphere of familiarity has revealed her radical incapacity to deal with anyone except on her own terms.

When Edna recalls that the friends of her youth had been of the self-contained type, the author notes: "She never realized that the reserve of her own character had much, perhaps everything, to do with this." Even Leonce Pontellier did not realize what was happening to his wife, "that she was becoming herself and daily casting aside that fictitious self which we assume like a garment with which to appear before the world." Only Mlle Reisz and Adele Ratignolle seemed to sense, though vaguely, what was actually happening. Mlle Reisz had warned Edna, "The bird that would soar above the level plain of tradition and prejudice must have strong wings." Thus, expectedly, when Edna walks to the beach at Grand Isle for the last time, a bird with a broken wing hovers above her, "reeling, fluttering, circling disabled down, down to the water." And Adele had pleaded with Robert, "Let Mrs. Pontellier alone. . . . She is not one of us."

Edna Pontellier's final revolt against nature, when she swims to her death in the sea, is certainly not an eventuality that the reader is unprepared for. Her innate sense of independence and her desire to assert her freedom, despite nature's refusal to satisfy her longing,

4. Daniel S. Rankin, *Kate Chopin and Her Creole Stories* (Philadelphia: University of Pennsylvania Press, 1932), p. 171.

have led her "step by inexorable step,"[5] in Stanley Kauffmann's phrase, to withdraw from life. The stages of her withdrawal into the solitude of complete isolation are symbolized, as we have seen, by the retreat from the home on Esplanade to the "pigeon-house," the garden, and the sea. The ultimate realization that she has awakened to is that the only way she can save herself is to give up her life. She cannot accept the restrictions that nature and man have conspired to impose upon her, the perpetual frustration of desire that living entails. And so, paradoxically, she surrenders her life in order to save herself.

Although it is difficult—perhaps presumptuous—to write with assurance about the essence of local color, it seems safe to say that a local color novel is one in which the identity of the setting is integral to the very unfolding of the theme, rather than simply incidental to a theme that could as well be set anywhere. *The Awakening* is clearly of the former type. The greater freedom of the new environment—with all of its characteristic sensuousness—has tempted Edna to reach for the unattainable because, in contrast with the severity of her Kentucky background, the summer at Grand Isle actually deluded her into thinking that her deepest longings could be satisfied. By the time she awakens to the cruel illusion nurtured by life in her new environment, her independent and selfish temperament—which supported her vain efforts—has led her irrevocably into abysses of solitude.

LEWIS LEARY

[Kate Chopin and Walt Whitman]†

* * * Through much of the novel like an obbligato refrain runs the voice of the sea—"the everlasting voice of the sea," that "broke like a lullaby" on her consciousness. When Edna is first introduced, returning from bathing in the sea with Robert, her husband's attitude toward her is defined by the remark, "You are burnt beyond recognition"; he looks at his wife "as one looks at a valuable piece of property which has suffered some damage." Four chapters later, when Robert invites her to go bathing again, the sea's "sonorous murmur reached her like a loving but imperative entreaty": the sea is "delicious," her companion tells her; "it will not hurt you." The voice of the sea invites the soul "to lose itself in mazes of inward

5. Stanley Kauffmann, "The Really Lost Generation, *The New Republic*, CLV (December 3, 1966), 38.
† From Lewis Leary, *Southern Excur-* *sions: Essays on Mark Twain and Others* (Baton Rouge: Louisiana State University Press, 1971), pp. 169–74. Footnotes are by the editor.

contemplation. . . . The touch of the sea is sensuous, enfolding the body in its soft, close embrace." These words that appear first in Chapter 6 are repeated almost exactly in the final chapter, as are these also: "The voice of the sea is seductive; never ceasing, clamoring, murmuring, inviting the soul to wander for a spell in the abysses of solitude."

Echoes of the poetry of Whitman[1] can be recognized in these recurrent murmurings of the sea, especially of his "Out of the Cradle Endlessly Rocking," in which the sea whispers the strong and "delicious" word *death*. Mrs. Chopin seems to have known Whitman's poetry well and to have had confidence that her readers did also, as is suggested in her quotation from Whitman's "Song of Myself" in her story "A Respectable Woman," where the quotation depends for its force on the reader's adding to the apparently innocent lines "Night of south winds—night of the large few stars! / Still nodding night—" the sensuous words which Whitman precedes and follows them: "Press close bare-bosom'd night . . ." and "mad naked summer night." Indeed the whole of *The Awakening* is pervaded with the spirit of Whitman's "Song of Myself." Edna Pontellier is awakened to her self, until with Whitman she might finally say, "I exist as I am, that is enough." As she who early in the novel shrinks almost prudishly from physical contact with other people is awakened to the joy of touch, a reader may be reminded of Whitman's "Is this then the touch? quivering me to new identity." And the ending of the novel is suggested in lines from Section 22 of "Song of Myself":

> You sea! I resign myself to you also—I guess what you mean.
> I behold from the beach your crooked inviting fingers,
> I believe you refuse to go back without feeling of me,
> We must have a turn together, I undress, I hurry out of sight
>   of the land,
> Cushion me soft, rock me in billowy drowse.

Not only does the sea sound an anticipatory refrain; incidents and characters early introduced in the novel often seem emblematic or teasingly suggestive of what will happen later. Some may find it significant that this narrative of self-discovery begins with the voice of an impertinent parrot and with a mockingbird "whistling his notes out upon the breeze with maddening persistence," and that it ends drowsily with "the hum of bees, and the musky odor of pinks." Others may wonder why Edna sleeps so often and so soundly, or

---

1. Walt Whitman (1819–1892), American poet whose *Leaves of Grass*, first published in 1855, generated controversy because of its unorthodox form and subject matter. The poetry was in free verse and at times employed frank sexual imagery.

whether her appetite for food and her shrugging off of niceness in eating are related, or supposed to be related, to other appetites. The silent woman clothed in black who appears six times in the first fifteen chapters may seem an ominous portent, as may also the pair of anonymous young lovers who roam the seaside, their courtship interrupted by children at play, much as Edna's adventuring toward freedom is disturbed—but how much?—by her concern for children. "I would give my life for my children," she says at one time; "but I wouldn't give myself." The significance of the Spanish girl Mariequita, who appears just before Robert Lebrun flees to Mexico and who appears again just before the final scene of the novel, is worthy of contemplation, as are the implications intended in the carefree and self-indulgent character of Victor Lebrun.

Bird images will be found throughout the novel, sometimes presented with quiet irony, as when Edna, seeking more freedom than her husband's house affords, takes a house of her own and calls it her "pigeon-house," allowing a reader then to recall that the pigeon of the kind she thought of was a domesticated, often a captive bird. The bird with the broken wing which, "reeling, fluttering, circling," is the only witness to Edna's final encounter with the sea may remind a reader that Mademoiselle Reisz had warned Edna earlier that "a bird that would soar above the level plain of tradition and prejudice must have strong wings," and is prefigured also (the ending of the novel may be discovered to be prefigured) in the vision which Edna has in Chapter 9 "of a man standing beside a desolate rock on the seashore. He was naked. His attitude was one of hopeless resignation as he looked toward a distant bird winging his flight away from him."

Things like this do not seem accidental. Almost every incident or reference in *The Awakening* anticipates an incident or reference that follows it or will remind a reader of something that has happened before. Other characters appear only in their relation to Edna Pontellier. Only such elements of background are introduced as contribute to her awakening. The narrative focus remains on her, as "blindly following whatever impulse moved her," she stumbles on finally "as if her thoughts had gone ahead of her. She is timid at first, almost cold: no trace of passion . . . colored her affection for her husband"; she is not accustomed to outward and spoken expression of affection. But as she is aroused by love outside of marriage, and by passion outside of love, she seems finally, not so much an enlightened woman, as "a beautiful, sleek animal waking up in the sun," uncaged and vulnerable.

Everything fits—the imagery and the reasons, gradually revealed, of the awakening. Among Mrs. Chopin's American contemporaries only Henry James[2] and perhaps Sarah Orne Jewett had produced fiction more artfully designed; there is a simpleness and a directness in *The Awakening* which has inevitably reminded readers of Flaubert's *Madame Bovary*, and an economy and mastery of incident and character which seem to forecast the lucid simplicity of Willa Cather's *Death Comes for the Archbishop*,[3] so different in theme, but comparable in technique. Few words are wasted; nothing is incomplete: it is a book about Edna Pontellier, and about her only.

To keep focus sharply on Edna, Mrs. Chopin needed somewhat to blur the supporting characters, revealing just enough about them to enable a reader to recognize their function. Most of them are familiar fictional types, familiarly realized: the kindly family doctor; the husband with a proprietary attitude toward his wife, a vacillating concern for his children, who enjoys weekend card games, and cares greatly for appearances; the irresponsible insolence of Victor Lebrun, which contrasts with the almost storybook concept of gallantry held by his brother; the misanthropy of Mademoiselle Reisz; and the almost professional charm of Alcée Arobin. Conventional characters like Madame Ratignolle, "a mother woman," are described in conventional, romantic terms: "There are no words to describe her," says Mrs. Chopin, "save the old ones that have served so often to picture the bygone heroine of romance and the fair lady of our dreams." Her hair is "spun gold," and her eyes "like nothing but sapphires; two lips that pouted, that were so red that one could only think of cherries or some other delicious fruit in looking at them. . . . Never were hands more exquisite than hers, and it was a joy to look at them when she threaded her needle or adjusted her gold thimble to her middle finger as she sewed on the little night drawers or fashioned a bodice or a bib."

Madame Ratignolle is "a sensuous Madonna," happily pregnant, motherly wise, and mindful of the future: in summer she prepares garments for the winter to come. Edna, obsessively concerned with herself, is careless about the future. Her thoughts are of herself, her concerns are her vague desires. But of all the characters she alone is described with precision, not in clichés but as an individual whose "graceful severity of poise and movement" made her "different from the crowd." She is not another mother woman, like those who "idolized their children, worshipped their husbands, and esteemed it a holy privilege to efface themselves as individuals." Her eyes "were

---

2. Henry James (1843–1916), master of the novel and short story, creator of a number of memorable female heroes.
3. Willa Cather (1876–1947), American novelist whose *Death Comes for the Archbishop* (1927) concerns the struggles of two French clergymen in the New Mexico territory. She wrote an early review of *The Awakening*. See page 153.

a yellowish brown, the color of her hair. . . . Her eyebrows were a shade darker. . . . They were thick and horizontal, emphasizing the depth of her eyes. . . . The lines of her body were long, clean and symmetrical; it was a body which occasionally fell into splendid poses; there was no suggestion of the trim stereotyped fashion plate about it."

Surrounded by other characters, most of whom are typical, Edna Pontellier gradually emerges as an understandable, though perhaps not completely admirable, individual reality. Whether she is weak and willful, a woman wronged by the requirements of society, or a self-indulgent sensualist, finally and fundamentally romantic, who gets exactly what she deserves—these are not considerations that seem to have concerned Mrs. Chopin. *The Awakening* is not a problem novel. If it seems inevitably to invite questions, these are subsidiary to its purpose, which is to describe what might really happen to a person like Edna Pontellier, being what she was, living when she did, and where.

Mrs. Chopin has presented a compelling portrait of a trapped and finally desperate woman, a drama of self-discovery, of awakening and doom, a tragedy perhaps of self-deceit. No questions are required, no verdict is given. Here is Edna Pontellier, a woman. She is awakened to possibilities for self-expression which, because she is what she is or because circumstances are what they are or because society is what it is, cannot be realized. Her awakening, only vaguely intellectual, is disturbingly physical. But wronged or erring, she is a valiant woman, worthy of place beside other fictional heroines who have tested emancipation and failed—Nathaniel Hawthorne's Hester Prynne, Gustave Flaubert's Emma Bovary, or Henry James's Isabel Archer.[4] Readers are likely to find something of themselves in her.

---

4. Nathaniel Hawthorne (1804–1864), author of *The Scarlet Letter* (1850), in which Hester Prynne suffers the scorn of her community for having borne a child by a man who is not her husband. Henry James's novel *Portrait of a Lady* (1881) concerns the fortunes of Isabel Archer, an American girl whose "awakening" occurs in Europe. See also p. 153, note 1.

JULES CHAMETZKY

[Edna and the "Woman Question"]†

* * *

From the opening images of a parrot in its cage and the marriage ring on the woman's finger, to the final images that flash before the drowning heroine—clanging spurs of a cavalry officer and "the hum of bees, and the musky odor of pinks"—the struggle is for the woman to free herself from being an object or possession defined in her functions, or owned, by others. Despite her middle-class advantages—money and the freedom to pursue a talent—Edna Pontellier, the heroine, is finally unable to overcome by herself the strength of the social and religious conventions and the biological mystique that entrap her.

Along the way, nevertheless, she is vouchsafed a glimpse of life as an autonomous self. She knows the joy of being able to say she would "never again belong to another than myself." Her young children, however, present a great problem. She says that she might die for her children, but would not give up her essential selfhood for them. This sentiment seems admirable but it is somewhat ambiguous, for at the end, in a muddled way, it is precisely the image of the children and her uncertainty about the nature of her role towards them that prove her undoing. Unconcerned herself about her new, freer attitude towards illicit sex, she fears the effects it will have upon her children when they learn about it. Mrs. Chopin had shown earlier how the husband uses the children and the mother's presumed duties towards them as a means of control and subjugation of the woman, but she is, finally, at a loss as to how to break through to newer and more humane conventions—a legitimate and recognizable dilemma. More startling to contemporaries must have been Edna's sentiments after her fall into adultery, and with a most unworthy lover. Whatever the conflicting emotions that assail her, she says, "there was neither shame nor remorse."

Edna's struggle towards a new state of awareness and independent being is to some extent understood and encouraged by only one other woman in the book—the pianist Mme. Reisz. But this strange woman's encouragement takes the form of urging a kind of self-sufficiency that is as selfless as the marriage vows: if Edna is

† From Jules Chametzky, "Our Decentralized Literature," *Jahrbuch fur Amerikastudien* (1972), pp. 56–72, an essay which treats four American writers— George Washington Cable, Abraham Cahan, Charles W. Chestnut, and Kate Chopin—who have been described as regional or "local color" writers. This designation served to minimize the stature of their work and the importance of their concerns.

serious about her work as an artist, then she must give herself to it entirely—a renunciation, really, of the flesh and conventional human relationships. That, of course, is an answer, but no answer to the woman's question posed in this book, how to be free in one's self and for one's self but still meaningfully connected to others. Posed in this way, the question, of course, applies to everyone. What makes it peculiarly related to the woman question in *The Awakening* is Mrs. Chopin's unwillingness to make her heroine's situation easier by removing from her selfness the burden and possibility of motherhood. As indicated earlier, Mrs. Chopin stumbles ambiguously on this question, as indeed we still do.

Awakened by a realization of her sensuous self, Edna Pontellier grows in self-awareness and autonomy. But it is a lonely and isolated autonomy that exacts a terrible price. Like Kate Chopin herself, who broke through to new perceptions and honesty as an artist, Mrs. Pontellier, in the context of her time and milieu, found no firm ground beneath her, either in theory or practice, and she went under.

* * *

DONALD A. RINGE

Romantic Imagery†

* * * *The Awakening* posits a double world, one within and one without. Early in the book, Edna Pontellier feels contradictory impulses impelling her, impulses that at first serve to bewilder her, but which also reveal that she is "beginning to realize her position in the universe as a human being, and to recognize her relations as an individual to the world within and about her." As with Emerson's theory,[1] moreover, it is through the eyes that these worlds meet and influence each other, the outer world perceived and colored by the unique nature that lies within, and the inner world brought to its self-awareness by the influences that enter from the world without. Thus, when Edna returns from Chênière Caminada on the fateful Sunday she spends there with Robert Lebrun, she begins to perceive a new self "in some way different" from her old one. Though Edna does not yet fully suspect what is happening, the author makes

† From Donald A. Ringe, "Romantic Imagery in Kate Chopin's *The Awakening*," *American Literature*, XLIII (January 1972), 580–88. Author's footnotes have been renumbered and some have been omitted.

1. The author is referring to Emerson's theory of correspondence. See *The Works of Ralph Waldo Emerson* (Boston and New York: Houghton Mifflin, 1883), I, 13–80. [*Editor.*]

abundantly clear that a process is occurring that closely resembles the transcendentalist theory of self-discovery: "she was seeing with different eyes and making the acquaintance of new conditions in herself that colored and changed her environment."

The process is triggered, moreover, by an experience that Edna has in the ocean, an experience described by Kate Chopin through imagery that has deep romantic roots. As W. H. Auden has pointed out in *The Enchafèd Flood*, the sea plays an important role in romantic iconography. It is "the place where there is no community," where "the individual . . . is free from both the evils and the responsibilities of communal life." It is the place, moreover, where "decisive events, the moments of eternal choice . . . occurs."[2] In *The Awakening*, the sea serves precisely this purpose, for it is in the Gulf that Edna experiences the crisis that determines her development throughout the rest of the book. As in much romantic art, however, the sea serves here a double purpose for the individual: it invites "the soul to wander for a spell in abysses of solitude; to lose itself in mazes of inward contemplation." In other words, it can turn the soul's attention outward to the infinity suggested by the endless expanse of encircling horizon and sky—to confront the universe alone—or it can cause, as it does to Pip in *Moby-Dick*, an "intense concentration of self" that can hardly be endured.[3]

Edna experiences both of these feelings on the night she learns to swim. When she pulls herself through the water for the first time, "a feeling of exultation [overtakes] her," as if she has received "some power of significant import . . . to control the working of her body and her soul." She turns away from shore "to gather in an impression of space and solitude, which the vast expanse of water, meeting and melting with the moonlit sky, conveyed to her excited fancy," and as she swims out into the Gulf, she seems "to be reaching out for the unlimited in which to lose herself." The expansive feeling of striving toward the infinite is not to last, however, for when she turns to look at the shore, which seems to her now to be far away, a "flash of terror" strikes her, a "quick vision of death [smites] her soul," and she hurries back to her waiting husband and friends. The fear of death, of a threat to the self, clearly reveals the intensification of self-awareness that the experience has given her—an awakening of the self as important, perhaps, as any other in the novel. For from this point on, Edna develops a growing self-awareness from which there is no turning back.

2. W. H. Auden, *The Enchafèd Flood; or The Romantic Iconography of the Sea* (New York, 1967), pp. 15, 13.
3. Herman Melville, *Moby-Dick; or The Whale*, eds. Luther S. Mansfield and Howard P. Vincent (New York, 1952), p. 412. We must not assume, of course, that *Moby-Dick* itself lies behind *The Awakening*, but that both Herman Melville and Kate Chopin drew upon a common tradition of romantic imagery.

The process, however, is not complete until she returns to New Orleans. This is the romantic "city" which, as Auden has pointed out, is the symbolic opposite of the sea. It is community, with all the demands that the social organization makes upon the individual, and which the self sometimes finds hard to accept after the expansive experience on the sea or, we may add, the innocent interlude on the "happy island," a third romantic symbol[4] which, in Edna's case, is Grand Isle. It is not surprising, then, that in keeping with the romantic imagery through which the book is developed, Edna's rebellion should become complete when she returns to society. She refuses to take seriously the social forms through which the community functions, but instead determines to go her own way, independent of both her family and the society in which they live. By this time, even Léonce, her husband, sees that Edna is "not herself," that is, not her old self. As Kate Chopin puts it, "he could not see that she was becoming herself and daily casting aside that fictitious self which we assume like a garment with which to appear before the world."

But if Edna's real self is revealed as a result of this process, we may legitimately ask what that real self is like. It is one that insists upon its own inviolability, that will brook no interference from others. Indeed, Edna carries this insistence upon her own integrity almost to an extreme. As she tells Adèle Ratignolle at one point, she would be willing to give up what she considers the unessential for her children—her money or even her life—but she would not give up herself. "Nobody has any right," she believes, to force her to do anything, and she frankly admits to Doctor Mandelet, "I don't want anything but my own way. That is wanting a good deal, of course, when you have to trample upon the lives, the hearts, the prejudices of others—but no matter . . ." Though Edna usually exempts the children—at least partially and hesitantly—from her sweeping statements on her individual inviolability, she is indeed willing to sacrifice everyone else to the demands of her sole self. As a consequence, her characteristic state in the latter half of the novel is solitude. For the most part, she is alone.

Kate Chopin compares and contrasts Edna's state with a number of others in the book, developing her theme through the polarities of self-absorption (Madame Reisz) and willing surrender of self to another (Adèle and Alphonse Ratignolle). In Madame Reisz, the consequences of insisting on the self alone are clearly developed. Though she is indeed a fine artist, she is also self-assertive, imperious, and disposed "to trample upon the rights of others." She is

4. Auden, *The Enchafèd Flood*, p. 20. That Grand Isle may serve this familiar function in *The Awakening* seems clear from the innocent relationships that the characters maintain there until Edna's awakening drives Robert away to Mexico.

venomous, disagreeable, and rude. Small wonder, then, that she is
more often than not alone. By contrast, the Ratignolles are a prime
example of two individuals who, like right hand and left, heart and
soul, have indeed become one. "The Ratignolles understood each
other perfectly. If ever the fusion of two human beings into one has
been accomplished on this sphere it was surely in their union."
Chopin, of course, makes no explicit judgment on these two ways of
life, but it is apparent that Edna lies between the two extremes.

Yet another contrast is symbolized by a recurring detail that
appears in the depiction of life on Grand Isle. Throughout this part
of the novel, a pair of lovers and a lady in black, who is usually
saying her rosary or reading her prayer book, are frequently seen in
the background. As symbolic figures, they cannot perhaps be as-
signed precise meanings. But the two lovers are indeed so lost in
each other as to be almost completely oblivious to what is going on
around them. There is surely no self-assertion here. Nor does there
seem to be any in the lady in black who, in praying to her God, is
surrendering herself to the Deity. Both the couple and the lady in
black represent a strong contrast to Edna, who never really achieves
the loss of self in love for another, and who is never portrayed as
submitting herself to worship God in communion with others. She
is pictured instead as running away from the Presbyterian service as
a girl, and as leaving the Catholic mass with "a feeling of oppression" on Chênière Caminada.

Edna stands apart from all these people, even those, like Madame
Reisz, whom she most resembles. She vacillates between the polar
positions, reaching out to her children on occasion, and even to her
old friend Adèle, who calls for her during her labor. But she turns
away from all of them eventually, and takes pleasure most often in
being alone. Edna, moreover, is hardly consistent in her behavior,
for she is unwilling to allow others the same freedom she demands
for herself. Though she insists that she will not be possessed by
anyone, it is clear that she wishes to possess Robert. She wants to
hold on to him when he decides to leave for Mexico, and she
accuses him of selfishness when he will not submit to her demands.
Indeed, when she returns from Adèle Ratignolle's confinement expecting to find Robert waiting for her, "she could picture at that
moment no greater bliss on earth than *possession* of the beloved
one. His expression of love had already *given him to her* in part"
(italics mine). She demands of others what none may demand of
her; she wishes to possess, who will not herself be possessed.[5]

Edna's reaching out to others is either brief and transitory (as

5. Unlike the Creole husbands, moreover, who never feel jealous, Edna
becomes jealous almost as soon as she
perceives that she loves Robert, and the
emotion recurs later—a clear sign of
her desire for possession.

with Adèle and the children) or colored by a selfish motive (as with Robert). Indeed, as the story develops, one begins to suspect that Edna's self is by its very nature a solitary thing, that she is utterly incapable of forming a true and lasting relationship with another. The men to whom she is attracted before her marriage are either such as might inflame a youthful imagination (the cavalry officer and the tragedian), or the kind she is told she must not covet (the young man who is engaged to the lady on a neighboring plantation). Forbidden fruit seems to appeal to her most, a sign, perhaps, of a certain perverseness in her character. She married Léonce Pontellier partly at least because her family was opposed to him, and one suspects that the appeal of Alcée Arobin—and even of Robert Lebrun—derives from the fact that she knows she should not become involved with them.[6] The result is that she either ends up as a possession—and both Léonce and Alcée treat her as one[7]— or she is herself overwhelmed with the desire to possess another. Both relationships are, of course, thoroughly destructive.

Edna's final awakening, her ultimate self-discovery, reveals an inner nature that is devoid of hope. After she learns that Robert has left her for good, she lies awake throughout the night, a sense of despondency that never lifts overwhelming her spirit. She faces the truth about herself, that for her no lasting union with anyone is possible. Though she may want Robert with her now, she "realized that the day would come when he, too, and the thought of him would melt out of her existence, leaving her alone." Even her children appear to her as enemies, as "antagonists who had overcome her; who had overpowered her and sought to drag her into the soul's slavery for the rest of her days." Since Edna cannot give herself to anyone, but instead remains aloof from any true relationship with another, she is doomed to stand completely alone in the universe, a position that is clearly symbolized by the final episode in the book: her solitary swim far out into the emptiness of the Gulf.

The sea is presented here in language almost identical with that of the passage quoted above. A very important clause, however, is omitted. In the former passage, the dual nature of the sea experience is suggested, the outward expansion into the infinite, and the intensification of self-awareness that can also result from finding oneself alone in the apparently limitless sea. Here, the second aspect of the experience is not included. By now, Edna has explored herself completely and has penetrated to her true nature, solitary and

6. Note too that one of the few women she associates with in New Orleans is Mrs. Highcamp, whom her husband had advised her not to encourage socially.

7. This relationship is suggested by parallel scenes. Once his affair with Edna is established, Arobin settles down to smoke a cigar and read his newspaper in her house, in much the same way Léonce does in the first chapter of the book.

aloof though it may be. The seductive voice of the sea, therefore, can only incite her spirit "to wander in abysses of solitude." This Edna does, swimming on and on, pleased with the thought that she is escaping the slavery represented to her imagination in the form of Léonce and the children. But the price she pays for her escape is death. In defending her self against the threat of community, she loses it in the infinity suggested by the expanse of the sea.[8]

Read in these terms, Kate Chopin's *The Awakening* is a powerful romantic novel.[9] It develops the theme of self-discovery so important in the works of the transcendentalists and does it in terms of imagery that is thoroughly appropriate to its presentation. Unlike the transcendentalists, however, Kate Chopin allows her character no limitless expansion of the self. She presents her, rather—in terms suggesting Melville—as a solitary, defiant soul who stands out against the limitations that both nature and society place upon her, and who accepts in the final analysis a defeat that involves no surrender. Chopin herself makes no explicit comment on Edna Pontellier's actions. She neither approves nor condemns, but maintains an aesthetic distance throughout, relying upon the recurring patterns of imagery to convey her meaning. It is not the morality of Edna's life that most deeply concerns her, nor even the feminist concept so obviously present in the book. It is, rather, the philosophic questions raised by Edna's awakening: the relation of the individual self to the physical and social realities by which it is surrounded, and the price it must pay for insisting upon its absolute freedom.

CYNTHIA GRIFFIN WOLFF

Thanatos and Eros†

* * * An astonishing proportion of that part of the novel which deals with Edna's sojourn at Grand Isle is paced by the rhythm of her basic needs, especially the most primitive ones of eating and sleeping. If one were to plot the course of Edna's life during this

---

8. Edna's death by drowning seems consistent with the sea imagery through which much of the theme is developed. According to Auden, once the island is left behind, "the only possible place of peace for the romantic is under the waters." *The Enchafèd Flood*, p. 24.
9. I am aware, of course, that both *The Awakening* and the whole local color school to which Kate Chopin is said to belong are usually classified as late nineteenth-century realism. That realistic detail is not inconsistent with romantic imagery, however, is amply illustrated by so thoroughly romantic a book as *Moby-Dick*.
† From Cynthia Griffin Wolff, "Thanatos and Eros: Kate Chopin's *The Awakening*," *American Quarterly*, XXV (October 1973), 449–71. The author's footnotes have been renumbered.

period, the most reliable indices to the passage of time would be her meals and her periods of sleep. The importance of these in Edna's more general "awakening" can be suggested if we examine the day-long boat trip which she makes with Robert.

There is an almost fairy-tale quality to the whole experience; the rules of time seem suspended, and the mélange of brilliant sensory experiences—the sun, the water, the soft breeze, the old church with its lizards and whispered tales of pirate gold—melts into a dreamlike pattern. It is almost as if Edna's fantasy world had come into being. Indeed, there is even some suggestion that after the event, she incorporates the memory of it into her fantasy world in such a way that the reality and the illusion do, in fact, become confused. Later on in the novel when Edna is invited to tell a true anecdote at a dinner party, she speaks "of a woman who paddled away with her lover one night in a pirogue and never came back. They were lost amid the Baratarian Islands, and no one ever heard of them or found trace of them from that day to this. It was pure invention. She said that Madame Antoine had related it to her. That, also, was an invention. Perhaps it was a dream she had had. But every glowing word seemed real to those who listened."

Yet even this jewel-like adventure with Robert is dominated by the insistence of the infantile life-pattern—sleep and eat, sleep and eat. Edna's rest had been feverish the night prior to the expedition; "She slept but a few hours," and their expedition begins with a hurried breakfast. Her taste for sight-seeing, even her willingness to remain with Robert, is so overwhelmed by her lassitude that she must find a place to rest and to be alone. Strikingly, however, once she is by herself, left to seek restful sleep, Edna seems somewhat to revive, and the tone shifts from one of exhaustion to one of sensuous, leisurely enjoyment of her own body. "Left alone in the little side room, [she] loosened her clothes, removing the greater part of them. . . . How luxurious it felt to rest thus in a strange, quaint bed, with its sweet country odor of laurel lingering about the sheets and mattress! She stretched her strong limbs that ached a little. She ran her fingers through her loosened hair for a while. She looked at her round arms as she held them straight up and rubbed them one after the other, observing closely, as if it were something she saw for the first time, the fine, firm quality and texture of her flesh." Powerfully sensuous as this scene is, we would be hard put to find genital significance here. Reduced to its simplest form, the description is of a being discovering the limits and qualities of its own body—discovering, and taking joy in the process of discovery. And having engaged in this exploratory "play" for a while, Edna falls asleep.

The manner of her waking makes explicit reference to the myth of the sleeping beauty. " 'How many years have I slept?' she inquired. 'The whole island seems changed. A new race of beings must have sprung up, leaving only you and me as past relics.' " Robert jokingly falls in with the fantasy: " 'You have slept precisely one hundred years. I was left here to guard your slumbers; and for one hundred years I have been out under the shed reading a book.' " In the fairy tale, of course, the princess awakens with a kiss, conscious of love; but Edna's libidinal energies have been arrested at a pre-genital level—so she awakens "very hungry"—and her lover prepares her a meal! "He was childishly gratified to discover her appetite, and to see the relish with which she ate the food which he had procured for her." Indeed, though the title of the novel suggests a re-enactment of the traditional romantic myth, it never does offer a complete representation of it. The next invocation is Arobin's kiss, "the first kiss of her life to which her nature had really responded"; but as we have seen earlier, this response is facilitated, perhaps even made possible, by the fact that her emotional attachment is not to Arobin but to the Robert of her fantasy world. The final allusion to an awakening kiss is Edna's rousing of Robert; and yet this is a potentially genital awakening from which both flee.

Edna's central problem, once the hidden "self" begins to exert its inexorable power, is that her libidinal appetite has been fixated at the oral level. Edna herself has an insistent preoccupation with nourishment; on the simplest level, she is concerned with food. Her favorite adjective is "delicious": she sees many mother-women as "delicious" in their role; she carries echoes of her children's voices "like the memory of a delicious song"; when she imagines Robert she thinks "how delicious it would be to have him there with her." And the notion of something's being good because it might be good to "eat" (or internalize in some way) is echoed in all of her relationships with other people. Those who care about her typically feed her; and the sleep-and-eat pattern which is most strikingly established at the beginning of the novel continues even to the very end. Not surprisingly, in the "grown-up world" she is a poor housekeeper, and though Léonce's responses are clearly petty and self-centered, Edna's behavior does betray incompetence, especially when we compare it (as the novel so often invites us to) with the nurturing capacities of Adèle. It is not surprising that the most dramatic gesture toward freedom that Edna makes is to move out of her husband's house; yet even this gesture toward "independence" can be comprehended as part of an equally powerful wish to regress. It is, after all, a "tiny house" that she moves to; she calls it her "pigeon house," and if she were still a little girl, we might call it a playhouse.

The decision to move from Léonce's house is virtually coincidental with the beginning of her affair with Arobin; yet even the initial stages of that affair are described in oral terms—Edna feels regret because "it was not love which had held this cup of life to her lips." And though the relationship develops as she makes preparations for the move, it absorbs astonishingly little of Edna's libido. She is deliberately distant, treating Arobin with "affected carelessness." As the narrator observes, "If he had expected to find her languishing, reproachful, or indulging in sentimental tears, he must have been greatly surprised." She is "true" to the fantasy image of Robert. And in the real world her emotional energy has been committed in another direction. She is busy with elaborate plans—for a dinner party! And it is on this extravagant sumptuous oral repast that she lavishes her time and care. Here Edna as purveyor of food becomes not primarily a nourisher (as Adèle is) but a sensualist in the only terms that she can truly comprehend. One might argue that in this elaborate feast Edna's sensuous self comes closest to some form of expression which might be compatible with the real world. The dinner party itself is one of the longest sustained episodes in the novel; we are told in loving detail about the appearance of the table, the commodious chairs, the flowers, the candles, the food and wines, Edna's attire—no sensory pleasure is left unattended. Yet even this indulgence fails to satisfy. "As she sat there amid her guests, she felt the old ennui overtaking her; the hopelessness which so often assailed her, which came upon her like an obsession, like something extraneous, independent of volition. It was something which announced itself; a chill breath that seemed to issue from some vast cavern wherein discords wailed." Edna, perhaps, connects this despair to the absence of Robert. "There came over her the acute longing which always summoned into her spiritual vision the presence of the beloved one, overpowering her at once with a sense of the unattainable." However, the narrator's language here is interestingly ambiguous. It is not specifically *Robert* that Edna longs for; it is "the presence of the beloved one"—an indefinite perpetual image, existing "always" in "her spiritual vision." The longing, so described, is an immortal one and, as she acknowledges, "unattainable"; the vision might be of Robert, but it might equally be of the cavalry officer, the engaged young man, the tragedian—even of Adèle, whose mothering attentions first elicited a sensuous response from Edna and whose own imminent motherhood has kept her from the grand party. The indefinite quality of Edna's longing thus described has an ominous tone, a tone made even more ominous by the rising specter of those "vast caverns" waiting vainly to be filled.

Perhaps Edna's preoccupation with the incorporation of food is but one aspect of a more general concern with incorporating that which is external to her. Freud's hypotheses about the persistence in some people of essentially oral concerns makes Edna's particular problem even clearer.

> Originally the ego includes everything, later it separates off an external world from itself. Our present ego-feeling is, therefore, only a shrunken residue of a much more inclusive—indeed, an all-embracing—feeling which corresponded to a more intimate bond between the ego and the world about it. If we may assume that there are many people in whose mental life this primary ego-feeling has persisted to a greater or less degree, it would exist in them side by side with the narrower and more sharply demarcated ego-feeling of maturity, like a kind of counterpart to it. In that case, the ideational contents appropriate to it would be precisely those of limitlessness and of a bond with the universe . . . the 'oceanic' feeling.[1]

A psychologically mature individual has to some extent satisfied these oral desires for limitless fusion with the external world; presumably his sense of oneness with a nurturing figure has given him sustenance sufficient to move onward to more complex satisfactions. Yet growth inevitably involves some loss. "The feeling of happiness derived from the satisfaction of a wild instinctual impulse untamed by the ego is incomparably more intense than that derived from sating an instinct that has been tamed."[2] To some extent all of us share Edna's fantasy of complete fulfillment through a bond with the infinite; that is what gives the novel its power. However, for those few people in whom this primary ego-feeling has persisted with uncompromising force the temptation to seek total fulfillment may be both irresistible and annihilating.

Everywhere and always in the novel, Edna's fundamental longing is postulated in precisely these terms. And strangely enough, the narrator seems intuitively to understand the connection between this longing for suffusion, fulfillment, incorporation, and the very earliest attempts to define identity.

> But the beginning of things, of a world especially, is necessarily vague, tangled, chaotic, and exceedingly disturbing. How few of us ever emerge from such a beginning! How many souls perish in its tumult!
> The voice of the sea is seductive; never ceasing, whispering, clamoring, murmuring, inviting the soul to wander for a spell in abysses of solitude; to lose itself in mazes of inward contemplation. The voice of the sea speaks to the soul. The touch of the sea is sensuous, enfolding the body in its soft, close embrace.

1. Sigmund Freud, "Civilization and its Discontents," in *The Standard Edition of the Complete Works*, James Strachey, ed. (London: Hogarth Press, 1971), 21:71.
2. Ibid., p. 160.

Ultimately, the problem facing Edna has a nightmarish circularity. She has achieved some measure of personal identity only by hiding her "true self" within—repressing all desire for instinctual gratification. Yet she can see others in her environment—the Creoles generally and Adèle in particular—who seem comfortably able to indulge their various sensory appetites and to do so with easy moderation. Edna's hidden self longs for resuscitation and nourishment; and in the supportive presence of Grand Isle Edna begins to acknowledge and express the needs of that "self."

Yet once released, the inner being cannot be satisfied. It is an orally destructive self, a limitless void whose needs can be filled, finally, only by total fusion with the outside world, a totality of sensuous enfolding. And this totality means annihilation of the ego.

Thus all aspects of Edna's relationship with the outside world are unevenly defined. She is remarkably vulnerable to feelings of being invaded and overwhelmed; we have already seen that she views emotional intimacy as potentially shattering. She is equally unable to handle the phenomenal world with any degree of consistency or efficiency. She is very much at the mercy of her environment: the atmosphere of Mademoiselle Reisz' room is said to "invade" her with repose; Mademoiselle Reisz' music has the consistent effect of penetrating Edna's outer self and playing upon the responsive chords of her inner yearning; even her way of looking at objects in the world about her becomes an act of incorporation; "she had a way of turning [her eyes] swiftly upon an object and holding them there as if lost in some inward maze of contemplation or thought." Once she has given up the pattern of repression that served to control dangerous impulses, she becomes engaged in trying to maintain a precarious balance in each of her relationships. On the one hand she must resist invasion, for with invasion comes possession and total destruction. On the other hand she must resist the equally powerful impulse to destroy whatever separates her from the external world so that she can seek union, fusion and (so her fantasies suggest) ecstatic fulfillment.

In seeking to deal with this apparently hopeless problem, Edna encounters several people whose behavior might serve as a pattern for her. Mademoiselle Reisz is one. Mademoiselle Reisz is an artist, and as such she has created that direct avenue between inner and outer worlds which Edna seeks in her own life. Surely Edna's own attempts at artistic enterprise grow out of her more general desire for sustained ecstasy. "While Edna worked she sometimes sang low the little air, 'Ah, si tu savais!' " Her work is insensibly linked with her memories of Robert, and these in turn melt into more generalized memories and desires. The little song she is humming "moved her with recollections. She could hear again the ripple of the water, the flapping sail. She could see the glint of the moon upon the bay, and could feel the soft, gusty beating of the hot south wind. A subtle current of desire passed through her body, weakening her hold upon the brushes and making her eyes burn." In some ways, Edna's painting might offer her an excellent and viable mode for coming to terms with the insistent demands of cosmic yearning. For one thing, it utilizes in an effective way her habit of transforming the act of observing the external world into an act of incorporation: to some extent the artist must use the world in this way, incorporating it and transforming it in the act of artistic creation. Thus the period during which Edna is experimenting with her art offers her some of the most satisfying experiences she is capable of having. "There were days when she was very happy without knowing why. She was happy to be alive and breathing when her whole being seemed to be one with the sunlight, the color, the odors, the luxuriant warmth of some perfect Southern day. . . . And she found it good to dream and to be alone and unmolested."

Yet when Edna tells Mademoiselle Reisz about her efforts, she is greeted with skepticism: " 'You have pretensions,' " Mademoiselle Reisz responds. " 'To be an artist includes much; one must possess many gifts—absolute gifts—which have not been acquired by one's own effort. And moreover, to succeed, the artist must possess the courageous soul. . . . The brave soul. The soul that dares and defies.' " One implication of Mademoiselle Reisz' half-contemptuous comment may well be the traditional view that the artist must dare to be unconventional; and it is this interpretation which Edna reports later to Arobin, saying as she does, however, " 'I only half comprehend her.' " The part of Mademoiselle Reisz' injunction that eludes Edna's understanding concerns the sense of purposiveness which is implied by the image of a courageous soul. Mademoiselle Reisz has her art, but she has sacrificed for it—perhaps too much. In any case, however, she has acknowledged limitations, accepted some and grappled with others; she is an active agent who has defined her relationship to the world. Edna, by contrast, is passive.

The words which recur most frequently to describe her are words like melting, drifting, misty, dreaming, shadowy. She is not willing (perhaps not able) to define her position in the world because to do so would involve relinquishing the dream of total fulfillment. Thus while Mademoiselle Reisz can control and create, Edna is most comfortable as the receptive vessel—both for Mademoiselle Reisz' music and for the sense impressions which form the basis of her own artistic endeavor. Mademoiselle Reisz commands her work; Edna is at the mercy of hers. Thus just as there are moments of exhilaration, so "there were days when she was unhappy, she did not know why,—when it did not seem worth while to be glad or sorry, to be alive or dead; when life appeared to her like a grotesque pandemonium and humanity like worms struggling blindly toward inevitable annihilation. She could not work on such a day, nor weave fantasies to stir her pulses and warm her blood." Art, for Edna, ultimately becomes not a defense against inner turmoil, merely a reflection of it.

Another possible defense for Edna might be the establishment and sustaining of a genuine genital relationship. Her adolescent fantasies, her mechanical marriage, her liaison with Arobin and her passionate attachment to the fantasy image of Robert all suggest imperfect efforts to do just that. A genital relationship, like all ego-relationships, necessarily involves limitation; to put the matter in Edna's terms, a significant attachment with a real man would involve relinquishing the fantasy of total fulfillment with some fantasy lover. In turn, it would offer genuine emotional nourishment—though perhaps never enough to satisfy the voracious clamoring of Edna's hidden self.

Ironically, Adèle, who seems such a fount of sustenance, gives indications of having some of the same oral needs that Edna does. Like Edna she is preoccupied with eating, she pays extravagant care to the arrangement of her own physical comforts, and she uses her pregnancy as an excuse to demand a kind of mothering attention for herself. The difference between Edna and Adèle is that Adèle can deal with her nurturing needs by displacing them onto her children and becoming a "mother-woman." Having thus segregated and limited these desires, Adèle can find diverse ways of satisfying them; and having satisfied her own infantile oral needs, she can go on to have a rewarding adult relationship with her husband. Between Adèle and M. Ratignolle there is mutual joining together: "The Ratignolles understood each other perfectly. If ever the fusion of two human beings into one has been accomplished on this sphere it was surely in their union." The clearest outward sign of this happy union is that the Ratignolles converse eagerly and clearly with each other. M. Ratignolle reports his experiences and thoughts to his wife, and she in turn "was keenly interested in everything he said, laying down her fork the better to listen, chiming in, taking the words out of his mouth." Yet this picture of social and domestic accord is indescribably dismaying to Edna. She "felt depressed rather than soothed after leaving them. The little glimpse of domestic harmony which had been offered her, gave her no regret, no longing."

Again, what has capitulated is the fantasy of complete and total suffusion; the Ratignolles have only a union which is as perfect as one can expect *"on this sphere"* (italics added). Yet the acme of bliss which Edna has always sought "was not for her in this world."

Edna wishes a kind of pre-verbal union, an understanding which consistently surpasses words. Léonce is scarcely a sensitive man (that is, as we have seen, why she chose to marry him). Yet Edna never exerts herself to even such efforts at communication with him as might encourage a supportive emotional response. She responds to his unperceptive clumsiness by turning inward, falling into silence. Over and over again their disagreements follow the pattern of a misunderstanding which Edna refuses to clarify. At the very beginning of the novel when Léonce selfishly strolls off for an evening of gambling, Edna's rage and sense of loneliness are resolutely hidden, even when he seeks to discover the cause of her unhappiness. "She said nothing, and refused to answer her husband when he questioned her." Perhaps Léonce could not have understood the needs which Edna feels so achingly unfulfilled. And he is very clumsy. But he does make attempts at communication while she does not, and his interview with the family doctor shows greater concern about Edna's problems than she manages to feel for his.

The attachment to Robert, which takes on significance only after he has left Grand Isle, monopolizes Edna's emotions because it does temporarily offer an illusion of fusion, of complete union. However, this love affair, such as it is, is a genuinely narcissistic one; the sense of fusion exists because Edna's lover is really a part of herself—a figment of her imagination, an image of Robert which she has incorporated into her consciousness. Not only is her meeting with Robert after his return a disappointment (as we have seen earlier); it moves the static, imaginary "love affair" into a new and crucial stage; it tests, once and for all, Edna's capacity to transform her world of dreams into viable reality. Not surprisingly, "some way he had seemed nearer to her off there in Mexico."

Still she does try. She awakens him with a kiss even as Arobin had awakened her. Robert, too, is resistant to genuine involvement, and his initial reaction is to speak of the hopelessness of their relationship. Edna, however, is insistent (despite the interruption telling her of Adèle's accouchement). " 'We shall be everything to each other. Nothing else in the world is of any consequence. I must go to my friend; but you will wait for me? No matter how late; you will wait for me, Robert?' " And at this point, Edna seems finally to have won her victory. " 'Don't go; don't go! Oh! Edna, stay with me,' he pleaded. . . . Her seductive voice, together with his great love for her, had enthralled his senses, had deprived him of every impulse but the longing to hold her and keep her." And at this moment, so long and eagerly anticipated, Edna leaves Robert!

Robert's own resolve weakens during the interval, and it would be all too easy to blame Edna's failure on him. Certainly he is implicated. Yet his act does not explain *Edna's* behavior. "Nothing else in the world is of any consequence," she has said. If that is so, why then does she leave? No real duty calls her. Her presence at Adèle's delivery is of virtually no help. The doctor, sorry for the pain that the scene has caused Edna, even remonstrates with her mildly for having come. " 'You shouldn't have been there, Mrs. Pontellier. . . . There were a dozen women she might have had with her, unimpressionable women.' " To have stayed with Robert would have meant consummation, finally, the joining of her dreamlike passion to a flesh and blood lover; to leave was to risk losing that opportunity. Edna must realize the terms of this dilemma, and still she chooses to leave. We can only conclude that she is unconsciously ambivalent about achieving the goal which has sustained her fantasies for so long. The flesh and blood Robert may prove an imperfect, unsatisfactory substitute for the "beloved" of her dreams; what is more, a relationship with the real Robert would necessarily disenfranchise the more desirable phantom lover, whose presence is linked with her more general yearning for suffusion and indefinable ecstasy.

The totality of loss which follows Edna's decision forces a grim recognition upon her, the recognition that all her lovers have really been of but fleeting significance. "To-day it is Arobin; to-morrow it will be some one else. . . . It makes no difference to me. . . . There was no one thing in the world that she desired. There was no human being whom she wanted near her except Robert; and she even realized that the day would come when he, too, and the thought of him would melt out of her existence, leaving her alone." Her devastation, thus described, is removed from the realm of romantic disappointment; and we must see Edna's final suicide as originating in a sense of inner emptiness, not in some finite failure of love. Her decision to go to Adèle is in part a reflection of Edna's unwillingness to compromise her dream of Robert (and in this sense it might be interpreted as a flight from reality). On the other hand, it might also be seen as a last desperate attempt to come to terms with the anguish created by her unfulfilled "Oceanic" longing. And for this last effort she must turn to Adèle, the human who first caused her to loosen the bonds of repression.

The pre-eminence of Adèle over Robert in Edna's emotional life, affirmed by Edna's crucial choice, is undeniably linked to her image as a nurturing figure and, especially here, as a mother-to-be. In this capacity she is also linked to Edna's own children—insistent specters in Edna's consciousness; and this link is made explicit by Adèle's repetition of the cryptic injunction to "think of the children."

Now in every human's life there is a period of rhapsodic union or fusion with another, and this is the period of early infancy, before the time when a baby begins to differentiate himself from his mother. It is the haunting memory of this evanescent state which Freud defines as "Oceanic feeling," the longing to recapture that sense of oneness and suffused sensuous pleasure—even, perhaps, the desire to be reincorporated into the safety of pre-existence. Men can never recreate this state of total union. Adult women can—when they are pregnant. Most pregnant women identify intensely with their unborn children, and through that identification in some measure re-experience a state of complete and harmonious union. "The biologic process has created a unity of mother and child, in which the bodily substance of one flows into the other, and thus one larger unit is formed out of two units. The same thing takes place on the psychic level. By tender identification, by perceiving the fruit of her body as part of herself, the pregnant woman is able to transform the 'parasite' into a beloved being. Thus, mankind's eternal yearning for identity between the ego and the nonego, that deeply buried original desire to reachieve the condition once experienced, to repeat the human dream that was once realized in the mother's womb, is fulfilled."[3] Adèle is a dear friend, yes; she is a nurturing figure. But above all, she is the living embodiment of that state which Edna's deepest being longs to recapture. Trapped in the conflict between her desire for "freedom," as seen in her compulsive need to protect her precarious sense of self, and her equally insistent yearning for complete fulfillment through total suffusion, Edna is intensely involved with Adèle's pregnancy.

Edna's compulsion to be with Adèle at the moment of delivery is, in the sense which would have most significance for her, a need to view individuation at its origin. For if pregnancy offers a state of total union, then birth is the initial separation: for the child it is the archetypal separation trauma; for the mother, too, it is a significant psychic trauma. It is the ritual re-enactment of her own birth and a brutal reawakening to the world of isolated ego. "To make it the being that is outside her, the pregnant mother must deliver the child from the depths of herself. . . . She loses not only it, but herself with it. This, I think, is at the bottom of that fear and foreboding of death that every pregnant woman has, and this turns the giving of life into the losing of life."[4] Edna cannot refuse to partake of this ceremony, for here, if anywhere, she will find the solution to her problem.

Yet the experience is horrendous; it gives no comfort, no reassuring answer to Edna's predicament. It offers only stark, uncompromising truth. Adèle's ordeal reminds Edna of her own accouchements. "Edna began to feel uneasy. She was seized with a vague

3. Helene Deutsch, *The Psychology of Women* (New York: Grune and Strat- ton, 1971), 2:139.

4. Ibid., p. 79.

dread. Her own like experiences seemed far away, unreal, and only half remembered. She recalled faintly an ecstasy of pain, the heavy odor of chloroform, a stupor which had deadened sensation, and an awakening to find a little new life to which she had given being." This is Nature's cruel message. The fundamental significance to Edna of an awakening is an awakening to separation, to individual existence, to the hopelessness of ever satisfying the dream of total fusion. The rousing of her sensuous being had led Edna on a quest for ecstasy; but the ecstasy which beckoned has become in the end merely an "ecstasy of pain," first in her protracted struggle to retain identity and finally here in that relentless recognition of inevitable separation which has been affirmed in the delivery, "an awakening to find a little new life." Edna is urged to leave, but she refuses. "With an inward agony, with a flaming, outspoken revolt against the ways of Nature, she witnessed the scene torture."

In this world, in life, there can be no perfect union, and the children whom Adèle urges Edna to remember stand as living proof of the inevitability of separation. Edna's longing can never be satisfied. This is her final discovery, the inescapable disillusionment; and the narrator calls it to our attention again, lest its significance escape us. " 'The years that are gone seem like dreams,' " Edna muses, " 'if one might go on sleeping and dreaming—but to wake up and find—' " Here she pauses, but the reader can complete her thought—"a little new life." " 'Oh! well! perhaps it is better to wake up after all, even to suffer rather than to remain a dupe to illusions all one's life.' "

One wonders to what extent Edna's fate might have been different if Robert had remained. Momentarily, at least, he might have roused her from her despondency by offering not ecstasy but at least partial satisfaction. The fundamental problem would have remained, however. Life offers only partial pleasures, and individuated experience.

Thus Edna's final act of destruction has a quality of uncompromising sensuous fulfillment as well. It is her answer to the inadequacies of life, a literal denial and reversal of the birth trauma she has just witnessed, a stripping away of adulthood, of limitation, of consciousness itself. If life cannot offer fulfillment of her dream of fusion, then the ecstasy of death is preferable to the relinquishing of that dream. So Edna goes to the sea "and for the first time in her life she stood naked in the open air, at the mercy of the sun, the breeze that beat upon her, and the waves that invited her." She is a child, an infant again. "How strange and awful it seemed to stand naked under the sky! how delicious! She felt like some new-born creature, opening its eyes in a familiar world that it had never known." And with her final act Edna completes the regression, back beyond childhood, back into time eternal. "The touch of the sea is sensuous, enfolding the body in its soft, close embrace."

SUZANNE WOLKENFELD

Edna's Suicide:
The Problem of the One and the Many†

The recent critical controversy as to the meaning and value of Kate Chopin's *The Awakening* is epitomized in the range of responses to Edna's suicide. This finale constitutes the critical crux of the novel, not only in that it is central to the interpretation of Edna's character and the theme of the story, but also because it is joined with the issue of Chopin's attitude to her protagonist and the artistic integrity of her work. It is primarily through the interpretation of the pattern of imagery by which Edna's suicide is dramatized, and of the tone of the narrative voice, that each critic decides whether or not to take the final swim with Edna and determines Chopin's complicity in the act.

The most emphatic affirmations of Edna's suicide are found in the criticism of Per Seyersted and Kenneth Eble. Each proclaims the nobility of Edna's achievements and the heroic grandeur of her final gesture. Seyersted, approaching the story through feminist and existentialist perspectives, sees Edna's death as motivated by an uncompromising desire for "spiritual emancipation." Her suicide is "the crowning glory of her development from the bewilderment which accompanied her early emancipation to the clarity with which she understands her own nature and the possibilities of her life as she decides to end it."[1] Eble, distinguishing Edna from such deluded romantics as Emma Bovary, places her with classical figures who "struggle with elemental passion." Her suicide, seen as an immersion in Eros, gives her "the power, the dignity, the self-possession of a tragic heroine."[2] Both Seyersted and Eble acclaim the artistry of Chopin and assert her sympathy for Edna.

Donald A. Ringe and George Arms, each focusing on Edna's romanticism, present more qualified views of the significance of her suicide and question the assumption of Chopin's sympathy for her protagonist. Ringe relates Edna's romanticism to the transcendental-

† A previously unpublished essay printed with permission of the author. All footnotes are by the author.
1. Per Seyersted, *Kate Chopin: A Critical Biography* (Baton Rouge: University of Louisiana Press, 1969), pp. 134–63.
2. Kenneth Eble, "A Forgotten Novel: Kate Chopin's *The Awakening*," *Western Humanities Review*, 10 (Summer 1956), 261–69.

ist theme of self-discovery and perceives her suicide as the consequence of her realization of her essentially solitary nature. Stressing Chopin's philosophic concern with the relation of the individual to external reality, he evaluates Edna's final act as "a defeat that involves no surrender."[3] Arms, despite the basic realism of Edna's sexual emancipation, sees her as a figure motivated by romantic ideals, who "drifts" aimlessly into death. Noting the irony that pervades Chopin's treatment of Edna, he distinguishes between the romantic heroine and the realistic writer.[4]

Daniel S. Rankin represents the negative pole of reaction in his verdict on the work as "exotic in setting, morbid in theme, erotic in motivation." Edna's suicide is a testimony to the fact that "human nature can be a sickening reality." He identifies Chopin with Edna and judges the writer as an impressionable victim of romantic literature.[5]

George M. Spangler also presents a forceful indictment of the conclusion, not as does Rankin in terms of moral perversity, but on purely aesthetic grounds. He regards Edna's suicide as a pathetic defeat that is inconsistent with the depiction of her previous strength and achievements and accuses Chopin of a lapse from psychological subtlety into banal sentimentality.[6]

Cynthia Griffin Wolff, acknowledging Chopin's insight into human nature, sees her depiction of Edna as a penetrating account of psychological disintegration. Wolff analyzes Edna's experiences in the contexts of Laing and Freud and defines her as a schizoid personality whose erotic development has been arrested at the oral stage. Her suicide is a regressive act coming from "a sense of inner emptiness" and a failure to fulfill in real life her infantile yearnings for fusion.[7]

Between the positive and negative responses to Edna's suicide stand the views of Kenneth M. Rosen and Ruth Sullivan and Stewart Smith. Rosen insists on a purposeful ambiguity in which the sea is seen as symbolizing both life and death.[8] Sullivan and Smith argue not for ambiguity but for ambivalence in Chopin's presentation of Edna through two distinct and irreconcilable points of view.

3. Donald A. Ringe, "Romantic Imagery in Kate Chopin's *The Awakening*," *American Literature*, 43 (January 1972), 580–88.

4. George Arms, "Kate Chopin's *The Awakening* in the Perspective of Her Literary Career," *Essays in American Literature in Honor of Jay B. Hubbell*, Clarence Gohdes, ed. (Durham, N.C.: Duke University Press, 1967), pp. 215–28.

5. Daniel S. Rankin, *Kate Chopin and Her Creole Stories* (Philadelphia: University of Pennsylvania Press, 1932),

pp. 171–76.

6. George M. Spangler, "Kate Chopin's *The Awakening*: A Partial Dissent," *Novel: A Forum of Fiction*, 3 (1970), 244–55.

7. Cynthia Griffin Wolff, "Thanatos and Eros: Kate Chopin's *The Awakening*," *American Quarterly*, 25 (October 1973), 449–71.

8. Kenneth M. Rosen, "Kate Chopin's *The Awakening*: Ambiguity as Art," *Journal of American Studies*, 5 (August 1971), 197–200.

The reader's response to Edna's suicide depends on whether he is compelled by the voice that indulges a romantic vision of life's possibilities or by the contrasting voice that insists on accommodation to the limitations of reality.[9]

Those critical views that distinguish between the realism of Chopin and the romanticism of Edna and question the value of her suicide reflect most closely the meaning and spirit of *The Awakening*. The vision of life that emerges from the novel constitutes an affirmation of the multiple possibilities of fulfillment, an affirmation made with a clear and profound grasp of the problematic nature of reality. Chopin's attitude to Edna involves the same mixture of irony and respect that marks her treatment of the other characters in the story. Her sympathy, and perhaps even identification, with Edna are most evident in her dramatization of Edna's struggle to face the realities of life and her partial achievements of selfhood. But ultimately Chopin places Edna's suicide as a defeat and a regression, rooted in a self-annihilating instinct, in a romantic incapacity to accommodate herself to the limitations of reality.

This approach has affinities with the interpretations of Donald A. Ringe and George Arms and corresponds at points to the psychoanalytic study by Cynthia Griffin Wolff. But Ringe and Arms do not probe Edna's romanticism far enough to the psychological core, and Wolff tends to impose a clinically schematic pattern that sometimes distorts Chopin's use of imagery and implicitly raises the question of the author's control over her material. A reading that remains faithful to the psychological implications of Chopin's imagery in terms of her own apprehension of reality will illuminate most fully the meaning of Edna's suicide.

The editorial commentary that Chopin introduces at the point of Edna's first intuition of her passion for Robert provides the key to the author's thematic intention and to the central symbol in which it is embodied:

> In short, Mrs. Pontellier was beginning to realize her position in the universe as a human being, and to recognize her relations as an individual to the world within and about her. . . .
>
> But the beginning of things, of a world especially, is necessarily vague, tangled, chaotic, and exceedingly disturbing. How few of us ever emerge from such beginning! How many souls perish in its tumult!
>
> The voice of the sea is seductive; never ceasing, whispering, clamoring, murmuring, inviting the soul to wander for a spell in abysses of solitude; to lose itself in mazes of inward contemplation.

9. Ruth Sullivan and Stewart Smith, "Narrative Stance in Kate Chopin's *The Awakening*," *Studies in American Fiction*, 1 (Spring 1973), 62–75.

The voice of the sea speaks to the soul. The touch of the sea is sensuous, enfolding the body in its soft, close embrace.

What Chopin defines here are the two paths open to Edna from the point at which her instinctual nature is roused. Ideally, Edna's growth could bring her to self-awareness and community with the external world. But aware of the complex and vulnerable nature of the human psyche, Chopin emphasizes the perils that attend Edna's awakening. She stresses the universal temptation to yield to the primitive lure of the unconscious, to return to the primal sea in which body and soul are one. This symbolic invocation of the seductive sea that calls one to the ecstasy of immersion corresponds to Freud's conception of the Oceanic feeling of absolute fusion of the infantile ego.[1]

Chopin repeatedly underlines Edna's particular susceptibility to the infantile yearning for regression and subtly weaves the patterns of imagery that will culminate in her final surrender. The struggle within Edna between the desire for selfhood in relationship with others and the longing for self-annihilation is enacted in the scene of her first swim. Stirred to passion by the music she has heard, she achieves her first mastery over the ocean and swims out far in a spirit of self-assertion. But her instinctual intoxication also makes her open to the regressive urge: "As she swam she seemed to be reaching out for the unlimited in which to lose herself."

Edna's regressive instincts are embodied in the series of fantasies of unattainable lovers that dominated her early life. The infantile core of her romanticism is revealed in the childhood memory reawakened by the sight of the "water stretching so far away." She recalls walking through a meadow of grass, feeling that she "must walk on forever, without coming to the end of it." She connects this experience of the infinite in "that ocean of waving grass" to her first passionate infatuation with a visiting cavalry officer.

Her uncertainty about her response to the incident—"I don't remember whether I was frightened or pleased"—suggests her ambivalence to her romantic yearnings. Sensing the impossibility of fulfilling such passions "in this world," Edna marries a man she does not love, "closing the portals forever behind her upon the realm of romance and dreams."

When Robert arouses these fantasies once again, Edna determines not to love hopelessly in secret but to turn the phantom lover into reality, to take "possession of the beloved one." Through Robert she hopes to actualize her romantic need for Oneness in the act of sexual consummation.

1. See Wolff, op. cit., for a fuller treatment of Freud's conception of the infantile ego and its relationship to the character of Edna.

Through her dramatization of the Sleeping Beauty motif, Chopin reveals the conflict between the basic reality of Edna's erotic desire for Robert and the impossibility of her romantic quest for fusion. When Edna awakens from a long sleep at Chênière, she sees Robert as the Prince who has waited "one hundred years" to achieve his bride. The fact that she finds herself "very hungry" reflects her longing for a new life of sensuous satisfaction. Wolff's interpretation of this hunger as an indication that Edna's "libidinal energies have been arrested at a pregenital level" contradicts Chopin's use of food imagery as a positive symbol of life's nourishment.[2] Edna's problem is that she believes she can attain the final, unlimited union of the fairy-tale lovers. Robert's departure forces her to face the fact that real life is quite different from the idealized realm of the fairy tale.

Edna does achieve the existential integrity to value her painful coming to consciousness:

> The years that are gone seem like dreams—if one might go on sleeping and dreaming—but to wake and find— Oh! well! perhaps it is better to wake up after all, even to suffer, rather than to remain a dupe to illusions all one's life.

She not only awakens to knowledge of external reality but succeeds in penetrating the core of her inner nature. She confronts the shattering truth that even had Robert stayed, he could never have ultimately satisfied her need for "one thing":

> There was no one thing in the world that she desired. There was no human being whom she wanted near her except Robert; and she even realized that the day would come when he, too, and the thought of him would melt out of her existence, leaving her alone.

Edna does not possess the strength to live her life alone and is therefore driven to seek the solitary security of death. Her view of her children as enemies who seek "to drag her into the soul's slavery for the rest of her days" is the hysterical response of a woman who, compelled by the instinct to return to the unbroken bond with her mother, must perforce renounce her own motherhood.

Edna's suicide is not a conscious choice reached through her achievement of self-awareness. She was "not thinking" as "she walked down to the beach." In the grip of the unconscious she responds to the call of the sea: "The voice of the sea is seductive,

---

2. Wolff, op. cit., imposes a Freudian context in interpreting Edna's preoccupation with food as an indication of her infantile nature. Chopin uses food imagery to represent Edna's desire for life in contrast to her regressive desire for death by her request for fish for dinner before she starts her final walk down to the sea.

never ceasing, whispering, clamoring, murmuring, inviting the soul to wander in abysses of solitude." Her act of stripping off her clothes is not a gesture of self-liberation but rather a regression to the animality of infancy: "She felt like some new-born creature. . . ." Her experience of rebirth is directed not forward to new life but backward to the womb. Her final memories before her death represent a return to childhood, to her first fantasy lover, and to her walk in the meadow of infinity:

> Edna heard her father's voice and her sister Margaret's. She heard the barking of an old dog that was chained to the sycamore tree. The spurs of the cavalry officer clanged as he walked across the porch. There was the hum of bees, and the musky odor of pinks filled the air.

Edna finds her union with the One in the sea. Chopin affirms the many possibilities for satisfaction to be found on the land. In her portraits of Adèle Ratignolle and Mademoiselle Reisz, she suggests the multiplicity of roles open to women. Adèle, the "mother-woman," the dutiful wife, embodies the fertility of nature and the harmony of marital union. Her forays into art are all family oriented: She continually sews clothes for her children and keeps up her music as "a means of brightening the home and making it attractive." She is raised above the level of mere bovine domesticity by her charm, her amiability, and the generosity of her nurturing capacities. She is counterpointed by Mademoiselle Reisz, the artist who is isolated by her unamiable and imperious disposition. The "artificial violets" that she perpetually wears in her hair reflect her discordance with nature. But she is strong enough to live alone on her own terms, giving enough to secure the friendship of Robert and later of Edna, and capable through her music of inspiring passion.

The richness of Chopin's vision of life comes from her awareness of the many paths to self-realization from which to choose, each one involving compromise and renunciation. Her realism is inherent in her refusal to endorse the sentimentality of a fairy-tale resolution or the feminist fatalism of presenting Edna as the victim of an oppressive society. Chopin, as wife, as mother of six children, and as writer, is herself an affirmation of the many modes of living a woman can attain—each limited, each problematic, each real.

In a personal essay on her writing, published in the same year as *The Awakening*, Chopin affords us a glimpse of her personal life:

> . . . I write in the morning, when not too strongly drawn to struggle with the intricacies of a pattern, and in the afternoon, if the temptation to try a new furniture polish on an old table leg is not too powerful to be denied; sometimes at night, though as I grow older I am more and more inclined to believe that night

was made for sleep. . . . I am completely at the mercy of unconscious selection. To such an extent is this true, that what is called the polishing up process has always proved disastrous to my work, and I avoid it, preferring the integrity of crudities to artificialities.[3]

In this image of a writer who prefers at times to "polish" a piece of furniture rather than a work of art, who balances her commitment to writing with an indulgence to her moods and physical needs, one sees a woman who has learned to mediate between the inner and outer worlds, between fantasy and reality.

MARGARET CULLEY

Edna Pontellier: "A Solitary Soul"

> One sees that dead, vacant look steal sometimes over the rarest, finest of women's faces—in the very midst, it might be, of their warmest summer's day; and then one can guess at the secret of intolerable solitude that lies beneath the delicate laces and brilliant smile.
> —Rebecca Harding Davis,
> *Life in the Iron Mills* (1861)

The Awakening, an existential novel about solitude, is distinguished from most of such fiction by its female protagonist. Because of her sex, Edna Pontellier experiences not only dread in the face of solitude, but also delight. As a woman, she has had so little sense of a self alone that new-found solitude suggests entirely new arenas and modes of activity. Solitude also brings a confrontation with the ultimate aloneness—death—and thus the threat of extinction of the fragile, newborn self. When dread of solitude possesses Edna, she seeks, as she has sought from her youth, the deliverance of the imagination; her sexual awakening now leads her to seek the deliverance of the flesh. When she understands that both these deliverers will fail her, she embraces death with the same mixture of dread and delight as when she first discovered her solitude.

Daniel S. Rankin states, "In 1899 Herbert S. Stone and Co. of Chicago published *The Awakening*, a novel the author intended to name *A Solitary Soul*." One early reviewer suggests that the title we know was furnished by "intelligent publishers."[1] In any case, when Chopin added the title *The Awakening* to her notebook, she did not cancel *A Solitary Soul*, as she usually did when changing a title; and Per Seyersted suggests she may have wished to retain it as a subtitle.

In 1895 Chopin published a translation of a Guy de Maupassant

---

3. As quoted in Rankin, p. 183.
1. Daniel S. Rankin, *Kate Chopin and Her Creole Stories* (Philadelphia: University of Pennsylvania Press, 1932), pp. 171 and 173n.

sketch called "Solitude." In this piece two friends talk after leaving a high-spirited dinner party and walk into the night. One reflects: "For a long time I have endured the anguish of having discovered and understood the solitude in which I live. And I know that nothing can end it; nothing! Whatever we may do or attempt, despite the embraces and transports of love, the hunger of the lips, we are always alone. I have dragged you out into the night in the vain hope of a moment's escape from the horrible solitude which overpowers me. But what is the use! I speak and you answer me, and still each of us is alone; side by side but alone."[2] With images of drowning and the night, he continues his description of his solitude: "You may think me a little mad, but since I have realized the solitude of my being I feel as if I were sinking day by day into some boundless subterranean depths, with no one near me, no other living soul to clasp my out-stretched, groping hands. There [are] noises, there are voices and cries in the darkness. Behold, I strive to reach them, but I can never discover where they come in the darkness, this life which engulfs me." The speaker continues that the illusion which love brings—that he is not alone—is the cruelest of all, for ". . . after each embrace the isolation grows, and how pungent it is. And after the rapturous union which must, it would seem, blend two souls into one being, how, more than ever before, do you feel yourself alone—alone!" In another essay of de Maupassant which Chopin translated, the speaker also awakens from the illusion that he is not alone to the reality of his solitude. In this essay, though the dreams and illusions have persisted for a long time, they have ultimately fled; it is the sketch entitled "Suicide."

What we feel most keenly about Edna is her remoteness from those about her—her husband, her children, her two female friends, her two male friends. And her solitude is underscored by the dramatic action of the novel as the significant persons in her life repeatedly leave her alone. At the end of the first chapter, Léonce Pontellier leaves Edna for his club; at the end of the third chapter, he leaves her for his business; he leaves her after a quarrel later in the novel, again the next morning for his business, and then, finally, for New York—not to appear again in the novel. Similarly, Robert leaves Edna repeatedly: he leaves her to herself after the evening of the moonlight swim, and again on the Chênière Caminada. He leaves her penultimately in going to Mexico, and finally with "Goodby—because I love you." Edna's children are also removed from her for the major action of the novel. The key scenes in the novel are the scenes where Edna is alone: alone on the porch weeping in chapter two; alone in her daring swim; alone in the hammock that

2. Guy de Maupassant, "Solitude," trans. Kate Chopin, *St. Louis Life,* XIII (December 28, 1895), 30. The quotations following appear on the same page.

evening; alone on Chênière Caminada; alone after Léonce leaves for New York; alone in the pigeon house; and, finally, alone in death. The word *alone* resounds like a refrain in the text, occurring some two dozen times.

On the evening of the swim, Edna listens to Mademoiselle Reisz play the piano. One piece moves her especially; Edna secretly calls it "Solitude." Later at the beach she feels like a child who "walks for the first time alone." She enters the water: ". . . intoxicated with her newly conquered power, she swam out alone." She swims, turning her face "seaward to gather in an impression of space and solitude" and returns to say, "I thought I should have perished out there alone." This climactic scene of learning to swim—where the waves of the music, the sea, and the passion seem to become one— captures the ambivalence Edna experiences toward her solitude. The solitude is "intoxicating," as it is when she is left alone on Chênière Caminada to sleep: "She looked at her round arms as she held them straight up and rubbed them one after the other, observing closely, as if it were something she saw for the first time, the fine, firm quality and texture of the flesh." Also when she is alone after Léonce's departure for New York, the solitude transports her: "A feeling that was unfamiliar but very delicious came over her. She walked all through the house, from one room to another, as if inspecting it for the first time." It is in these moments of exhilaration that Edna discovers her body, her freedom, her will, her self. But just as childbirth for the nineteenth-century woman occurred in the shadow of death, the birth of Edna's new life, occurring as it does in the "abyss of solitude" which is the sea, brings with it its attendant vision of death.

Edna connects the ocean with a memory from her childhood: ". . . a meadow that seemed as big as the ocean to the very little girl walking through the grass, which was higher than her waist. She threw out her arms as if swimming when she walked, beating the tall grass as one strikes out in the water. . . . 'I could see only the stretch of green before me, and I felt as if I must walk on forever, without coming to the end of it. I don't remember whether I was frightened or pleased.' " Likely she was both. She tells of her first deliverance from that vast expanse: "At a very early age—perhaps it was when she traversed the ocean of waving grass—she remembered that she had been passionately enamored of a dignified and sad-eyed cavalry officer who visited her father in Kentucky." The cavalry officer is followed by another young gentleman and by the "face and figure of a great tragedian." The tragedian is undoubtedly Edwin Booth, who began "to haunt her imagination and stir her senses." His portrait is in her room and "when alone she sometimes picked it up and kissed the cold glass passionately."

Edna's marriage to Léonce ends this life of fancy until Robert loves her and then leaves for Mexico, thus taking his place among the presences in her imagination which deliver her from her solitude. When she feels most alone, she summons Robert to her as she had summoned the romantic figures before him. In the midst of her high-spirited dinner party Edna "suggested the regal woman, the one who rules, the one who looks on, who stands alone." The next paragraph tells us of her characteristic deliverance from this solitary position: "But as she sat there amid her guests, she felt the old ennui overtaking her; the hopelessness which so often assailed her, which came upon her like an obsession, like something extraneous, independent of volition. It was something which announced itself; a chill breath that seemed to issue from some vast cavern wherein discords wailed. There came over her the acute longing which always summoned into her vision the presence of the beloved one, overpowering her at once with a sense of the unattainable."

The unattainable quality of the vision is its essence. Robert's return to Edna is doomed, for his actual presence can never match the fantasy; and she knows even the fantasy will fail her. Just before she dies, she realizes this: "There was no human being whom she wanted near her except Robert; and she even realized that the day would come when he, too, and the thought of him would melt out of her existence, leaving her alone."

Alcée Arobin has offered Edna another escape from solitude, the deliverance of the flesh. Victor, who is associated with Arobin in his escapades with women, becomes transformed into a Bacchanalian figure, with a garland of roses on his black curls, his cheeks "the color of crushed grapes," well flushed with wine. Observing him, a dinner guest quotes the first two lines from this Swinburne sonnet:

A Cameo

There was a graven image of Desire
    Painted with red blood on a ground of gold
    Passing between the young men and the old,
And by him Pain, whose body shone like fire,
And Pleasure with gaunt hands that grasped their hire,
    Of his left wrist, with fingers clenched and cold,
    The insatiable Satiety kept hold,
Walking with feet unshod that pashed the mire.
The senses and the sorrows and the sins,
    And the strange loves that suck the breasts of Hate
Till lips and teeth bite in their sharp indenture,
Followed like beasts with flaps of wings and fins.
    Death stood aloof behind a gaping grate,
Upon whose lock was written Peradventure.

Placed thus, the allusion to the rather brutal Swinburne poem about the insatiety of fleshly desire and the final victory of time and death over passion, foretells the impossibility of such deliverance for Edna. Again, just before her death, she realizes the futility of this route: "To-day it is Arobin; to-morrow it will be someone else."

Having dismissed both possibilities of deliverance from her solitude, and unable to sustain the delight it brings her, Edna embraces death whose voice she has heard in her aloneness: "The voice of the sea is seductive, never ceasing, whispering, clamoring, murmuring, inviting the soul to wander in the abysses of solitude." She watches the Icarian figure fall from its lonely flight to its lonely death and "there beside the sea, absolutely alone, she cast the unpleasant, pricking garments from her. . . ."

Chopin's study of "A Solitary Soul" is particularly poignant because the soul is a female soul, characteristically defined as someone's daughter, someone's wife, someone's mother, someone's mistress. To discover solitude in the midst of this connectedness is surely among the most painful of awakenings, because the entire social fabric sustains the dream and the illusion. As Edna says to the doctor before her death: "The years that are gone seem like dreams —if one might go on sleeping and dreaming—but to wake up and find— Oh! well! perhaps it is better to wake up after all, even to suffer, rather than remain a dupe to illusions all one's life."

We feel the tragedy of Edna Pontellier because we see so many brave moments of delight she takes in her solitary self. We glimpse the ecstasy of the discovery of the power of the self and the refusal to adjure it. To Madame Ratignolle she says, "I would give up my life for my children; but I wouldn't give up myself." Having resolved "never again to belong to another than herself," she tells Robert: "I am no longer one of Mr. Pontellier's possessions to dispose of or not. I give myself where I choose. If he were to say 'Here, Robert, take her and be happy; she is yours,' I should laugh at you both." But Edna cannot sustain these moments of resolve and when her two deliverers, the imagination (Robert) and the flesh (Arobin), have failed her, she begins to understand something of what Mademoisele Reisz's presence and words have told her about the price of solitude, and thinking that Mademoiselle would have laughed, perhaps sneered, she swims out alone.

Selected Bibliography

KATE CHOPIN: WORKS

Seyersted, Per, ed. *The Complete Works of Kate Chopin*. Two volumes. Baton Rouge: Louisiana State University Press, 1969.

BIOGRAPHY

Deyo, C. L. "Mrs. Kate Chopin," *St. Louis Life*, IX (June 9, 1894), 11–12.
Dondore, Dorothy. "Kate O'Flaherty Chopin," *Dictionary of American Biography*. New York: Scribners, 1930.
Rankin, Daniel S. *Kate Chopin and Her Creole Stories*. Philadelphia: University of Pennsylvania Press, 1932.
Schuyler, William. "Kate Chopin," *The Writer*, VII (August 1894), 115–17.
Seyersted, Per. *Kate Chopin: A Critical Biography*. Baton Rouge: Louisiana State University Press, 1969.

BIBLIOGRAPHY

Potter, Richard H. "Kate Chopin and Her Critics: An Annotated Checklist," *The Bulletin—Missouri Historical Society*, XXVI (July 1970), 306–17.
Springer, Marlene. *Kate Chopin and Edith Wharton: An Annotated Bibliographical Guide to Secondary Materials*. Boston: G. K. Hall, 1976.

CRITICISM

Arnavon, Cyrille. "Les Débuts du Roman Réaliste Américain et l'Influence Française," in *Romanciers Américains Contemporains*, ed. Henri Kerst (*Cashiers des Langues Modernes*), I, Paris, 1946, 9–35.
——, ed. *Edna* [*The Awakening*]. Paris, 1953, pp. 1–22.
Cantwell, Robert. "*The Awakening*, by Kate Chopin," *Georgia Review*, X (Winter 1956), 489–94.
Forrey, Carolyn. "The New Woman Revisited," *Women's Studies*, II (1974), 37–56.
Kauffmann, Stanley. "The Really Lost Generation," *The New Republic*, CLV (December 3, 1966), 22, 37–38.
Milliner, Gladys W. "The Tragic Imperative: *The Awakening* and *The Bell Jar*," *Mary Wollstonecraft Newsletter*, II (December 1973), 21–27.
Rocks, James E. "Kate Chopin's Ironic Vision," *Louisiana Review*, I (Winter 1972), 11–20.
Rosen, Kenneth M. "Kate Chopin's *The Awakening*: Ambiguity as Art," *Journal of American Studies*, V (August 1971), 197–99.
Seyersted, Per. "Kate Chopin: An Important St. Louis Writer Reconsidered," *The Bulletin—Missouri Historical Society*, XIX (January 1963), 89–114.
Skaggs, Peggy. "Three Tragic Figures in Kate Chopin's *The Awakening*," *Louisiana Studies*, XIII (Winter 1974), 345–64.
Sullivan, Ruth, and Stewart Smith. "Narrative Stance in Kate Chopin's *The Awakening*," *Studies in American Fiction*, I (Spring 1973), 62–75.
Toth, Emily. "The Independent Woman and 'Free Love,'" *Massachusetts Review*, XVI (Autumn 1975), 647–64.
Wheeler, Otis B. "The Five Awakenings of Edna Pontellier," *Southern Review*, XI (January 1975), 118–28.
Zlotnick, Joan. "A Woman's Will: Kate Chopin on Selfhood, Wifehood, and Motherhood," *Markham Review*, III (October 1968), 1–5.

NEWSLETTER

The Kate Chopin Newsletter, edited by Emily Toth. [Notes, short articles, bibliography, work in progress.]

NORTON CRITICAL EDITIONS